THE MODERN LIBRARY
OF THE WORLD'S BEST BOOKS

GREAT GERMAN SHORT NOVELS AND STORIES

GREAT GERMAN

SHORT NOVELS

AND STORIES.

EDITED, WITH AN INTRODUCTION, BY **VICTOR LANGE**

PROFESSOR OF GERMAN LANGUAGE AND LITERATURE,

CORNELL UNIVERSITY

THE MODERN LIBRARY · NEW YORK

Random House is the publisher of *The Modern Library*

BENNETT A. CERF · DONALD S. KLOPFER · ROBERT K. HAAS

Manufactured in the United States of America

By H. Wolff

CONTENTS

INTRODUCTION

By Victor Lange

THE German short story or, as it is usually called, the Novelle, is one of the most impressive achievements of modern German literature. It is, perhaps, the only form which can claim a distinct tradition and which has produced a remarkably homogeneous body of excellence. From Goethe to Thomas Mann and Kafka, from the end of the eighteenth century to our own day no literary form—neither the drama nor the lyric nor, indeed, the novel itself—has attracted an equal number of first-rate German writers, and in no other area of the creative imagination is it so rewarding to trace the development of the form from an early pattern of anecdotal purpose to the subtle and intricate texture of our contemporary kind of narrative.

The two writers who first determined the manner and purposes of European fiction and of the short story in particular are Boccaccio and Cervantes. In the *Decameron* Boccaccio recounts a series of striking incidents that occur in a clearly defined social setting; Cervantes was, in his *Novelas Ejemplares,* more concerned with the psychological make-up of an individual human being and his relationship to the increasingly puzzling world about him. On both of these distinct yet complementary forms much of the narrative art of the seventeenth and eighteenth centuries continued to depend. As, towards the end of the eighteenth century, the interest in "manners" and "characters" began to blend, the main ingredients of the classical Novelle—the plausibly coherent social background and the stable emotional structure of the human being—became problematical.

When Goethe suggested, as a comprehensive definition of the Novelle, that it should relate a single, unheard-of incident, *eine sich ereignete unerhörte Begebenheit*, this formula must already have seemed inadequate to the younger —romantic—practitioners of German fiction. Although Goethe was not insensitive to the social and intellectual changes that his own revolutionary era brought about, he held all the more deliberately to the belief that the short story should reflect the convictions of an articulate and self-conscious social elite, and that the "unheard-of incident" should illuminate both the conditions of life in that society and the limits within which deviation from it or submission to it seemed possible or desirable. The Novelle was for Goethe essentially a moral tale, and its moral ends could be maintained and represented only within a clearly defined frame of social convention.

But such an advantage of stability and of a distinctly stratified society could in Germany, in the early nineteenth century, no longer be assumed and it is, in large part, the process of diversification and even disintegration of social attitudes and beliefs that produced the remarkable literature of the romantic period. The key to this new, romantic, sensibility is the ever-deepening sense of conflict between emotional and intellectual individualism and a political and social life that was, if not authoritarian, at any rate attached to rigorously conservative ideals. This discrepancy was felt more and more clearly by the German artist, and it was recognized not merely as a pragmatic political issue but as a far-reaching spiritual dilemma. In the best examples of the German Novelle in the nineteenth century it supplies the recurrent though not always obvious impulse. For what the great German writers between Goethe and Thomas Mann attempted to do was far more than to give expression to any sense, however urgent or noble, of political uneasiness: to attack directly or obliquely the suspect and distasteful social inadequacies. On an altogether more significant level of artistic seriousness they moved beyond the conflict of social ideals to the representation of ever greater and subtler intellectual and emotional complexity.

These classic representatives of the German Novelle are

all, in varying measure and intention, interested in the realities about them. But if that notion—and the term "realistic"—is to have any useful meaning beyond the obvious, it must suggest to us that they are intensely concerned with the complicated and forever more puzzling character of reality, and that, if they are to represent this elusive "reality," they can do so only by representing it in its fullness and multiplicity. It is not the portraying of one stable and self-evident view of life, but of the infinitely differing kinds, levels, shades, and aspects of reality which is the subject matter of nearly all the stories in the present volume.

This feeling for the powerfully disturbing ambivalence of life is not difficult to recognize in the very themes of these stories. Again and again we find the artist asking—openly or implicitly—whether any one given and perhaps widely accepted sort of reality—a belief, a way of coping with life, a point of view, an attitude—might not prove to be brittle and unreliable especially when under extreme stress it is tested as to its durability. The radical emotionalism of Werther, the momentary idyll of humaneness and love in Kleist's story, the deceptive ring of the word "honor" in *Casper and Annie,* the greed for possessions and money in *The Jews' Beech Tree,* the barren routine of Flagman Thiel's life, the web of romantic and sensuous illusion in Heinrich Mann's *Three Minute Novel,* the solemnly acquired self-discipline of Aschenbach in *Death in Venice*—in every instance it is not a feeling of cynicism or defeatism or, least of all, escapism that is to remain with us as the gist of the story. We are to gain, on the contrary, a positive and heightened awareness of the complexity of what we might, all too confidently, regard as an unambiguous matter or a simple alternative. Contrasting concepts of law and order, of human or transcendental values, of faith and unbelief, of normalcy and disorder are offered and examined throughout these examples of a varied and revealing literary form.

Even though we cannot and should not judge these tales by any unequivocal formal criterion, it is in their form, their literary devices, as much as in their subject matter, that they prove remarkably interesting. As it is the purpose of every significantly realistic work of art to explore a wide range of life and thereby to go beyond the limited conditions of experience, the artist must forever be in search of adequate ways of representing this roving curiosity. He will, therefore, not hesitate to blur the line of demarcation between observed truth and imagination, to move freely from the natural to the supernatural, to mingle the sober reporting of an everyday event with the suddenly intruding fantasy of a dream. Especially the modern writer—increasingly caught in wonderment or doubt, yet expected to remain objective, to suspend his judgment—assumes a variety of different roles: he may be sympathetically stirred by what he sees, he may even (*in Casper and Annie*) find himself an unexpected member of the cast, or he may maintain a pointedly ironic detachment. Not in order to indulge in an evasive sort of unreality but, rather, to remind us of the many possible forms in which life may present itself, and be presented, he uses the fairy tale, the chronicle, the parable, or the legend. Reality and spirituality are for him no longer separate realms of meaning; in the modern Novelle they are interlocked to the point of becoming indistinguishable.

Throughout the nineteenth century the short story proved to be an exceptionally popular and effective form; indeed, in Germany it usurped some of the appeal which at other times was excited by the drama; it retarded, certainly, the development of a truly significant and cosmopolitan kind of German novel. The reason for this historical preference is not simply the pointedly dramatic structure of the Novelle or the brevity with which it could accomplish an often difficult narrative purpose. What made the German Novelle so strikingly attractive was its unhackneyed, experimental quality and the scope it offered for the poetic representation of new dimensions of experience. Long before European and, especially, German fiction was to abandon the single focus of a psychological portraiture, the Novelle had evolved its own devices for indicating depth and complexity. Kleist, Brentano, Hoffman, Droste—and, among those who cannot be included in the present volume, Gotthelf with his *Black Spider* and Adalbert Stifter—are the great forerunners of the modern symbolic novel. If we want to do justice to these masters we cannot regard their short stories as mere accounts of "unheard-of incidents" or, as the Cervantean tradition of character fiction would demand it, as case histories, however elaborately embroidered, of an interesting individual. Whether we take a romantic tale such as Brentano's *Casper and Annie* or a naturalistic narrative such as Hauptmann's *Flagman Thiel* or Thomas Mann's *Death in Venice* or Kafka's *A Country Doctor*, the form-giving movement within the story which will supply the fitting key is not simply the chronological sequence of action but the gradual unfolding of relationships within the carefully wrought network of symbolic statements. Thus, in its finest examples the modern German Novelle, from Kleist to Kafka, offers us—no less effectively than the larger form of the contemporary novel—an understanding of our own complex conditions of life through continuous effort at symbolic illumination.

II

The history of modern German fiction begins with Goethe's *Werther* (1774), a short novel of astonishing emotional power and, behind its deceptively simple plot, of great subtlety of design. It is the story, not merely of a disappointed lover, but of a human being who finds himself inescapably caught in an experience of the discrepancy between his own all-consuming inner intensity and the obtuseness and conventionality of the world about him. His whole existence is a desperate struggle to transcend life itself and he desires nothing more than to communicate his extreme state of mind. But all attempts at sharing it, indeed even at describing it, must fail. With the inexorable pace of a Greek tragedy, Werther's tremendous gamble at a radical assertion of his own energies ends logically in his surrender to Nature and God—their presence, at first idyllic and later de-

monic, remains the only reality that he will accept. All forms
of human communication—love, friendship, social institu-
tions, even art—gradually prove meaningless to Werther; he
denies the value, indeed the possibility, of human life and
in a last suicidal gesture he draws the consequence of his
radical loneliness. Werther is the prototype of the romantic
egotist, and Goethe, then a young man of only twenty-four,
portrays that state of mind with extraordinary artistry, with
a beautiful command of the revealing symbols, and even
something of the irony that alone makes such a vortex of
crisis bearable for us.

While *Werther* is a superb document of the emancipation
of feeling and its profoundly disturbing consequences, it
still remains a late product of the bourgeois eighteenth century. With its subtlety of texture it surpasses by far such a
conventional yet characteristic "true story" as Schiller's
Sport of Destiny (1788), but it also differs widely from the
monumental grandeur of perspective which we find in
Kleist's *Earthquake in Chile* (1807), the first narrative work
of one of Germany's great dramatists. Kleist's world is one
of extreme and barely relieved tensions. The human being
is here at the mercy not only, as in *Werther,* of his own unsettling insights, but of natural forces which he cannot control and of explosive and incalculable outbursts of social
fanaticism that pervert the very meaning of the moral convictions which they seem to defend. Among these instances
of inhumanity it is nearly impossible to find a place of security; the poet can conceive and represent it only as an
idyllic interlude between two moments of destruction, the
earthquake and the lynching. Yet even though the lovers
are expelled from the community and cruelly destroyed by
it, the integrity of their devotion is reasserted: the child of
their love remains a symbol of promise in an apparently
meaningless world. Kleist's theme, presented without moral-
izing or sentimentality, is an immensely powerful one; it is,
at the same time, remarkably close to our own experience.

The tragic effect which Kleist achieved with an utmost
degree of objectivity and self-denial on the part of the nar-

rator is produced in Brentano's *Casper and Annie* (1817) by involving the poet directly in a strange sequence of events. The poet listens, at first baffled but with ever-deepening compassion, to an old woman who tells of the pathetic fate of her grandson and of the imminent execution of the unhappy Annie. With her deeply religious sense of honor— that same "honor" which, in its spurious and worldly form, has driven Casper and Annie to their death—she hopes not for a pardon but for their decent burial. Speaking in the cool, starry summer night, she gradually emerges as an almost mythical symbol of faith, love, work, and sacrifice. With a wonderful command of an infinite variety of poetic effects from the sweetly lyrical to the gruesome and terrifying, Brentano, drawing on motifs of the folk song, the ballad, the legend, and the hymn, weaves a delicately romantic design. But his imagination is by no means irresponsible: no turn in the story is more revealing than the narrator's embarrassment at being thought a mere poet; he resolves—and this is a beautiful touch of irony—to put his skill as a writer, as a scribe, to the test and, although the petition which he composes cannot save Annie, he contributes in the end to the (somewhat melodramatically achieved) contrition of the Duke and his mistress.

What Brentano and Hoffmann have in common—their stories were written in the same year, though from very different artistic impulses—is their faith in the incredible, their feeling for the presence of the improbable or, to put it more simply, the realism with which they represent the supernatural. Even more definitely than in *Casper and Annie,* where the role of the artist seemed to become problematical, it is the ambiguity of art, of inspiration, of creativity, which disturbed Hoffman. He deals with this problem in a number of stories of which *The Cremona Violin* (1817) is an excellent example. In the eccentric personality of Krespel there lies concealed an extraordinary sensitiveness to disturbing, indeed fearful and overpowering, universal forces. This susceptibility is as alive and troublesome to him as it appears bizarre to the world about him. But if Krespel differs from other men, it is for a significant reason: "There are men," he remarked, "from whom nature or a special destiny has taken away the cover behind which the mad folly of the rest of us runs its course unobserved. They are like thin-skinned insects, which, as we watch the restless play of their muscles, seem to be misshapen, while nevertheless everything soon comes back into its proper form again. All that remains thought with us passes over with Krespel into action." In this pathological state Krespel recognizes not only the bliss but the terror of the spiritual force that reveals itself in the vessels of art, in his violin and Antonia's voice. What seems uplifting is in reality destructive: Antonia's voice destroys her body—ecstasy and physical frailty are closely linked—and it is not in the opposition but the surrender to this spiritual reality, in the ultimate performance of the purest act of art which is death-in-love, that Antonia achieves peace. This strikingly modern feeling for the ambivalent nature of art, for the relationship between disease and creativity, by which Hoffmann anticipates Poe, Baudelaire, Nietzsche, and Thomas Mann, is dramatized with an impressive array of technical devices. As he describes with the most accurate sort of realism the puzzling incongruities in and about Krespel, as he invokes all kinds of scientific evidence, as he reminds us of magnetism and somnambulism, of the "double" and the split personality, Hoffmann creates the adequate symbols for his highly differentiated perception. And by attempting to demonstrate this imaginative vitality against a background of bourgeois normalcy, he performs implicitly and with the legitimate irony of the artist, an act of social criticism.

This aspect of social criticism is, of course, ever present in the Novelle of the nineteenth century. It is sometimes pointed, witty, and specific, as in Heine's *Gods in Exile* (1851). But more often it is part of a larger poetic purpose. If Brentano deals lyrically and in a romantic mood with the problem of honor, Annette von Droste-Huelshoff, some twenty-five years later, transposes the same theme from a minor to a major key, and moves it from the releasing atmosphere of Christian grace to the somber setting of old-testamentarian retribution. She emphasizes, like Brentano, the appropriate provincial setting and transforms, like him, the reported evidence of a true occurence into a statement of compelling poetic logic. *The Jews' Beech Tree* (1842) is a mystery story in which, as in our contemporary mystery fiction, the criminal hero is not convicted by law, but destroyed; its motivating and propelling issue is a moral dilemma which is ultimately referred to the transcending decision of conscience. As we follow the tense succession of deliberately unexplained events against a dark setting of local custom, we are reminded of the same rich and violent mood in Emily Brontë's *Wuthering Heights*. But the fate of Merkel, this unexceptional yet, as we see him, remarkable character, is told without any romantic flourishes; instead of listening to the flowing, urgent talk of Brentano's old woman, we are here in the company of an absolutely sober chronicler whose dispassionate account we must follow to the final sentence in order to feel the full tragedy of Merkel's state of mind. It is the very presence of objects and circumstances which need, in the manner of the true myth, only be named to exercise their powerful influence upon the figures of the story and upon us (most impressive, of course, the symbol of the beech tree itself) that makes this one of the finest specimens of the German realistic Novelle.

The term "realistic," as we have seen, is deceptive, and it is only moderately helpful if we compare the work of Keller, Meyer, and Storm, three mid-century authors, who come closest to representing human beings and attitudes with the reconciliating ease and the wise acceptance of the world about us that is sometimes attached to the word "realism." If Storm in his popular *Immensee* (1851) is not free of routine sentimentality, he nevertheless infuses the Novelle with a lyrical feeling for nature and thus anticipates the later impressionists. The idyll of love, which in Kleist was set in relief and given its grandeur by scenes of monstrous inhumanity, is here shown, in the manner of the romantics, as a melancholy though imperishable incident in the stream of remembered time. This sense of passing in all experience and of the elusive chance by which we might, but seldom actually do, grasp happiness distinguishes Storm's "poetic realism" from that of his two Swiss contemporaries, Keller and Meyer. Where Storm is musical and picturesquely diffuse, Keller is vividly pictorial; Meyer, most calculating in his effects, is sculpturesque and a master of the carefully staged scene. In *Saint Vitalis* (1872) Keller is gently satirical of the mawkish clichés which increasingly trivialized the popular retelling of medieval legends. But instead of assuming a solemn pose, he endows the religious incident with delicious humorous reality. There is no other German storyteller in the nineteenth century who has Keller's steadiness of eye and cheerful sympathy with all living things. He chides without condescension and maintains in his art, his religion, and his politics an attitude of positive realism without ever resorting to the banal.

The world of C. F. Meyer is no less definitely shaped and colorful. Yet it is viewed by a far less instinctive philosophic temperament. *Plautus in the Convent* (1882) has the surface character of a classical, convivial Novelle in the manner of Boccaccio; it is actually, in theme and form, a demonstration of ambiguity: the facetious anecdote is only the frame for a much more stirring and involved incident which dramatizes the unresolvable fluidity between truth and falsehood and which culminates in the narrator's reflections upon the protean character of conscience. From beginning to end Meyer insists upon this dualism of experience: it is suggested in the central figure of the elegant humanist Poggio: "the expression on this brilliant face was a curiously mixed one: the serenity of his brow and his smiling lips were overshadowed by a sad experience"; and the first and last paragraphs place this theme of ambiguity—without irony—in a magnificently firm Renaissance setting of grandeur and permanence.

What Gerhart Hauptmann attempts to show in *Flagman Thiel* (1887) may, in one respect, seem to be related to Meyer's intention. Both are concerned with the peculiarly modern experience of the precariousness of moral judgment. But Meyer is still able, as it were, to control and evaluate this experience and to project it in an almost classical dramatic tableau. Hauptmann presents a clinical analysis of the crisis in which an individual not only comes to realize his own human insecurity, but finds himself—different from Meyer's humanist—unable to cope with it and eventually overwhelmed by it. Thiel's whole life is a process of alienation from the world of certainty; it can, we are made to feel, only be borne by a person of extraordinary insensitiveness. But as Thiel is beset, first by various grotesquely accidental misfortunes and later by the crushing evidence of cruelty and inhumanity, he begins, slowly, to grasp the terrifying pressure of forces outside and beyond himself. There is no escaping, no rallying; he is the victim of an appalling destiny which, as if bestowing a cynical grace, opens his eyes only to blind him by the horror of what his mystical insight reveals to him. The style of this early but unsurpassed prose work of a distinguished playwright is "naturalistic" only in the sense that Hauptmann carefully confines himself to the observable external evidence of psychological processes: his attitude towards this pathetic middle-class fate is rigorously detached; he does not moralize or soften the impact of the case history upon us. But the depth and force of the story, the sense of shock and urgency which we derive from this ordeal of disintegration is achieved by Hauptmann's own compassion and his poetic strategy in showing everyday objects and incidents in the gradually gathering light of symbolic meaning.

A different sensibility, a more cautious and more class-conscious sort of social philosophy, produced Schnitzler's *A Farewell* (1895). It is one of the most characteristic of his studies in loneliness, set, as is nearly all of Schnitzler's work, against the unmistakable local and psychological background of Vienna. The longing for a simple and uncomplicated love, for happiness, for peace, which in the normal but devitalized social order seem impossible to attain, proves, even where it is nearly attained, a melancholy delusion—a delusion which becomes all the more real and all the more agonizing as it is experienced with the nervous sensitiveness of one who finds himself the center of a shockingly revealing dream. The fatal sickness of the woman he loves envelops and unsettles the young man and seems to lend reality to what was before only a life of self-indulgence. Now, his vanity and his cowardice are challenged, most critically when this "artist in deception" is eventually brought to the deathbed of the one person whose love, while she lived, had for a short time created an illusion of true happiness. But an ironic smile on the lips of his dead mistress seems to remind him of his weakness; he fails the imaginary test, he remains irresolute between dream and reality, he betrays her. Full of shame he hurries away through the streets "for it seemed to him as if he were not privileged to mourn with the others—as if his dead love was driving him away because he had disowned her."

The theme of longing, unfulfilled and unattainable, which Schnitzler represents lyrically and with an appropriate reliance on muffled impressions, becomes taut and breathlessly kaleidoscopic in Heinrich Mann's *Three Minute Novel* (1904). If the inner monologue of *A Farewell* proceeds with definite psychological plausibility, Heinrich Mann's *tour-de-force* has something of the jolting imaginative rhythm of the expressionist poet; the disintegration of the "normal" sequence of time and space has here gone even further than before. By a sliding succession of momentary but exactly focused flashes we are expected not so much to contemplate an individually interesting character or incident as—in keeping with expressionistic intentions—to identify ourselves with a human situation that might, eventually, be our own. The dazzling speed with which the images flare up before us conveys the sense of a continuously fluctuating life in which it is impossible to fix a point of fulfillment. Yet even in this flickering stream of images every effort is made to maintain, in detail, an exact and symbolically charged objectivity. For it is, of course, the special difficulty of the modern writer, whether in poetry or fiction, to render his ever more differentiating and unsettling insight into the complexity of life in a manner which must suggest his own ability as an artist to assume the indispensable creative detachment. In Wedekind's *Burning of Egliswyl* (1905), this effort at objectivity is especially important as the violence, the heat of the animalistic passion which consumes the apparently normal, provincial characters and their world might well have become melodramatic. Wedekind is careful not himself to intrude or to explain motives in the telling of events which must speak for themselves; he revives the classic Kleistean Novelle but narrows the motivating forces from a transcendental fate to ineluctable primitive instincts that are, in their immediacy, no less powerful and no less frightening.

There is none of the anxious seriousness of the surrounding stories in Rilke's *How Old Timofei Died Singing* (1900). It conveys delightfully and without pretense the charm of the *skazki* and *bylini,* the Russian fairy tales and legends, whose simple religious appeal had so impressed Rilke during his visit to Russia. In the parable of Timofei, "the best singer within ten days' journey," and his son and successor, Yegor, he demonstrates the power of community that rests in these folk motifs.

The two remaining works reveal with singular success the new poetic dimensions of the contemporary tale. Thomas Mann's *Death in Venice* (1913) and Kafka's *A Country Doctor* (1919) are magnificent achievements in themselves; they also indicate the direction in which the Novelle has extended its resources far beyond its initial possibilities.

Death in Venice casts light upon an involved and even paradoxical spiritual process. Von Aschenbach, the masterly and disciplined artist, finds himself sucked into a whirl of incidents which bring about his moral and physical destruction; but as he yields to the seductive forces which, by acquiescing in a deceptively normal and successful life, he had hitherto kept at a safe distance, he recognizes that his perception, his judgment, his artistry are immeasurably deepened. The fascination with disorder and impropriety and the unexpected spiritual consequences of sensuality produce in him an experience of overpowering force. He comes to realize that the staggering adventures of his innocently undertaken journey are only the progressive stages toward a truly profound vision of life—a vision which must ultimately be paid for by the radical sacrifice of all that health and beauty, success and stability had seemed to offer. *Death in Venice* is a work of superb organization and astonishing intricacy of symbolic interrelations. By a process of constant echoing of motifs on several increasingly subtle levels, each image, each sentence is made to contribute its resonant meaning to the design of the whole.

Such an act of poetic vision, still more radically felt and rendered than in *Death in Venice,* is Kafka's *A Country Doctor.* It is a puzzling but almost classic example of the modern idiom. As we read it, we must remember that its "unheard-of" intention demands on our part not merely attention to the customary "incidents" of normal fiction but a readiness to evaluate each element of the story as a poetic statement. Yet, we must not strain the function of its detail; if we regard this story primarily as a series of metaphors, if we force the analogical meaning of each phase, we do injustice to Kafka. It is more revealing to take the constituent elements as true poetic symbols: through the events of his story Kafka illuminates the ultimately inescapable human situation of helplessness. Since this sense of inadequacy is always present and not merely the result of any special or accidental circumstances, Kafka points to it in every line of the parable; and since the insight into this feeling of utter helplessness is not a slowly developing process, he projects it in a series of sudden and leaping dreamlike images. That the doctor, in a blinding snowstorm, has no ready means of reaching the—other—sick human being, that he insists at first that the patient's illness is trivial, that the family holds the naïve hope that close physical contact may bring "relief," that too late the doctor becomes aware of the woman whose presence he had never before taken seriously, that his own "sheltering" home is lost—these and many others are the equivalent symbols of the complete and irreparable state of human insecurity. The wound is the pivotal image of this incurable weakness which the doctor at every turn of his completely unhinging crisis learns to recognize and accept.

With Kafka a long history of experience and form has come to an end. It is a history of ideas and attitudes, of changing assumptions and offered solutions which is not easily surveyed or summarized. From the end of the eighteenth century to our own day the intellectual and physical resources of the human being have become vastly extended, and with the larger perspectives and an increasing awareness of the potentialities of man, there has emerged an ever sharper perception of the elements of risk and ambiguity that provide the challenging climate of our life. The balance between thought and action, good and evil, hope and despair is now perhaps more precariously suspended than ever before, and it is this disturbing but revealing modern sensibility that characterizes the stories offered in this volume by an impressive company of German writers.

GREAT GERMAN

SHORT NOVELS AND STORIES

THE SORROWS OF YOUNG WERTHER[1]

Johann Wolfgang von Goethe

(1749-1832)

WHATEVER I have been able to discover of the story of poor Werther I have industriously collected, and put it now before you, and I know that you will thank me for it. You will not be able to withhold your admiration and love for his mind and character or your tears for his fate.

And you, good soul, who are labouring under the same distress as he, draw consolation from his sufferings and, if you should be prevented by fate or your own fault from finding one more intimate, let this little book be your friend.

4 May, 1771.

How glad I am to have got away! My dear friend, what a thing is the heart of man! To leave you whom I love so much, from whom I was inseparable—and yet be cheerful! I know you will forgive me. Were not all my other friendships veritably chosen by Fate to oppress a heart like mine? Poor Leonore! And yet the blame was not mine! Could I help it if her poor heart conceived a passion for me while the capricious charms of her sister afforded me agreeable entertainment! And yet—am I altogether blameless! Did I not feed her emotions? Did I not myself find pleasure in the sincere manifestations of Nature which so often made us laugh, however little conducive they were to laughter! Did I not— Oh! what is man, that he may bewail his lot?—I will, dear friend, I promise you, I will mend my ways; I will no longer chew the cud of misfortune that Fate ekes out to us, as I have always done. I will enjoy the present, and the past

[1] Translated by William Rose.

3

shall be done with. You are surely right, my best of friends. The sufferings of men would be less if they did not so busily engage their imagination—God knows why they are so constituted—in recalling the memory of bygone ills, rather than bear an indifferent present.

Will you be so good as to tell my mother that I shall look after her business as well as I can and that I shall write to her about it in a day or two ? I called on my aunt and did not by any means find the ill-tempered woman that they make her out to be at home. She is lively, impetuous and very warm-hearted. I explained to her my mother's grievances about the legacy that had been held back. She told me the reasons that had impelled her to do it and the terms under which she would be ready to hand everything over—more, in fact, than we asked.—In short, I don't want to write about it now, but tell my mother everything will be all right. And in dealing with this little matter I have again found that misunderstandings and indolence are perhaps the cause of more disturbance in the world than cunning or malice. At any rate the last two are certainly more rare.

For the rest, I am quite happy here. Solitude is delicious balm to my heart in this heavenly spot, and this youthful season pours the fulness of its warmth into my oft-shivering heart. Every tree, every hedge is a nosegay, and one would like to turn into a cockchafer to float in a sea of fragrance and find in it all the nourishment one needs.

The town itself is not very agreeable, but it lies amidst the most inexpressible natural beauty, which led the late Count von M. to lay out a garden on one of the intersecting hills which form the most charming valleys in the loveliest diversity of Nature. The garden is simple, and one feels as soon as one enters that it was planned not by a scientific gardener but by an impressionable soul that wanted here to take its pleasure. I have shed many a tear for the departed owner in the crumbling arbour which was his favourite sojourn, and is also mine. Soon I shall be the master of the garden. The gardener has become devoted to me during the few days I have been here, and he will not do at all badly by it.

10 May.

My whole soul is imbued with a wondrous serenity, like the pleasant Spring mornings which I enjoy with all my heart. I am completely alone and find life so enjoyable in this spot which was created for souls like mine. I am so happy, so absorbed in the sensation of a tranquil existence, that my art is suffering. I could not draw a line at this moment, and yet I have never been more of a painter than I am now. When the mist is rising from the lovely valley and the sun is high above the impenetrable shade of my wood, so that only now and then a ray steals into the inner sanctuary, and I lie in the tall grass by the falling brook, and discover a thousand different grasses on the surface of the earth; when I feel nearer to my heart the teeming little world among the blades, the innumerable, unfathomable creatures in the shape of worms and insects, and when I feel the presence of the Almighty Spirit Who created us all in His image, the breath of the All-loving One who sustains us as we float in illimitable bliss—Oh! friend, when the world then grows dim before my eyes and earth and sky are absorbed into my soul like the form of a beloved, I am often consumed with longing and think, ah! would that I could express it, would that I could breathe on to paper that which lives so warm and full within me, so that it might become the mirror of my soul as my soul is the mirror of the eternal God! My friend—but it is beyond my power, and I succumb to the splendour of what lies before me.

12 May.

I know not whether deluding spirits are hovering round this spot, or whether it is the divine and ardent fancy of my heart which turns everything round me into a Paradise. Right in front of the gate is a spring, a spring by which I am enchanted like Melusine and her sisters. On descending a small hill you come to an arch, with about twenty steps going down to where the clearest of water gushes from the marble rock. The little wall above, which encloses it, the tall

trees all round, the coolness of the place—there is something
so attractive, so awesome about it all. Hardly a day passes
without my sitting there for an hour. Then the girls come
from the town to fetch water, the most innocent and necessary of services which once even the daughters of kings performed. As I sit there I am reminded vividly of the days of
the patriarchs, all striking up acquaintance or plighting their
troth at the well, and kindly spirits hovering round the
springs and fountains. Oh! he can never have refreshed himself at the coolness of a spring, after a hard walk on a summer's day, who is unable to sympathise with my emotion.

13 May.

You ask whether you are to send my books along? I entreat you, for the Lord's sake, do not bother me with books.
I no longer want to be guided, enlivened or excited. This
heart is in sufficient of a ferment without their help. I need
lullabies and I have found them in abundance in my Homer.
How often do I lull my stormy spirit, for never have you seen
anything so restless, so changeable as this heart. Dear friend!
do I need to tell *you* who have so often borne the burden of
my transition from grief to excessive joy, from gentle melancholy to devastating passion? I treat my heart like a sick
child and gratify its every whim. Don't repeat this, there are
people who would take it amiss.

15 May.

The poor folk here know me already and have an affection
for me, especially the children. I have noticed something
which saddens me. When I first mixed with them and asked
in a friendly manner about one thing or another, some of
them thought I wanted to scoff, and they put me off very
rudely. I did not take offence, but I felt very keenly, what I
have often noticed, that people in a better position always
keep coldly aloof from the common folk as though they
feared to lose something by proximity, and there are even
heedless, mischievous wags who appear to act condescend-
ingly in order to make poor people all the more sensitive *tr*

their arrogance. I know quite well that we are not all equal, and that we never can be so. But I maintain that anyone who thinks it necessary to hold himself aloof from the so-called rabble, in order to keep its respect, is quite as blameworthy as a coward who hides from the enemy because he is afraid of defeat.

A little while ago I came to the spring and found a young maidservant who had put her pitcher on the lowest step and was looking round for one of her friends to help her lift it on to her head. I went down and looked at her. "Shall I help you, young woman?" I asked. She blushed to the roots of her hair. "Oh no sir!" she said. "Come, don't stand on ceremony."—She adjusted her head piece and I helped her. She thanked me and went up the steps.

17 May.

I have made all sorts of acquaintances but have not yet got into any circle. I do not know what there is about me that attracts people, so many like me and become attached to me, and it always grieves me when our paths are the same for only such a very short distance. When you ask what the people here are like, I must reply, like everywhere else. The human race does not vary much. Most people pass the greater part of their lives in work, in order to live, and the modicum of free time they have to themselves makes them so uneasy that they seek every means they can to kill it. Alas, the destiny of man!

But they are a very worthy type of folk! When I on occasion forget myself, and am able to enjoy with them the pleasures that still remain to man, to exchange jests in all candour and sincerity at a well-set board, to arrange a walk or a dance at the proper time and so on, it has a good effect on me, so long as I do not remember all the other forces lying dormant in me, all untried and becoming atrophied, which I must carefully conceal. Oh! all this clutches at my heart—and yet! It is the fate of a man like me to be misunderstood.

Alas! that the friend of my youth is gone, alas! that I ever knew her! I would say to myself "You are a fool! You are seeking what does not exist down here." But she was mine, I felt the heart, the great soul in whose presence I seemed to myself to be more than I really was, since I was everything that I could be. God! was there a single force in my soul that remained untried, was I not able to develop in her presence all the wondrous perception with which my heart embraces Nature, was not our intercourse an endless weaving of the most delicate feeling, the keenest wit, whose variations were all stamped, even to the extent of extravagance, with the impress of genius? And now—Alas! she descended before me to the grave, for she had the advantage in years. Never shall I forget her, never shall I cease to recall her steadfast mind and divine fortitude.

A few days ago I met a young man named V., a straight-forward youth with very pleasing features. He has just come down from the University, does not exactly consider himself a sage but yet thinks he knows more than other people. He was very diligent, as I can tell from various signs, in short, he is pretty well informed. As he had heard that I draw a great deal and know Greek (two unusual phenomena in these parts) he came to me and dug out his store of learning, from Batteux to Wood, from de Piles to Winckelmann, assuring me that he had read right through the first part of Sulzer's *Theory* and possessed a manuscript of Heyne's about the study of antiquity. I did not pursue the subject.

I have made the acquaintance of another very worthy fellow, the prince's bailiff. A straightforward, simple man. They say it does one's heart good to see him among his children, of whom he has nine. In particular they talk a great deal about his eldest daughter. He has invited me to come and see him, and I am going to call on him very soon. He lives in one of the prince's hunting lodges, an hour and a half from here, to which he received permission to move after the death of his wife, since he found staying here in the town, in the bailiff's lodge, too painful.

In addition I have come across a few eccentric oddities whom I find quite insufferable, most insupportable of all being their attestations of friendship.

Farewell! you will like this letter, it is all about things that have happened.

22 May.

That the life of man is only a dream has already occurred to many, and I also am always haunted by this feeling. When I see the restrictions by which the active, speculative powers of man are hemmed in, when I see how all activity is directed toward the satisfaction of needs which themselves have no other purpose than to prolong our wretched existence, and that the only way to meet certain speculations is by a dreamy resignation, in which we paint the walls of our prison with coloured figures and bright prospects—all this, Wilhelm, makes me dumb. I turn in upon myself and find a world! But again more with presentiment and obscure craving than plastic power and vital force. Everything swims before my senses and I continue on my way through the world with a dreamy smile.

All learned teachers and instructors are agreed that children do not know the reason for their desires. But nobody likes to believe that grown-ups are also walking unsteadily upon this earth, that, like children, they do not know whence they come nor whither they are going, that their actions are equally devoid of true purpose, that they are ruled in the same way by the promise of biscuits, cake or the birch, and yet it seems to me the thing is evident.

I willingly admit, for I know what your reply will be, that the happiest mortals are those who, like children, live for the day, drag about their dolls, don and doff their clothes, creep respectfully round the cupboard where mother keeps the tarts and, when they at last snatch what they are after, stuff their cheeks and cry for more.—Such beings are happy. And they also are well-off who give high-sounding names to their miserable pursuits, or even their passions, and attribute to them a colossal influence on the welfare and prosperity of the human race. He is lucky who can do so! But whoever in his humbleness recognizes what all this leads to, who sees how neatly every contented citizen trims his little garden into an

Eden, and how even unhappy mortals pant along patiently under their heavy load and everybody alike is eager to see the light of the sun for another minute—such a man is tranquil and likewise creates his world out of his own soul, happy because he is a human being. And then, circumscribed as he is, he yet always preserves in his heart the sweet feeling of freedom and the thought that he can leave this prison when he will.

26 May.

You know of old the way I settle down, build myself a cabin in some intimate spot and take up my modest quarters there. I have again found a corner that attracts me.

About an hour's journey from the town lies a hamlet called Wahlheim.[1] It is very interestingly situated on a hill and, when you walk out of the village by the footpath above, you see the whole valley spread out at your feet. A kindly landlady, obliging and cheerful in her old age, dispenses wine, beer and coffee and, what is most delightful of all, there are two limes whose spreading branches cast their shade over the little open space in front of the church, which is closed in on all sides by the cottages of the peasants, their barns and farmyards. I have rarely found a spot more intimate or cosy, and I have my little table and chair brought out from the inn, drink my coffee and read my Homer. The first time I came by accident upon the limes one fine afternoon, the place was a solitude. Everybody was in the fields. Only one little boy about four years of age was sitting on the ground, holding a child of about six months between his feet, clasping him with both arms to his breast so that he formed a kind of armchair for him and, in spite of the vivacity which sparkled in his black eyes, he was quite still. The sight pleased me and, sitting down on a plough opposite them, I amused myself by drawing their brotherly attitude, including the neighbouring hedge, the doorway of a threshing-floor and some broken cartwheels, just as they all stood, so that in an hour I had

---

[1] The reader need not exert himself to find out which are the places referred to here, as it has been necessary to change the names mentioned in the original letters.

made a well-grouped and very interesting sketch without adding anything at all that was not in my model. This strengthened my resolution to keep to Nature in the future. Nature alone is infinitely rich, and Nature alone forms the great artist. Much can be adduced in favour of rules that can be applied with more or less equal justice in praise of middle-class society. The man who models himself on them will never produce anything inferior or in bad taste, just as one who allows his life to be fashioned by precepts and the laws of propriety will never become a disagreeable neighbour or a remarkable villain; on the other hand, whatever people may say, rules destroy the true feeling for Nature and its true expression. You will say, "That is too severe! they only act as a check, prune the rank tendrils, and so on." My good friend, shall I submit a parable to you? It is like love. A youth cleaves wholly to a maid, passes all his hours in her company, expends all his forces, all his fortune, to express to her at every moment that he is completely devoted to her. And then there comes a Philistine, a man engaged in a public office, who says to him, "Young Man, to love is human, only you must love in a human way! Divide up your hours, giving some to work, and your hours of recreation you may dedicate to your maid; calculate your fortune, and from whatever you have beyond your needs you may offer her a gift, say on her birth or name day, only not too often, and so on." If he obeys, he will become an efficient young man and I would advise any prince to give him a post in the government service; but there will be an end to his love and, if he is an artist, to his art. Oh my friends! Why does the stream of genius break forth so rarely, so rarely roar down in a raging torrent, mountain high, to convulse your wondering souls? My friends, there are tranquil fellows dwelling on both banks whose arbours, tulip-beds and cabbage-plots would be devastated, and so they are able to ward off the threatening danger by timely damming and draining.

27 May.

I see that I have lapsed into parable and ecstatic declamation, and have quite forgotten to tell you the sequel to my adventure with the children. I had been sitting on my plough for about two hours entirely absorbed in perceptions of the picturesque which my letter of yesterday will have transmitted to you in a very fragmentary manner. Towards evening a young woman comes up to the children, who during all this time had not moved, with a little basket on her arm, and calls out when she is still some distance away, "Philip, you are a very good boy." She greeted me, I thanked her, stood up, went up to her and enquired whether she was the mother of the children. She said she was and, giving the older one half a roll, she picked up the baby and kissed it with every sign of maternal affection. "I gave my Philip the baby to hold," she said, "and went into the town with my eldest boy to buy white bread and sugar and an earthenware saucepan for porridge." I saw all this in the basket from which the lid had fallen off. "I want to cook Hans (that was the name of the baby) some broth before he goes to bed; my scamp of an eldest broke my saucepan yesterday as he was quarrelling with Philip over what was left of the porridge." I enquired about the eldest boy, and she had hardly told me that he was chasing a couple of geese on the common when he came running up with a hazel switch for Philip. In further conversation with the mother I learned that she was the daughter of the schoolmaster, and that her husband was on his way to Switzerland to fetch a legacy that had been left him by a cousin. "They tried to cheat him out of it," she said, "and did not answer his letters, so he has gone there himself. I hope nothing has happened to him, as I have not heard from him since." I found it difficult to tear myself away. I gave each of the children a *Kreuzer*, including one for the baby which I gave to the mother to buy him a roll for his broth when she went into the town, and so I left them.

I tell you, my dear fellow, when my mind is all a riot, it is soothed by the sight of such a mortal pursuing in tranquil contentment the narrow round of her existence, making both ends meet from day to day, and with no other thought, when she sees the leaves falling, but that winter is near.

I have often gone out since, and the children have become

quite used to me. When I drink my coffee they have their share of the sugar, and they share my bread and butter and sour milk in the evening. On Sundays they never fail to receive their *Kreuzer*, and if I am not there after the hour of prayer the landlady has orders to pay it to them.

I have won their confidence and they tell me all sorts of things. I find it particularly delightful to watch them vent their passions and express their desires so naïvely when a number of children from the village are collected together.

I had a lot of trouble to relieve the mother of her apprehension lest they might "incommode the gentleman."

16 June.

Why don't I write to you? You ask me that though you are also numbered among the scholars! You should be able to divine that I am well, and indeed—in short, I have met someone in whom my heart is interested. I have—I do not know.

To tell you in proper order how it happened that I made the acquaintance of one of the most charming of beings will be no easy matter; I am content and happy, so am not likely to be a satisfactory narrator.

An angel! By Heaven, everybody says that of his mistress! Doesn't he? And yet I am incapable of telling you how perfect she is, or why she is perfect; enough, she has taken complete possession of my mind.

So much naïvete combined with such intelligence, such kindness and such resolve, such tranquillity of soul in such an active life.

This is all hopeless twaddle that I am saying about her, mere abstractions which fail to express a single feature of her real self. Another time—No, not another time, I will tell you now, immediately. If I don't do it now, I never shall. For, between ourselves, since I began this letter I have been three times on the verge of laying down my pen, saddling my horse and riding off though I vowed early this morning that I would not—and yet every minute I go to the window to see how high the sun stands. . . .

I could not help it, I had to go out to her. I am back once

more, Wilhelm, and will eat my supper and finish this letter. How it enraptures my soul to see her among the dear happy children, her eight brothers and sisters.

If I continue like this, you will be no wiser at the end than you were at the beginning, so listen, I will force myself to give you details.

I wrote to you recently that I had made the acquaintance of the bailiff S., and that he had invited me to come and visit him soon at his hermitage, or rather his little kingdom. I neglected to do so and would perhaps never have gone, if there had not been revealed to me by accident the treasure concealed in that tranquil spot.

The young people here had arranged a ball in the country, and I gladly agreed to go. I offered my escort to a nice, good-looking, but not otherwise interesting girl in this town, and it was settled that I was to hire a coach to drive out to the scene of the festivities with my partner and her cousin, and that we were to pick up Charlotte S. on the way. "You will make the acquaintance of a beautiful girl," my partner said, as we drove through a broad avenue in the wood towards the hunting lodge. "Take care," her cousin added, "that you don't fall in love." "What do you mean?" I asked. "She is already betrothed," the former replied, "to a very worthy man who has gone to put his affairs in order after his father's death and to apply for an important post." The information did not interest me particularly.

The sun was still a quarter of an hour from the hilltop when we reached the lodge gate; it was very sultry and the ladies expressed their anxiety lest we should be overtaken by a storm which we could see gathering in heavy, whitish-gray little clouds round the horizon. I relieved their fears by pretending to a knowledge of the weather, though I began myself to have a foreboding that our festivities would be interrupted.

I had alighted, and a maid who came to the gate begged us to wait a moment, Mamselle Lottchen would be with us straightway. I went across the courtyard to the well-built house and, when I had ascended the steps in front and entered at the door, I caught sight of the most charming scene that I have ever witnessed. In the entrance hall there swarmed six children, from two to eleven years of age, round a handsome girl of middle height, who wore a simple white frock with pink bows on the breast and arms. She was holding a loaf of black bread and cutting a slice for each of the children round her in proportion to its age and appetite, offering it with such an amiable air and each one crying "Thank you!" so artlessly, after he had stretched his little hands up as high as he could before his slice was cut, and then springing away contentedly with his supper or, if he was of a quieter nature, walking tranquilly towards the gate to see the strangers and the coach in which their Lotte was to drive away.—"I beg your pardon," she said, "for giving you the trouble of coming in and making the ladies wait. While I was dressing and making all sorts of arrangements for the house in my absence, I forgot to give my children their supper, and they won't have their bread cut by anyone but me." I paid her some harmless compliment while my whole soul was absorbed in the contemplation of her figure, her voice, her bearing, and I had just time to recover from my surprise when she ran into the room to fetch her gloves and fan. The children kept at a little distance, casting sidelong glances at me, and I went up to the youngest who was a most pleasant looking child. He had just drawn back when Lotte appeared in the doorway and said, "Louis, shake hands with your cousin." The boy did so with a very frank air, and I could not refrain from kissing him heartily in spite of his dirty little nose. "Cousin?" I said, as I offered her my hand. "Do you consider that I deserve the happiness of being related to you?" "Oh!" she said, with a roguish smile, "our circle of cousins is very extensive, and I should be very sorry if you were the least worthy among them." As we went she ordered Sophie, the next oldest sister to herself, a girl of about eleven, to keep an eye on the little ones, and greet their father when he came back from his ride. The little ones she admonished to obey their sister Sophie as they would herself, and some of them expressly promised to do so. A pert little blonde, however, of about six years, said, "But it isn't you, after all, Lottchen! we like you better." The two eldest boys had climbed up behind the coach, and at my request she allowed them to travel with us until we reached the edge of the wood, so long as they promised not to tease each other and to hold on firmly.

Hardly had we fitted ourselves in and the ladies greeted one another, each in turn expressing her views about the others' costumes, particularly bonnets, and duly passing in review the company that they expected to meet, when Lotte stopped the coach for her brothers to descend; they asked to kiss her hand once more, and the older one did so with all the delicacy that could be expected of a boy of fifteen, the other with impetuousness and levity. She bade them give her love once more to the little ones, and the coach rolled on.

The cousin enquired whether she had finished the book she had recently sent her. "No," said Lotte. "I do not like it; you can have it back. The one you sent me before was no better." When I asked what the books were, I was amazed at her reply.[1] There was so much character in all she said, and with every word I discovered fresh charms, saw new flashes of intelligence lighting up her features, which appeared gradually to brighten with pleasure because she felt that I understood her.

"When I was younger," she said, "I liked nothing so much as novels. Heaven knows I felt happy when I could sit in some corner on Sundays and share with my whole heart the fortune or distress of some Miss Jenny. Nor do I deny that this kind of romance still has some charm for me. But since I now so seldom have time for a book, it must be suited to my taste. And the author I most prefer is the one in whom I find my own world again, who describes happenings such as I see around me and yet whose story I find as interesting, as sympathetic as my own domestic existence, which is, to be sure, not a Paradise, but nevertheless on the whole a source of inexpressible bliss."

[1] It has been thought necessary to suppress this passage in the Manuscript so as not to afford anyone grounds for complaint. Although, as a matter of fact, no author can be much concerned at the judgment of a single girl and an unbalanced young man.

I did my best to conceal my emotions at these words. I was not, it is true, very successful, for when I heard her speak incidentally, but with such truth, about the Vicar of Wakefield and about—,[1] I lost my control and told her everything that forced itself to my lips, and only noticed after some time, when Lotte directed her remarks to the others, that these had been sitting there the whole time with wide-open eyes, as though they were not there at all. The cousin looked at me more than once with a mocking air, which however was of little consequence to me.

The conversation turned upon the pleasure of dancing. "If this passion is a fault," said Lotte, "I willingly confess I know nothing that excels dancing. And when I have something on my mind and drum out a quadrille on my squeaky old harpsichord, then everything is all right again."

How I gazed into her black eyes as she spoke, how her vivacious lips and her fresh, lively mien drew my whole soul on, how totally absorbed I became in the glorious feeling of listening to her, so that I often did not even hear the words by which she expressed herself!—Of this you can have some idea, since you know me. In short, I descended from the coach as though in a dream when we came to a halt in front of the summer house, and I was still so immersed in dreams amid the darkling world around me that I hardly noticed the music which was wafted down to us from the brightly lit hall.

Two gentlemen named Audran and a certain N.N.—who can remember everybody's name!—who were the partners of Lotte and the cousin, met us at the coach door, took charge of their ladies, and I escorted mine upstairs.

We glided round one another in minuets, I engaged one lady after another, and it was just the least attractive ones who could not manage to change hands and end the figure. Lotte and her partner began an English quadrille, and you can imagine how happy I was when the turn came for her to begin the figure with us. You should see her dance! She is so

[1] The names of some of our native authors have been omitted here also. Whoever shares Lotte's appreciation will certainly feel in his own heart who they are, if he should read these lines. And there is no necessity for anybody else to know.

absorbed in it, heart and soul, her whole body *one* harmony, as care-free, as unaffected, as though nothing else mattered, as though she thought or felt nothing else, and it is certain that at such moments everything else has ceased to exist for her.

I asked her for the second quadrille, but she promised me the third, and with the most charming ingenuousness in the world she assured me that she was very fond of dancing in the German way. "It is the fashion here," she continued, "that each couple who are together remain together in the German dance, but my partner is an indifferent waltzer and he will be grateful if I relieve him of the labour. Your lady can't waltz either and doesn't like it, and I saw during the quadrille that you waltz well; if you care to be my partner for the German dance, go and ask leave of my partner while I go and ask your lady." I agreed, and it was soon arranged that her partner should sit out the waltz with mine.

We then began, and took delight in interlacing our arms in diverse ways. What charm, what fleetness of movement! And when we came to the waltz, and the dancers revolved round each other like planets, there was at first a certain amount of confusion since very few are expert at it. We were prudent and let them wear themselves out, and when the clumsiest couples had left the floor we joined in and held out valiantly to the end together with another pair, Audran and his partner. Never have I danced so easily. I was no longer a mortal. To have the most charming creature in the world in my arms and to fly around with her like lightning, so that everything round about ceased to exist—Wilhelm, to be candid, I *did* vow that the girl I loved, on whom I had claims, should never waltz with another, even if it meant the end of me. You understand!

We took a turn or two round the room after the dance in order to recover our breath. Then she sat down, and the lemons I had stolen when the punch was being brewed, which were now the only ones left and which I brought her cut into slices with sugar, had an excellent refreshing effect, except that with every slice the lady sitting next to her took out of the cup a stab went through my heart, though for the sake of decency I had to offer it to her also.

In the third quadrille we were the second couple. As we danced through the ranks and I, God knows with what rapture, kept my eyes, as she hung upon my arm, fixed upon hers, in which shone the sincerest expression of frank and pure enjoyment, we reached a lady who had attracted my attention on account of her sympathetic mien, though her face was no longer exactly young. She looked at Lotte with a smile, lifted a minatory finger, and mentioned the name Albert twice with considerable emphasis as she whirled past.

"Who is Albert," I asked Lotte, "if it is not presumption on my part?" She was about to reply when we had to separate to make the figure of eight, and it seemed to me that I saw a certain pensiveness shade her brow as we crossed in front of each other. "Why should I keep it from you?" she said, as she gave me her hand for the promenade. "Albert is a worthy man to whom I am as good as betrothed." This was not news to me, for the girls had told me in the carriage, and yet it *was* entirely new to me, since I had not thought of it in connection with her who had come to mean so much to me in such a short time. Enough—I became confused, forgot the steps, and danced in between the wrong couple so that everything became mixed up and Lotte's whole presence of mind and pulling and tugging were necessary to restore order.

The dance had not yet come to an end when the flashes of lightning, which we had for some time seen gleaming on the horizon and which I had pretended were sheet lightning, began to grow more pronounced and the thunder drowned the music. Three ladies ran out of the ranks, followed by their partners, confusion became general, and the music ceased. It is natural, when our pleasure is interrupted by an accident or something terrifying, that the impression made upon us should be stronger than usual, partly because of the contrast which is felt so vividly, partly and even more because our senses are susceptible and receive an impression all the more quickly. To these causes must be attributed the wondrous grimaces which I saw appear on the faces of several ladies. The wisest of them sat down in a corner with her back to the window and held her hands over her ears, another knelt down and buried her face in the lap of the first one, a third pushed her way in between them both and clasped her little sisters to her with a thousand tears. Some wanted to drive home, others, who were even less aware what they were doing, had not sufficient presence of mind to avoid the impertinences of some of the young gentlemen who had had a little to drink, and who appeared to be busily engaged in capturing from the lips of the beauties in distress the timorous prayers which were meant for Heaven. Some of the gentlemen had gone downstairs to smoke a quiet pipe, and the rest of the company did not refuse when the hostess hit upon the clever idea of showing us into a room which had curtains and shutters. Hardly had we entered when Lotte began to arrange chairs in a circle, to seat the guests and suggest a game.

I saw more than one gentleman purse his lips and stretch his limbs in expectation of a luscious forfeit. "We are going to play at Counting," she said, "so pay attention. I am going round in a circle from right to left, and each of you must also count round the number that comes to him, but it must go like wildfire, and whoever hesitates or makes a mistake receives a box on the ears, and so on to a thousand."—It was a merry sight. She went round the circle with her arm stretched out. "One," cried the first, his neighbor "two," "three" the next and so on. Then she began to go more quickly, more and more quickly. One man missed his number, *smack!* a box on the ears; the next man laughed so much that he also missed, *smack!* And more and more quickly. I received two slaps on the face myself, and with secret pleasure I thought I felt that they were harder than those she gave the others. A general uproar and outburst of laughter brought the game to an end before the thousand was counted. Those who were most intimate with each other drew aside, the storm was over, and I followed Lotte into the ballroom. On the way she said, "During the ear-boxing they forgot the weather and everything!" I did not know what to reply. "I was one of the most timorous," she said, "and by pretending to be brave in order to give the others courage I became courageous myself." We stepped to the window, the thunder could be heard away to the side, and the glorious rain was pattering down on to the earth, while the most refreshing fragrance rose up to us in a full, warm vapour. She stood leaning on her elbow, her gaze searching the landscape; she looked up to the heavens and then at me, I saw her eyes fill with tears, she put her hand on mine and murmured—*Klopstock!* I became submerged in the flood of emotions which this name let loose upon me. I could not bear it, I bent over her hand and kissed it amidst the most ecstatic tears. And looked up again into her eyes—Noble Poet! would that thou hadst seen thy apotheosis in that gaze, and would that I might never hear again thy so oft desecrated name!

19 June.

I no longer know where I broke off my story. All I know is that it was two o'clock in the morning when I went to bed, and that if, instead of writing, I had been able to babble to you, I should probably have kept you up till daybreak.

I have not yet told you what happened on our way home from the ball and I haven't time to tell you to-day either.

There was a lovely sunrise. The dripping wood and the freshened fields round about. Our companions in the coach were nodding off. She asked if I did not want to join them, as far as she was concerned I need not be embarrassed. "As long as I see your eyes open," I said, looking at her firmly, "there is no danger of that." And we both held out until we reached the gates of her home, when the maid opened gently and assured her, in answer to her enquiries, that her father and the little ones were all right and were still asleep. Then I took leave with the protestation that I would see her that same day, and I kept my promise; and since that time sun, moon and stars can journey calmly on their round, I know not whether it is night or day and the whole world about me has ceased to have any existence.

21 June.

My days are as happy as those God allots to His saints; and whatever the future may have in store for me, I shall not be able to say that I have not experienced the joys, the purest joys of life. You know my Wahlheim. I am quite settled there. It is only half an hour away from Lotte, and there I feel I am myself and possess all the happiness that is granted to mankind.

Had I but thought, when I selected Wahlheim as the goal of my walks, that it lies so near to Heaven! How often in the course of my long wanderings did I see the hunting lodge, which now encompasses all my desires, either from the hill or in the plain across the river.

Dear Wilhelm, I have pondered over so many things, man's craving to extend, to make new discoveries, to rove about; and then again his inward urge to submit willingly to his limitations, to travel along the path of custom and have no thought for the right hand or the left.

It is wonderful how I came here and gazed down from the hilltop into the lovely valley, how I was enchanted by everything round about. There the little wood! Oh could you but mingle in its shade! There the summit of the mount! Oh could you but survey from there the broad landscape! The chain of hills and intimate valleys! Oh could I but lose myself in them! I hurried thither and returned, and had not found that which I sought. Oh! distant vistas are like the distant future! A vast darkling whole lies before our soul, our emotions merge into it, like our gaze, and we yearn to surrender our entire being, to be filled with all the rapture of a single great glorious feeling.—And oh! when we rush up to it, when the distant *there* becomes *here*, everything is as it was before, and we stand hemmed in by our poverty, while our soul pants for the draught that is beyond its reach.

And so even the most restless wanderer longs at last for his native land, and finds in his poor cabin, at the breast of his wife, amidst his children and the occupations necessary for their sustenance, all the rapture which he sought in vain in the wide and dreary world.

When I set out at daybreak to walk to my Wahlheim and pick peas for myself in the garden of the inn, and sit down and shell them while I read my Homer; when I then go into the little kitchen to find a pot, cut off a piece of butter, put my peas on the fire, cover the pot and sit down to keep turning them—then I feel so vividly how the glorious haughty suitors of Penelope slaughtered oxen and swine, cut them up and roasted them. Nothing so fills me with a sincere, calm emotion as the features of patriarchal life which I, thanks be to God, am able without affectation to weave into my mode of living.

How happy I am that my heart can feel the simple, innocent joy of the man who brings to his table a cabbage that he has grown himself, and enjoys at the same moment not only the cabbage but also all the fine days, the beautiful morning when he planted it, the pleasant evenings when he watered it and when he rejoiced in its increasing size.

29 June.

The physician came here from the town the day before yesterday to visit the bailiff and found me on the floor among Lotte's children, some crawling over me and the others teasing me while I was tickling them, and we all made a great uproar. The doctor, who is a very dogmatic puppet and arranges the folds of his cuffs while he is discoursing and pulls out his frill as far as his navel, thought this beneath the dignity of an intelligent person, as I could see by the way he turned up his nose. I did not let myself be put out, however, but let him pursue his wise disquisition, and continued to rebuild a house of cards that the children had knocked down. He afterwards went about the town complaining that the bailiff's children were sufficiently badly brought up without that fellow Werther spoiling them completely.

Yes, Wilhelm, children are nearer to my heart than anything else on earth. When I watch them and see in the little creatures the germs of all the virtues and all the powers that they will one day find so indispensable, when I see in their obstinacy all the future constancy and firmness of character, in their wantonness all the future good humour and facility in gliding over the hazards of life, all so unspoilt, so undiminished—I always, always repeat the golden words of the Teacher of men, "Unless ye become even as one of these!"

And yet we treat them, who are such as we, whom we should look upon as our models, after the manner of inferior beings. They are said to be lacking in will!—Have we then none? And in what lies our superiority? In our age and maturer wisdom? God in Heaven, Thou seest old children and young children, and that is all, and Thy Son has long since proclaimed in which Thou findest greater joy. But they do not believe in Him and do not hear Him—that is also out of fashion!—and they model their children upon themselves, and—Adieu, Wilhelm, I have no wish to continue this idle talk.

1 July.

What Lotte must be to a sick man I feel in my own poor heart, which is worse off than many a one which is languishing on a bed of sickness. She is to pass some days in the town at the bedside of an honest woman who, so the doctors say, is nearing her end, and who wishes to have Lotte near her in her last moments. I went with her last week to visit the pastor of St., a hamlet an hour's journey away in the mountains. We arrived about four. Lotte had brought her second sister with her. When we entered the courtyard of the parsonage, which is shaded by two tall walnut trees, we found the good old man sitting on a bench before the house door, and when he saw Lotte it was as though he were imbued with new life. He forgot his knotted stick and made an effort to rise and come towards her. She ran towards him and made him sit down, while she took a seat at his side, gave him her father's best greetings, and embraced his youngest child, an unclean, ugly lad but the darling of his father's old age. You ought to have seen her occupying the old man's attention, raising her voice to reach his half-deaf ears, telling him about robust young people who had unexpectedly died, how excellent Karlsbad was and praising his resolve to go there next summer, and how she thought that he looked much better and more cheerful than the last time she had seen him. I had meantime paid my respects to the pastor's wife. The old man became quite cheerful, and since I could not help praising the handsome walnut trees that shaded us so pleasantly, he began, though with a little difficulty, to tell us their history. "The old one," he said, "we don't know who planted that, some say one pastor, some say another. But the young one over there is the same age as my wife, fifty years next October. Her father planted it the morning of the day she was born. He was my predecessor in the living, and I cannot tell you how much he loved that tree; it is in truth no less dear to me. My wife was seated beneath it on a log with her knitting when I first entered this courtyard as a poor student seven and twenty years ago." Lotte enquired after his daughter, and he told her that she had gone out to the workmen in the meadow with Mr. Schmidt; then, continuing his narrative, he explained how his predecessor had grown fond of him, and the daughter as well, and how he had first become his curate and then his successor. He had hardly finished his story when his daughter came through the garden with the said Mr. Schmidt. She welcomed Lotte with considerable warmth, and I must admit that I found her by no means unattractive. A lively brunette with a good figure, who would have been quite entertaining company during a short stay in the country. Her suitor, for as such Mr. Schmidt soon presented himself, was a cultivated but reserved individual, who did not show any desire to join in our conversation, although Lotte kept turning to him, and what most depressed me was that I thought I could gather from his expression that it was caprice and ill-humour rather than limited intelligence which prevented him from being more communicative. In the sequel this unfortunately grew only too evident, for when Friederike, as we walked along, kept to the side of Lotte or occasionally came over to me, the gentleman's face, which was in any case of a brownish hue, darkened so visibly that it was time for Lotte to tug me by the sleeve and advise me to refrain from making myself agreeable to Friederike. Now nothing aggravates me more than when people torment each other, especially when young couples, who might be most receptive to all the joys that come in the prime of life, spoil the few days that might be so pleasant with crotchets, and only realise when it is too late that they have wasted what cannot be recovered. It vexed me mightily, and when we returned to the parsonage towards evening and were supping at a table in the courtyard on bread dipped in milk, I could not help taking up the subject when the conversation turned on the joys and sorrows of this world, and attacking most heartily the vice of ill-humour. "We mortals frequently complain," I began, "that the days of our happiness are too few and those of our sorrow too many, and I think we are generally wrong. If our hearts were always open to enjoy the good which God gives us each day, then we should also have sufficient strength to bear misfortune when it comes." "But we have not control over our natures," replied the pastor's wife. "How much depends on our bodies! When we feel unwell, everything seems wrong." I admitted that. "Then let us regard it as a disease and enquire whether there is no remedy for it." "That is worth considering," said Lotte. "I believe at least that much depends on ourselves. I know it from my own nature. When anything worries me and is inclined to make me depressed, I jump up and sing a couple of quadrille airs up and down the garden, and it goes immediately." "That is just what I wanted to say," I rejoined. "Ill-humour is like laziness, for it is a kind of laziness; our natures are strongly inclined that way, and yet, when we only have the strength to assume control of ourselves, our tasks are done with no difficulty and we find a real pleasure in activity." Friederike was very attentive, and her young suitor objected that man is not his own master, having control least of all over his emotions. "We are referring here to a disagreeable emotion," I replied. "Everyone is anxious to get rid of it, and nobody knows the extent of his strength until he has tried. A sick man will certainly consult all the physicians and will not reject the greatest trials, the bitterest medicines, in order to win back the health he desires." I noticed that the worthy old man was straining his hearing to take part in the conversation, and I raised my voice as I directed my remarks to him. "People preach against so many vices," I said, "but I have never heard anyone denouncing ill-humour from the pulpit."[1]

[1] We now possess an excellent sermon by Lavater on this text, among those on the Book of Jonah.

"The pastors in the towns ought to do that," he answered, "the peasants are never ill-tempered. Though it would not hurt occasionally and would at least be a lesson to our wives—to say nothing of the bailiff." Everybody burst out laughing, and he joined in heartily until he fell into a fit of coughing, which interrupted the conversation for a time, before the young man again took up the thread. "You called ill-humour a vice, I think that is an exaggeration." "Not at all," I declared, "if that which harms oneself and one's dear ones deserves the name. Is it not enough that we cannot make each other happy; must we in addition deprive each other of the pleasure that each heart is able at times to afford itself? And I should like to know the name of the man who is in an ill-humour and yet has the virtue to conceal it, to bear it alone without destroying the happiness of those around him. Is it not rather an inward displeasure at our own unworthiness, a dissatisfaction with ourselves which is always combined with an envy that a foolish conceit has incited? We see happy people whose happiness has not been caused by *us*, and we cannot bear it." Lotte smiled at me when she saw the vehemence with which I spoke, and a tear in the eye of Friederike spurred me on to continue. "Woe be to those," I said, "who abuse their power over the heart of another to deprive it of the simplest joys that spring up in it. All the gifts, all the good-will in the world, cannot replace a moment of pure pleasure which the envious constraint of a tyrant has embittered."

My whole heart was full at this moment, the memory of so much that had happened in the past rushed into my soul, and my eyes filled with tears.

"If people would only think to themselves every day," I cried, "that you can do nothing for your friends save leave them their pleasure and augment their happiness by enjoying it with them. Have you the power, when their inmost soul is tortured by an agony of passion, torn with grief, to offer them a drop of comfort? And when the last fatal sickness overtakes the being whom you helped to wear away in the days of her youth, and she lies there in pitiable exhaustion, her eyes raised unseeingly to Heaven, the death-sweat coming and going on her brow, and you stand at the bedside like one of the damned, with the feeling in your inmost soul that with all your power you can do nothing, you are inwardly convulsed with the agonising thought that you would give your all to be able to instill into the dying being a particle of vigour, a spark of courage."

The memory of such a scene, at which I had been present, took possession of me with undiminished force as I uttered these words. I put my handkerchief to my eyes and left the company. Only the voice of Lotte, who called to me that it was time to go, brought me to myself. And how she scolded me on the way home for taking too warm interest in everything, declaring that it would be my ruin, that I should spare myself!—Oh angel! For thy sake I must live!

6 July.

She is still looking after her dying friend and is always the same, always the devoted, lovely creature who soothes pain and spreads happiness wherever she goes. She went for a walk yesterday evening with Marianne and little Amalie. I knew of this and went to meet them. After an hour and a half we had come back to the town and the spring which is so precious to me, and which became a thousand times more precious when Lotte sat down on the wall beside it. I gazed around, and alas! the time when my heart was so solitary again came vividly into my mind. "Beloved spring," I said, "I have not rested since then in thy cool shade, and often have I hastened past thee without a glance." I looked down and saw that Amalie was ascending the steps with a glass of water. I looked at Lotte and felt all that she means to me. Amalie meanwhile approached with the glass and Marianne wanted to take it from her, but "No!" cried the child with the sweetest expression, "no, you shall drink first, Lotte!" I was so enraptured with the sincerity, the goodness with which she said this, that I found no other way to express my emotion but to take the child up in my arms and kiss her so violently that she straightway began to scream and weep. "That was wrong of you," said Lotte. I was disconcerted. "Come, Amy," she continued, taking the child by the hand

and leading her down the steps, "quick, wash your face in the running water and it won't hurt you." As I stood there and watched the child busily rubbing her cheeks with her wet hands; when I saw the faith she had that the miraculous spring would wash away all defilement and prevent the disgrace of growing an ugly beard; how she even continued to wash away after Lotte had said, "It's enough!", as though too much was better than too little—I tell you, Wilhelm, I have never felt more reverent at a baptism. And when Lotte came up, I would have liked to cast myself at her feet as before a prophet who has washed away in consecrated water the sins of a nation.

That evening I could not help, in the happiness of my heart, relating the incident to a man from whom I expected human understanding, since he is a man of common sense. But what did I find! He said it was very wrong of Lotte, that children should not be told such stories, since they gave rise to all sorts of misconceptions and superstitions, against which children should be guarded at an early age. It occurred to me, however, that he had had a child of his own baptised a week previously, so I said nothing and silently kept to my conviction that we ought to treat children as God treats us.— He makes us happiest when He lets us wander on under the intoxication of agreeable illusions.

8 July.

What children we are! How we crave a glance! What children we are! We had gone to Wahlheim. The ladies were driving out, and during our walks I thought I could see in Lotte's black eyes—I am foolish, forgive me, but you should see these eyes. In short, for I can hardly keep my eyes open, the ladies were getting into the coach round which young W., Selstadt, Audran and I were standing. They were talking through the window to the fellows who were, to be sure, pretty thoughtless and frivolous. I sought Lotte's eyes! Alas! they were glancing from one to the other! But on me! me! me! who stood there absorbed in her alone, they did not fall! My heart bade her a thousand adieux! And she did not see me! The coach drove past and a tear stood in my eye. I gazed after her! And I saw Lotte's coiffure leaning out of the window as she turned to look back. Oh! at me?—It is in this uncertainty that I hover! It is this which is my consolation. Perhaps it was I at whom she turned to look. Perhaps—good night! Oh! how childish I am!

10 July.

You should see what a foolish figure I make when she is spoken of in company. And when I am asked how I like her—like! I hate the word. What sort of a fellow must he be who likes Lotte and whose whole mind, whose whole heart is not entirely absorbed by her. Like! The other day someone asked me how I liked Ossian!

11 July.

Mrs. M. is very ill. I pray for her, for I suffer with Lotte. I see her rarely at a friend's, and to-day she told me of a marvellous happening. Old M. is a miserly curmudgeon who has curbed and harassed his wife pretty well during her life, though she has always been able to manage tolerably. A few days ago, when the doctor said there was no hope for her, she sent for her husband while Lotte was in the room and spoke to him thus: "I must confess something that might cause you confusion and vexation after my death. Hitherto I have kept house in as orderly and economical a manner as possible, but you will forgive me for having deceived you these thirty years. When we first married, you allowed me a trifling sum for food and other domestic expenses. When our household became larger and our business grew, I could not move you to increase my weekly allowance to meet the altered circumstances. In short, you know that when our expenses were greatest I had to manage with seven florins a week. I accepted this amount without protest and abstracted the remainder from the receipts every week, since no one had any suspicion that your wife would steal from the till. I have never been extravagant and would have gone tranquilly to my eternal rest without confessing this, if it were not that the one who follows me in keeping house for you will not know how to make both ends meet, and yet you might still insist that your first wife had been able to manage."

I talked with Lotte concerning the incredible delusion of the human mind, which can prevent a man from suspecting that there is something wrong when seven florins suffice to cover an obvious outlay of possibly twice as much. I have, however, myself known people who would not have been surprised at the presence in their house of the widow's inexhaustible cruse.

13 July.

No, I am not deceiving myself! I can read in her black eyes a real interest in me and my destiny. Yes, I feel (and in this matter I can trust my heart) that she—Oh! may I, can I express the Paradise that lies in these words?—that she loves me.

Loves me! How the thought exalts me in my own eyes! How I—I may tell you, perhaps, for you can sympathise with such an emotion—how I worship myself since she loves me.

And be it presumption or perception of the true state of affairs—I do not know the man whose rivalry I would have to fear in Lotte's heart. And yet—when she speaks of her betrothed with such warmth, with such affection, I feel like one who has been deprived of all his honours and dignities and has had to yield up his sword.

16 July.

Oh! how the blood rushes through my veins when my finger accidentally touches hers, when our feet meet under the table. I draw back as from a flame, and a secret force thrusts me forward again. All my senses swim. And oh! her innocence, her pure soul, does not feel the torment which these little intimacies occasion me. When she lays her hand on mine as we converse, and moves nearer to me as she grows more interested, so that her divine breath is wafted to my lips—I feel that I am about to sink to the ground as though struck by lightning. And, Wilhelm, if I should ever dare to—but no, my heart is not so depraved! Weak! weak enough! Is that not depravity?

She is sacred to me. All lust ceases in her presence. I am

never aware what I feel when I am with her; it is as though my soul were revolving in all my nerves. There is a melody which she plays on the harpsichord with the touch of an angel, so simple and spiritual. It is her favourite song, and I am cured of all my harassing bewilderment and melancholy so soon as she strikes the first note.

I do not find it difficult to believe the stories of the magic power of music in ancient times. How this simple song fascinates me! And how well she knows when to play it, often at a time when I feel like putting a bullet in my brain! All the confusion and gloom in my soul are dispersed, and I breathe more freely again.

18 July.

What meaning has the world for our souls without love, Wilhelm? It is a magic lantern without its lamp. Hardly have you inserted the lamp when the most colourful pictures appear on the white screen. And even if that were all there is, nothing but passing phantoms, yet it makes us happy when we stand in front like simple children and are enraptured by the wonderful pictures. I was unable to visit Lotte to-day, being detained by an unavoidable engagement. What could I do? I sent my lad out, just to have somebody about me who had been in her presence to-day. How impatiently I awaited his return, how glad I was to see him again! I would have liked to take him in my arms and embrace him, had I not been ashamed to do so.

It is said of the Bologna stone that when it is placed in the sun it attracts the rays, and is luminous for a time by night. So it was with the lad. The feeling that her eyes had rested on his face, his cheeks, his coat buttons, the collar of his surtout, made them all so sacred and precious to me that I would not at that moment have exchanged the lad for a thousand *Talers*. I felt so happy in his presence.—May God preserve you from laughing at this. Can these be phantoms, Wilhelm, that make us so happy?

19 July.

"I am going to see her!" I cry aloud every morning, when

I am aroused and gaze happily at the glorious sun. "I am going to see her!" And I have no further wish for the rest of the day. Everything, everything is absorbed in this prospect.

20 July.

I cannot yet accept your suggestion that I should accompany the ambassador to * * *. I am not fond of discipline, and we all know that he is, in any case, a disagreeable fellow. You write that my mother would like to see me occupied? It makes me laugh. Am I not now occupied? And is it not, at bottom, a matter of indifference whether I count peas or lentils? Everything in this world ends in nothingness, after all, and a fellow who wears himself out for somebody else's sake, without its being his own ambition, in order to achieve wealth or dignity or anything else, is simply a fool.

24 July.

Since you are so anxious that I should not neglect my drawing, I would rather say nothing about it than confess that hitherto I have done little.

I was never happier, never has my sympathy with Nature down to the stones and blades of grass been fuller and more ardent, and yet—I know not how to express myself, but my powers of perception are so weak, everything swims and trembles before my soul so that I cannot seize the outline; but I think, if I had clay or wax, I could probably fashion it out. If this lasts much longer I shall procure some clay and mould it, even if all I can make is cakes.

I have begun Lotte's portrait three times, and each time I have made a mess of it, which vexes me all the more since I got it quite successfully some time ago. Then I cut out her silhouette, and that will have to suffice.

26 July.

I have often made up my mind not to see her so frequently. If I could only keep to my resolution! Every day I succumb to temptation and promise myself sacredly that I will stay away next day, and when the morning comes I again discover some irresistible reason and find myself there before I am aware of it. Either she has said the evening before, "You will come to-morrow, won't you?" (who could remain away under such circumstances?)—or the day is so very lovely, I walk to Wahlheim, and when I am there it is only half an hour to her. I am too near to her presence—in a trice I am there. My grandmother used to tell me a story of a magnetic mountain. The ships which approached too closely to it were suddenly deprived of all their ironwork, the nails shot towards the mountain, and the poor wretches sank amidst the collapsing planks.

30 July.

Albert has arrived, and I shall go. Even if he were the best, the most noble of men, to whom I were prepared in every respect to give way, it would be intolerable to see him before my eyes in possession of so many perfections. Possession!— Enough, Wilhelm, her betrothed has arrived. A worthy, agreeable fellow, whom one cannot help liking. Luckily, I was not present when she welcomed him. It would have torn my heartstrings. He is so honourable and has never even kissed Lotte when I was there. May God reward him for it! I must love him for the respect with which he treats the girl. He is well-intentioned towards me, but I suspect that is due to Lotte more than to his own disposition, for in this matter women are delicate, and rightly so. If they can keep two admirers on good terms with each other, the advantage is always theirs, though it is seldom practicable.

Meanwhile I cannot deny Albert my esteem. His outward calm is in very vivid contrast to the restlessness of my character, which I am unable to conceal. He is a man of feeling and knows what he possesses in Lotte. He appears rarely to be in an ill-humour and, as you know, that is the sin I hate more than any other.

He considers me a man of intellect, and my attachment to Lotte, with the ardent pleasure I take in all her actions, increases his triumph, and he loves me all the more. Whether he does not sometimes plague her privately with petty jealousy is a matter about which I will offer no opinion. At any rate, I should not in his place be altogether free from the demon.

Be that as it may, my pleasure in Lotte's company is gone. Am I to call it foolishness or infatuation? What do names matter? The thing itself is evident. I knew everything that I know now before Albert came. I knew that I could have no claim on her, nor did I make any, that is to say, as far as it is possible to be without desire in the case of so many charms. And the ridiculous fellow opens his eyes wide now that the other man has arrived and takes the girl away.

I grit my teeth and mock at my wretchedness, and mock doubly and trebly at those who might say I should be resigned, since it cannot be helped.—Rid me of these fellows!— I wander about in the woods, and when I come to Lotte's and Albert is sitting with her in the summer house in the garden, and I can get no further, I behave in an extravagant manner, practise all sorts of crazy buffoonery. "For Heaven's sake," Lotte said to me to-day, "I beg of you! no more scenes like that of yesterday evening! You are dreadful when you act so wildly." Between ourselves, I wait till he is occupied elsewhere; *presto!* I am there in a trice, and I am always happy when I find her alone.

8 August.

Please Wilhelm, I did not mean you when I wrote, "Rid me of the fellows who say I ought to be resigned." I really did not think that you could be of that opinion. And at bottom you are right. Only one thing, my dear friend! In this world it is rarely possible to settle matters with an "either, or," since there are as many gradations of emotion and conduct as there are stages between a hooked nose and one that turns up.

So you will not take it amiss if I grant you your whole argument and nevertheless try to steal my way between your "either, or."

Either I have hopes of Lotte, you say, or I have not. Good! In the former case I must seek to realise them, seek to achieve the fulfilment of my desires; in the latter case I must pull myself together and try to rid myself of a wretched emotion which is bound to consume all my energies. That is well said, my friend, and—soon said.

Can you demand of the unhappy man whose life is gradually and irremediably ebbing under the influence of an insidious malady, can you demand of him that he should put an end to his torture with a dagger? Does not the disease which is consuming his energies at the same time rob him of the courage to procure his own deliverance?

You can of course answer me with a similar allegory—who would not rather submit to the amputation of an arm than risk his life by doubts and hesitations? I do not know. And we will not attack each other with allegories. Enough . . . Yes, Wilhelm, I often have such moments of bounding, vehement courage, and then, if I only knew whither, I would probably go.

10 August.

I could lead the happiest and best of lives were I not a fool. Such a combination of favourable circumstances is rarely found for the delight of a man's heart as that in which I am now placed. Alas! how true it is that our heart is alone responsible for its own happiness. To be a member of this charming family, loved by the old man like a son, by the little ones like a father, and by Lotte . . . and now this worthy Albert, who never disturbs my happiness by any display of ill-humour, who regards me with sincere friendship, who, next to Lotte, loves me more than anything in the world. Wilhelm, it is a joy to hear us on our walks, when we talk about Lotte. There has never been anything more ridiculous than this relationship, and yet it often brings the tears to my eyes.

When he tells me about her righteous mother, how she entrusted her house and children to Lotte on her deathbed and confided Lotte to his care, how since then Lotte has been imbued with a new spirit, how in her concern for the household she has really become a mother, how not a moment of her time but has been occupied or absorbed in some task of affection, and yet she has not lost her cheerful lighthearted-ness. I walk along beside him and pluck flowers by the way-side, bind them very carefully into a nosegay and—cast them into the brook that flows past to watch them gently float along. I do not know whether I have written to you that Albert is to remain here and receive a post at a handsome sal-ary from the Court, where he is in very good favour. I have rarely seen his equal for regularity and diligence at his oc-cupation.

12 August.

Albert is certainly the most excellent of men. There was an extraordinary scene between us yesterday. I went to his house to take leave of him, for I had conceived a desire to ride into the hills, whence I am now writing to you, and as I was walking up and down the room I caught sight of a pair, of pistols. "Lend me your pistols," I said, "for my journey." "Certainly," he replied, "if you will take the trouble to load them; I only keep them here *pro forma*." I took one of them down, and he continued, "Since my prudence played me such a scurvy trick, I don't like having anything more to do with the things." I was curious to hear the story. "When I was staying with a friend in the country for about three months," he told me, "I had a brace of unloaded pocket-pistols with me and slept unperturbed. One rainy afternoon, as I was sitting idly thinking, it occured to me for some rea-son or other that we might be attacked, that we might have need of the pistols and—you know the sort of thing I mean. I gave them to the servant to clean and load. He dallies with the maidservants, tries to frighten them, and, the Lord knows how, the pistol goes off with the ramrod still in it, and shoots the latter through the ball of the thumb of the right hand of one of the girls, smashing it. I had to bear the lamentation and pay the surgeon into the bargain, and since that time I leave my pistols unloaded. My dear fellow, what's the use of precautions? One cannot guard against every peril. To be sure. . . ." Now, you know, I am very fond of the man until he says "to be sure . . ."; for is it not a matter of course that every general proposition is subject to exceptions? But he is so anxious to justify his opinion, that when he thinks he has said anything rash, made a general statement, or uttered a half-truth, he never ceases to qualify, modify, add to, or subtract from what he has said, until finally there is nothing left of his original assertion. On this occasion he dilated at great length on the subject, till I at last ceased to listen to him, subsided into a state of melancholy, and pressed the mouth of the pistol with a flourish to my forehead above the right eye. "Come!" said Albert, snatching at the pistol. "What is the meaning of this?" "It is not loaded," I said. "And even so, what is the meaning of it?" he asked impatiently. "I cannot imagine how a man can be so foolish as to shoot himself. The very thought is repellent."

"Why do you people," I cried, "when you speak of anything, declare immediately 'this is foolish, this is wise, this is good, this is bad!' What is the meaning of it all? Have you discovered the inward circumstances of an action? Can you determine exactly why it happened, why it was bound to happen? Had you done that, you would be less hasty in your judgments."

"You will admit," said Albert, "that certain actions are vicious from whatever motive they may occur."

I shrugged my shoulders and granted him that. "But, my dear fellow," I continued, "even in that case there are exceptions. It is true that thieving is a vice, but does a man who sets out to steal in order to preserve himself and his family from a miserable death by starvation, deserve punishment or sympathy? Who will be the first to cast a stone at the man who sacrifices an unfaithful wife and her worthless seducer to his righteous wrath? Against the girl who in a moment of rapture loses herself amid the impetuous joys of love? Even our laws, those cold-blooded pedants, are not insensible, and refrain from punishment."

"That is a very different matter," Albert replied, "because a man who is swept away by passion is deprived of all power of reflection and is in the same category as a drunkard or a madman."—"Oh you men of reason!" I cried with a smile. "Passion! Drunkenness! Madness! You stand there so calmly, you moral creatures, so unsympathetic, scolding the drunkard, abhorring the lack of reason, passing by like the priest and thanking your God like the Pharisee that he has not made you like one of these. I have been drunk more than once, my passions were never far from madness, and for neither do I feel remorse, for I have learned in my own measure to understand that all men above the ordinary who have done anything great or seemingly impossible have invariably been decried as drunkards or madmen.

"But even in our daily life it is intolerable to hear it said of a man who has done anything at all generous, noble or unexpected, 'The fellow is crazy,' or 'The fellow is drunk.' Shame upon you sober beings! Shame upon you sages!"

"This is another of your crotchets," said Albert. "You exaggerate everything, and here at least you are certainly wrong in comparing suicide, which we are now discussing, with exalted actions, since it is not possible to regard it as anything but a weakness, for it is surely easier to die than to bear a life of agony without flinching."

I was about to break off, for no argument in the world so disconcerts me as when a fellow comes out with some insignificant platitude when I am speaking with my whole heart. But I contained myself, for it had often occurred to me and I had often been vexed at it, and rejoined with some heat, "You call that weakness? I beg of you not to be deceived by appearances. When a nation is groaning under the intolerable yoke of a tyrant, can you term it weak if it finally rises up and bursts its fetters? When a man, under the influence of horror at seeing his house break out in flames, is able to put forth all his strength and bear with ease burdens which in a calmer mood he can scarcely move—when a man, in a rage at some injury, attacks half a dozen foes single-handed and conquers them—are these to be called weak? And, my friend, if exertion is strength, why should over-tension be the reverse?"

Albert looked at me and said, "Do not take it amiss, but

the instances you quote appear to me to be quite inapplicable." "It may be so," I replied, "I have often been informed that my method of argument verges on the absurd. Let us see then whether we can in any other way depict the state of mind of a man who has resolved to cast off the burden of life, which is generaly so agreeable, for only in so far as we experience his emotions can we have the right to discuss the matter."

"Human nature," I continued, "has its limits; it can bear joy, sorrow and pain to a certain degree, but it succumbs when this is exceeded.

"The question, therefore, is not whether a man is strong or weak, but whether he can endure the measure of his suffering, moral or physical, and I find it just as extraordinary to say that a man is a coward who takes his own life, as it would be improper to call a man a coward who dies of a virulent fever."

"Paradoxical, very paradoxical," cried Albert. "Not so much as you imagine," I replied. "You will admit we call it a mortal disease when nature is so seriously affected that its forces are partly consumed, partly so put out of action that it cannot be set right, that the ordinary course of life cannot by any happy transformation be restored.

"Well, let us apply this to the mind. Let us see how man is circumscribed, how he is affected by impressions, obsessed by ideas, until finally a growing passion robs him of the power of calm reflection and brings him to grief.

"It is in vain that a cool, reasoning individual perceives the unhappy man's condition and talks to him in a persuasive manner, just as a healthy man is unable to inspire an invalid with even a modicum of his own vigour."

This was speaking in terms too general for Albert. I reminded him of a girl who had been found dead in the water some time previously, and recapitulated her story. "A respectable young creature, who had grown up within the restricted sphere of her domestic occupations, with no other prospect of amusement than being able to walk out on a Sunday in the best clothes which she had gradually accumulated, her companions being girls in a similar situation to herself, with an occasional dance on the chief holidays, or the opportunity of whiling away an hour or two by a lively chat with a neighbour about the cause of a quarrel or some scandalous rumour; whose ardent nature eventually felt more inward cravings, which were intensified by the flatteries of men. All her former pleasures gradually grew insipid, till she finally met a man to whom she was irresistibly attracted by some hitherto unknown emotion, on whom she cast all her hopes, forgetting the world about her, hearing nothing, seeing nothing, sensing nothing but him alone, longing for nothing but him alone. Unspoilt by the empty pleasures of an inconstant vanity, her desire marches straight to its fulfilment; she wants to be his, to find in an indissoluble union all the happiness which she has missed, to experience all the combined joys for which she has longed. Reiterated promises, which seal the certainty of all her hopes, bold caresses, which intensify her cravings, encompass her whole being; she hovers in a semi-conscious state of bliss, with the premonitory feeling of supreme rapture, worked up to the highest pitch, until at last she stretches forth her arms to embrace her desires—and is abandoned by her lover. Stupefied, out of her mind, she stands on the verge of an abyss, everything is dark around her, with no hope for the future, no solace, since he has left her with whom alone her existence was bound up. She is blind to the world which lies before her, to those who could replace what she has lost, she feels herself alone, abandoned by all the world. And unseeingly, oppressed by the dreadful agony in her soul, she hurls herself down to still her torment in an encircling death. —That, Albert, is the story of so many mortals, and tell me, is it not analogous to the condition of an invalid? Nature can find no way out of the entangled labyrinth of confused and contradictory instincts, and the mortal must die.

"Woe to him who would say, 'Foolish woman! Had she but waited till time had exerted its healing effect, her despair would have abated and another would have come to give her solace.' That is as though one would say, 'The fool!

to die of a fever! Had he but waited till his strength was restored, his humours were adjusted, the tumult of his blood
had subsided, all would have been well and he would still be
alive today!' "

Albert, who was still unwilling to accept my analogy,
continued to put forward objections, among others, that I
had only adduced the case of a simple girl; and he wanted to
know what excuse could be found for a reasoning being who
was not so circumscribed and understood better the con-
nections of things.

"My friend," I cried, "a man is a man, and the little reasoning power he may possess is of small advantage, or of
none at all, when passion rages and he is oppressed by the
limits of humanity. Much rather—but another time," I said,
and seized my hat. Oh! my heart was so full. And we parted,
without having understood each other. How difficult it is for
one to understand the other in this world!

15 August.

It is, after all, certain that nothing in the world renders a
man indispensable save love. I feel that Lotte would not
willingly lose me, and the children have no other notion but
that I shall return every morning. I went out to-day to tune
Lotte's harpsichord, but I was unable to set to work at it,
for the children besought me to tell them a fairy tale, and
then Lotte herself asked me to comply with their wish. I
cut the bread for their supper, which they now accept almost as eagerly from me as from Lotte, and told them their
favourite tale of the princess who was served by hands. It
teaches me a great deal, I assure you, and I am amazed at
the impression it makes on them. Since I often have to invent
an episode, which on the next occasion I forget, they tell me
at once that it was different at the previous telling, so that
I now practise reciting it mechanically in a sort of chant.
This has taught me that an author must necessarily spoil his
book when he alters the story for a second edition however
much it may be improved from the artistic point of view.
The first impression finds us receptive, and man is so constituted that he can be convinced of the most extravagant

incidents; these, however, are immediately embedded in his mind, and woe to him who attempts to erase and obliterate them.

18 August.

Was it ordained by Fate that that which renders a man happy becomes later the source of his misery?

My heart's full and ardent sympathy with Nature, which flooded me with such bliss and made the world round about into a Paradise, has now become an unbearable torment, a torturing spirit which pursues me everywhere. When I used to stand upon the rock and survey the fertile valley across the river as far as the distant hills, when I saw everything about me surge forth and germinate, the mountains clad thickly from foot to summit with tall trees, all the vales in their manifold windings shaded by the most delightful forests, with the river gently flowing among the whispering reeds, mirroring the clouds which were wafted along by the gentle evening breeze; when I heard the birds awakening the forest and the myriad swarms of midges danced merrily in the red rays of the setting sun, whose last quivering glance roused the humming chafer from his grassy bed, while the whirring life about me drew my attention to the ground, where the moss, which wrests its nourishment from the hard rock, and the broom, which grows down the arid sandhill, revealed to me the inward, fervent, sacred life of Nature—how I took all this into my ardent heart, lost myself in its unending abundance, while the glorious forms of the unending world stirred within my animated soul. Vast mountains surrounded me, precipices lay at my feet, torrents poured down, rivers streamed below me, and forest and hills resounded. I saw all the unfathomable forces at their interweaving work of creation in the depths of the earth. Above the earth and below the sky there swarm the innumerable species of creatures. Everything, everything populated with a thousand kinds of shapes, and mankind secures itself in little houses and settles down and rules in its own way over the wide world. Poor fool! you who deem everything of little significance because you are yourself so small. From the inaccessible mountain, across the wilderness which no foot has ever trod, to the end of the unknown ocean there breathes the spirit of the Eternal Creator Who rejoices at every speck of dust that receives it and lives. How often have I longed to be borne on the wings of the crane which flew above my head to the shores of the immeasurable ocean, to quaff the swelling rapture of life from the foaming goblet of the infinite, and to feel for but a moment the curbed forces of my soul extended by one drop of the bliss of that Being Who brings forth all things in and through Himself.

Brother, it is only the memory of those hours that gives me ease. Even the exertion of recalling and again clothing in words those inexpressible emotions, exalts my soul above itself, only to let me feel in double measure the anguish of my condition.

It is as though a curtain has been drawn from before my soul, and the scene of eternal life is being transformed before my eyes into the abyss of the ever open grave. Can you say *This is,* when everything is transitory, everything rolls past with the speed of lightning, only rarely endures till its life force is spent, but is carried away by the current, submerged and smashed against the rocks? Not a moment but consumes you and yours, not a moment when you do not yourself destroy something, and inevitably so. The most innocent stroll costs a myriad tiny creatures their lives, one step annihilates the laborious construction of a nation of ants and crushes a world in little to ignominious ruin. It is not the great occasional catastrophes of the world, the floods that sweep away your villages, the earthquakes that devour your cities, by which I am moved. It is the consuming force latent in universal Nature, that has formed nothing that has not destroyed its neighbour and itself, which saps my soul. And so I reel along in anguish, surrounded by earth and sky and all the weaving forces of Nature. I see nothing but a monster, eternally devouring, eternally chewing the cud.

21 August.

In vain I stretch out my arms towards her in the morning when I wake from troubled dreams. In vain I seek her at night in my bed when an innocent dream has made me happy with the illusion that I am sitting beside her in the meadow, holding her hand and covering it with a thousand kisses. Oh! when I put out my hand to touch her, still drunk with sleep, and rouse myself by doing so, a stream of tears wells up from my oppressed heart, and I weep for the hopelessness of the gloomy future.

22 August.

My condition is wretched, Wilhelm! All my energies are reduced to a restless inactivity. I cannot be idle, and yet I am unable to take up any task. I have no power of imagination, no interest in Nature, and my books all repel me. When we lose ourselves, we have lost everything. I vow I could sometimes wish to be a labourer, so as to have every morning, when I awake, some prospect for the ensuing day, some urge, some hope. I often envy Albert, whom I see buried to the ears in his documents, and pretend to myself that I should like to be in his place. More than once it has suddenly occurred to me to write to you and the minister in order to apply for the post at the legation which you assure me I should not fail to obtain. I believe so too. The minister has long been fond of me, and used frequently to urge me to take up some profession. For an hour or so I occupy myself with the notion, but later, when I think about it again, I remember the fable of the horse that was tired of its freedom, allowed itself to be saddled and bridled, and was ridden to death. I do not know what to do, and is not perhaps my longing for a change in my situation a deep-seated, uneasy impatience which will pursue me wherever I may go?

28 August.

Truly, if my malady could be cured, these people would do it. It is my birthday to-day, and very early this morning I received a packet from Albert. As soon as I opened it I caught sight of one of the pink bows that Lotte was wearing on her bosom when I first met her, and which I had since then more than once asked her for. There were also two little books in duodecimo in the packet, the Wetstein edition of Homer, which I had so often wanted to possess so as not to have to drag about the edition of Ernesti on my walks. You see! that is how they anticipate my desires, how they think of all the small friendly services which are a thousand times more appreciated than the brilliant presents that humiliate us and are due to the vanity of the giver. I kiss the bow a thousand times, and with every breath I drink in the memory of the rapture which more than filled those few happy days that can return no more. The blossoms of life are only a mirage. It is so, Wilhelm, and I do not complain. How many fade and do not leave a trace behind; how few bear fruit, and how little of the fruit reaches maturity! And yet sufficient remain, but—Oh my brother! can we neglect, despise the ripened fruit, let it wither and rot without having been enjoyed?

Farewell! The summer is glorious and I often sit in the fruit trees in Lotte's orchard, picking pears from the highest branches with a long rod. She stands below and receives them when I reach them down.

30 August.

Foolish wretch that I am! Do I not deceive myself? What is the purpose of all this endless raging passion? I offer no prayers now save to her; no form appears before my mind save hers; and everything in the world about me I see only in relation to her. And this affords me so many happy hours —till I must again tear myself away from her. Oh! Wilhelm, whither does my heart so often urge me! When I have sat with her thus for two hours or three, feasting my eyes on her form, her bearing, listening to the divine words that come from her lips, and then gradually all my senses become taut, my eyes grow dim, I hardly hear what is said, and I feel as though some assassin were gripping me by the throat, while my heart beats wildly in the endeavour to free my oppressed senses but only increases their confusion—Wilhelm, I am scarcely aware at such times whether I am in this world! And often, if melancholy does not gain the ascendancy and Lotte offer me the wretched solace of pouring forth my anguish in tears upon her hand, I am compelled to rush away, out into the fields where I rove about, or to find pleasure in climbing a steep hill, thrusting my way through a trackless wood, being wounded by hedges and torn by thorns. Then I feel somewhat relieved. Somewhat! And when I some-times sink down on the way, overcome with weariness and thirst, in the dead of night when the full moon is floating above my head, or sit on a crooked tree in the lonely forest to rest the aching soles of my feet, and fall asleep in the lulling stillness of the half light. . . . Oh! Wilhelm, a solitary cell, a hair-shirt and a belt of thorns were the relief for which my soul is languishing. Adieu! I see no end to all this misery but the grave.

3 September.

I must away. I thank you, Wilhelm, that you have con-firmed my wavering resolve. For a fortnight I have been trying to make up my mind to leave her. I must. She is again in the town on a visit to a friend. And Albert—and—I must away.

10 September.

What a night that was! Now, Wilhelm, I can surmount anything. I shall not see her again. Oh! that I cannot fly to your breast, tell you amid a thousand tears and transports all the emotions which are assailing my heart. Here I sit and gasp for air, try to calm myself, and await the morning. The horses are to be ready at dawn.

She sleeps peacefully and does not think that she will never see me again. I have torn myself away, was strong enough, during a conversation lasting two hours, not to re-veal my purpose. And God! what a conversation!

Albert had promised me that he would be in the garden with Lotte immediately after supper. I stood on the terrace beneath the tall chestnuts and gazed at the sun, which I saw for the last time sinking over the lovely valley and the gentle stream. How often I had stood with her at this spot watch-ing the same glorious scene, and now. . . . I walked to and fro along the avenue which was so dear to me; I had so often been bound here by some mysterious, sympathetic attraction before ever I knew Lotte—and how we rejoiced when we discovered, at the beginning of our friendship, our mutual inclination for the place, which is really one of the most romantic productions of art that I have ever seen.

First, you have the broad prospect between the chestnut trees—Oh! I remember I have, I think, already written you a lot about how one is finally closed in by a high rampart of beeches and the avenue grows darker and darker on account of a plantation that adjoins it, until one at last emerges into a confined clearing over which there hovers the awe of solitude. I can still feel the queer emotion by which I was stirred when I first entered it one high noon; I had a faint presentiment of all the pain and bliss of which it was to be the scene.

I had been revelling for about half an hour in the sweet languishing thoughts of parting and seeing her again, when I heard them coming up the terrace, ran towards them, seized her hand with an inward shudder and kissed it. We had just reached the top when the moon rose behind the tree-clad hill; we spoke of a diversity of things and approached imperceptibly the gloomy recess. Lotte entered and sat down, Albert at her side, and I also seated myself, but my restlessness soon made me start up again; I stood in front of her, walked to and fro, sat down again and was most distressed. She drew our attention to the beautiful effect of the moonlight which illuminated the whole terrace at the end of the rampart of beeches, a glorious sight which was rendered all the more striking by the deep twilight which closed us in all round. We were silent, and after a time she said, "I never go for a walk in the moonlight without being accompanied by the thought of my dead ones, without being oppressed by the feeling of death, of what is to come. We shall exist, Werther," she continued with the most exalted emotion in her voice, "but shall we meet again? and recognise one another? What do you surmise, what do you say?"

"Lotte," I replied, giving her my hand, my eyes filling with tears, "we shall meet again! Here and beyond!"—I could say no more. . . . Wilhelm, why did she have to ask me that, at the moment when I bore the anguish of this parting in my heart?

"And do our dear departed ones know anything about us?" she continued. "Do they feel, when it fares well with us, that we remember them with warm affection? Oh! my mother's form is always hovering about me, in the quiet evenings when I am sitting among her children, my children, and they are gathered round me as they were once gathered round her. When I gaze yearningly up to Heaven with tears in my eyes and wish that she might for a moment be able to look down and see how I am keeping the promise I gave on her deathbed to be a mother to her children. A hundred times I cry out, 'Forgive me, dearest one, if I am not to them what you were. Oh! I do whate'er I can, they are clad, fed, and oh! what is more than all, cared for and loved. Could you but see the harmony in which we live, dear saint! You would glorify with the most fervent gratitude the God Whom you entreated with your last bitter tears to protect your children!"

That is what she said. Oh! Wilhelm! who can repeat her words, how can the dead cold letter depict the divine effloresence of her spirit? Albert broke in gently, "It affects you too deeply, dear Lotte; I know your soul clings strongly to these notions, but I beg of you . . ." "Oh! Albert!" she said, "I know you do not forget the evenings when we sat together at the small round table, when father was away on a journey and we had sent the little ones to bed. You often had a good book with you, but you seldom succeeded in reading anything. Was not intercourse with this splendid soul more than all else? The beautiful, gentle, cheerful, ever busy woman! God knows with what tears I often cast myself before Him as I lay in bed, and entreated Him to make me as she was."

"Lotte!" I cried, throwing myself at her feet and seizing her hands, which I moistened with a thousand tears. "Lotte!

the blessing of God and the spirit of your mother rest upon you." "If you had known her," she said, pressing my hand, "she was worthy to be known by you." I thought I should swoon. Never had anything so exalted, so proud been said in my praise. She continued, "And this woman was taken away in the prime of her life, when her youngest son was not yet six months old. Her illness did not last long, she was tranquil, resigned, regretting only her children, especially the babe. As the end drew near she said to me, 'Let them come up to me,' and I brought them in, the little ones who did not understand, and the older ones who were beside themselves; they stood round the bed and she raised her hands and prayed over them, and kissed them one after the other and sent them away, and said to me, 'Be a mother to them!' I gave her my hand as I made the vow. 'It is no little thing which you are promising, my daughter,' she said, 'the heart of a mother and the eye of a mother. I have often seen by your grateful tears that you know what that means. Let your brothers and sisters find them in you, and show to your father the faithfulness and obedience of a wife. You will afford him consolation.' She asked after him, but he had gone out to conceal from us the unbearable grief he felt. His heart was lacerated.

"You were in the room, Albert! She heard someone walking, inquired who it was, and asked you to approach. And as she gazed at you and at me, with a tranquil look, confident that we should be happy, happy together. . . ." Albert fell on her neck and kissed her, and cried, "We are! we shall be!" The usually serene Albert had entirely lost his self-possession, and I myself was on the verge of losing consciousness.

"Werther," she began, "this is the woman that we have lost! God! when I think, as I so often do, how we thus let the dearest thing in our life be taken away, and no one feels it so keenly as the children; who long continued to complain that the black men had carried away their mama."

She rose, but I was agitated and shaken and remained seated, holding her hand. "We must go," she said, "it is growing late." She wished to withdraw her hand, but I held it more firmly. "We shall meet again," I cried. "We shall come together, under whatever form we shall recognise one another. I go, I go willingly, and yet, if I had to say 'for ever,' I could not bear it. Farewell, Lotte! Farewell, Albert! We shall meet again." "To-morrow, I think," she replied jestingly. I was affected by this "to-morrow." Oh! she did not know as she withdrew her hand from mine . . . They went out along the avenue, I stood, looked after them in the moon-light, then threw myself on the earth and wept my fill, sprang up, ran out on to the terrace and could still perceive below, in the shadow of the tall limes, her white frock gleaming on the way to the garden door, I stretched out my arms, and it disappeared.

20 October.

We arrived at this place yesterday. The ambassador is un-well, & will therefore keep to the house for some days. If only he were not so ungracious, all would be well. I per-ceive, I perceive that Fate has hard trials in store for me. But I must be of good courage! A light heart can bear every-thing. A light heart! I cannot help laughing as the word falls from my pen. A little more lightness of heart would make me the happiest being under the sun. What! where other men, with their modicum of energy and talent, are strutting around me in complacent self-assurance, do I despair of my energy, of my talents? God in Heaven, Who didst endow me with all this, why didst Thou not withhold the half and give me instead self-confidence and contentment!

Patience! Patience! Things will mend. For I tell you my friend, you are right. Since I have been compelled to move about among the people like this every day, and see what they do and how they go about things, I am on much better terms with myself. To be sure, since we are, after all, so con-stituted that we compare everything with ourselves and our-selves with everything, happiness or misery lies in the things with which we establish the analogy, and so nothing is more dangerous than solitude. Our power of imagination, forced by its nature to assert itself, nourished by the fantastic visions of poetry, raises for itself a series of beings of which we are the lowest, and where everthing that is external to ourselves appears more splendid, everyone else more perfect. And the process is quite natural. We feel so often that there is something lacking in us, and it is just what we lack that often appears to us to be possessed by someone else, to whom we then impute, in addition, everything that we have ourselves and a certain ideal ease to boot. And so the happy being is perfect, the creature of our own imagination.

When, on the other hand, weak as we are, we only continue laboriously with our work, we very often find that with all our dawdling and tacking we get further than others with their sails and oars—and—it does impart a feeling of self-confidence when one keeps up with or even outstrips others.

10 November.

I am beginning to settle down tolerably well here so far. The best of it is that there is enough to do, and then the various kinds of people, the diversity of new faces, present a motley scene to my soul. I have made the acquaintance of Count C., a man whom I learn to esteem more every day. A broad and lofty mind, making allowances for much and therefore by no means unsympathetic. One's connection with him is illumined by such feeling for friendship and affection. He took an interest in me when I had some business to arrange with him, and he perceived at the opening of our conversation that we understood one another, that he could talk to me as he could not talk to everybody. And I cannot sufficiently praise his frank bearing towards me. There is no real ardent pleasure to equal that of being given access to a great soul.

24 December.

The ambassador causes me much chagrin, as I anticipated. He is the most meticulous fool that can be imagined. He proceeds step by step and is as fussy as an old woman. A

man who is never satisfied with himself and whom therefore
nobody can please. I like to work quickly, and as a thing
turns out so I leave it, but he is capable of giving me back a
memorandum and saying, "It is good, but look through it
again, there is always a better word, a more precise particle." It is enough to drive me crazy. No "and" or other con-
junction may be omitted, and he is a mortal enemy of all
the inversions which occasionally escape me. If one's periods are not ground out in accordance with the time-
honoured rhythm, he is unable to understand them. It is a
penance to have to deal with such a man.

The confidence of Count von C. is the only thing which
compensates me. He confessed to me quite openly the other
day how dissatisfied he is with the dull-witted scrupulous-
ness of my ambassador. Such people make things more difficult for themselves and for others. "But," he said, "we must
be resigned, like a traveller who has a mountain to cross.
Of course, if the mountain weren't there, the way would be
easier and shorter, but it *is* there and it has to be got over."

My chief probably feels, also, the preference the Count
gives me over him, and that vexes him, so that he seizes
every opportunity to speak ill of the Count to me. I oppose
him, of course, and thereby only render matters worse. Yesterday he even made me fly into a passion, for he included
me in his remarks—that the Count was quite good for affairs of the world, being a very quick worker and having a
facile pen, but he was lacking in solid erudition, like all
literary folk. I would have liked to thrash him for this, for
there is no other way of reasoning with such fellows, but
since this was not possible, I disputed with some heat and
told him that the Count was a man who inspires esteem not
only on account of his character but also of his knowledge.
"I have never known anyone," I said, "who has so succeeded
in enlarging his mind, to embrace matters innumerable,
without surrendering his activity in ordinary life." This was
all Greek to his brain, and I took my leave to avoid having to
choke down more choler at further nonsensical talk.

You are all responsible for this, who talked me into as-

suming the yoke and prated so much of 'activity.' Activity!
If the man who plants potatoes and rides to town to sell his
corn, is not doing more than I, then I will wear myself out for
another ten years in the galley to which I am now fettered.

And the gilded misery, the boredom among the loath-
some people who are assembled here! Their love of rank,
the way they keep watch and guard to steal the smallest
march upon each other, their most wretched and pitiable
passions which they make no attempt to conceal. There is a
woman, for instance, who tells everybody about her noble
birth and her country, so that every stranger must think,
"What a fool she is with her conceited notions of her trivial
patent of nobility and the fame of her country." That isn't
the worst of it, however, for this very woman is the daughter
of a district clerk in these parts. I cannot understand the
human race that has so little sense as to make such a downright fool of itself.

To be sure, I perceive more clearly every day how foolish
it is to judge others by oneself . . . And since I have so much
to occupy me in myself, and my heart and mind are so tempestuous—oh! I would gladly let the others go their way, if
they could only let me go my way too.

What irritates me most of all is the odious social conditions. To be sure, I am as well aware as anybody of the
necessity for class distinctions and of the advantages that I
myself receive from them; but they ought not to stand in my
way just when I could enjoy a little pleasure, a gleam of happiness on this earth. During one of my walks recently I made
the acquaintance of a Fräulein von B., a charming creature,
who has preserved considerable naturalness in spite of the
stiff conventional life here. We found one another's conversation agreeable and, when we parted, I asked permission to call upon her. This she granted with such frankness,
that I could hardly await the appropriate hour to go to her.
She does not come from this part, and is staying with an
aunt, an old maid whose physiognomy was displeasing to
me. I paid the latter much attention, applied my conversation mostly to her, and in less than half an hour I had pretty

well conjectured what the young lady herself afterwards admitted to me—that the aunt, lacking everything, with neither a respectable fortune nor qualities of mind, has no support in her old age other than her ancestral tree, no protection other than the rank behind which she barricades herself, and no pleasure except to look down from her height and ignore the middle classes. She is said to have been beautiful in her youth and to have trifled away her life, first tormenting many a poor young man with her capriciousness, and in later years bowing to the domination of an elderly officer, who, in return for this and a passable income, passed the brass age with her and then died. And now she has reached the iron age, she is alone, and would not receive any consideration, if her niece were not so charming.

8 January, 1772.

What creatures they are whose whole soul is bound up with ceremonial, whose thoughts and aims are for years directed towards the means of worming their way on to a chair which is one move higher up the table! And it is not as though the fellows had no other opportunities. No! there is work in abundance, for the very reason that the petty vexations hinder the progress of the important matters. Last week there was a quarrel during a sledge drive and all the fun was spoilt.

Fools, not to see that the place does not really matter at all, and that he who occupies the first very rarely plays the chief part! How many kings are ruled by their ministers, and how many ministers by their secretaries! And who is then the first? The one, it seems to me, who can take in the others at a glance, and has sufficient power or cunning to harness their energies and passions to the execution of his plans.

20 January.

I must write to you, dear Lotte, here in the taproom of a poor rustic inn where I have taken refuge from a heavy storm. Since I have been moving about in that wretched hole of a town, among strangers, complete strangers to my heart, there has not been a moment, not a single one, when my heart bade me write to you. And now in this hut, in this solitude, where I am so hemmed in, and snow and hail are beating furiously against the window panes, here my first thought was of you. As I entered, your form appeared before my mind. Oh, Lotte! with such sacred fervour! God! the first happy moment recaptured!

If you could see me now, in this deluge of distraction! How dried up my senses are becoming, not one moment when I can allow my heart full play, not one single hour of tearful bliss! Nothing! Nothing! It is as though I am standing in front of a raree show, watching the mannikins and the little horses moving about, and I often ask myself whether it is not an optical illusion. I join in the general movement, or rather I am moved like a marionette, and often seize the wooden hand of my neighbour and start back with a shudder.

I have only discovered a single feminine being here. A Fräulein von B. She resembles you, Lotte, if it is possible for anyone to resemble you. "Ah!" you will say, "the fellow is paying compliments!" There is some truth in that. For some time I have been very well-mannered, since, after all, I cannot help myself. I have a ready wit, and the ladies say nobody utters such delicate compliments as I do (and lies, you will add, for otherwise they cannot be successful, do you follow me?). I was speaking about Fräulein B. She has much soul which shines from her blue eyes, and is oppressed by her rank which does not satisfy any of her heart's desires. She longs to escape from the turmoil, and we pass many an hour in fanciful conversation about rural scenes of unalloyed happines—and about you. How often does she have to pay you homage! There is no 'must,' she does it with all her heart, likes so much to hear about you, loves you.

Oh! would that I were sitting at your feet in the dear familiar room, and our little ones were tumbling about round me, and when they grew too noisy for you I would collect them round me and quieten them with a weird fairy tale. The sun is setting gloriously over a gleaming, snow-white earth, and the storm has passed on. And I—must again shut muself up in my cage. Adieu! Is Albert with you? And how—? God forgive me the question!

17 February.

I fear that my ambassador and I will not stay together much longer. The fellow is perfectly unbearable. His way of working and doing business is so ridiculous, that I cannot refrain from contradicting him and frequently doing a thing in my own way and to my own mind, which, of course, then never suits him. He recently complained of me at Court on this account, and the minister reproved me, mildly to be sure, but nevertheless it was a reproof, and I was about to send in my resignation when I received a private letter[1] from him, a letter before which I sank on my knees and worshipped the lofty, wise and noble mind that knows so well how to correct my too great sensitiveness, respecting, indeed, my exaggerated notions of activity, of influence over others, of getting the mastery in affairs, as a praiseworthy, youthful spirit, trying not to eradicate them, but only to temper them and guide them to where they can have full scope and achieve their most useful purpose. I am now fortified for a week, and in harmony with myself. Tranquillity of soul is a glorious thing, and joy in oneself. Dear friend, if only the thing were not just as fragile as it is beautiful and precious.

20 February.

God bless you, my dear ones, and grant you all the happy days that He takes from me.

I thank you, Albert, for deceiving me; I was awaiting news when your wedding day was to be, and had intended on that day solemnly to take down Lotte's silhouette from the wall and bury it under other papers. Now you are married, and

---

[1] This letter, together with another which is referred to later on, has been withdrawn from this collection out of respect for this excellent man, as it was not thought that such boldness could be excused by the gratitude, however warm, of the public.

her portrait is still here! Well, it shall stay! Why not? I know
that I am also with you, that I am in Lotte's heart, without
prejudice to you. I have, yes, I have the second place in it,
and will and must retain it. Oh! I would go mad, if she were
able to forget. . . . Albert, hell lies in the thought. Albert, farewell! Farewell, angel from heaven, farewell, Lotte!

15 March.

I have been subjected to a mortification that will drive me
away from here, and makes me gnash my teeth. The Devil!
It cannot be made good, and the whole fault is yours, all of
you who spurred me on, and drove me and worried me to accept a post that was not to my mind. Well, here I am! You
have got your way! And in order that you may not tell me
again that my exaggerated notions spoil everything—here,
my dear Sir, is a story, clear and simple, as a chronicler would
record it.

Count von C. is fond of me, pays me special attention, that
is well known and I have already told you so a hundred times.
I was dining with him yesterday, on the particular day when
the aristocratic company of ladies and gentlemen assembles
at his house in the evening. I had forgotten this, and it never
occurred to me that we of inferior rank are not acceptable on
such occasions. Good. I dine with the Count, and after table
we walk up and down the great hall, I converse with him and
with Colonel B. who puts in an appearance, and thus the
hour for the party approaches. God knows, I suspect nothing.
Then there enters the more-than-gracious Madame von S.
with her consort and her nobly hatched little goose of a flat-
chested, tight-laced daughter. They widen their eyes and
nostrils in the traditional, highly-aristocratic manner *en pas-
sant*, and, as I loathe the herd with all my heart, I was about
to take my leave, waiting only until the Count should be free
from the exchange of dreadful twaddle, when suddenly my
Fräulein von B. entered. Since it always raises my spirits a
little when I see her, I remained, took my place behind her
chair, and only noticed after some time that she was talking
to me with less frankness than usual, indeed with some em-

barrassment. I was struck by this. If she is like all these
people, I thought to myself, may the Devil take her! I was
irritated and wanted to depart, and yet remained, for I was
intrigued and wished for more light on the matter. Meanwhile the room was filling up. Baron F., wearing his whole
wardrobe dating from the coronation of the Emperor Francis
the First, Hofrat R., here called *in qualitate* Herr *von* R.,
with his deaf wife etc., to say nothing of J., who is badly off,
his antiquated garments contrasting strangely with the fashionable oddments he wore with them—all these were arriving, and I was conversing with some of the people I knew,
who were all very laconic. I was occupied with my thoughts,
and only concerned with my Fräulein B. I did not notice that
the women were whispering to each other at the end of the
room, that this infected the men, that Frau von S. was talking to the Count (Fräulein B. told me all this afterwards),
until finally the Count came up to me and led me to a
window. "You are aware," he said, "of our odd conventions.
The company, I observe, is displeased to see you here. I
would not for anything in the world...." "Your Excellency," I
interrupted, "I beg a thousand pardons. I should have
thought of it before, but I know you will forgive my *faux pas*.
I was about to take my leave some time ago, but," I added
with a smile as I bowed, "an evil genius held me back." The
Count pressed my hand with a sympathy which said more
than words. I made my bow to the distinguished company
and took a coach as far as M. to see the sun setting from the
top of the hill, and read in my Homer the glorious canto
where Ulysses is entertained by the worthy swineherd. This
was all delightful.

In the evening I returned home to sup. There were only a
few people left in the coffee-room, and they had turned back
the table cloth and were throwing dice in a corner. Then
Adelin came in, put down his hat, as he glanced at me, came
up and said softly, "You were rebuffed?" "*I* was?" I said.
"The Count asked you to leave the company." "The Devil
take them," I said. "I was glad to get out into the fresh air."
"Good," he said, "that you treat it lightly. But I am annoyed.

Everybody is talking about it." Now for the first time the matter began to vex me. I thought everyone who looked at me at table did so because he knew about it. This began to rouse my choler.

And now, when I am pitied wherever I go, when I hear those who are jealous of me exclaiming triumphantly that one could see what happened to arrogant fellows who boasted of their modicum of intellect and thought it gave them a right to set themselves above all conventions, and that sort of twaddle—it is enough to make a man stick a knife in his heart. For whatever people may say about independence, I would like to see who can bear scoundrels talking about him when they have him at a disadvantage. If it is only empty talk, oh! then one can easily ignore them.

16 March.

Everything is combining to provoke me! To-day I met Fräulein B. in the avenue. I could not refrain from addressing her, and showing her, as soon as we were some distance from the rest of the company, that I was hurt at her recent behaviour. "Oh! Werther!" she said, in a tone of deep sincerity, "could you thus interpret my confusion, knowing my heart as you do? How I suffered for your sake, from the moment when I entered the room! I foresaw everything, a hundred dred times it was on the tip of my tongue to warn you, I knew that Madame von S. and Madame von T., together with their husbands, would rather take their departure than stay in your company, I knew that the Count would not venture to fall out with them—and now all this fuss . . ." "What do you mean?" I asked, and concealed my dismay, for everything that Adelin had told me the day before yesterday coursed through my veins like boiling water at this moment. "How much it has already cost me!" said the sweet creature, with tears in her eyes. I could no longer control myself, was about to throw myself at her feet. "Tell me what you mean," I cried. The tears ran down her cheeks. I was beside myself. She dried them without any attempt at concealment. "You know my aunt," she began. "She was there, and oh! how she opened her eyes! Werther, I endured last night and this morning a sermon about my intercourse with you, and have to listen to you being disparaged, degraded, and was only half able to defend you."

Every word she uttered pierced my heart like a sword. She did not see what a mercy it would have been to hide all this from me, and she now told me all the further gossip there would be, how all the malicious fellows would be triumphant. How from now on they would proclaim that my arrogance and disdain of others, which they had long blamed in me, was now punished and humbled. To hear all this from her lips, Wilhelm, in a tone of sincerest sympathy—I was overcome, and am still raging inwardly. I wish someone would dare to cast it in my teeth, that I might thrust my sword through his body! If I were to see blood I should feel better. Oh! I have taken up a knife a hundred times to let air into my suffocating heart. It is related of a noble species of horses that, when they are frightfully heated and at their last gasp, they instinctively bite open a vein to help them to breathe. I often feel like that. I would like to open a vein and achieve eternal freedom.

24 March.

I have handed in my resignation at Court and hope it will be accepted. You will forgive me for not asking your permission first. I *had* to go away, and I already know everything you would say to persuade me to stay, so—sugar the pill for my mother. I cannot help myself so she must put up with it, though I cannot help her either. It will certainly grieve her. To see the brilliant career which was leading her son to a privy councillorship or an embassy suddenly interrupted and the horse put back in its stable! Make of it what you will and add up the possible eventualities which might have made it possible for me to stay, or obliged me to do so. Enough, I am going. And that you may know whither I am going, Prince * * *, who relishes my society, is here, and asked me, when he heard of my intention, to accompany him to his estates and spend the beautiful Spring there. He has promised that I shall be left entirely to myself and, since we understand each other up to a certain point, I will try my luck and go with him.

19 April.

For your Information.

I thank you for your two letters. I did not reply, since I was leaving this letter until my resignation had been accepted at Court, for I feared my mother might apply to the minister and render my purpose difficult. Now, however, it is all over, and I have my discharge. I hardly like to tell you how unwillingly they gave it me, and what the minister has written; you would break out into fresh lamentations. The hereditary prince has sent me a parting gift of twenty-five ducats, with a letter that moved me to tears. So my mother need not send me the money I wrote for recently.

5 May.

I leave here to-morrow, and since the place where I was born is only a few miles away, I would like to see it again, and recall the happy days I used to dream away. I will enter by the very gate from which I drove out with my mother when she left the dear, familiar spot after my father's death, to shut herself up in her unbearable town. Adieu, Wilhelm, you shall have news of my progress.

9 May.

I have fulfilled the pilgrimage to my home with a pilgrim's reverence and have been affected by many an unexpected emotion. I stopped at the great lime tree, a quarter of an hour's journey outside the town on the way to S. I alighted and bade the postillion take the coach on, that I might go on foot to savour each memory anew, vividly, and in my own way. There I stood beneath the lime which used to be the goal and boundary of my walks as a boy. How different the circumstances! Then, in my blissful ignorance, I had yearned to go out into the unknown world, where my heart hoped to find all the nourishment, all the enjoyment of which I so often felt the lack in my bosom. Now I was coming back

from the wide world—with oh! how many hopes miscarried,
how many plans shattered!—I saw the range of mountains in
front of me, that had times without number been the object
of my desires. I had sat here for hours at a time, yearning to
be there, fervently absorbed in the woods and valleys which
appeared before me in an intimate halflight—and then, when
the time came to return home, how unwillingly I left the beloved spot! I approached the town, greeted all the old familiar summer houses, and disliked the new ones as well
as all the other changes which had taken place. I went in
through the gate and there I found myself again completely.
I will not give you all the details, for, charming as they were
to me, the record would only be monotonous. I had made up
my mind to take a lodging in the market-place, next door to
our old house. As I walked along I noticed that the little
school, where our childhood had been penned up by an
honest old dame, was turned into a shop. I recalled the restlessness, the tears, the mental apathy and heartaches I had
endured in that den.—Every step I took was fraught with
interest. No pilgrim in the Holy Land comes across so many
shrines of pious memory, and the souls of few are so filled
with sacred emotion. One more detail that must suffice for
a thousand. I went down the river to a certain farm, which
used also to be one of my walks, and looked at the places
where we boys tried who could make the flat stones rebound
most often as we skimmed them along the surface of the
water. I remember most vividly how I often stood there and
gazed at the stream, the wondrous presentiments with which
I followed it, how romantic the country appeared to me to
which it was flowing, how I soon found that there were limits
to my imagination and yet I had to penetrate further, ever
further, until I had completely lost myself in the illimitable
distance. Is that not just what the glorious patriarchs felt!
When Ulysses speaks of the immeasurable ocean and the
unbounded earth, is not that more true, more human, more
fervent, than nowadays when every schoolboy thinks himself a miracle of wisdom because he can repeat that the world
is round?

Here I am in the Prince's hunting-box. He is quite agreeable to live with, being simple and sincere. I am often pained, however, when he talks about things that he only knows from hearsay or reading, and always from a second-hand point of view.

And he has more understanding for my intellect and talents than for my heart, which is, after all, my only pride, the sole source of everything, all vigour, all bliss and all misery. Oh! anyone can know what I know.—My heart is my own.

25 May.

I had something in my mind about which I was unwilling to tell you anything until it had been put into execution but, now that it has come to nothing, I may just as well do so. I wanted to go to the wars! My heart was long intent on it. It was the chief reason why I came here with the Prince, who is a general in the *** service. I revealed my intention to him during one of our walks, he dissuaded me, and it would have had to be a passion rather than a whim to prevent me listening to his arguments.

11 June.

Say what you will, I cannot stay any longer. What is the use? I am finding it tedious. The Prince treats me as an equal and yet I do not feel at home. And we have not really anything in common. He is a man of intellect, but of a low order, and I find his conversation no more entertaining than a well-written book. I shall stay another week and then resume my wanderings. The best thing I have done here is my sketching. The Prince has a feeling for Art, though this would be deeper if he were not limited by the abominations of science and the usual terminology. It often makes me gnash my teeth when, upon my introducing with warmth and imagination topics of Nature and Art, he thinks he is doing quite well as he suddenly blunders in with some conventional technical term.

18 June.

Where am I going? I will tell you in confidence. I have to remain here another fortnight after all, and then I pretend to myself that I am going to visit the mines in * * *. Nothing of the sort, however. I only want to see Lotte again. That is all. And I ridicule my own heart—but shall do what it demands.

29 July.

No, it is all right! Everything is all right! I—her husband! Oh! God, Who made me, if Thou hadst granted me that bliss, my whole life would be one continual prayer. I will not complain, and crave pardon for these tears, pardon for my vain desires.—She—my wife! If I had the dearest being under the sun enfolded in my arms—a shudder goes through my whole body, Wilhelm, when Albert embraces her slender waist.

And—ought I to say it? Why not, Wilhelm? She would have been happier with me than with him! Oh! he is not the man to fulfil all the longings of that heart. A certain lack of delicacy, a lack—take it as you will, that his heart does not beat in sympathy at—oh!—at a passage in a beloved book where my heart and Lotte's meet as one. In a hundred other cases, when it happens that we express our feelings at the action of someone else. Dear Wilhelm!—He *does* love her with his whole soul, and what is such a love not worth. . . .

I have been interrupted by an insupportable fellow. My tears are dried. I am distracted. Adieu, dear friend!

4 August.

I am not the only one to suffer thus. All men find their hopes deceived, their expectations betrayed. I visited the good woman who lives by the lime tree. Her eldest boy ran towards me, and his shouts of joy attracted his mother, who looked very downcast. Her first words were, "Good Sir! Alas, my Hans is dead."—He was the youngest of her sons. I was silent.—"And my husband," she continued, "has returned from Switzerland with empty hands, and were it not for some kind people he would have had to go a-begging. He fell ill of a fever on the way." I knew not what to say to her, and gave something to the little one. She asked me to accept some apples, which I did and left the place of melancholy memory.

21 August.

I change in a flash. Sometimes I find a gleam of joy in life once more, but alas! only for a moment. When I thus lose myself in my dreams, I cannot avoid the thought—'What if Albert were to die! You would, she would—,' and then I pursue the will o' the wisp till it leads me to the verge of abysses before which I shudder back.

When I go out at the town gate, the way I first went when I fetched Lotte to the ball—how different it all was! All, all is over. Not a vestige of the former world, not a throb of the emotion I then felt. I feel like a ghost that has returned to the burnt-out castle which it once built in its princely glory and bequeathed on its death-bed, splendidly furnished, to a beloved son.

3 September.

I am sometimes unable to comprehend how another can, or may love her, when I love her so singleheartedly, so fervently, so completely, and know nothing, am aware of nothing, have nothing but her.

6 September.

I had a difficult struggle before I was able to make up my mind to put aside the simple blue coat in which I first danced with Lotte, but it grew at last too shabby. I have had a new one made, just like the last, with collar and facings, and another yellow waistcoat and pair of breeches.

But it has not quite the same effect. I do not know—perhaps, with time, I shall grow to like it more.

15 September.

It is enough to make one resign oneself to the Devil to see

all the hounds that God tolerates on this earth, without sense or feeling for what little there is of value on it. You know the walnut trees beneath which I sat with Lotte at the honest old clergyman's in St., the glorious walnut trees which, God knows, always filled my soul with the greatest content. How intimate and cool they made the courtyard, how glorious their branches were. And the memories they held, back to the good clergymen who had planted them so many years ago. The schoolmaster often mentioned the name of one of them, which he had learned from his grandfather. He is said to have been such a worthy man and his memory was always sacred to me under the trees. I tell you there were tears in the schoolmaster's eyes yesterday when we discussed their having been cut down.—Cut down! The thought makes me frenzied, I could murder the hound who struck the first blow. I, who could pine away with grief if a few trees stood in my courtyard and one of them withered with age—I have to look on at this. But there is one point worth mentioning. What a thing is human feeling! The whole village is muttering, and I hope the minister's wife will feel the difference in the way of butter, eggs and other presents, to show how she has wounded the villagers. For it is she who is to blame, the wife of the new minister (the old one is dead), a scraggy, sickly brute with very good cause to take no interest in the world, since no one takes any in her. An ugly creature who puts forth pretensions to learning, takes a hand in the examination of the canon, works a great deal at the new-fangled critico-moral reformation of Christianity and shrugs her shoulders at the enthusiasms of Lavater, is quite shattered in health and therefore without joy on God's earth. Only such a creature could find it possible to cut down my walnut trees. I cannot keep cool! Just imagine, the falling leaves make the courtyard dank and dirty, the trees take away the light and, when the nuts are ripe, the boys throw stones at them and that jars her nerves, disturbs the profundity of her meditations when she is pondering the differing views of Kennicott, Semler and Michaelis. When I saw how discontented the villagers were, especially the old ones, I asked why they had suffered it. "When the mayor wants a thing hereabouts," they replied, "what can we do?" But one justice was done at least. The mayor and the parson, who at any rate wanted to make something out of his wife's whims, which don't bring him in much profit, thought of sharing the proceeds, but the revenue-office heard of it and said, "This way please!", and sold the trees to the highest bidder. There they lie! Oh if I were but a Prince! The parson's wife, the mayor and the revenue-office would be—Prince!—Well, if I were a Prince, would I worry about the trees in my country!

10 October.

If I only look into her black eyes, I am already cured! And what mortifies me is that Albert does not appear to be as happy as he—expected—as I—thought I would be—if—I am not fond of dashes, but it is the only way I can express myself here—and I think it is clear enough.

12 October.

Ossian has crowded Homer out of my heart. To what a world this glorious poet has introduced me! To wander over the heath, with the storm wind howling round me, carrying along in the steaming mists the ghosts of ancestors under the light of the moon. To hear from the mountains, amid the roaring of the forest river, the fading groans of spirits in their caves and the laments of the maiden pining with grief by the four moss-covered, grass-grown stones that mark the grave of her noble lover. Then when I find him, the wandering grey bard, who seeks on the broad heath the foot-steps of his fathers, and finds alas! their tombstones, and then gazes lamenting at the evening star which is hiding in the rolling ocean, and ages long gone by re-awaken in the soul of the hero, when the friendly beam shed its light upon the perils of the brave ones and the moon illumined their ship returning wreathed in victory; when I read the deep sorrow on his brow, see the last forlorn hero tottering exhausted to the grave, drinking in ever fresh, grievously glowing joys in the impotent presence of the shades of his departed ones, and looking down on the cold earth and the high waving grass, crying out: "The traveller will come, will come, who knew me in my beauty and will ask, 'Where is the minstrel, Fingal's worthy son?' His foot-step will pass over my grave and he will ask for me upon the earth in vain."—Oh Friend! I would like to draw my sword like a noble armour-bearer and free my lord with one blow from the quivering torment of this slowly receding life, and send my soul to follow the freed demi-god.

19 October.

Oh! this void, this dreadful void within my breast. I often think—if you could but press her once, only once, to your heart, the void would all be filled.

26 October.

Yes, I am growing certain, friend, certain and ever more certain, that the existence of any creature matters little, very little. One of Lotte's friends came to see her, and I went into the next room to find a book, but could not read, so took up a pen to write. I heard them speaking softly, exchanging trifling gossip, news of the town, how one girl had married, another was very sick. "She has a dry cough, the bones are sticking out of her face, she gets fainting fits, I wouldn't give a penny for her life," said the friend. "So and so is also in a bad way," said Lotte. "He has swollen up already," said the other. My vivid imagination set me at the bedsides of these poor people, I saw how reluctantly they turned their backs on this life, how they—and Wilhelm, these ladies were discussing the matter in the way we usually discuss a stranger's death. And when I look round, and see the room, with Lotte's clothes lying about, her ear-rings here on the table, and Albert's papers and the furniture with which I am so familiar, even this ink-pot, and think to myself, "See what you are to this house! All in all. Your friends esteem you. You often make them happy and your heart feels that it could not exist without them; and yet—if you were to go? if you were to leave this circle? would they, and for how long, feel the void which your loss would make in their lot? for how long?"—Oh! man is so transitory that even where he finds the actual certainty of his existence, where he leaves the only true impress of his presence, in the memory, in the soul of those he loves—even there he must be extinguished, must disappear, and oh! how soon!

27 October.

I would often like to tear my breast and dash out my brains at the thought that two mortals can be so little to one other. The love, the joy, the ardour, the rapture that do not come from myself will not be given me by another, and though my whole heart be full of bliss I cannot make another happy if he stands before me cold and limp.

30 October.

If I have not a hundred times been on the verge of embracing her! The great God knows what it feels like to see so much charm about one and not be able to grasp it. And that is yet the most natural of human instincts. Do not children grasp at everything they see?—And I?

3 November.

God knows, I lie down to sleep so often with the wish, sometimes with the hope, that I shall not wake again; and in the morning I open my eyes, see the sun again and am wretched. Oh! that I could be peevish, could shift the blame to the weather, to a third party, to an unsuccessful venture; the intolerable burden of ill-humour would then only half rest upon myself. Woe is me, I feel only too truly that the whole fault is mine alone—not fault! Enough that the source of all my misery lies concealed within myself, as formerly was the source of all my happiness. Am I not still the same who formerly hovered amidst all the abundance of emotion, with a Paradise following on every step, with a heart able to embrace a whole world with love? And this heart is now dead, no more delights flow from it, my eyes are dry, and my faculties, no longer revived by refreshing tears, draw uneasy furrows across my brow. I am suffering much, because I have lost what was the sole delight of my life, the holy vivifying power with which I created worlds around me. It has gone!—When I look out of my window at the distant hill, as the morning sun pierces the mist above it and illumines the tranquil meadows in the valley, and the gentle stream winds towards me between its leafless willows—oh! when this glorious scene appears before me as fixed as a varnished picture and all this rapture is incapable of pumping a single drop of happiness from my heart up into my brain, and my whole churlish self stands before the face of God like a dried-up spring, like a cracked pitcher! I have so often cast myself upon the ground and implored God to send me tears as a husbandman prays for rain, when the sky is brazen overhead and the earth about him is parched.

But oh! I feel that God does not send rain and sunshine at our impetuous bidding, and those times, the memory of which torments me, why were they so happy if not because I patiently awaited His spirit and received with a grateful fervent heart the rapture which He caused to descend upon me!

8 November.

She has reproached me with my lack of control, and oh! so gently! That I sometimes allow myself to be seduced by a glass of wine into drinking the whole bottle. "Don't do it," she said, "think of Lotte!" "Think!" I said. "Do you need to bid me do that? I think!—or do not think! You are always present to my soul. I sat to-day at the spot where you alighted lately from the coach. . . ." She changed the topic, to stop me pursuing the subject further. Friend, I am lost! She can do with me what she will.

15 November.

I am grateful to you, Wilhelm, for your sincere sympathy, for your well-meant advice, and would beg you to be tranquil. Let me endure it to the end; with all my lassitude I have strength enough to see it out. I have respect for religion, as you know, I feel that it is a staff for many a weary soul, refreshment for many who are faint. But—can it, must it then be for everyone? When you look at the great world, you see thousands for whom it has not been, thousands for whom it will not be—preached or not preached—must it then be for me? Does not even the Son of God say that those would be about Him whom His Father has given to Him? Supposing our Father wishes to keep me for Himself, as my heart tells me? I beg you, do not interpret this falsely, do not look for mockery in these innocent words; it is my whole soul that I am baring to you. Otherwise I would rather have remained silent, for I do not willingly waste words about things of which no one knows any more than I do. What is it but the fate of man to endure his lot, to drain his cup?—And if the cup was too bitter for the human lips of the God Who came from Heaven, why should I brag and pretend it tastes sweet to me? And why should I be ashamed, in the dread moment when my whole existence is trembling between being and not being, when the past is gleaming like lightning over the dark abyss of the future, when everything round me is falling away and the world crashing to ruin over my head?—Is it not the voice of the mortal who is thrust wholly in upon himself, insufficient unto himself, plunging headlong into the chasm, which grates from the secret recesses of his vainly upward-striving soul: "My God, My God, why hast Thou forsaken me?" And should I be ashamed to say this, should I stand in dread of the moment when even He did not escape it Who rolls the Heavens together like a cloth?

21 November.

She does not see, she does not feel that she is preparing a poison which will bring us both to grief. And I am voluptuously draining the cup that she is handing me for my destruction. What is the meaning of the kindly glance with which she often—often?—no, not often, but nevertheless sometimes looks at me, the favour with which she receives an involuntary expression of my feeling, the sympathy with my suffering that I see on her brow?

Yesterday, as I was leaving, she gave me her hand and said,

"Adieu, dear Werther!" Dear Werther! It was the first time that she called me "dear," and it penetrated to my very marrow. I repeated it to myself a hundred times, and last night, as I was going to bed, as I was chattering to myself about nothing in particular, I suddenly said, "Good night, dear Werther!" and had to laugh at myself afterwards.

24 November.

She feels what I am suffering. Her gaze went deep into my heart to-day. I found her alone. I said nothing, and she looked at me. And I no longer saw in her the charming beauty, no longer saw the shining of her fine spirit; all that disappeared from before my eyes. The gaze which affected me was far more glorious, full of an expression of the most ardent interest, the sweetest sympathy. Why could I not cast myself at her feet? Why could I not embrace her in reply with a thousand kisses?—She took refuge at the harpsichord, and in a sweet, soft voice breathed harmonious sounds to accompany her playing. Never have I seen her lips so alluring; it was as though they opened thirstily to drink in the sweet tones that welled forth from the instrument, and only the secret echo was returning from her sweet mouth—if I could only tell you what it was like! I no longer resisted; I bowed my head and vowed that I would never venture to imprint a kiss on those lips on which the spirits of Heaven are hovering. And yet—I will—Ha! you see, it stands like a barrier before my soul—this bliss—and then to go down to do penance for my sin—sin?

30 November.

I cannot, I cannot regain command of myself. Wherever I go I encounter an apparition which totally deranges me. To-day! Oh fate! Oh humanity!

At noon I went down to the river, I had no desire for food. Everything was so dreary. A damp, cold west wind was blowing from the mountains and the gray storm clouds were being wafted along the valley. From the distance I saw a man in a shabby green coat crawling about among the rocks and appearing to search for herbs. When I came close to him, and the noise I made caused him to turn round, I saw a very interesting physiognomy of which the chief feature was a quiet melancholy, but which otherwise expressed only a good and frank disposition; his black hair was held in two coils by pins, and the rest woven into a thick plait which hung down his back. Since his dress seemed to me to denote a man of inferior rank, I thought he would not take it amiss if I betrayed an interest in his occupation, so I asked him what he was looking for. "I am looking for flowers," he replied with a deep sigh, "and can find none." "This is not the season for them," I said with a smile. "There are so many flowers," he said, coming down towards me. "In my garden there are roses and two kinds of honeysuckle, one of which my father gave me; they grow like weeds; I have been searching for two days and cannot find any. Out there also there are always flowers, yellow and blue and red, and the centaury has a beautiful flower. I cannot find any at all." There seemed to be something queer about this, so I asked him in a roundabout way, "What do you want the flowers for then?" His mouth twitched with an odd wry smile. "If you will not give me away," he said, pressing his finger to his lips, "I have promised to take a nosegay to my sweetheart." "That is fine," I said. "Oh!" he replied, "She has a lot of other things, she is rich." "And yet she would like your nosegay," I said. "Oh!" he continued, "she has jewels and a crown." "What is her name?" "If the States General were to pay me," he replied, "I should be another man. Yes, there was once a time when I was so well off. Now it is all over with me, now I am . . ."—a tearful gaze at the heavens expressed everything. "So you were happy?" I asked. "Oh! I wish I were so again!" he said, "then I was so well off, so gay, as happy as a fish in water." "Heinrich!" cried an old woman who came along the path, "Heinrich, where have you been? We have looked for you everywhere. Come and eat." "Is he your son?" I asked, going up to her. "Yes, my poor son," she replied. "God has given me a heavy cross to bear." "How long has he been like this?" I asked. "He has been as quiet as this for half a year now. Thank God he has got so far! Before that he was in a frenzy for a whole year, and he lay in chains in the mad-house. Now he would not harm anybody, and is only oc-cupied with kings and emperors. He was such a good quiet boy, who helped to keep me and wrote a good hand; but sud-denly he grew melancholy, fell into a violent fever, then into a frenzy, and now he is as you see him. If I were to tell you, Sir . . ." I broke in upon her stream of reminiscences by ask-ing what he meant by the time when he was so happy and well off. "The crazy fellow," she cried with a smile of com-passion. "He means the time when he was out of his mind; he always praises it. That was when he was in the madhouse, when he was unaware of his condition."—I was thunder-struck. I pressed a piece of money in her hand and rushed away.

"When you were happy!" I cried aloud, as I hastened towards the town. "Happy as a fish in water.—God in Heaven! hast Thou made it the fate of man that he is only to be happy when he has come to his senses and when he loses them again! Poor fellow! yet how I envy your melancholy, the confusion of mind in which you are languishing! You set out hopefully to pluck flowers for your queen—in Winter—and are sad that you can find none, and cannot comprehend why you can find none. And I—and I set out without hope or purpose, and return home as I came. You indulge your fancy of what you would do if the States General were to pay you. Blissful being, who can impute his lack of happiness to an earthly obstacle. You do not feel! you do not feel that your misery springs from your ravaged heart, from your unhinged brain, and that all the kings on earth cannot help you."

He should perish without hope who mocks a sick man for travelling to the furthermost spring that will only intensify his malady and render his death more painful, who assumes himself superior to an oppressed being when the latter, to rid himself of remorse and the sufferings of the spirit, makes a pilgrimage to the Holy Tomb. Every footprint on an un-trodden path is a drop of balsam for the anguished soul, and with every day's toilsome journey he lies down relieved of so much affliction. And can you call that madness—you arm-chair windbags?—Madness!—Oh God! Thou seest my tears! Why didst Thou, Who createdst man in wretchedness enough, put brothers at his side to rob him of his morsel of wretchedness, the morsel of trust he has in Thee, in Thee, Thou All-loving One? For what is trust in a healing root, in the tears of the vine, but trust in Thee, that Thou hast laid in all the things about us the power to heal and soothe which we need at every step? Father, Whom I do not know! Father, Who didst formerly fill my whole soul and now hast turned away Thy face from me! Call me to Thee! Break Thy silence! Thy silence cannot sustain this thirsting soul—and could a man, a father, be angry whose son returned before his time and fell upon his neck and cried, "I am returned, my father. Be not angry that I have broken off my journey which, according to thy will, I should have prolonged. The world is everywhere the same, for work and toil, reward and joy, but what is that to me? I am only well where thou art, and in thy presence I will suffer and rejoice."—And Thou, dear Heavenly Father, wouldst *Thou* turn him from Thee?

1 December.

Wilhelm! the man I wrote to you about, the happy un-happy one, was a clerk in the employ of Lotte's father, and an unhappy passion for her which he nourished, concealed, and then revealed, so that he was dismissed from his office, sent him mad. Feel, fellow, at these dry words, the distraction with which I listened to this story when Albert related it as calmly as you, perhaps, will read it.

4 December.

I beg of you—you see, it is all over with me—I can bear it all no longer. I sat by her to-day—sat, she played on the harpsichord, various melodies, with such expression! such expression!—what will you?—her little sister sat on my knee and dressed her doll. Tears came into my eyes. I bent my head and caught sight of her wedding ring.—My tears flowed.—And suddenly she played the divine old melody, suddenly, and through my soul there coursed a feeling of solace and memory of all the past, all the occasions when I had heard the song, all the dismal intervals of chagrin and hopes miscarried, and then—I walked up and down the room, my heart suffocating under it all. "For God's sake," I said, going up to her in a violent outburst. "For God's sake, stop!" She ceased playing and gazed at me fixedly. "Werther," she said, with a smile that went to my soul, "Werther, you are very ill, you have taken a dislike to your favourite dishes. Go, I beg you! Calm yourself!" I tore myself away, and—God! Thou seest my misery and wilt put an end to it.

6 December.

How her form pursues me! Waking and dreaming she absorbs my soul. Here, when I close my eyes, here in my forehead, at the focus of inward vision, are her black eyes. Here! I cannot explain it to you. When I close my eyes, they are there, like an ocean, like an abyss they lie before me, in me, absorb my mental faculties.

What is man? The lauded demi-god! Are not his powers deficient just when he has most need of them? And when he soars up in bliss or sinks down in suffering, is he not held back, is he not again restored to cold dull consciousness, just at the moment when he longed to lose himself in the fulness of the infinite?

8 December.

Dear Wilhelm, my condition is that in which those unhappy beings must have been who were believed to be driven about by evil spirits. I am often possessed by something which is not fear, not craving. It is an unknown inward raging that threatens to tear my breast, that clutches my throat. I am wretched! wretched! And then I wander about the dread nocturnal countryside of this inhuman season.

Last night I was impelled to go out. I had heard in the evening that the stream had overflowed, and all the brooks, and that the whole of my dear valley, from Wahlheim down-

wards, was inundated. At night, some time after eleven, I
hastened out. A dreadful scene. To see the turbulent flood
whirling down from the rock in the moonlight over fields,
meadows and hedges, and up and down the broad valley a
raging sea lashed by the howling wind. When the moon came
out again and illumined the black clouds and the booming
flood rolled out in front of me in the dreadful glorious reflection, I was overcome by awe and longing. Oh! I faced the
abyss with widespread arms and breathed, 'Down! down!',
and was immersed in the rapture of hurling down there all
my torment and all my suffering, to rage along like the torrent. And oh! I was incapable of raising my foot from the
ground to put an end to all my affliction!—My clock has not
yet run down—I feel it! Oh Wilhelm! how willingly would I
have surrendered all my humanity to tear the clouds apart
with the storm wind, to embrace the flood. Ha! Will not perhaps the prisoner one day share this rapture?—

And as I gazed down pensively at a spot where I had
rested with Lotte beneath a willow when we were heated
with our walk, it was also submerged, and I could hardly
make out where the willow was. And I thought of her
meadows, and the whole region round her hunting-lodge!
how our summer house was now scattered by the raging
stream! And a sunbeam from the past gleamed out as when
a captive dreams of herds, meadows and cornfields. I
stayed.—I do not blame myself, for I have the courage to
die.—I should have. . . . Now I am sitting here like an old
woman gleaning wood from hedges and begging bread at
doors to prolong and alleviate her wasting, joyless life for yet
another moment.

17 December.

What is this, my friend? I start back in terror from myself!
Is not my love for her the holiest, purest, most brotherly love?
Have I ever borne in my soul a culpable desire?—I will not
maintain . . . and now—dreams! Oh! how true a perception
they had when they ascribed such contradictory effects to
strange forces! Last night, I shudder to say it, I held her in

my arms, clasped her tightly to my bosom and covered her love-lisping lips with unending kisses. My eye swam in the intoxication of hers. God! am I to blame that I even yet feel an ecstasy in recalling with all their fervour these glowing joys. Lotte! Lotte!—And it is all over with me! My senses are confused. For a week I have lost my powers of deliberation, my eyes have been filled with tears. I am at ease nowhere and everywhere. I desire nothing, require nothing. It is better that I should go.

THE EDITOR TO THE READER

In order to supply the detailed story of our friend's last remarkable days, I am compelled to interrupt his letters by a narration, the material for which I gathered from the mouth of Lotte, Albert, his servant and other witnesses.

Werther's passion had gradually undermined the peace of Albert and his wife. The latter loved her with the tranquil faithfulness of an honourable man, and his amiable intercourse with her was in time subordinated more and more to his profession. To be sure, he did not want to admit to himself the difference which distinguished the present situation from the days when they were betrothed, but he felt a certain inward resentment at Werther's attentions to Lotte, which must have seemed both an interference with his privileges and a silent reproach. This increased the ill-humour which was often generated by overwork in his hampered and badly-paid profession, and, since Werther's situation made him also a depressing companion, the anguish of his heart having consumed his remaining spiritual faculties, his vivacity and his acumen, it was unavoidable that at last Lotte should also be infected and that she fell into a kind of melancholy in which Albert thought he could perceive a growing passion for the lover, and Werther a deep chagrin at the changed demeanour of her husband. The distrust with which the two friends regarded one another rendered their mutual presence very embarrassing to them. Albert avoided his wife's room when Werther was with her, and the latter, noticing it, after some fruitless attempts to keep away from her altogether, seized the opportunity of visiting her when her husband was detained at his office. This gave cause for fresh discontent, their tempers grew more and more exasperated, until at last Albert said rather curtly to his wife that she should at least for people's sake give a different turn to her relations to Werther, and put an end to his too-frequent visits.

It was about this time that the resolve to quit the world had taken shape in the poor youth's soul. It had always been a favorite idea of his, which had occupied him particularly since his return to Lotte.

It was, however, to be no precipitate, rash act; he wanted to take the step with the firmest conviction, with the most tranquil resolution.

His doubts, his struggle with himself, can be seen in a note that is probably the beginning of a letter to Wilhelm, and was found undated among his papers.

Her presence, her fate, her sympathy with mine, press the last tears from my parched brain.

To raise the curtain and step behind, that is all! So why this fear and hesitation?—Because we do not know what it is like behind?— And because there is no return?—And because it is the quality of our mind to forebode confusion and darkness where we know nothing definite.

He could not forget the rebuff at the embassy. He rarely mentioned it, but one could feel imperceptibly that he considered his honour irretrievably outraged, and that the episode had inspired him with a dislike for a profession or political activity. He therefore resigned himself totally to the odd emotional and mental idiosyncrasies with which we are acquainted from his letters, and to a bottomless passion which was bound to cause the eventual extinction of all his vital energies. The eternal monotony of a melancholy attachment to the charming and beloved being whose peace of mind he was upsetting, the tempestuous wearing down of his vitality, without hope or purpose, drove him at last to the dreadful act.

20 December.

I am grateful, Wilhelm, for the affection that has prompted you to accept my remark as you have. Yes, you are right, it is better that I should go. Your suggestion that I should return to you does not please me altogether; at least, I would like to come by a roundabout way, especially as it is to be expected that the frost will last and the roads be good. I am glad that you will come to fetch me, but postpone it for a fortnight until you have received a letter from me with further news. Nothing should be plucked until it is ripe. And a fortnight more or less can do much. Ask my mother to pray for her son, and to forgive all the trouble I have caused her. It was my fate to sadden those to whom I owed happiness. Farewell, my dearest friend. All the blessing of Heaven be upon you! Farewell!

On that very day—it was the Sunday before Christmas—he came to Lotte in the evening, and found her alone. She was occupied in arranging some toys that she had prepared as Christmas presents for her little brothers and sisters. He talked about the pleasure the little ones would experience, and about the times when the unexpected opening of the door and the appearance of a decorated Christmas tree with wax candles, sweetmeats & apples inspired a heavenly ecstasy. "You also," said Lotte, concealing her embarrassment with a sweet smile, "you also are to receive Christmas presents, if you behave properly, a little roll of wax tapers and something else." "And what do you call behaving properly?" he cried. "What am I to do, what can I do, dearest Lotte?" "Thursday evening," she said, "is Christmas Eve, when the children are coming, and my father also, then everyone will receive his present, and you are to come as well—but not before." Werther was taken aback. "I beg of you," she continued, "that is how things are, and I beg you for the sake of my peace of mind, we cannot, we cannot continue like this!"—He turned his eyes away from her, went up and down the room, and muttered, "We cannot continue like this!" between his teeth. Lotte, who perceived the terrible state these words had put him in, tried to divert his thoughts by asking him all manner of questions, but without avail.

"No, Lotte," he cried, "I shall not see you again!"—"Why?" she rejoined, "you can, you must see us again, only control yourself. Oh! why were you born with this impetuosity, this persistent passion for everything that you once touch! I beg of you," she continued, taking his hand, "control yourself. Your intellect, your knowledge, your talents—what diverse enjoyments do these not offer you! Be a man. Rid yourself of this melancholy attachment to a person who can do nought but pity you." He grated his teeth and looked at her gloomily. She held his hand. "Only one moment of calm thinking, Werther," she said. "Do you not perceive that you are deceiving yourself, that you are the voluntary cause of your own undoing? Why me, Werther? Just me, who belong to another? Just this? I fear, I fear it is only the impossibility of possessing me that makes this desire so alluring." He withdrew his hand from hers, gazing at her with a fixed and angry look. "Clever!" he cried. "Very clever! Did Albert say that, I wonder? Subtle! Very subtle!"—"Anyone might say it," she replied. "Is there then no maiden in the wide world who could fulfill the desires of your heart? Bring yourself to look for her, and I swear to you that you will find her. For a long time I have feared for you and for us the restriction you have imposed upon yourself. Bring yourself to it! A journey will and must distract you! Seek and find a worthy object for all your love, then return and let us enjoy together the happiness of a true friendship."

"That ought to be printed," he said with a cold laugh, "and recommended to all tutors. Dear Lotte, let me have just a little repose, and everything will be all right."—"Only this, Werther! that you do not come back till Christmas Eve."— He was about to reply, when Albert entered the room. They bade one another a frigid good evening, and walked up and down the room together with some embarrassment. Werther began some trifling conversation, which soon petered out. Albert did the same and then asked his wife about some commissions and, when he heard that they had not yet been carried out, returned a sharp answer that cut Werther to the heart. He wanted to go, could not, and delayed till eight o'clock. Their irritation and ill-humour with one another increased more and more until the table was laid and he took his hat and stick, when Albert, with conventional politeness, invited him to take pot-luck with them.

He arrived at his lodging, took the candle from his servant who wanted to light him on his way, and went alone to his room, where he wept aloud, spoke in an excited manner to himself, strode violently up and down, and finally threw himself, fully clad, on his bed, where he was found by his man who ventured about eleven o'clock to go in and ask whether he should take off his master's boots. This he let him do, and then ordered him not to come into the room the next morning until he was called.

On Monday morning, the twenty-first of December, he wrote the following letter to Lotte, which was found sealed on his writing-desk after his death and brought to her. I will insert it here at intervals, just as—and this is evident from what happened—he wrote it.

My mind is made up, Lotte. I intend to die, and I am writing you this calmly, without romantic exaltation, on the morning of the day when I shall see you for the last time. When you read this, my dearest, the cool grave will already cover the stiffened remains of the restless, unhappy man who knows no sweeter bliss in the last moments of his life than to converse with you. I have had a terrible night, which has strengthened, has fixed my wavering resolve. I intend to die. When I tore myself away from you yesterday, with my senses in a state of fearful excitement, when it all rushed in upon my heart, and the thought of my hopeless, joyless existence at your side seized hold of me with chill horror— I was hardly able to reach my room, beside myself I fell upon my knees, and oh! God! Thou didst grant me the final boon of bitter tears! A thousand plans, a thousand possibilities coursed through my brain, and at last it was there, firmly, wholly, the one ultimate thought—I intend to die!—I lay down, and this morning, in all the tranquillity of my awakening, it is still firm, still strong in my heart—I intend to die!—It is not despair, but the certainty that I have reached the end, and that I am sacrificing myself for you. Yes, Lotte! Why should I not say it? One of us three must go, and I will be the one. Oh! my dearest, the frenzy has often crept

through my torn heart, often—to murder your husband!—You!—
Myself! So let it be then!—When you climb up the hill, on a
beautiful summer evening, remember me, how I often came thus
up the valley, and then gaze across at the churchyard to my
grave, as the wind gently waves the grass to and fro in the rays
of the setting sun.—I was calm when I began, and now I am
weeping like a child when I see it all so vividly.

Towards ten o'clock Werther called his servant, and said
to him as he dressed that he was going away in a few days,
and his clothes should therefore be turned out and made
ready for packing. He also ordered him to ask everywhere
for bills to be sent in, to collect some books that had been
lent, and to pay two months advance to some poor people
to whom he was accustomed to give something every week.

He had his meal brought to his room, and rode out afterwards to the bailiff, whom he did not find at home. He
walked pensively up and down the garden, and appeared to
want to bury himself at the last moment under all his melancholy memories.

The little ones did not long leave him in peace, but pursued him, sprang up at him, told him that when to-morrow
had come, and then another day, and another day after that,
they were going to Lotte's to fetch their Christmas presents,
and spoke of the wonders that their little imaginations
promised them. "To-morrow!" he cried, "and then another
day, and another day after that!" And he kissed them all
affectionately, and was about to go when the smallest one
tried to whisper something in his ear. He confided to him
that his big brothers had written beautiful New Year greetings, so big! one for papa, one for Albert and Lotte, and
also one for Herr Werther. They were going to hand them
over early on New Year's Day.

This overcame him. He gave each one something,
mounted his horse, asked them to give his regards to the old
man, and rode away with tears in his eyes.

He reached home towards five, ordered the maid to see to
the fire and to keep it going till night time. He told his servant to pack his books and linen in his trunk downstairs

and to sew his clothes up in a bale. Then he probably wrote the following passage in his last letter to Lotte.

You do not expect me. You think I shall obey you and not see you again till Christmas Eve. Oh, Lotte! To-day or never again. On Christmas Eve you will hold this letter in your hand and tremble as you moisten it with your sweet tears. I will, I must! Oh! how glad I am that I have made up my mind!

At half past six he went to Albert's house, and found Lotte alone, very alarmed at his visit. She had told her husband in the course of conversation that Werther would not return until Christmas Eve. Soon after he had had his horse saddled, saying he was riding to an official in the neighbourhood with whom he had some business to settle, and had gone out in spite of the inclement weather. Lotte, who knew quite well that he had long postponed this matter and that it would keep him from home all night, understood the pantomime only too well, and was very depressed. She sat alone, her heart was touched, she thought of the past, feeling how precious it had been, and her love for her husband, who now, instead of the promised happiness, was beginning to make her life wretched. Her thoughts came back to Werther. She blamed him, but could not hate him. A mysterious trait had attracted her to him from the beginning of their friendship and now, after so long, after having lived through so many experiences, the impression on her heart was bound to be inextinguishable. Her oppressed heart at last found relief in tears, and she fell into a quiet melancholy in which she became more and more deeply immersed. But how her heart hammered when she heard Werther ascending the steps and asking for her outside! It was too late to say she was not at home, and she had only half recovered from her confusion when he entered the room. "You have not kept your word!" she cried. "I made no promise," was his answer. "Then you should at least have acceded to my request," she said, "it was for both our sakes." As she spoke, she made up her mind to send for some girl friends. These should be witnesses to her conversation with Werther and, since he would have to see them home, she would be able to get rid of him early. He had brought her back some books, and she enquired about some others, trying to keep the conversation on a general level until her friends arrived, when the maid returned and informed her that they both begged to be excused, one of them having some relations visiting her whom she could not send away, and the other not wanting to dress and go out in such wretched weather.

This made her ponder for a few minutes, until the feeling of her innocence roused her pride. She decided to defy Albert's crotchets, and the purity of her heart fortified her, so that she did not, as she at first intended, call her maid into the room but, after she had played a number of minuets on the harpsichord to recover herself and allay the confusion of her heart, sat down calmly on the sofa at Werther's side. "Have you nothing to read?" she said. He had nothing. "In my drawer there," she began, "is your translation of some of the songs of Ossian. I have not read them yet, for I hoped to hear you recite them, but ever since you haven't been fit for anything." He smiled, fetched the songs, a tremor ran through him as he took them in his hand, and his eyes filled with tears as he looked at them. He sat down and read:[1]

Star of descending night! fair is thy light in the west! thou liftest thy unshorn head from thy cloud: thy steps are stately on thy hill. What dost thou behold in the plain? The stormy winds are laid. The murmur of the torrent comes from afar. Roaring waves climb the distant rock. The flies of evening are on their feeble wings; the hum of their course is on the field. What dost thou behold, fair light? But thou dost smile and depart. The waves come with joy around thee: they bathe thy lovely hair. Farewell, thou silent beam! Let the light of Ossian's soul arise!

And it does arise in its strength! I behold my departed friends. Their gathering is on Lora, as in the days of other years. Fingal comes like a watry column of mist! his heroes are around: and see the bards of song, grey-haired Ullin! stately Ryno! Alpin, with the tuneful voice! the soft complaint of Minona! How are ye changed, my friends, since the days of Selma's feast? when we

[1] This extract from Ossian's *The Songs of Selma* is here reproduced in the original—(Translator's note).

contended, like gales of spring, as they fly along the hill, and bend by turns the feebly-whistling grass.

Minona came forth in her beauty; with down-cast look and tearful eye. Her hair flew slowly on the blast, that rushed unfrequent from the hill. The souls of the heroes were sad when she raised the tuneful voice. Often had they seen the grave of Salgar, the dark dwelling of white-bosomed Colma. Colma left alone on the hill, with all her voice of song! Salgar promised to come: but the night descended around. Hear the voice of Colma, when she sat alone on the hill!

COLMA

It is night; I am alone, forlorn on the hill of storms. The wind is heard on the mountain. The torrent pours down the rock. No hut receives me from the rain; forlorn on the hill of winds!

Rise, moon! from behind thy clouds. Stars of the night, arise! Lead me, some light, to the place, where my love rests from the chase alone! his bow near him, unstrung: his dogs panting around him. But here I must sit alone, by the rock of the mossy stream. The stream and the wind roar aloud. I hear not the voice of my love! Why delays my Salgar, why the chief of the hill, his promise? Here is the rock, and here the tree! here is the roaring stream! Thou didst promise with night to be here. Ah! whither is my Salgar gone? With thee I would fly, from my father; with thee, from my brother of pride. Our race have long been foes; we are not foes, O Salgar!

Cease a little while, O wind! stream, be thou silent a while! let my voice be heard around. Let my wanderer hear me! Salgar! it is Colma who calls. Here is the tree, and the rock. Salgar, my love! I am here. Why delayest thou thy coming? Lo! the calm moon comes forth. The flood is bright in the vale. The rocks are grey on the steep. I see him not on the brow. His dogs come not before him, with tidings of his near approach. Here I must sit alone!

Who lie on the heath beside me? Are they my love and my brother? Speak to me, O my friends! To Colma they give no reply. Speak to me: I am alone! My soul is tormented with fears! Ah! they are dead! Their swords are red from the fight. O my brother! my brother! why hast thou slain my Salgar? why, O Salgar! hast thou slain my brother? Dear were ye both to me! what shall I say in your praise? Thou wert fair on the hill among thousands! he was terrible in fight. Speak to me; hear my voice; hear me, sons of my love! They are silent; silent for ever! Cold, cold are their breasts of clay! Oh! from the rock on the hill; from the top of the windy steep, speak, ye ghosts of the dead! speak, I will not be afraid! Whither are ye gone to rest? In what cave of the hill shall I find the departed? No feeble voice is on the gale: no answer half-drowned in the storm!

I sit in my grief; I wait for morning in my tears! Rear the tomb, ye friends of the dead. Close it not till Colma come. My life flies away like a dream: why should I stay behind? Here shall I rest with my friends, by the stream of the sounding rock. When night comes on the hill; when the loud winds arise; my ghost shall stand in the blast, and mourn the death of my friends. The hunter shall hear from his booth. He shall fear but love my voice! For sweet shall my voice be for my friends: pleasant were her friends to Colma!

Such was thy song, Minona, softly-blushing daughter of Torman. Our tears descended for Colma, and our souls were sad! Ullin came with his harp! he gave the song of Alpin. The voice of Alpin was pleasant: the soul of Ryno was a beam of fire! But they had rested in the narrow house: their voice had ceased in Selma. Ullin had returned, one day, from the chase, before the heroes fell. He heard their strife on the hill; their song was soft but sad! They mourned the fall of Morar, first of mortal men! His soul was like the soul of Fingal; his sword like the sword of Oscar. But he fell, and his father mourned: his sister's eyes were full of tears, Minona's eyes were full of tears, the sister of car-borne Morar. She retired from the song of Ullin, like the moon in the west, when she foresees the shower, and hides her fair head in a cloud. I touched the harp with Ullin; the song of mourning rose!

RYNO

The wind and the rain are past: calm is the noon of day. The clouds are divided in heaven. Over the green hills flies the in-constant sun. Red through the stony vale comes down the stream of the hill. Sweet are thy murmurs, O stream! but more sweet is the voice I hear. It is the voice of Alpin, the son of song, mourning for the dead! Bent is his head of age; red his tearful eye. Alpin, thou son of song, why alone on the silent hill? why complainest thou, as a blast in the wood; as a wave on the lonely shore?

ALPIN

My tears, O Ryno! are for the dead; my voice for those that have passed away. Tall thou art on the hill; fair among the sons of the vale. But thou shalt fall like Morar; the mourner shall sit on thy tomb. The hills shall know thee no more; thy bow shall lie in thy hall unstrung!

Thou wert swift, O Morar! as a roe on the desert; terrible as a meteor of fire. Thy wrath was as the storm. Thy sword in battle, as lightning in the field. Thy voice was a stream after rain; like thunder on distant hills. Many fell by thy arm; they were consumed in the flames of thy wrath. But when thou didst return from war, how peaceful was thy brow! Thy face was like the sun after rain; like the moon in the silence of night; calm as the breast of the lake when the loud wind is laid.

Narrow is thy dwelling now! dark the place of thine abode! With three steps I compass thy grave, O thou who wast so great before! Four stones, with their heads of moss, are the only memorial of thee. A tree with scarce a leaf, long grass, which whistles in the wind, mark to the hunter's eye the grave of the mighty Morar. Morar! thou art low indeed. Thou hast no mother to mourn thee; no maid with her tears of love. Dead is she that brought thee forth. Fallen is the daughter of Morglan.

Who on his staff is this? who is this, whose head is white with age? whose eyes are red with tears? who quakes at every step? It is thy father, O Morar! the father of no son but thee. He heard of thy fame in war; he heard of foes dispersed. He heard of Morar's renown; why did he not hear of his wound? Weep, thou father of Morar! weep; but thy son heareth thee not. Deep is the sleep of the dead; low their pillow of dust. No more shall he hear thy voice; no more awake at thy call. When shall it be morn in the grave, to bid the slumberer awake? Farewell, thou bravest of men! thou conqueror in the field! but the field shall see thee no more; nor the dark wood be lightened with the splendour of thy steel. Thou hast left no son. The song shall preserve thy name. Future times shall hear of thee; they shall hear of the fallen Morar!

The grief of all arose, but most the bursting sigh of Armin. He remembers the death of his son, who fell in the days of his youth. Carmor was near the hero, the chief of the echoing Galmal. Why bursts the sigh of Armin? he said. Is there a cause to mourn? The song comes, with its music, to melt and please the soul. It is like soft mist, that, rising from a lake, pours on the silent vale; the green flowers are filled with dew, but the sun returns in his strength, and the mist is gone. Why art thou sad, O Armin, chief of sea-surrounded Gorma?

Sad! I am! nor small is my cause of woe! Carmor, thou hast lost no son; thou hast lost no daughter of beauty. Colgar the valiant lives; and Annira fairest maid. The boughs of thy house ascend,

O Carmor! but Armin is the last of his race. Dark is thy bed, O Daura! Deep thy sleep in the tomb! When shalt thou awake with thy songs? with all thy voice of music?

Arise, winds of autumn, arise; blow along the heath! streams of the mountains roar! roar, tempests, in the groves of my oaks! walk through broken clouds, O moon! show thy pale face, at intervals! bring to my mind the night, when all my children fell; when Arindal the mighty fell; when Daura the lovely failed! Daura, my daughter! thou wert fair; fair as the moon on Fura; white as the driven snow; sweet as the breathing gale. Arindal, thy bow was strong. Thy spear was swift in the field. Thy look was like mist on the wave: thy shield, a red cloud in a storm. Armar, renowned in war, came, and sought Daura's love. He was not long refused: fair was the hope of their friends!

Erath, son of Odgal, repined: his brother had been slain by Armar. He came disguised like a son of the sea: fair was his skiff on the wave; white his locks of age; calm his serious brow. Fairest of women, he said, lovely daughter of Armin! a rock not distant in the sea, bears a tree on its side; red shines the fruit afar! There Armar waits for Daura. I come to carry his love! She went; she called on Armar. Nought answered, but the son of the rock, Armar, my love! my love! why tormentest thou me with fear? hear, son of Arnart, hear: it is Daura who calleth thee! Erath the traitor fled laughing to the land. She lifted up her voice; she called for her brother and her father. Arindal! Armin! none to relieve your Daura!

Her voice came over the sea. Arindal my son descended from the hill; rough in the spoils of the chase. His arrows rattled by his side; his bow was in his hand: five dark grey dogs attend his steps. He saw fierce Erath on the shore: he seized and bound him to an oak. Thick wind the thongs of the hide around his limbs; he loads the wind with his groans. Arindal ascends the deep in his boat, to bring Daura to land. Armar came in his wrath, and let fly the grey-feathered shaft. It sung; it sunk in thy heart, O Arindal my son! for Erath the traitor thou diedst. The oar is stopped at once; he panted on the rock and expired. What is thy grief, O Daura, when round thy feet is poured thy brother's blood! The boat is broken in twain. Armar plunges into the sea, to rescue his Daura, or die. Sudden a blast from the hill came over the waves. He sunk, and he rose no more.

Alone, on the sea-beat rock, my daughter was heard to complain. Frequent and loud were her cries. What could her father do? All night I stood on the shore. I saw her by the faint beam of the moon. All night I heard her cries. Loud was the wind; the rain beat hard on the hill. Before morning appeared, her voice was weak. It died away, like the evening-breeze among the grass of the rocks. Spent with grief she expired; and left thee, Armin, alone. Gone is my strength in war! fallen my pride among women! When the storms aloft arise; when the north lifts the wave on high; I sit by the sounding shore, and look on the fatal rock. Often by the setting moon, I see the ghost of my children. Half-viewless, they walk in mournful conference together.

A stream of tears, which gushed from Lotte's eyes and afforded relief to her oppressed heart, interrupted Werther's reading. He threw down the sheets, seized her hand and wept bitterly. Lotte supported herself on her other arm and hid her eyes in her handkerchief. The agitation of both of them was terrible. They felt their own misery in the fate of those noble ones, felt it together, and their tears mingled. Werther's lips and eyes burned on Lotte's arms, a tremor ran through her, she tried to withdraw, and all her grief, all her pity lay heavy as lead upon her. She took a deep breath to recover herself and begged him with a sob to continue, begged him with the whole voice of Heaven. Werther trembled, his heart felt as though it would burst, he picked up the sheet and read in a broken voice:[1]

"Why dost thou awake me, O breath of Spring, thou dost woo me and say: 'I cover thee with the drops of heaven.' But the time of my fading is near, the blast that shall scatter my leaves. To-morrow shall the traveller come; he that saw me in my beauty shall come. His eyes will search the field, but they will not find me."

The whole force of these words deprived the unhappy man of his self-possession. He threw himself at Lotte's feet in utter despair, seized her hands, pressed them against his eyes, against his forehead, and a foreboding of his dreadful intention appeared to flash through her soul. Her mind grew confused, she clasped his hands, pressed them against her breast, bent over him with a sorrowful air, and their burning cheeks touched. They were lost to the world, he twined his arms round her, pressed her to his breast, and covered her

[1] From Ossian's *Berrathon*. (Translator's note.)

trembling, stammering lips with frenzied kisses. "Werther!" she cried in a suffocating voice, turning away her face, "Werther!", and she thrust him away from her breast with a nerveless hand. "Werther!" she cried in a calm tone with noble dignity. He did not resist, released her from his embrace, and threw himself madly at her feet. She got up hastily and, in nervous confusion, trembling between love and anger, she said, "This is the last time, Werther! You shall not see me again." With a look, fraught with love, at the unhappy man, she rushed into the next room and locked the door behind her. Werther stretched his arms out towards her, not daring to hold her back. He lay on the ground, his head on the sofa, and in this attitude he remained for half an hour, until a sound recalled him to himself. It was the maid who wanted to lay the table. He walked up and down the room and, when he saw that he was alone again, went to the door of the cabinet and called gently, "Lotte! Lotte! only one word more, in farewell!"—She was silent, he waited—and begged—and waited, then tore himself away and cried, "Farewell, Lotte! Farewell for ever!"

He came to the town gate. The watchmen, who were used to him, let him out without a word. There was a drizzle, half rain half snow, and it was getting on for eleven when he knocked at the gate again. His servant noticed, when Werther returned home, that he was without his hat. He did not venture to say anything and undressed him. Everything was wet. The hat was found afterwards on a rock, on the slope of the hill towards the valley, and it is inconceivable how he managed to climb up there on a wet dark night without falling headlong.

He lay down in bed and slept for many hours. His servant found him writing, when, at his call, he brought in his coffee next morning. He added the following to the letter to Lotte:

For the last time then, for the last time I open these eyes. They are alas! to see the sun no more; it is hidden by a dark and misty day. Mourn then, Nature! thy son, thy friend, thy lover nears his end. Lotte, it is a feeling without compare, and yet it is most akin to a twilight dream, to say to oneself, 'This is the last morning.'

The last! Lotte, I have no conception of the word—the last! Do I not stand here in all my strength, and to-morrow I shall lie stretched out and inert on the ground! Die! What does that mean? We are dreaming when we speak of death. I have seen many people die, yet humanity is so limited that it has no conception of the beginning and end of its existence. Still mine, thine! thine! beloved, and the next moment—separated, parted—perhaps for ever.—No, Lotte, no.—How can I pass away, how can you pass away, do we not exist!—Pass away!—What does that mean? It is again a word! an empty sound, that awakes no echo in my heart.— Dead, Lotte! Interred in the cold earth, so narrow, so dark!—There was a girl who was everything to me in my helpless youth; she died, and I followed her corpse and stood beside her grave. As they let down the coffin and pulled up the whirring ropes again from under it, as the first shovelful of earth thudded down and the fearful shell gave back a muffled sound, becoming more and more muffled till it was at last entirely covered—I sank down beside the grave—moved, shaken, in anguish, my soul torn, but I knew not what had happened to me—what will happen to me— Death! The grave! I do not understand the words!

Oh, forgive me! Yesterday! It should have been the last hour of my life. Oh, you angel! for the first time, for the first time there glowed through the depths of my soul, without room for doubt, the feeling of rapture: She loves me! She loves me! The sacred fire that streamed from your lips still burns on mine, a fresh rapturous warmth is in my heart. Forgive me, forgive me.

Oh, I knew that you loved me, knew from the first soulful glances, the first hand pressure, and yet when I went away again, when I saw Albert at your side, I again despaired with feverish doubtings.

Do you remember the flowers you sent me, when you were unable to say a word to me, or give me your hand, at that odious party? Oh! I have knelt in front of them half the night and they put the seal on your love for me. But alas! these impressions faded, as the believer gradually loses the sense of his God's loving kindness which was accorded him with all Heaven's abundance in sacred and visible symbols.

All this is transitory, but no eternity can extinguish the glowing essence that I imbibed yesterday from your lips, that I feel within me. She loves me! This arm has embraced her, these lips have trembled on her lips, this mouth has stammered against hers. She is mine! You are mine! Yes, Lotte, for ever!

And what does it mean, that Albert is your husband? Husband!—That is to say in this world—and in this world it is a sin that I love you, that I would like to snatch you from his arms into mine? A sin? Good! I am punishing myself for it. I have tasted this sin in all its divine rapture, have drunk restoring balsam and strength into my heart. From that moment you were mine! mine, Lotte! I go ahead! to my Father and to yours. To Him I will bring my plaint, and He will solace me till you come and I can fly to you, clasp you, stay with you before the face of the Infinite in an eternal embrace.

This is no dream, no delusion! On the verge of the grave I saw more clearly. We *shall* exist! We shall see one another again! See your mother! I shall see her, find her, and oh! pour out all my heart before her. Your mother, bearing the semblance of yourself.

Towards eleven o'clock Werther enquired of his servant whether Albert had yet returned. The servant said that he had, for he had seen his horse being led. His master then gave him an unsealed note with the following contents:

Would you lend me your pistols for a journey I am about to undertake? Farewell.

Lotte had slept little that night; she was in a state of feverish agitation, and her heart was ravaged with a thousand emotions. In spite of herself, she felt deep within her breast the passion of Werther's embraces, and at the same time she saw with double beauty the days of her artless innocence, of her care-free confidence in herself. She already feared beforehand her husband's gaze and his half-vexed, half-mocking questions, when he should hear of Werther's visit. She had never dissembled, she had never lied, and now she was faced, for the first time, with the unavoidable necessity of doing so. The reluctance, the embarrassment she felt, made the fault all the greater in her eyes, and yet she could neither hate him who was the cause of it nor promise herself never to see him again. She wept till morning, when she sank into a sleep of exhaustion, from which she had hardly risen and dressed when her husband returned, whose presence for the first time she found quite unbearable. For she trembled lest he should discover in her the traces of a sleepless night spent in tears, and this increased her confusion, so that she greeted him with an impetuous embrace which was more expressive of consternation and remorse than passionate delight, thereby attracting the attention of Albert, who asked her curtly, after he had opened some letters and packets, whether anything had happened, whether any one had called. She answered hesitatingly that Werther had been there for an hour on the previous day.—"He chooses his time well," he replied, and went to his study. Lotte remained alone for a quarter of an hour. The presence of her husband, whom she loved and honoured, had made a fresh impression on her heart. She remembered all his kindness, generosity and affection, and reproached herself for having so ill requited them. An obscure impulse made her follow him; she took her work, as she was sometimes wont to do, and went to his room. She asked him whether he needed anything, but he said that he did not and sat down at his desk to write, while she sat down to do her knitting. They had been together for an hour in this way, when Albert began to walk up and down the room. Lotte spoke to him, but he made little or no reply, only sitting down at his desk again, and she fell into a train of melancholy thoughts which were all the more distressing since she tried to hide them and to stay her tears.

The appearance of Werther's boy plunged her in the greatest embarrassment. He handed the note to Albert, who turned coldly to his wife and said, "Give him the pistols."— "I wish him a good journey," he said to the youth. This was like a thunderclap to her. She faltered in an attempt to rise. She could not understand her feelings. Slowly she went to the wall, took them down trembling, wiped off the dust and hesitated, and would have delayed still more if Albert's enquiring glance had not impelled her. She gave the fatal weapons to the boy, without being able to utter a word, and when he had gone she gathered her work together and went to her room in a state of the most inexpressible anguish. Her heart prophesied all sorts of catastrophes. At first she was on the verge of throwing herself at her husband's feet and revealing everything—what had happened on the previous evening, her own fault and forebodings. Then she could not see what would be the advantage of such a step. Least of all could she hope to persuade her husband to go to Werther. The table was laid, and a friend of Lotte's, who only came to make some enquiry but was not allowed by Lotte to leave, made conversation bearable during the meal. They constrained themselves, discussed sundry matters, and were able to forget.

The boy brought the pistols to Werther, who took them from him in a transport of delight when he heard that they had been handed to him by Lotte. He had bread and wine brought in, told the boy to go and have his dinner, and sat down to write.

They have passed through your hands, you have wiped the dust from them, I kiss them a thousand times for you have touched them. Thou, Spirit of Heaven, dost favour my resolve! And you, Lotte, offer me the weapon, you, at whose hands I wished to encounter death and alas! now encounter it! Oh! I made my servant tell me everything—you trembled when you handed them to him, you bade me no farewell!—Alas! Alas!—no farewell! Is it possible that you have closed your heart to me on account of the moment which sealed me to you for ever? Lotte, a thousand years cannot wipe out the impress! And I feel that you cannot hate him who burns for you thus.

After the meal he ordered his boy to finish packing everything, destroyed a number of papers, and went out to settle some small debts. He returned home, went out again beyond the gate, in spite of the rain, as far as the Count's garden, roved about the neighbourhood, came back as night fell, and wrote:

I have seen field, wood and sky for the last time, Wilhelm. I bid you farewell, also! Forgive me, mother! Console her, Wilhelm. God bless you both! My affairs are all in order. Farewell! We shall meet again in happier circumstances.

I have ill rewarded you, Albert, but you will forgive me. I have ruined the peace of your house and sowed distrust between you. Farewell, I am about to make an end. Oh! that my death might restore your happiness! Albert! Albert! Make the angel happy. And may God's blessing rest upon you!

He spent much time turning out his papers during the evening, tore many of them up and threw them in the stove, and sealed a number of packages which he addressed to Wilhelm. They contained small essays and disconnected ideas, several of which I have seen. After having the fire made up and a flask of wine brought in, he sent his servant, who slept some distance away, as did the other domestics, to bed. The boy lay down in his clothes in order to be at hand at an early hour, for his master had told him that the coach horses would be at the door before six.

after eleven.

All is so still around me and my soul so calm. I thank thee, Lord, for these last moments of strength and ardour.

I step to the window, my dearest, and still see some stars shining through the fleeting storm-clouds. No, you will not fall! The Eternal One bears you at his heart, and me. I saw the wheeler stars of Charles's Wain, the loveliest of all the constellations. When I left you at night, as I went out at the gate, it was in front of me. With what intoxication have I so often gazed at it, raised aloft my hands and made it a symbol, a sacred token of the bliss I felt, and still—Oh! Lotte, what is there that does not remind me of you! Are you not about me always! And have I not always, like a child, insatiably, seized every trifle that your saintly hands had touched!

Beloved silhouette! I now return it to you at my death, Lotte, and beg you to hold it in honour. I have pressed a thousand, thousand kisses on it, waved a thousand greetings to it when I went out or returned.

I have left a note for your father entreating him to protect my body. In the churchyard there are two lime trees, at the back in a corner, towards the field, and there I wish to lie. He can and will do this for his friend. Add your entreaties to mine. I will not ask pious Christians to allow their bodies to rest beside that of a poor wretch. Oh! I could wish to be buried by the wayside, or in the lonely valley, that priest and Levite might cross themselves as they passed by the stone which marked the spot, and the Samaritan shed a tear.

Here, Lotte! I do not shudder to take the dread cold cup from which I am to drink the ecstasy of death! It is you who have handed it to me, and I do not fear. All! All! thus are all the desires and hopes of my life fulfilled! To knock so cold, so stiff, at the brazen gate of death.

That I might have been granted the happiness to die for you! To sacrifice myself for you, Lotte! I would die with a stout heart, I would die gladly, if I could restore the tranquillity, the rapture of your life, But alas! it was granted to but few noble souls to shed their blood for those they loved, and by their deaths to kindle for them a new life enhanced an hundredfold.

I wish to be buried in these clothes, Lotte. You have touched and sanctified them. I have asked your father to grant me this favour. My soul will hover over my coffin. Let them not search my pockets. This pink bow which you wore on your bosom, when I met you first among your children—Oh! kiss them a thousand times and tell them the fate of their unhappy friend. The darlings, how they swarm about me. Oh! how I attached myself to you, could not keep away from you from the first moment! Let this bow be buried with me. You gave it me on my birthday! How eagerly I accepted it all!—Alas, I did not think that the way would lead to this!—Be calm! I beg you, be calm!—

They are loaded—it is striking twelve!—So be it then—Lotte! Lotte, farewell! Farewell!

A neighbour saw the flash of the powder and heard the shot, but as everything remained still he paid no more attention.

At six next morning the servant entered with a candle and found his master stretched on the floor, with blood about and the pistol by him. He called to him, seized hold of him, but there was no answer, only a rattling in the throat. He ran for a doctor, for Albert. Lotte heard the bell, all her limbs began to tremble. She woke her husband, they got up, the servant stammered the news amid sobs, Lotte sank to the ground in a swoon in front of Albert.

When the physician arrived, he found the unhappy youth on the floor beyond all hope; his pulse was still beating but all his limbs were paralysed. He had shot himself through the head above the right eye, and his brains were protruding. He was bled in the arm, the blood flowed and he still breathed.

From the blood on the arm of his chair it was concluded

that he had committed the deed sitting at his desk. He had then sunk down and twisted convulsively round the chair. He lay on his back in the direction of the window, deprived of strength, fully dressed in boots, blue coat and yellow waistcoat.

The house, the neighbours, the whole town were in a turmoil. Albert entered. Werther had been laid on the bed, his forehead tied up, his face already like that of a dead man, without moving a limb. A dreadful rattling noise still came from his lungs, now faintly, now more loudly; the end was near.

He had only drunk one glass of the wine. *Emilia Galotti* lay open on his desk.

I cannot describe Albert's dismay, Lotte's grief.

The old bailiff came galloping up at the news, and he kissed the dying youth as the hot tears coursed down his cheeks. His eldest sons arrived soon afterwards on foot and sank beside the bed with expressions of the most unrestrained sorrow, kissed his hands and mouth, and the eldest, of whom he had been the most fond, clung to his lips and had to be torn away by force. He died at noon. The presence of the bailiff and the arrangements he made prevented a crowd from assembling. He had him buried towards eleven o'clock at night at the spot that he had chosen. The old man and his sons followed the body. Albert could not. Lotte's life was in danger. He was carried by workmen. There was no pastor present.

THE SPORT OF DESTINY [1]

A Fragment of a True Story

FRIEDRICH VON SCHILLER

(1759-1805)

ALOYSIUS VON G＿＿ was the son of a commoner of some
note in the ＿＿ Company's service. He had great ability
which was so well developed by an excellent education that,
at an unusually early age, he entered the military service of
his native Prince. Both were in the full glow of their youth
and both were possessed of rash and enterprising natures,
which soon endeared G＿＿ to the Prince. Gifted with wit,
charm and good humor, as well as information, G＿＿ soon
became an agreeable addition to every circle in which he
moved, while the Prince had the good sense to appreciate his
virtues. Added to these, he showed a great spirit of perseverance and all these qualities were heightened by a very pleasing figure, and an appearance of blooming health and power.
He combined, in his demeanor, high spirits and natural dignity, relieved by a due share of modesty of manner. The
Prince was charmed with both the inward and exterior
qualities of his new associate, and the similarity of age, of
inclination, and of character soon led to a great degree of
intimacy between the two. G＿＿ was advanced very
rapidly, though to the Prince, even this rate of promotion
seemed all too slow, so high was his opinion of his friend.
When he was not yet twenty-two, G＿＿ had reached
heights which would have been envied by the most venerable
statesmen at the close of their careers. But his active spirit

[1] Translated by Marian Klopfer. Copyright, 1933, by The Modern
Library, Inc.

was incapable of contentment or repose and while the Prince was engaged in his pleasures, the young favorite would devote himself with unwearying assiduity to important affairs. He became, in time, so skillful and judicious that his talents were more and more constantly employed, so that, from the mere companion of his pleasures, he soon became counselor and Minister, and finally, the director of his Prince. In a short time, the only way to obtain the royal favor was through him. He had the disposal of all ranks and offices, as well as the distribution of all rewards and remunerations.

G——, however, was far too young and inexperienced, and had risen by too rapid strides, to use his power with moderation. The respectful humility and attentions shown him by the first nobles of the land, who all surpassed him in birth, fortune and reputation, awoke the slumbering embers of his pride and tyranny and he began to show a hardness of character which remained through all the vicissitudes of his fortunes. There was no service, however great, which his friends might not venture to solicit; but woe be to his enemies! He was less solicitous to enrich himself than a number of his creatures, but his choice of them was dictated by sheer whim rather than by justice. Yet, by exacting too much, by the haughtiness of his commands, and by his whole demeanor, he alienated from him even those who were most in his debt, while his rivals, and those who envied him were quickly converted into his deadliest enemies. These men, watching his every act with jealousy, were collecting materials for his future accusation and were slowly planning to undermine his greatness. Among them was a Piedmontese Count, named Joseph Martinenzo, belonging to the Prince's suite. G—— himself had promoted him, as a harmless, obedient creature, to his present post—that of attending the pleasures of his princely master, which he began to find too irksome now that he was engaged in more important occupations.

Viewing this man merely as the work of his own hands, and thinking that he could at any time again reduce him to his original unimportance, he felt assured, through motives of fear and gratitude, of the fidelity of his creature. He thus fell into the same error as was committed by Richelieu in entrusting Louis the Thirteenth to the care of the young Le Grand. Lacking Richelieu's ability of repairing so great a mistake, he had, further, to deal with a far bitterer enemy than the French Minister had to encounter. Instead of boasting of his good fortune, or allowing his patron to feel that he could dispense with his further patronage, Martinenzo was only the more cautious to maintain a show of dependence, and to bind himself constantly closer in the alliance with his benefactor. Meanwhile, he ignored no opportunity afforded him by his office to ingratiate himself with the Prince, until, from being useful, he became indispensable to him. Discovering all the avenues to his confidence and favor, he gradually made himself master of the Prince's mind. All those arts which pride and a natural elevation of character had taught the Minister to hold in contempt were brought into play by the Italian, who was utterly unscrupulous about the attainment of his object as well as about the means he employed. He was well aware that nothing is so conducive to unreserved confidence as participation in common vices and with this knowledge he proceeded to play upon the Prince, exciting passions hitherto dormant and directing them to the worst of purposes. By a train of the most seductive arts, he plunged him into excesses which admitted of no outside participation and no witnesses, and thus finally became the master of the most incriminating secrets. He then began to lay the foundation of his own fortunes upon the progressive degradation of the Prince's character; the secrets which rendered him so formidable obtained him complete domination over the Prince's feelings before G——— even suspected that he had a rival.

It may appear strange that so important a change should escape the attention of the Minister; but he had, unluckily, too high an opinion of his own worth to suspect that a man like Martinenzo would dare to become his opponent, while the latter was too cautious to commit the least error which might rouse his patron from his security. The same overweening confidence which had caused the downfall of so many of his predecessors from the summit of royal favor, was fast preparing the Minister's ruin. The confidential terms upon which he saw Martinenzo with his master gave him no uneasiness; he was glad to resign a species of favor which he despised, and which left his ambition unsatisfied: it was only as it smoothed his path to power that he had ever valued the Prince's friendship, and he foolishly threw down the ladder by which he had risen to his goal.

Martinenzo was not the man to play a subordinate part. At each step in the Prince's favor, his hopes rose higher, and his ambition, growing in a friendly soil, began to strike deeper and stronger roots. The greater his reputation grew, the more his role of humility toward his benefactor irked him. On the other hand, the Minister's deportment toward him, far from becoming more tactful as he rose in the Prince's favor, aimed at humbling his pride by admonitions reminding him of his dependence. This tryanny finally grew so intolerable to Martinenzo that he boldly plotted the destruction of his rival at a single blow. Under an impenetrable veil of dissimulation, he brought his plan to completion, still not venturing to enter into open competition with his rival. Though the first glow of the Minister's favor was at an end, the slightest circumstance could still have restored it, since the Prince showed the greatest respect for his mind and his advices and if he had once been dear to his master as a friend, he was now equally powerful as a Minister.

Fully realizing the situation, the Italian knew that the blow which he was about to strike must succeed, or else prove fatal to himself. The means by which he gained his object remained a secret with the few who aided him. It was reported that he had detected a secret correspondence of a treacherous nature, carried on by the Minister with a neighboring court; but whether his proposals had been listened to or rejected, remained a matter of doubt. The Prince felt that G_____ was one of the most ungrateful and treacherous of men—that his delinquencies were fully proved and only awaited punishment. This was secretly arranged between

the new favorite and his master; G____ was unconscious of
the gathering storm, and continued wrapt in his fatal security
until the final tragic moment, which precipitated him from
the summit of princely honors into the depth of obloquy and
contempt.

On the appointed day, G____ appeared as usual upon the
parade. Not many years ago an ensign, he was now an
officer of distinguished rank and even this was only meant as
a screen for the exercise of his political power, which actually
placed him above the foremost of the land. The parade was
his stage—here he indulged in all the pride of patronage;
here he received the obsequious attentions of his creatures,
thus rewarding himself for the exertions and labors of the
day. His chief dependents, all men of rank, were seen gathering around him, eager to offer their obeisance, yet evidently
anxious as to the kind of reception they might meet with. The
Prince himself, as he passed by, beheld his chief Minister
with a relenting eye; he felt how much more dangerous it
well might be to dispense with the services of such a man
than with the friendship of his rival. Yet this spot, where he
was flattered and adored, almost like a god, was that which
had been chosen for the scene of his tragic disgrace. The
Prince rejoined the Italian, and the affair was suffered to
proceed. G____ mingled carelessly among his friends who,
not suspecting any more than he, offered him their respects
and awaited his commands. Suddenly, Martinenzo appeared,
accompanied by some State officers. He was no longer the
same meek, cringing, smiling courtier; the presumption and
insolence of a lackey suddenly elevated into a master were
visible in his haughty step and fiery eye. He marched straight
up to the Prime Minister and confronted him, with his hat
on, for some moments, without uttering a word; then in the
Prince's name, he demanded his sword. This was handed to
him with an expression of terrific emotion; then, thrusting the
naked point into the ground, he split it into shivers with his
foot—the fragments lay at G____'s feet. At this signal the
two adjutants seized him; one strove to tear the order of the
cross from his breast, the other pulled off the shoulder knots,

the facings of his uniform, and even the plume of feathers from his hat. During this cruel and humiliating proceeding, which took scarcely an instant, not a single voice was raised; a breathless silence reigned throughout the immense throng. The hundreds of nobles who were present, all stood motionless, with pale cheeks and beating hearts, an expression of pained surprise on every face. Throughout this trying ordeal, G____, though anguished, bore himself with fortitude and composure.

When this procedure was ended, he was conducted through many rows of spectators, to the very end of the parade ground, where a covered carriage was waiting for him. He was motioned to ascend, an escort of mounted hussars being ready to attend him. Meanwhile, the report of what had occurred was spread on all sides; windows were opened, the streets were filled with throngs of curious people pursuing the carriage—their cries of triumph, of scorn, or of indignation, echoing far and wide.

He escaped the frightful din at last, only to meet a more fearful trial. The carriage turned out of the high road into a narrow, unfrequented by-way, towards the place of judgment and then into a more public path. Exposed to the sultry summer heat, without hearing any accusation, without attendance or consolation, he passed seven hours of misery and affliction, before he arrived at his destination. Late in the evening the carriage stopped and G____, unconscious, his gigantic strength having yielded at last to twelve hours' fast, was dragged from his seat. When he regained consciousness, he found himself consigned to a subterranean dungeon, dimly lit by the rising moon whose rays entered through a few grated openings from a great height above. Near him he found a portion of coarse bread, with a bowl of water, and a heap of straw for his bed. He endured this plight without any interruption, until noon the following day, when he heard the sash of one of the iron windows in the center of the tower drawn aside; two hands were visible, lowering down a basket like that which had contained his food the day before. For the first time since his arrest he felt some inclination to

inquire into the cause, and also into the nature of his future
destiny. But he received no answer from above; the hands
disappeared and the sash was closed. Thus, without behold-
ing the face, or hearing the voice of a fellow-creature; without having the least light thrown on his destiny, left in utter
ignorance both as to the future and the past; never feeling
the warmth of the sun nor the freshness of the air; he spent
four hundred and ninety days of agony, only sustained by a
small allowance of coarse bread. But this was not all, for he
made a discovery one day which increased and intensified
his wretchedness. He recognized the place; he had ordered
it constructed only a short while ago, in a rage of vengeance
against a worthy officer who had had the misfortune to dis-
please him, and he had even suggested the manner in which
it might be made more horrible and revolting. What added
the last bitter sting to his punishment was that the same
officer who had been destined to occupy it, had just succeeded the late commander of the fortress, and by a sort of
retributive justice, was made the master of his enemy's
destiny. He was deprived of the last poor comfort, the right
of commiserating with himself. He knew he did not deserve it; he felt himself an object of disgust and of the
bitterest self-contempt; and, worst of all, dependent upon
the magnanimity of a man to whom he had shown none.

His jailer was, fortunately for him, a man of noble feelings,
who scorned to take a mean revenge. He felt sorry at the
idea of fulfilling the part assigned to him; yet, as a faithful
subject and an old soldier, he did not think himself justified
in departing from the usual rules, and he feared to swerve
from his instructions. Still, he pitied him, and pointed him
out to a benevolent assistant, the preacher of the prison, who,
having been able to ascertain nothing against the prisoner
beyond mere report, resolved, as far as possible, to mitigate
his sufferings. This excellent man, whose name I willingly
suppress, believed that he could best fulfill his pious charge
by bestowing his spiritual support and consolations upon a
being deprived of all other hopes of mercy.

As he could not obtain permission from the commandant

himself to visit the prisoner, he proceeded to the capital to solicit the consent of the Prince. He fell at his feet, appealing for some mitigation of the prisoner's sufferings. He insisted, in the name of his pious calling, on free admittance to the prisoner, whom he claimed as a penitent, and for whose soul he was responsible. His subject made him eloquent and he soon made some impression upon the Prince, who had at first refused his request. The result of his efforts won him, at last, full permission to visit the wretched prisoner and administer to his spiritual needs.

The first human face G____ saw, after a lapse of sixteen months, was that of his new benefactor and he was eloquent in his gratitude, for this was the only friend he had in the world; all his prosperity had never brought him one. The pastor was filled with horror and astonishment on entering the vault. His eyes sought a human form, but beheld, creeping towards him, a white and wild-looking living skeleton, whose couch resembled the den of a beast of prey rather than a human resting-place. All signs of life seemed absent from his countenance; on which despair and grief had traced deep furrows; his beard and nails had grown to a frightful length; his clothing was falling about him in tatters and, due to the lack of water and all means of cleanliness, the air was foul and contaminated. Almost terrified at the terrible state in which he found the prisoner, the pastor quickly hastened back to the Governor to solicit a second alleviation of his sufferings, since he feared that without it, the first concession would be of little use. Since this, however, was in opposition to the strict letter of the Governor's instructions, the pastor resolved on a second journey to the capital, in the hope of obtaining some further concessions from the Prince. He declared that he could not, without violating the sacred character of the sacrament, administer it to a wretch who had not even the semblance of a human being. He gained his object and from that day on, the prisoner's lot was much ameliorated.

For many subsequent years, however, G____ continued to languish in captivity, though its trials were much less agonizing than those he had suffered previously; especially after the short reign of the new favorite was over and he was succeeded by others, who either were more humane or had no motive for revenge. Yet ten years passed, without any judicial investigation or any formal acquittal, before he was finally released. He was presented with his freedom as a sort of princely gift, but was requested at the same time, to banish himself from his native country. Here, the oral traditions which I have been able to collect begin to fail and I find myself compelled to omit an intervening period of about twenty years. During this period, he took up his military career once more, this time in foreign service, and by combined skill and industry he achieved the same heights which he had formerly attained in his native land. Time, likewise, helped; the Prince's days of pleasure and of passion were over; humanity gradually resumed its sway over him, and when his hair turned white, and he trembled at the brink of the grave, the friend of his youth appeared to him and constantly haunted his rest. He invited the banished man to revisit his native land, in order to repair, so far as possible, the injuries which had been done him. G——, of course, had long been anxious to return, but the meeting, though apparently warm and cordial, was extremely trying. The Prince gazed earnestly, as if trying to recall features so well known and yet so strange; he seemed to be numbering the deep furrows which he himself had traced there. But nowhere in that aged, grief-worn countenance could he recognize the features of his former companion and friend. The welcome and the looks of confidence were quite evidently forced on both sides; mutual shame and dread had separated them irrevocably. A single look, which brought back to his soul the full sense of his guilt, hurt the Prince, while G—— felt that he could no longer have any regard for the author of his misfortune.

The Prince attempted to salve his conscience by reinstating him in all his old honors and authority, but he never succeeded in winning back the sincere good-will and fondness which had characterized their friendship. His failure so distressed him that he found his heart closed to all the enjoyments of life and ended his days in the shadow of unhappiness.

G——, on his part, continued his troubled existence for nineteen years: neither time nor fate had quenched the fire of passion, nor wholly obscured the lively spirit of his character. In his seventieth year, he was still in pursuit of the shadow of a happiness which he had really possessed when he was only twenty. He died, finally, as the Governor of a fortress for the confinement of State prisoners. It was to be expected that he would behave with true humanity towards these unfortunates but, on the contrary, he treated them with the greatest harshness and ill-temper. If he remembered his own miseries as a prisoner, he gave not the slightest sign of it either by word or action. It was in one of his increasingly frequent fits of temper, in his eightieth year, that G—— collapsed and died without regaining consciousness, a victim, finally, to the passions that had wrecked his character and his career.

THE EARTHQUAKE IN CHILE[1]

Heinrich von Kleist

(1776-1811)

At the very moment of the great earthquake of 1647 during which many thousands perished in Santiago, the capital of the kingdom of Chile, a young Spaniard, Jeronimo Rugera, leaning against a pillar of the prison where he was held, was about to hang himself. A year before, Don Henrico Asteron, one of the wealthiest noblemen of the town, had removed him from his house where he was employed as a tutor, because he was discovered to be in love with Don Henrico's only daughter, Josepha. Through the malice and vigilance of his proud son a secret message between the lovers had been betrayed to the old Don, and as he had earlier given his daughter strict warnings, he was now so outraged that he sent her to the Carmelite covent of Our Lady of the Mountain. By happy chance Jeronimo had managed to see her there, and, one night, in the convent garden, they found their happiness. On Corpus Christi Day, as the solemn procession of the nuns followed by the novices, started, and the bells began pealing, Josepha collapsed in birth pains on the steps of the cathedral. This created an extraordinary stir; without regard for her condition the young sinner was at once taken to prison and, on the orders of the Archbishop, was tried soon after the child was born. The townspeople talked with such bitterness about this scandal, and so severely criticized the convent where it had happened, that neither the influence of the Asteron family, not even the intercession of the abbess herself, who had grown fond of the young girl because of her otherwise im-

[1] Translated by Victor Lange.

peccable behavior, could alleviate the harsh ecclesiastical punishment she faced. The only leniency that could be extended was that the death at the stake to which she had been condemned, was, much to the indignation of the matrons and maidens of Santiago, commuted by vice-regal decree, to death by beheading. All along the streets through which the execution procession was to pass, windows were leased, indeed, roofs were opened up, and the pious daughters of the town invited their friends to witness this spectacle demonstrating divine retribution. Jeronimo, who had meanwhile been imprisoned, nearly lost his mind when he learned of this terrible turn of events. In vain did he ponder ways of escape: wherever the wings of even the boldest imagination carried him, he met only walls and bolted doors, and when he tried, actually, to file through the bars of his window, he was detected and locked in all the more tightly. He threw himself down before the image of the Holy Mother and fervently prayed to Her Who alone could help him. But the dreaded day arrived, and with it the realization of the utter helplessness of his position. As he heard the bells that accompanied Josepha to her execution, despair overcame him. Life seemed hateful to him and he decided to hang himself with a rope which had been left by chance. He stood, as mentioned earlier, by a pillar, fastening to an iron bracket in the ledge the rope that was to take him from this miserable world, when suddenly the greater part of the city collapsed as though the entire firmament were crashing down, burying everything under its debris. Jeronimo Rugera was rigid with horror, and as if his consciousness had been shattered, he now clung for life to the pillar on which he had planned to die. The ground swayed under his feet, the prison walls tore open, the whole structure tilted and would have fallen if the opposite building had not also slowly tipped forward, forming a sort of vault, and preventing the total destruction of the prison. Trembling, his hair standing on end and his knees nearly giving way under him, Jeronimo slid across the slanting floor to the opening which had been torn in the front wall by the coming together of the two buildings. No

sooner was he outside, than, at the second tremor of the
earth, the entire street caved in. Nearly out of his mind he
did not know how to save himself in this universal disaster.
While death attacked him from all sides he hurried across
rubble and timbers towards the nearest city gate. Houses
crashed and falling debris forced him into a side street;
flames shot from the roofs, flashing through clouds of smoke,
and drove him, horrified, into another; there, the Mapocho
river, burst from its bed, surged towards him and forced him
into a third street. The dead lay piled high; from under the
rubble one could hear groans, people screamed from burning
rooftops; men and animals struggled with the waters of the
river. Some tried, courageously, to help, others stood, speechless and pale as death, stretching their trembling hands towards heaven. When Jeronimo had reached the gate and
climbed a hill on the other side, he collapsed. He lay completely unconscious for perhaps a quarter of an hour; then
he awoke again and, with his back to the city, half rose from
the ground. He felt his forehead and chest, not knowing
what to make of his state: as the west wind, blowing in from
the sea kindled his returning life, and as he saw the lovely
countryside near Santiago spreading before him, an indescribable feeling of bliss seized him. He was disquieted only
by the crowds that he noticed everywhere: he could not
understand what had brought him—and them—to this place.
And not until he turned around and saw the city in ruins, did
he recall the terrible moment he had experienced. He bowed
down so low that his forehead touched the ground, to thank
God for his miraculous rescue; and as if that one ghastly impression had pushed away all earlier ones, he cried with delight that he could still enjoy life in all its color and abundance. Then, noticing a ring on his hand, he remembered
Josepha and his own imprisonment, and the bells that he had
heard, and the moment preceding the crash of the building.
Again, deep melancholy seized him; he began to regret having prayed, and he could think only with terror of the Being
Who reigns above the clouds. Mingling with the crowds
that came hurrying from the gates, bent on saving their be-

longings, he enquired cautiously after Asteron's daughter and whether the execution had actually taken place. But there was no one who could give him reliable information. A woman with her back weighed down under an immense load of utensils, and holding two children, said, as she passed— and as if she had witnessed it—that Donna Josepha had been beheaded. Jeronimo turned away, and since, calculating the elapsed time, he could not doubt that the execution had been performed, he sat down in a lonely part of the forest and surrendered to his grief. He wished that the destructive power of nature should once more be unleashed against him. He did not understand why he had escaped death for which his grief-stricken soul yearned even as it offered itself everywhere to him. He resolved not to struggle, though the oaks about him should be uprooted and crush him. When he had stopped crying and, from the burning tears, hope had re-emerged, he roamed the fields; he visited every hilltop where people gathered, and wherever the stream of refugees was still moving he joined it. Anxiously he hurried after every dress fluttering in the wind: but none belonged to the beloved daughter of Asteron. The sun was about to set, and with it his hopes; he stepped to the edge of a rock and from there he gained a view into a wide valley that only a few people had reached. Uncertain what to do, he scanned the groups and was about to turn away again when suddenly he noticed at the spring that supplied the valley with water a young woman cleaning a child. At this sight his heart leaped with joy; he quickly climbed down the rocks and, filled with expectation, shouted: "Mother of God!" He recognized Josepha as she turned around, startled by the sound of his voice. How blissful was the embrace of the two unhappy lovers whom a miracle had saved. Josepha had almost reached the place of execution when the procession had been dispersed by the crash of the collapsing buildings. Horrified she ran towards the nearest city-gate; but she soon regained her senses and hurriedly turned toward the convent where her helpless little baby boy had been left behind. She found the whole establishment in flames, and the abbess, who during those moments that were to have been Joespha's last, had promised to care for the child, now stood outside, crying for someone to save him. Josepha ran without fear through the smoke into the crumbling building and, as if all the angels of Heaven guarded her, carried the little child unharmed from the house. The abbess' amazement knew no bounds, and Josepha was about to rush into her arms when the roof of one of the buildings crashed, killing the abbess and nearly all her nuns. Josepha drew back in horror, quickly closed the abbess' eyes and, terrified, fled to save the beloved child whom Heaven had returned to her. She had gone only a few steps when she came upon the body of the Archbishop which had just been pulled from under the rubble of the cathedral. The vice-regal palace, too, had crumbled, the courts of law where she had been sentenced stood in flames, and on the spot where her father's house had stood, there was now a lake that boiled forth reddish steam. Josepha gathered her strength and, putting all distress from her mind, walked bravely with her precious load from street to street. She had almost reached the city-gate when she saw that Jeronimo's prison, too, was destroyed. She faltered and nearly fainted; but at that very moment a building that had been seriously weakened by the tremors collapsed behind her, and this fresh shock drove her on. She kissed her child, wiped the tears from her eyes and, paying no attention to the ghastly horrors about her, she found the gate. When she had reached the open it occurred to her that not everyone who had lived in one of the destroyed buildings would necessarily have been crushed under it. She stood still at the next crossroads and waited to see if the being whom next to little Philipp, she loved most might not somehow appear. But he did not come and, as the crowds grew larger, she moved on, stopped once more, turned around, and finally, shedding bitter tears, walked along a dark valley where, in the shadow of the pine trees, she prayed for his soul which she assumed had departed. But there she found him, her beloved, and bliss, in this valley, as if it has been the valley of Eden.

All this she now told Jeronimo with deep emotion, and

when she had finished she gave him the boy so that he might kiss him. Jeronimo took him and fondled him with a father's joy; and as the child cried, afraid of the strange face, he closed his lips with unending caresses. Meanwhile, the night in all its beauty, mildness and fragrance had fallen, so brilliant and silvery and still as only a poet can imagine it. Everywhere around the spring people had settled down in the light of the moon and prepared their beds of moss and leaves to find rest from the anguish of the day. And since so many unfortunates were still crying because they had lost their house, or their wife and child, or everything, Josepha and Jeronimo slipped away into the thicket so that their secret rejoicing would not disturb anyone. They found a magnificent pomegranate tree with its branches full of fragrant fruit spread wide, and a nightingale at the top fluting its voluptuous song. There Jeronimo stopped and, taking Josepha in his lap and Philipp in hers, they settled down to rest, covered by his coat. The scattered shadows of the tree passed across them and the moon paled before the dawn ere they fell asleep. For there was no end to their tales of the convent garden and the prisons, and the worry they had suffered on one another's behalf; and they were deeply moved at the thought of how much misfortune had to befall the world before they could be happy. They decided to go as soon as the earth tremors had stopped, to La Conception, where Josepha had a close friend from whom they hoped to obtain some money; they would then take a boat to Spain, the home of Jeronimo's mother's relatives, and there live happily to the end of their days. With these thoughts and many kisses they fell asleep.

When they awoke the sun stood high and they noticed several families nearby preparing their scant morning meal over a fire. Jeronimo was just wondering how he could obtain food for his family when a well-dressed young man with a child in his arms approached Josepha, and asked her modestly whether she would not give her breast to this poor little creature whose mother lay injured over there under the trees. To her surprise Josepha recognized him as an acquaintance; the young man misunderstood her confusion and continued: "It is only for a few moments, Donna Josepha; the child has had no food since that hour that has made us all desolate." "I was silent for another reason, Don Fernando," she replied; "in times as dreadful as these no one refuses to share whatever he may have." She gave her own child to his father, took the little stranger and put him to her breast. Don Fernando was very grateful for this kindness and asked her whether they would not join his friends who were just then preparing some food. Josepha answered that she would gladly accept this offer and since Jeronimo had no objection either they followed Don Fernando to his family where she was received most tenderly by Fernando's two sisters-in-law whom she knew as highly respected young ladies. Donna Elvira, Don Fernando's wife, lay on the ground, her feet seriously injured. When she saw their famished child at Josepha's breast, she invited her most kindly to sit down next to her. His father-in-law, Don Pedro, who was wounded in the shoulder, also nodded graciously towards her. In Jeronimo and Josepha there stirred curious feelings: finding themselves treated with such confidence and kindness they hardly knew what to think of the past, of the place of execution, of the prison, of the bells——had they only dreamt it all? It was as if the terrible blow that had shaken them all had brought about universal harmony; and beyond that point their memories would not go. Only Donna Elizabeth whom a friend had invited to watch yesterday's spectacle, but who had refused the invitation, regarded Josepha from time to time with a dreamy glance. But she was at once pulled back to the present from which she had momentarily escaped, by the account of some other dreadful incident. The city, someone said, had immediately after the first tremor been crowded with women who had given birth to children before the eyes of the men; monks had rushed about, crucifixes in their hands, shouting that the end of the world had come; the guards who had demanded that, upon orders from the viceroy, a church should be cleared, were told that there was no longer any viceroy of Chile; at the height of the disaster the viceroy had gallows put up to stop the looting; an innocent man who had tried to save himself by running through a burning house was rashly seized by the owner and immediately hanged. Donna Elvira, whose wounds Josepha attended, took the opportunity when the conversation was most lively, to ask her how she had fared on this terrible day. And as Josepha, with heavy heart, gave her a brief account, she noticed with something like joy that the tears welled up in that lady's eyes; Donna Elvira seized her hand, pressed it, and asked her not to go on. Josepha felt extraordinarily happy. She could not help thinking that the past day with all its misery had brought her bliss such as Heaven had never before bestowed upon her. In the midst of those fearful moments when all earthly goods had perished and all of nature threatened to be buried, the spirit of humanity itself seemed to blossom like a lovely flower. As far as the eye reached one could see people of all ranks resting side by side, princes, beggars, matrons and peasant women, high-ranking officials and day laborers, monks and nuns—all pitying one another, extending help, and sharing readily what they might rather have saved for their own support. It was as if the common misfortune had made them all one single family. Instead of indulging in empty tea-table talk for which the fashionable world usually supplied the material, they related examples of astounding deeds: people of whom before not much notice had been taken had now shown Roman fortitude; there were countless examples of fearlessness, of proud contempt for danger, of self-denial and supreme sacrifice, of life being thrown away unhesitatingly as though, like the least precious object, it could easily be recovered at the next step. There was not one who had not on that day been most touchingly helped or who had not himself acted generously; and sorrow was in everyone mixed with so much sweet happiness that it would have been difficult to say whether the sum of universal happiness had not increased as much on the one side as it had diminished on the other.

After many such reflections Jeronimo took Josepha's arm

and led her, unspeakably elated to and fro under the shadowy bower of the pomegranate trees. He told her that in view of the general friendliness and the changed circumstances, he had given up his plan to go to Europe; that if the viceroy was still alive he would in person plead for mercy before him—especially since the viceroy had always looked on him with favor; and that he hoped—he kissed her—to remain in Chile with her. Josepha replied that she had had similar thoughts and that, if her father was still alive she would undoubtedly be able to win his forgiveness; but she would advise that instead of appearing in person before the viceroy, they go to La Conception and from there attempt to reconcile the viceroy in writing. There they would in any case be near a port and if all went well, could easily return to Santiago. Jeronimo, after brief consideration, applauded the wisdom of her plan; they walked about a little longer, thinking of the happiness that was before them, and then rejoined the company.

Meanwhile it was afternoon and as the tremors grew less and less frequent the minds of the refugees had calmed; then the news spread that in the Dominican church—the only church that the earthquake had spared—a solemn mass would be celebrated by the prelate of the monastery. Heaven was to be implored to prevent further disaster. Crowds of people everywhere hurried towards the town. There was some question whether Don Fernando's group should also join and take part in this ceremony. Somewhat uneasy, Donna Elizabeth reminded them of yesterday's events in the church and suggested that such prayers of thanks would surely be repeated and that when the danger had definitely passed one could surrender to that feeling of gratitude all the more happily and confidently. Josepha on the other hand, enthusiastic and at once ready to go, insisted that she had never before felt the impulse to give thanks to her Creator more vividly than now that He had revealed His inconceivable and sublime power. Donna Elvira readily agreed with Josepha. She urged that they should attend mass, and asked Don Fernando to lead the group. Thereupon all of them arose, even Donna Elizabeth, though she seemed disturbed and, evidently, made her simple preparations for their departure with some hesitation. When she was asked what distressed her she said that she felt an indistinct presentiment; but Donna Elvira reassured her and suggested that she stay with her and her ailing father. Josepha said: "Will you take this little darling, Donna Elizabeth? he seems again to have attached himself to me." "Certainly," replied Donna Elizabeth and was about to take him; but as the child began to cry pathetically at this injustice, and would not acquiesce, Josepha kissed him and agreed with a smile that she would keep him. Don Fernando was much impressed by the dignity and gracefulness of her manner and offered her his arm; Jeronimo, carrying little Philipp, took Donna Constanza; the others followed, and in that order the group started for the city. They had hardly gone fifty paces when they heard Donna Elizabeth call after Don Fernando; she had meanwhile vehemently though barely audibly spoken with Donna Elvira, and now ran hastily after the group. Don Fernando turned and, without letting go of Josepha, waited for Donna Elizabeth. But since she stopped at some distance as if to wait for him, he asked her what she wanted. Donna Elizabeth came closer though apparently with some reluctance, and whispered, so that Josepha could not hear her, a few words into his ear. "Well?" he asked, "and what harm could come of it?" Donna Elizabeth continued to whisper to him, much disturbed. A touch of anger flashed across Don Fernando's face; he replied that all was well and that Donna Elvira should calm down; whereupon he continued with his lady.

When they reached the church of the Dominicans the organ was intoning with magnificent splendor. An immense crowd had gathered inside, indeed, it overflowed far out into the square in front of the church portals. Boys crouched in the frames of the pictures high up on the walls, and, in devotion and expectancy, held their caps in their hands. A brilliant light fell from the chandeliers; in the beginning dusk the pillars cast mysterious shadows. The huge rosette of stained glass at the extreme end of the nave glowed like the very evening sun that illuminated it. The organ ceased; there was absolute silence—not a single breath came from the congregation. Never before had such a flame of devotion gone out from any Christian cathedral as on this day from this Dominican cathedral at Santiago; and no human souls had ever burned more fervently than Jeronimo's and Josepha's. The ceremony began with a sermon that was delivered from the pulpit by one of the oldest members of the chapter in full ecclesiastical ornament. His trembling hands raised to Heaven and the sleeves of his robe flowing splendidly, he began with praise and gratitude that in this devastated part of the world there should still be men left able to stammer their prayers to God. He described what had happened upon His command: Judgment Day could not be more dreadful. And as he called yesterday's earthquake a mere precursor of that day—pointing at the same time to a gash in the wall of the cathedral—a shudder ran through the congregation. From there his oratory led him on to the moral depravity of the city; he blamed it for horrors such as Sodom and Gomorrha had not witnessed: it was due only to God's infinite patience that it had not been completely wiped from the face of the earth. But it was as if a dagger had stabbed at the hearts of our two lovers who were already deeply moved by this sermon, when the preacher, in this context, referred insistently to the infamy that had been committed in the garden of the Carmelite Convent. The leniency which the world had shown on this occasion was godless; and in an aside that could not have been more damning, he committed the souls of the evil-doers—and he called them by their names—to all the princes of hell. Donna Constanza pulled at Jeronimo's arm and cried: "Don Fernando!" but he answered as firmly and as quietly as possible: "Keep silent, Donna, don't move an eye, and pretend to faint. We'll try to leave the church." Before Donna Constanza had a chance to carry out this ruse that might have saved them, a loud voice, interrupting the sermon, shouted: "Keep away, citizens of Santiago! Here they are, those godless creatures!"

Another terrified voice in a widening circle of horror asked:
"Where?" and a third one replied: "Here" and, full of pious
brutality, dragged Josepha by the hair so that, with Don
Fernando's son in her arm, she would have stumbled, if Don
Fernando himself had not steadied her. "Are you mad?" he
cried, and put his arm around Josepha. "I am Don Fernando
Ormez, the son of the commandant of the city whom you all
know!" "Don Fernando Ormez?" shouted close to him a shoe-
maker who had done work for Josepha and knew her at
least as well as he knew her small feet. "Who is the father of
this child?" he turned impudently to Asteron's daughter. Don
Fernando paled at this question. He looked, hesitating, at
Jeronimo and scanned the crowd to find someone who might
recognize him. Josepha, caught in this terrifying situation,
said: "This is not my child, as you believe, master Pedrillo,"
and, looking with infinite anguish at Don Fernando, "that
young man is Don Fernando Ormez, the son of the commandant of the city whom you all know." The cobbler asked:
"Who among you citizens knows this young man?" And
several among those standing by repeated: "Who knows
Jeronimo Rugera? Let him come forward!" It happened that
at this moment little Juan, frightened by the tumult, turned
away from Josepha and cried for Don Fernando. Thereupon
a voice shouted: "It *is* his father!" and another: "It *is* Jeronimo Rugera!" and a third: "Here they are, those godless,
blasphemous people!" and finally the whole congregation
assembled in the temple of Christ roared: "Stone them!
Stone them!" Jeronimo called out: "Stop, you monsters! If
you are looking for Jeronimo Rugera—here I am! Let that
man go; he is innocent." The furious mob hesitated, confounded by what Jeronimo said. Some of them took their
hands off Don Fernando. At the same moment a high-ranking
naval officer came pushing through the crowd and asked:
"Don Fernando Ormez! What happened to you?" "Look at
them," Don Fernando replied, "those fiends! I would have
been lost if this man had not pretended to be Jeronimo Rugera in order to appease the mob. Arrest him, if you will, together with this young lady, for their own protection. And,"

seizing master Pedrillo, "take along this fellow who started the whole uproar!" The cobbler cried: "Don Alonzo Onoreja —I am asking you on your honor: is not this girl Josepha Asteron?" Since Don Alonzo, who knew Josepha well, hesitated for a second with his answer, several voices, infuriated once more, screamed: "It is she, it is she!" and "Kill her! Kill her!" Josepha put little Philipp whom Jeronimo had carried, and little Juan, on Don Fernando's arm and said: "Go, Don Fernando, save your two children and leave us to our fate." Don Fernando took both children and said that he would rather perish than tolerate that anything should happen to his friends. He asked the naval officer for his sword, offered Josepha his arm and told the other couple to follow him. With a certain measure of respect the crowd made room for them. They managed to leave the church and thought that they were now safe. But they had hardly stepped out into the square which was equally filled with worshippers when a voice from among the mad crowd that had pursued them shouted: "This is Jeronimo Rugera, citizens! I know it for I am his own father," and with a tremendous blow he struck Jeronimo to the ground. "Jesus Maria!" cried Donna Constanza and ran towards her brother-in-law; but "You whore of a nun!" someone screamed from another side, and with a second blow of the club beat her down lifeless next to Jeronimo. "You are mad!" shouted someone else, "that was Donna Constanza Xares!" "Why did they lie to us?" replied the cobbler. "Find the right one and kill her!" When Don Fernando saw Constanza's body he burned with fury. He drew his sword, raised it and struck, and would have split the fanatical murderer who had started this horror, had the cobbler not been able to dodge the savage stroke. But as he obviously could not cope with the crowd pressing close to him, Josepha called out: "Farewell, Don Fernando and the children!" and "Here, you bloodthirsty tigers—kill me!" and she threw herself among them in order to finish the massacre. Master Pedrillo struck her dead with his club. Splattered with her blood he screamed: "Send the bastard to hell after her!" and with unstilled lust for murder he advanced again.

Don Fernando now stood, divinely heroic, with his back against the church, in his left arm the children, in his right the sword. With every stroke he slashed one to the ground. A lion could not have fought better. Seven of the beasts now lay dead before him and the leader of the satanic mob was himself wounded. But master Pedrillo would not rest until he had grabbed one of the children by the legs, swung it around high above his head, and smashed it against one of the pillars. Thereupon everything became silent and the crowd dispersed.

As Don Fernando saw his little Juan lying dead before him, his brains dashed from his skull, he lifted his eyes in unspeakable horror to Heaven. The naval officer came to him once again trying to console him, and assuring him that he regretted not having acted in this misfortune—although, he said, this was justified by several circumstances. Fernando replied that there was nothing to reproach himself for, and asked him to help carry away the bodies. They were taken in the dark of the evening to Don Alonzo's house, and Don Fernando followed, covering little Philipp's face with his tears. He spent the night with Don Alonzo and for a long time he postponed telling his wife of the full extent of the disaster; using all sorts of pretexts: after all, she was ill, and he was not quite sure how she would judge his role in the event. But shortly afterwards she learned from a visitor what had happened. She wept in solitude with all the sorrow of a mother, and one morning, her tears still fresh, she embraced and kissed him. Don Fernando and Donna Elvira adopted the child and when Don Fernando compared Philipp with Juan and how they had become his, it almost seemed to him that he had reason to be happy.

THE STORY OF THE JUST CASPER AND FAIR ANNIE[1]

Clemens Brentano

(1778-1842)

IT was early summer. The nightingales had only just begun to sing, but on this cool night they were silent. The breath of distant storms was in the air. The night watchman called out the eleventh hour. Homeward bound I saw before the door of a large building a group, just out of the taverns, gathered about someone, who was sitting on the doorsteps. The bystanders seemed to show such lively concern, that I augured a mishap and joined the group.

On the steps sat an old peasant woman. Despite the animated concern the onlookers displayed, she turned a deaf ear to the inquisitive questions and good-natured proposals, that came from all quarters. There was something quite uncanny, yes, even a touch of majesty about the way the good old woman knew just what she wanted; while she was making herself comfortable for a night under the open sky, as little abashed by her audience, as though she were at home in her own little bedroom. She threw her apron about her as a protection, drew her large, black, lacker hat over her eyes, placed the bundle containing her belongings under her head, and was silent to all questions.

"What ails the old woman?" I asked one of the onlookers. Hereupon replies came from every hand: "She has walked in eighteen miles from the country; she is exhausted; she doesn't know her way about in the city; she has acquaintances at the other end of town, but can't get there alone."—"I was

---

[1] Translated by Carl F. Schreiber. From *Fiction and Fantasy of German Romance*, edited by F. E. Pierce and Carl F. Schreiber. Copyright 1927 by Oxford University Press, Inc.

going to take her," said one, "it's a long way though, and I've left my housekey at home. Besides she wouldn't know the house she's looking for."—"Still, the woman can't stay here over night," remarked a newcomer. "But she insists," replied the first; "I told her more than once, that I'd take her home, but she talks only nonsense, she must be drunk."—"I think she's weak-minded. At any rate, she can't stay here," repeated the former, "the night is cool and long."

During all this chatter the old woman, just as if she were deaf and blind, had gone on unconcerned with her preparations for the night. When the last speaker again stressed the point: "At all events she can't stay here," she replied in a strangely deep and earnest tone:

"Why am I not to stay here? is this not a ducal house? I am eighty-eight years old, and the duke certainly won't drive me from his threshold. Three of my sons have died in his service, and my only grandson has taken his leave.—God, I'm sure will forgive him, and I want to live until he is honorably buried."

"Eighty-eight years old and has walked in eighteen miles!" exclaimed the bystanders. "She is tired and childish; at that advanced age one weakens."

"But, mother, you might catch cold and take sick here; then too, how lonesome you'll be," said one of the group as he bent down to her.

Then the old woman spoke again in her deep voice, half entreating, half commanding:

"Oh leave me in peace and be sensible! I'm in no need of a cold, nor need I be lonely; it is already late, I am eighty-eight years old, morning will dawn soon, then I'll pick up and go to my friends. If one is pious, has his own cross to bear, and can pray, he can surely live through these few short hours too."

Gradually the crowd had dispersed. The last who had remained now hastened away also, because the night watchman was approaching and they wanted him to unlock their doors for them. I alone remained. The street-noises died away. Under the trees of the square lying opposite I paced back and forth thoughtfully. The manner of the peasant woman, her certain, earnest way of expressing herself, her self-reliance, despite her eighty-eight years; all this made it appear as though she considered this long span of life but as the vestibule to the sanctuary. I was greatly moved. "What are all the pangs, all the desires of the heart? Unmindful the stars continue in their course. To what purpose do I seek meat and drink, and from whom do I seek to secure them and for whom? Whatever I may strive for here, and love, and gain, will it ever teach me so to live that I can with as much composure as this good pious soul, spend the night on a doorstep? There to await the morrow? And will I then find my friend, as she is certain to find hers? Ah, I'll not have the strength to get as far as the city; footsore and exhausted I'll collapse in the sands before the gates, or perchance fall into the hands of robbers." Thus I spoke to myself. A bit later, when I was walking under the linden trees in the direction of the old woman, I heard her praying half aloud to herself with head bowed. I was strangely affected, stepped to her side and said: "Good mother, include me in your prayers, just an entreaty for me!" With these words I slipped a silver coin into her apron.

Perfectly composed, the old woman exclaimed: "A thousand thanks, my dear Master, that you have answered my prayer."

I thought that she was speaking to me and said: "Mother, did you ask me for something? if so, I wasn't aware of it."

Surprised the old woman raised herself and spoke: "Good sir, do go home, say your prayers and lie down to sleep. Why are you roaming the streets at this hour? That's not good for young fellows, for the enemy goeth about and looketh, where he may seize upon you. Many a one has come to grief through being abroad at such hours of the night. Whom are you seeking? The Lord? He is in the hearts of men, if they be righteous, and not on the streets. But if you seek the enemy, be assured, you have him already. Go home now and pray that you may be rid of him. Good night."

At these words she turned quietly on her other side and put the coin in her bundle. Whatever the old woman did

made a peculiar, serious impression on me. Again I addressed
myself to her: "Good mother, what you say is perfectly
true, but it is you yourself that keep me here. I overheard
you praying, so I made bold to beg you to include me in your
prayers."

"That's already done," said she. "When I noticed you walking back and forth under the linden trees, I prayed to God,
that He grant you clean thoughts. Now you have them, go
home and sleep well."

Instead I sat down upon the steps beside her, seized her
wrinkled hand and spoke: "Let me sit here beside you
through the night, while you tell me all about your home, and
what brought you so far to the city. Here you have no one
to stand by you, at your age one is nearer God than men. The
world has greatly changed since you were young."—

"I'm aware of it," replied the old woman, "my life long I
have found it pretty much the same. You are still young; at
your age everything seems new and strange. I have lived
and relived so much, that I look upon life now only with
pleasure, because God is so faithful in all things. But one
should never turn goodwill away, even though one doesn't
stand in need of it, lest the good friend fail to appear another
time when he would be most welcome. Sit where you are,
perhaps you can be of some help. I'll tell you what has urged
me over these long miles into the city. I never thought I
should see this place again. Seventy years ago I served as a
maid in this very house, on the doorstep of which I now sit.
Since then I have never again been in the city. How time
flies, like the turn of a hand. How often did I sit here of an
evening seventy years ago waiting for my sweetheart, who
was then serving as a soldier. Here we became engaged. If
he—but shh—, the guard is making the rounds."

Then she began in a subdued voice to sing, as young maids
and servants are wont on bright moonlight nights before
the doors, and I heard with great delight this old sweet song
from her lips:

"When the last Great Day shall be,
　　The stars shall fall on land and sea.
　　Ye dead, ye dead shall then arise,

And stand before the Last Assize;
There, far in front your feet shall go
Where blesséd angels sit in row;
God, newly come, shall wait you there,
A beauteous rainbow round His chair.
There those false Jews shall trembling stand,
Who gave the Christ to Pilate's hand.
Tall trees shall shed a glory near,
Hard stones shall crush their hearts with fear.
Who then can pray this simple prayer
Will surely pray it then and there,
The soul before its God is tried,
When Heaven's doors shall open wide."

When the guard came nearer, the good old woman exclaimed with a show of emotion: "Ah, to-day is the sixteenth of May; there's but little difference, it's just as in the past, only they wear different caps now, and the cues are gone. What matters that, if the heart is pure!" The officer of the guard stopped at the doorstep. Just as he was on the point of asking what was our business here at that late hour, I recognized in him an acquaintance, corporal, Count Grossinger. I explained the situation to him briefly; whereupon he replied, signally stirred: "Take this coin for the old woman and a rose too"—he held it in his hand—"old peasants of her type are fond of flowers. To-morrow ask the old woman to repeat the song so that you may write it down and bring it to me. I have searched far and near for that song, but never have I been able to come upon the complete version." Then we parted, for from the headquarters toward which I had accompaneid him over the square, the nearby guard shouted: "Who's there!" As Grossinger turned, he told me that he was in command of the guard at the castle, I should look him up there. I returned to the old woman, and gave her the rose and the coin.

She seized the rose with a touching impetuousness and fastened it in her hat, while in a low voice almost weeping she repeated:

"Roses as flowers on the cap I wear,
Had I but gold I'd have no care,
Roses and my dear one."

I said to her: "Come, mother, you have grown quite merry," and she recited:

> "Merry, merry,
> Reckless, very,
> Much did dare he,
> High did fare he,
> Then miscarry.
> Wherefore stare ye?"

"See, dear sir, is it not well that I remained here? It's all the same, you may well believe. It is seventy years ago to-day, I was sitting here on the doorstep. I was an hard-working maid and was fond of singing all the old songs. I was just in the midst of the Judgment Day song that I sang to-night, when the guard went by. A grenadier in passing threw a rose into my lap—I have it now between the pages of my Bible—. That was the beginning of my acquaintance with my husband long since dead. Next morning I wore the rose to church; he saw me there, and soon we were on good terms. How great is my pleasure, that again I hold a rose on this anniversary day. It is a sign, I'm to come to him! How happy it makes me to be invited this way! Four sons and a daughter have gone on before me; day-before-yesterday my grandson took his leave—may God help him and have mercy on him! —To-morrow another good soul will leave me; but why do I say to-morrow, is it not already past midnight?"

"The clock has indeed struck twelve," I replied, astonished at her words.

"God grant her comfort and peace these four short hours to come!" said the old woman, and waxed silent, folding her hands as in prayer. I too was speechless; her words and her behavior had gripped me so. Since, however, the silence became prolonged and the coin of the officer still lay in her lap, I addressed her again: "Mother, put the coin away, lest you lose it."

"I'll not put this one away, I'm going to give it to my friend in her last great suffering," she replied. "The first coin, I'll take home with me to-morrow, my grandson shall have it, it's his to enjoy. You see, he was always a splendid boy; he had a deal of pride in his person and in his soul—Oh, God, in his soul!—The whole long way to the city I prayed for him; the dear Lord certainly will have mercy on him. Of the lads at school he was always the cleanest and most hard-working but the astonishing thing was his sense of honor. His lieutenant often remarked: 'If my company has a high sense of honor, then Casper Finkel's responsible.' He was a lancer. The first time he returned from France he had a great deal to tell, but rarely did he venture a story that did not savor of honor. His father and step-brother served with the militia. There was many a quarrel about honor, for where he had an excess of it, they had not enough. God forgive me my great sin, I don't mean to speak evil of them. Everyone has his burden to bear; but my dead daughter, his mother, worked herself to death for that sluggard. Try as she might, she couldn't pay off his debts. The lancer said his bit about the Frenchmen, and when his father and step-brother had not a good word to utter for them, the lancer said with emphasis: 'Father, you don't understand, they do have a high sense of honor.' Angrily the step-brother retorted: 'Why babble so much about honor to your father? Wasn't he a petty-officer of company N? He ought to know more about it than you, you private!'—'Yes,' old Finkel chimed in, 'to be sure I was a petty-officer, and many an insolent fellow got his twenty-five stripes; if I'd had Frenchmen in the company, they'd have felt them even more, with their sense of honor!' These remarks irritated the lancer, and he said: 'I'll tell you an incident of a French petty-officer, that's more to my taste. During the reign of the former king there was much talk of introducing corporal punishment into the French army. An order of the war minister was proclaimed at Strassburg on the occasion of a large parade, and the troops in rank and file listened grimly to the proclamation. Now at the close of the parade a private did something against military rules, so his petty-officer was ordered to advance and adminster twelve blows to him. Sternly he was commanded to perform his duty, so there was no getting around it. But scarcely had he finished when he grasped the musket of the private, whom he had just finished beating, placed the butt of it on the ground before him, and discharged it with his foot, so that the bullet raced through his head and he fell dead to the pavement. The incident reached the ears of the king, who immediately ordered that corporal punishment be discontinued. Mind, father, that chap had a real sense of honor!'— 'He was a fool,' exclaimed the brother.—'Eat your honor, if you're hungry,' grumbled the father. Then my grandson took his sabre, left the house and came straight to tell me the incident, tears of anger rolling down his cheeks. I couldn't cheer him up, although I didn't entirely discredit his story; still I always came back to the same conclusion: 'to God alone be honor!' I gave him my blessing, for his furlough expired on the day following, and it was his wish to ride away a mile to the place where a god-child of mine was in service on an estate. He thought a good deal of this girl and wanted to see her once more:—they'll soon be united, if God hears my prayers. He has already taken his leave, my god-child will get hers to-day. Her dower I have brought with me. No one shall be present at her marriage but me." Here the old woman lapsed into silence and seemed to be praying. My mind was confused through sheer meditation on honor. Would a Christian consider the death of the petty-officer noble and proper? How I wished some one would tell me a sufficient solution to this problem!

When the watchman sang out one o'clock, the old woman remarked: "Two hours more! Ah, you're still here, why don't you go home to bed? To-morrow you'll not be fit to work and you'll not get on well with your employer. What's your trade, friend?"

The thought of explaining to her that I was an author put me to some embarrassment. I couldn't very well tell her that I was a scholar without lying. It is remarkable that a German always feels a bit ashamed to call himself an author (*Schriftsteller*); especially wary is he in using this term when speaking with the lower classes, because it so readily conjures up in their minds the scribes and the Pharisees of the Bible. The word *Schriftsteller* has not been so generally accepted among the Germans, as the *homme de lettres* among the French. In France there exists a sort of author's guild, and in their works one traces a good deal of professional tradition. Not infrequently the question is asked: *Où avez-vous fait votre Philosophie?*—where have you "made" your philosophy?—which leads us to venture the pun, that there is a good deal of the "made" man about the Frenchman. But it isn't this un-German custom alone, that makes it so embarrassing to pronounce this word when at the city-gate you are asked your occupation. A certain inner humiliation makes us reticent, a feeling that comes over all those who barter in free spiritual capital, the immediate heavenly gifts. Scholars are less embarrassed than poets, for as a rule they have paid their tuition, are for the most part state officials, and perform such tasks as produce more or less tangible results. But the so-called poet is verily in a bad way, because as a rule he has played truant from school to climb Parnassus. Thus suspicion enshrouds the poet by vocation; perhaps he who writes as an avocation is a shade the better. It is an easy matter to say reproachfully to the former: "Sir, every mother's son has a bit of poetry in his make-up as he has brains, a heart, a stomach, a spleen, a liver and the like; but he who feels it to excess, pampers or fattens one of these members, and develops it at the expense of the others, or even goes to the length of making it a means of livelihood; he has cause to be ashamed of himself in the presence of his fellow men. One who lives by poetry, has lost his balance; and an enlarged goose's liver, no matter how delicate to the taste, does posit a sick goose. Every one who does not earn his bread by the sweat of his brow must feel a measure of humiliation. That humiliation is especially felt by one who has not yet been dubbed a knight of the quill, when he is forced to speak of himself as a *Schriftsteller*." Such thoughts passed through my mind, as I bethought myself what my reply to the old woman should be. She was surprised at my hesitancy, looked me in the face, and said:

"What's your trade? I ask. Why don't you tell me? If your trade be not honest, then apprentice yourself properly; an honest trade has its own reward. I trust you're not a hangman or a spy, who is on my trail. For my part you may be what you may be; speak, who are you! If you were lounging about this way by day, I'd think you a sluggard or a do-nothing, who props himself against the houses, not to fall over from sheer laziness."

At that a word came to me, that might perhaps bridge the gap between us: "Good mother," said I, "I am a clerk."—"Well," she replied, "you might have told me that sooner; you're a man of the quill then. You must have a good hand, nimble fingers and a good heart, otherwise you wouldn't get far. So you're a clerk? Fine! In that case you can write a petition to the duke for me, but such a petition as will surely come to his notice and find favor with him. Most such writings are bandied about in the antechambers."

"Indeed, I'll write a petition for you, good mother," said I, "and I'll take great pains, to make it as forceful as possible."

"That's good of you," she replied, "God reward you for it. May you arrive at a riper old age than I, and in your old age may He grant you a like composure, as happy a night with roses and coins, as I; and in addition a friend, who will write a petition for you, if there be need of it. But do go home now, good sir, and get some paper so that you may write the petition. I'll wait here for you one hour longer before I go to my god-child. You can go with me to witness her pleasure in the petition. Her heart is pure, but God's judgments are incomprehensible."

After these words the old woman said no more; she bowed her head and appeared to be praying. When she began to weep, I enquired: "Mother, what has come over you? What brings the tears to your eyes?"

"Why shouldn't I weep? The coin, the petition, everything has moved me to tears. But to what purpose? The world is still much, much better than we deserve, and tears as bitter as gall are still much too sweet. Just look at that golden camel over there on the apothecary's sign! How strange and glorious God has created everything, only man is not mindful of it, and a camel like that can sooner pass through the eye of a needle than man enter the kingdom of heaven.—But you're still sitting here, why don't you go get the paper and fetch me the petition?"

"Good mother," I rejoined, "how can I frame this petition for you, if you don't tell me what I'm to put in it?"

"I'm to tell you that?" she replied; "then petition-writing isn't an art, and I'm no longer surprised that you were ashamed to call yourself a clerk, if I have to tell you all that. Well, I'll do my best. Put into the petition, that two lovers are to be laid to rest side by side; that the one of them is not to be dissected but left so that his limbs shall be assembled at the cry: 'Ye dead, ye dead, shall arise, ye shall come to judgment!' " Then she began weeping bitterly again.

I augured that a great sorrow was crushing her, but despite the burden of her years she broke down only for brief intervals. Her weeping was devoid of complaint, her utterance was at all times calm and dispassionate. Once more I begged her to tell me the full purpose of her mission to the city, and she spoke:

"My grandson, the lancer, of whom I made mention before, loved my god-child, as you will recall. He was constantly speaking to the fair Annie—so people called her because of her beauty—about honor, and he repeatedly told her that she must cherish her honor, and his too. As a result, the girl took on a something quite distinctive in feature and in her dress. She was more genteel and better mannered than all the other girls of her class. She grew more sensitive, and if a lad clasped her too tightly at the dance, or swung her higher than the bridge of the bass-viol, then she came to me in tears repeating over and over, that such things were contrary to her honor. Ah, Annie was always a peculiar girl. Sometimes when no one was aware of it, she seized upon her apron with both hands and tore it off, as though it were ablaze, and then burst into violent tears. But there's a reason for that; teeth tore at it; the fiend won't rest. Would that the child had not been so possessed of honor and had put a stronger trust in the dear Lord; would that she had clung to Him in all tribulation, had suffered disgrace and contempt for His sake, instead of laying such store by worldly honor.

The Lord would have had mercy, and will still show mercy. Ah, I know they'll meet; God's will be done!

The lancer had returned to France. Never a line did he write, so we quite believed him dead and shed many a hot tear for him. In a hospital he lay, sick of a dangerous wound, but when he returned to his comrades and was advanced to a petty-officer, he remembered how his step-brother had insulted him two years before, calling him nothing but a private and his father a corporal. Then he reflected on the story of the French petty-officer, and his many, many urgings to Annie about honor, when he was on the point of saying good-bye. Then his peace was gone; home-sickness seized upon him. He said to his commanding officer, who had noticed the change that had come over him: 'Ah sir, I feel as though I were being drawn home by the teeth!' He was granted leave to ride home on his horse, for all his officers trusted him. Three months was his furlough; he was to return when the cavalry got its fresh quota of horses. Now he hastened as fast as was possible, without harm to his mount, of which he was more chary than ever, because it had been entrusted to him. One day he felt a special urge to hasten homeward; it was the day before the anniversary of his mother's death, and he seemed to see her running alone before his horse crying: 'Casper, do me the honor!' Ah, on that very day I sat on her grave all alone and thought, if Casper were only here too. I had woven forget-me-nots into a wreath and had hung it on the sunken cross. Then I measured the space round about and thought to myself: 'I'd like to rest here, and there let Casper be buried, if God grant him a grave at home. Then we could all be together when it shall be said: 'Ye dead, ye dead, shall arise, ye shall come to judgment!' But Casper didn't come. I couldn't know that he was so near at hand and might have arrived. He felt an unusually urgent desire for haste, for while in France he had often thought of the day. He had brought along a little wreath of everlasting, to decorate the grave of his mother, and also a wreath for Annie, which she was to keep against her day of honor."

Here the old woman ceased and shook her head; but when

I repeated her last words: "which she was to keep against her day of honor,"—she continued: "Who knows, perhaps they will let me have it still. Ah, if I might but wake the duke!"—"To what purpose?" I queried, "what is your request, mother?" Then she continued seriously: "Oh, what were there to life, if one's days were not numbered; what were there to life, if it were not eternal!" She went on:

"Casper could well have been in our village at noon, but that morning the hostler had pointed out to him that he had ridden his horse sore, and added: 'My friend, that runs contrary to the honor of horsemanship.' Casper felt the force of the reproof, loosened the girth and did everything to heal the wound. Afoot, leading the horse by the bridle, he continued his journey. So he came late at night to a mill, three miles from our village. Since he knew the miller as an old friend of his father, he put up there for the night, and was received as a welcome guest just come from distant parts. Casper led his horse into the stable, placed the saddle and his valise in a corner and entered the living-room of the miller. Then he asked after his relatives and was told that I, his old grandmother, was still alive, that his father and stepbrother were well and were prospering. Yesterday they had brought grain to the mill. The father had turned a hand to trading in horses and oxen and was doing well at the business. As a result he had some regard for his honor and had laid aside his torn and patched clothing. Casper was delighted to hear this. When he asked about fair Annie, the miller replied he didn't know her, but if his guest had reference to the girl who had been in service at Roseacres, he had heard that she had taken a place in the capital, because she could get much more experience there, and more honor went with such service. This he had learned a year ago from a hand at Roseacres. That too was pleasant news for Casper. He grieved at the postponement of seeing her, but he hoped to find her in the capital very soon, pretty and neat, so that it would prove a real honor for him, an officer, to go walking with her of a Sunday. Then he told the miller this and that about France, they ate and drank together, and he helped his host pour in some grain. Finally the miller took him up-stairs to bed, while he himself lay down to rest on some sacks on the floor below. The clatter of the mill and his great desire to be home kept Casper awake, even though he was very tired. He was restless, thinking much of his dead mother and of fair Annie, and about the honor, that he anticipated, when he came back as an officer. At last he fell off into a light slumber, but started up often out of disturbing dreams. Time and again he saw his dead mother approach him and, wring-ing her hands, implore him for aid. Then he dreamed that he had died and was about to be buried, but as a corpse he him-self walked along to his burial, fair Annie beside him. He wept bitter tears that his comrades did not escort him, and when he had arrived at the church-yard, he saw that his grave was beside his mother's. Annie's grave was there too, and he gave Annie the wreath he had brought for her, and he hung his mother's on the cross over her grave. Then he looked about him and saw no one there but me. Then he saw Annie dragged into her grave by the apron, and after that he too climbed down into his grave exclaiming: 'Isn't there anyone here, who'll do me the last honors, and shoot into my grave as becomes a brave soldier?' Then he drew his pistol and himself shot into his grave.

"At the ring of the shot he awoke in great fear, for it seemed to him that the windows rattled. He peered about the room, then he heard another shot, then a tumult in the mill and cries through the mill's clatter. With a bound he was out of bed and seized his sabre; his door opened, and in the full moon-shine he saw two men with blackened faces, armed with cudgels, rush on him, but he defended himself and struck one of them a blow on the arm. Then both fled, bolt-ing the door, that opened outwards, behind them. Casper tried in vain to pursue them. Finally he succeeded in kicking out one of the door-panels. Hastily he crept through the hole and ran down the stairs, where he heard the miller whimper-ing, gagged and lying among the grain sacks. Casper loosed him and hurried off into the stable in search of his horse and valise. Both were gone. In great anguish he hastened back to the miller and lamented to him his misfortune, that all his belongings were gone, and the horse entrusted to him had been stolen. That the horse had been taken drove him to distraction. Then the miller appeared with a great bag of money; he had fetched it from a closet in the room above and now said to the lancer: 'Dear Casper, be content, to you I owe it that my entire fortune was not carried away. The robbers had laid their plans to make off with this bag, which was up in your room. The bold defence you put up has saved me all; I have lost nothing. The thieves who took your horse and valise from the stable must have been a part of the look-out, for they gave warning by their shots that danger was near, because in all probability they saw by your saddle that a cavalryman was lodging with me. On my account then you shall not come to grief. I shall take every pains and spare no money to get back your horse, and if I do not find this one, I'll buy you another, cost what it may.' Casper replied: 'I'll take no presents, that runs counter to my honor, but if in these hard straits you will advance me seventy thalers, I'll give you my note, to return you the sum within two years.' This was agreed; and the lancer took his leave so that he could hasten to his village and report the matter to a magistrate who represented the nobility of the surrounding region. The miller staid at home awaiting his wife and son, who had gone to a wedding in one of the neighboring places. As soon as they had returned, he would follow the lancer with his statement for the magistrate too.

"You can well imagine, my dear Mr. Clerk, with what a heavy heart poor Casper hastened on his way to our village, on foot and poor, where it had been his ambition to make his appearance proudly riding a-horseback. He had been robbed of fifty-one thalers, which he had saved, his letter-patent as petty-officer, his furlough and the wreaths for his mother's grave and for fair Annie. He was desperate. In this state of mind he arrived at one in the morning in his home village. No time did he waste, but immediately knocked at the door of the justice, whose house is the first as you enter the town. The minute he was let in, he reported the robbery and care-

fully listed everything that had been taken from him. The
justice advised him to go at once to his father, who was the
only peasant in the place that kept horses. With him and his
brother he might patrol the region, to see whether some trace
of the robbers could not be found. Meanwhile the justice
himself would send others out on foot, and interview the
miller for any further evidence. Casper now turned his back
on the justice's house and proceeded toward his father's
farm. His way led past my hut where through the window
he heard me singing a religious song. I had not been able to
close an eye for thoughts of his dear, dead mother, so he
tapped on the window and said: 'Praise be to Jesus Christ,
dear grandmother, Casper is here.' Ah, how those words
struck into the marrow of my bones. I hastened to the window, opened it, and kissed and embraced him with unending
tears. Briefly he told me of his misfortune, then of the commission he had to his father from the justice. This errand
would brook no delay, the sooner they got on the trail of the
thieves the better, for he would forfeit his honor, if he did not
recover his horse.

"Strange, but that word honor shook me from head to foot,
for I knew the trials he had to face. 'Do your duty, and to
God alone be the honor,' I said, as he left me to hurry away
to Finkel's farm at the other end of the village. When he had
gone, I sank on my knees to pray God, He might protect my
Casper. Ah, I prayed with a fear as never before, and repeated over and over: 'Lord, Thy will be done on earth even
as it is in heaven.'

"Casper, mad with fear, ran toward his father's place. He
climbed in over the garden wall; he heard the creaking of the
pump, and a neighing in the stall, that chilled his blood. He
stopped stone-still. By the light of the moon he saw two men
washing themselves. Casper thought his heart would break.
One of them exclaimed: 'This confounded stuff won't come
off!' Then the other said: 'Let's go into the stall first to bob
the nag's tail and trim its mane. Did you bury the valise
deep enough in the dung-heap?'—'Yes,' replied the first. Then
both went into the stable; and Casper, mad for sheer misery,

rushed up, locked the stable-door behind them and shouted: 'In the name of the duke, surrender! If you resist, I'll shoot you dead!" Ah, so he had caught his father and his step-brother as the robbers of his horse. 'My honor! my honor! it's gone!' he cried, 'I am the son of a dishonorable horse-thief!' When the two within heard those words they were greatly frightened. 'Casper, dear Casper,' they shouted, 'for God's sake don't bring ruin upon us! Casper, we'll give up every-thing on the spot; for your dear mother's sake, whose death-day's to-day, have mercy on your father and brother!' But Casper was desperate. He kept on exclaiming: 'My honor, my duty!' Then as they tried to force the door and had kicked a hole in the dirt wall in order to escape, Casper shot his pistol into the air as he cried out: 'Help, help, thieves, help!' The peasants awakened by the justice were approaching in order to make their plans as how best to pursue the thieves. At the sound of the shot and the cries they rushed to the scene. Old Finkel was still pleading with his son to open, but he per-sisted: 'I am a soldier, and must act as the law commands.' Here the justice, surrounded by peasants, came up. Casper cried: 'God's mercy, justice, my own father, my own brother are the thieves. Oh, that I had never been born! I have locked them here in the barn, my valise lies buried in the dung-heap.' Then the peasants made their way into the stall, bound old Finkel and his son and dragged them into the house. But Casper dug up his valise, took from it the two wreaths, and did not go into the house; he went to the church-yard to the grave of his mother. Dawn was in the east; I had been out upon the meadow and had woven for me and for Casper two wreaths of forget-me-nots. I thought to myself, 'we two shall decorate his mother's grave when he returns from his search.' Strange noises came from the village; and since every hub-bub is unpleasant to me, and I prefer to be alone, I skirted the village and went toward the church-yard. I heard a shot, the smoke rose up before me. I hurried toward it. Oh, Lord of Heaven! have mercy on him! Casper lay dead on his mother's grave. He had sent a bullet through his heart over which he had fastened to a button the wreath he had brought for fair Annie—through this wreath he had sent the bullet into his heart. The wreath for his mother hung on the cross. I felt as though the earth yawned under my feet at sight of this. On to his dead body I threw myself and cried out: 'Casper, poor boy, what have you done? Ah, who acquainted you with your misery; oh, why did I let you go before I told you all! Oh God! what will your poor father, your brother say, when they find you so?' I didn't know that he had taken this step on account of them; I was thinking of quite another matter. But worse was in store. The justice and the peasants brought old Finkel and his son bound with ropes. Misery made me dumb, I couldn't utter a sound. The justice asked me whether I had seen my nephew. I pointed to the spot where he lay. The justice drew nearer, for he thought that Casper was weeping on his mother's grave. He shook the prostrate form, then he saw the blood gush forth. 'Jesus, Mary!' he exclaimed, 'Casper has done away with himself.' At these words the two captives looked at one another in horror. Casper's corpse was now lifted and carried along beside his father and brother to the house of the justice. The village resounded with cries of lament; good peasant women helped me to follow. Ah, that was the most woeful journey of my life!"

Here the old woman ceased, and I said to her: "Good mother, your sorrow is great, but God loves you; whom he tries sorely, they are His dearest children. Tell me now, good mother, what has induced you to make the long journey hither, and what is the purpose of your petition to the duke?"

"Ay, you must have an inkling of that by now," she continued calmly, "to get an honorable burial for Casper and fair Annie. This wreath, I have brought along, she shall have; it was meant for her day of honor; it is drenched with Casper's blood. Just look at it, sir!"

Here she drew a little wreath of gold tinsel out of her bundle and held it before me. By the faint light of the dawn I could see that it was blackened with powder and spattered with blood. My heart ached at the great trials of this dear old woman, and the dignity and steadfastness with which she bore up under them filled me with awe. "Ah, dear mother," said I, "how will you acquaint poor Annie with her sorrow lest she fall down dead of fright, and what manner of day of honor is it for which you are bringing Annie this woeful wreath?"

"Good sir," spoke she, "come with me, you may take me there. I can't walk very fast, and so we shall find her just in time. On the way I'll tell you about her."

Then she rose, said her morning prayer very calmly, and arranged her clothing. But her bundle she hung over my arm. It was two o'clock in the morning, the day was dawning as we walked along through the quiet streets together.

"You see," the old woman continued her story, "when Finkel and his son were locked up, the justice summoned me into court. Casper's body was laid upon a table and, covered with his lancer's coat, carried into the court-room. Then I had to tell the justice all I knew about my nephew, also what he had said to me through the window that morning. Every word of mine went down on the paper that lay before the official. When he had finished with me, he examined the memorandum book that had been found among Casper's effects. There were records of his expenses in it, several stories about honor, among them that one about the French petty-officer—and just after it something written in pencil." Here the old woman gave me the booklet, and I read these last words of poor Casper: "I too cannot outlive my disgrace; my father and my brother are thieves, they have robbed me, their nearest of kin. My heart was sore, yet what could I do but seize them and bind them over to justice, for I am a soldier of my duke, and my sense of honor will allow of no leniency. I have given my father and my brother over to vengeance for honor's sake. Ah, may many lips intercede for me that I be granted an honorable burial, here beside my mother, where I have fallen. I ask my grandmother to send fair Annie the wreath through which I shot myself, and my greetings too. Ah, her sad lot chills me to the bone, but she shall not become the wife of a horse-thief's son, for honor has always been most dear to her. Dear, fair Annie, I hope you will not take my death too hard; it has to be, and if ever you liked me, then don't speak evil of me now. My disgrace is not of my doing! I tried so hard my life long to keep myself honorable. I had already been advanced to a petty-officer and was well thought of by every one. Surely I would have become an officer sometime, and Annie, truly I would not have given you up to court a grand lady—but the son of a horse-thief, who for honor's sake must have his own father seized and convicted, cannot outlive his disgrace. Annie, dear Annie, do accept the little wreath; I have always kept the faith with you, as surely as God will have mercy on me! I give you your freedom again, but do me the honor never to marry anyone who might be considered inferior to me. And if it is in your power, then intercede for me, that I may be granted honorable burial beside my mother, and should you die here in our village, ask that your grave be beside ours. My dear grandmother will rest here too, then we'll all be to-gether. I have fifty thalers in my valise, they shall be let out at interest for your first baby. The pastor shall have my sil-ver watch, if I receive honorable burial. My horse, the uni-form and the arms belong to the duke, this my brief-case is for you. Farewell, dearly beloved; farewell, dear grand-mother, pray for me and to all farewell—God have mercy on me—ah, my despair is great!"

These last words of an assuredly noble, afflicted human being I could not read without shedding bitter tears.— "Cas-per must have been a very good person, dear mother," I said to the old woman. At these words she stopped still, pressed my hand, and replied in a deeply moved voice: "Yes, he was the best person on earth. But he shouldn't have writ-ten those last few words about despair; they'll rob him of his honorable burial; they'll put him on the dissecting table. Ah, dear Clerk, if you could only be of help on this point!"

"How, of help, dear mother?" I asked, "of what weight can these last few words be?"—"Yes, yes," she replied, "the justice told me quite plainly. An order has gone out to all courts that only suicides out of melancholy shall have hon-orable burial, but all such as lay hands on themselves from despair shall be used for dissection. And the justice told me that he should have to send Casper to the laboratory as one who had admitted his despair in so many words."

"That is certainly a strange law," I said, "for in the case of every suicide a suit could easily be brought, as to whether death resulted from melancholy or despair, and the suit might be of such long duration that the judge and the advocates would be brought to melancholy and despair, and themselves be sent to the laboratory. But be of good cheer, dear mother, our duke is a kind and just ruler; if the whole matter is brought to his attention he will most certainly grant Casper a resting place beside his mother."

"God grant that!" replied the old woman. "You see, dear sir, when the justice had written down all the evidence, he gave me the brief-case and the wreath for fair Annie, and with these I came the long way here yesterday, so that on her day of honor I might give her this comfort for her journey.—Casper died just in time; had he known all, he would have grown mad with grief."

"Do tell me what has happened to fair Annie?" I asked the old woman. "Now you say that she has but a few hours more, now you mention her day of honor, and that she will have comfort from your sad message. Do tell me plainly, is she about to marry another, is she dead, or incurably sick? All this I must know if I am to write out the petition."

To this the old woman replied: "Ah, dear Clerk, these are the facts; God's will be done! You see, when Casper returned I was not as happy as might be. When Casper took his life I wasn't as sad as I should have been. I should never have survived if God had not had mercy on me and sent me even a greater sorrow. Yes, hear me, a stone had been placed before my heart like an ice-breaker, and all the pangs which like floating ice rushed upon me and would most certainly have torn my heart away, they broke against the stone and drifted by almost without notice. I'll tell you now a sad story.

"When my godchild, the fair Annie, lost her mother, a cousin of mine, who lived some twenty-one miles from our place, I was taking care of the sick woman. She was the widow of a poor peasant. In her youth she had fallen in love with a huntsman, but had rejected him because of his wild ways. Finally the huntsman had come to such a pass that he was jailed because of a murder and sentenced to die. This news came to my cousin upon her sick bed, and she grieved so deeply at this that from day to day she grew worse. Just before she passed away she intrusted dear, fair Annie to me as my godchild, and then in her last moments with parting breath she said to me: 'Dear Anna Margaret, when you pass through the city where the huntsman is held captive, send a message to him through the jailor, that on my death-bed I entreat him to turn to God, and that with my last breath I have prayed for him fervently, and that I send him my greetings.'—Not long after these words my good cousin died. When she had been buried I lifted little Annie—she was only three then—on to my arm and started on my homeward journey.

"At the edge of the city, through which our way led, I came to the house of the headsman. He had some skill in doctoring cattle, so our burgomaster had asked me to bring back a medicine that the headsman prepared. When I entered his house and told him what I wanted he said that I should go up to the attic with him, where he kept his store of herbs, and help him select. I left little Annie below in the living-room and followed him up. On our return little Annie was standing before a small cabinet that was fastened to the wall, and kept saying: 'Grandmother, there's a mouse in there, listen, how it rattles; there's a mouse in there!'

"These words of the child made the headsman look very serious. He opened the cabinet and said: 'God have mercy on us!' for he saw his headsman's sword, which hung quite alone in the cabinet on a nail, sway back and forth. He took down the sword. I was all atremble. 'Good woman,' he continued, 'if you love the dear little Annie, then do not start if I slit the skin a bit all around her neck with my sword. The sword, you see, set itself in motion in her presence. It thirsts for her blood, and if I don't slit her neck with it, the child will face grave misery in her life.' Then he took hold of the child, who began to cry unmercifully. I too cried out and clasped Annie to me. Here the burgomaster of the city came in; he was just returning from the hunt and had brought a sick dog to be cured. He asked the cause of the outcry. Annie screamed in reply: 'He's going to kill me!' I was beside myself with fear. The headsman told the burgomaster what had happened. The latter reproved him for his superstition, as he called it, and added some threats. The headsman, however, did not lose his composure and said: 'So was the custom of my fathers, I shall not depart from it.' To this the burgomaster made reply: 'Headsman Franz, if you had believed that your sword moved because I here and now give you notice that to-morrow morning at six the huntsman Jürge shall be beheaded by you, then I would see some reason in it; but when you set out to draw conclusions as regards this child, that is quite unreasonable and the part of madness. An expereince such as this might drive one to despair should he recall later in life that it had occurred in his youth. You should lead no one into temptation.'—'The like is true of a headsman's sword,' murmured Franz, and hung the sword back in the cabinet. Then the burgomaster kissed little Annie and gave her a roll out of his hunting-pouch. Next he turned to me and asked who I was, where I had come from, and whither I was going. When I had informed him of my cousin's death and her message to the huntsman Jürge, he said to me: 'You shall deliver your greeting in person. I myself will take you to him. His heart is hard, it may be, the memory of this good woman dying will touch his heart in his last moments.' The good gentleman then took us into his cart that was before the door and drove us into the city.

"He bade me go to his cook, where we got a good meal, and toward evening he accompanied me to the poor sinner. When I had brought the condemned man my cousin's last message, bitter tears began to flow from his eyes as he cried: 'Ah, God, if she had become my wife I should never have ended so.' Then he begged that the pastor be sent for after all, he wished to pray with him. The burgomaster promised to do his bidding, praised him for his change of heart, and asked him whether he had one last wish that might be granted. To this the huntsman Jürge exclaimed: 'Ah, do beg this good old mother to be present to-morrow at my execution. That will give me strength in my dying hour.' Then the burgomaster put this last wish to me, and gruesome as it was, I could not refuse the poor miserable man. He begged my hand in pledge, and as I solemnly promised he sank back weeping on the straw. From there the burgomaster took me to his friend, the pastor. Before this good man could be prevailed upon to visit the jail, I had to tell him all that had happened.

"That night I spent with the child in the mayor's house, and on the next morning I went the hard road to the execution of the huntsman Jürge. I stood beside the burgomaster in the circle and saw how he broke the little staff. Now the huntsman Jürge said a few parting words, all the people wept; and, deeply touched, the condemned man looked at me and little Annie, who was standing just in front of me. Then he kissed the headsman Franz, the pastor prayed with him, his eyes were blinded, and he knelt down. In a flash the headsman gave him the deathblow. 'Jesus, Mary, Joseph!' I cried; for Jürge's head bounded along right toward little Annie and set its teeth in the little girl's apron. She shrieked with fear. I tore off my apron and threw it over the gruesome head. As I did this Franz rushed up, tore the head loose and said: 'Mother, mother, what did I tell you this morning? I know my sword, it has life.'—I was unnerved with fear; little Annie never stopped crying. The burgomaster was completely bewildered and had me and the child driven to the house, where his wife gave each of us a change of clothing. After dinner the burgomaster made us a present of some money, and many people of the city, who were curious to see the girl, did likewise, so that I came away with twenty thaler and many clothes for her. In the evening the pastor visited the house and solemnly charged me to bring little Annie up in the fear of the Lord, and as a comfort bade me pay no attention to all these ominous signs. They were clearly the snares of Satan which must be scorned. At parting he gave me a fine Bible for little Annie, which she has kept to this day. On the following morning the burgomaster saw us on our way some nine miles in the direction of home in his own horse and cart.—Ah, Thou my God, and now all has come just as predicted!" the old woman concluded and was silent.

A fearful premonition was upon me; the old woman's narration made my heart bleed. "In the name of God, mother," I cried, "what has become of poor Annie; is there no help for her?"

"She was drawn to her fate with teeth," said the old woman, "to-day she must die; but it was an act of despair. Honor, honor, was back of it all! A passion for worldly honor brought her disgrace. She was seduced by one in high standing; he left her; she strangled her child in the very apron that I had thrown over the head of Jürge, the huntsman. Secretly she had taken it from me. Ah, fate dragged her to it with teeth! She was not in her right mind when she did it. The seducer had promised to marry her. He had won her by saying that Casper lay buried in France. Gradually despair clutched her poor soul, and she smothered the babe. She gave herself up to the law. At four she will be executed. She wrote me to come to her. That's what I'm about now. The wreath and poor Casper's last greetings I am taking to her—and the rose, that I got to-night; these will be of some comfort. Ah, dear Clerk, if only you can bring it about through your petition, that her body and Casper's too may find their last resting place in our church-yard."

"Everything, everything in my power, I'll do," I cried. "Without a moment's delay I'll hasten to the castle. My friend, who gave you the rose, is in charge of the guard there to-night; I'll beg him to waken the duke. I'll sink on my knees beside the royal bed and beg a pardon for Annie."

"Pardon?" said the old woman coldly. "You don't understand; fate dragged her to it with teeth. Listen, good sir, justice is better than pardon. Of what profit is pardon on earth? We must all appear before the final Judgment:

"Ye dead, ye dead shall then arise,
    And stand before the Last Assize.

"You see, she doesn't seek a pardon; she was offered that if she would name the father, but Annie replied: 'I have murdered his child and I want to die, but he must not suffer. I'll bear the penalty, to be with my babe, but all will go wrong, if I name its father.' Then she was convicted to die by the sword. But make haste to the duke and beg him for Casper and Annie, that they may rest in an honorable grave. Go! Go now! See there, the pastor's just entering the jail. I'll ask him to take me in with him to the fair Annie. If you are spry, maybe you can meet us out at the place of execution with the comforting news that honorable burial has been granted to the just Casper and fair Annie."

Now we had come up with the pastor. As soon as the old woman told him her relationship to the condemned, he readily allowed her to accompany him into the jail. But I ran as never before to the castle. On the way I got an inkling of comfort; it seemed like a hopeful sign, as I dashed by the house of Count Grossinger, to hear out of an open window of the garden-house a sweet voice singing to the accompaniment of a lute:

Though Mercy went a-wooing,
    Yet Honor watches well,
Respectful love renewing,
    She breathes to-night farewell.
If Love gives roses to her
    The veil let Mercy take,
Then Honor greets the wooer,
    With love for Mercy's sake.

Ah, and there were further good omens! A hundred paces on I found a white veil in the street; I picked it up, it was filled with fragrant roses. I clasped it tightly in my hand and hurried on, thrilled with the thought: "Ah God, this is Mercy." As I turned the corner, I saw a man who drew his coat up around him as I hastened past and swiftly turned his back on me in order not to be seen! These were unnecessary precautions, for I saw nothing and heard nothing. My heart alone cried out: "Mercy! mercy!" I rushed in through the iron gate into the court-yard. God be praised, corporal Count Grossinger, who was pacing up and down under the blooming chestnut trees before the guard-house, came forward to meet me.

"Dear Count," I cried impetuously, "you must lead me to the duke immediately, on the spot, or it will be too late. All will be lost!"

He seemed embarrassed at this request and said: "Are you in your right mind? See the duke at this unaccustomed hour! It can't be. Return when the duke reviews the guard, then I'll present you."

The ground burned like coals under my feet. "Now," I shouted, "or never! You must! A life hangs in the balance!"

"It's impossible now," replied Grossinger sharply in a tone of finality. "My honor is at stake. I have strict orders to-night to let nobody up."

The word honor brought me close to desperation. I thought of Casper's honor and fair Annie's honor and exclaimed: "Damn this honor! I must to the duke as a last resort in a case where just such honor has failed. You must announce me or I'll cry out for the duke."

"If you so much as stir," said Grossinger sternly, "I'll have you thrown into the guard-house. You are a dreamer. You have no sense of conditions."

"Oh, I know conditions, frightful conditions! I must speak to the duke. Every moment is precious!" I retorted. "If you'll not announce me now, I'll find my way to him alone."

This said, I was on the point of making for the steps that led up to the duke's apartments when I espied the same muffled figure which I had just encountered hastening toward them. Grossinger forced me about so that I might not see the person. "What are you up to, rashling?" he whispered into my ear. "Be still, quiet, I say, or you will bring me to grief."

"Why didn't you halt that man, who just went up to the duke?" I asked. "He can have no request more urgent than mine. Ah, it is so urgent. I must, I must see the duke! The fate of a poor, deceived, unhappy creature is at stake."

Grossinger replied: "You saw that man ascend those steps; if you ever breathe a word about it you will face the blade of this sword. Just because he went up you cannot; the duke has business with him."

A light shot forth from the duke's windows. "God, there's a light, he's up!" I cried. "I must speak with him. In the name of heaven let me go, or I'll cry for help."

Grossinger seized me by the arm and said: "You're drunk, come into the guard-house. I'm your friend, come, sleep it off. Give me the song that the old woman sang to-night at the doorstep as I marched by with the guard. I'm burning to hear it."

"It's of the old woman and her kin, that I must speak to the duke!" I said.

"Of the old woman?" asked Grossinger. "Tell me about her. Those higher up take no interest in such matters. Come, come to the guard-house!"

He was on the point of pulling me along when the castle-clock pealed down three-thirty. The sound pierced my soul like a cry of anguish, and I shouted with all my strength up to the duke's windows: "Help! in God's name help! for a miserable, deceived creature!" Grossinger flew into a rage, he tried to clasp his hand over my lips, but I freed myself. He thumped me in the back of the neck. He cursed. I felt and heard none of it. He called the guard. A corporal rushed up with several soldiers to seize me. The duke's window was thrown open, and a voice called out:

"Corporal Count Grossinger, what's all the noise? Bring the person up, without delay!"

I did not wait for the corporal. Up the steps I rushed and prostrated myself at the feet of the duke. Embarrassed and out of sorts he bade me arise. He had on his boots and his spurs, although he was still in a bath-robe, which he carefully drew together at the breast.

As briefly as possible I related to the duke all that the old woman had told me of the suicide of the lancer and of fair

Annie's history. I entreated him to delay the execution a few short hours and begged for an honorable burial for the two unfortunates, in case a pardon could not be had.—"Ah, mercy, mercy!" I cried as I drew forth from my bosom the white veil filled with roses. "This veil, that I found on the way, seemed to give promise of mercy."

Impetuously and shaken with emotion, the duke seized upon the veil, he clasped it between his palms. I pressed my advantage. When in terse phrases I added that the poor girl was the victim of a false sense of honor; that a person in high standing had deceived her and promised to wed her; that her nobleness was such that she preferred death to exposing the father—then with tears in his eyes the duke interrupted and cried: "Cease, in the name of Heaven, cease!"—Abruptly he turned to the corporal, who stood at the door, with quick sharp commands: "Go! both of you ride. Don't spare the horses! Away to the place of execution! Fasten the veil to your sword, wave it and shout, Mercy! mercy! I follow."

Grossinger took the veil. An utter change had come over him. Like a ghost he looked for fear and haste. We ran into the stall, mounted, and off we were in a gallop. He charged out of the gate like one possessed. As he fastened the veil to the point of his sword he exclaimed: "Lord Jesus, my sister!" These words were dark to me. He rose in his stirrups, waved the veil and kept shouting: "Mercy! mercy!" On the hilltop we saw the crowd assembled for the execution. My horse shied at the streaming veil. I am a poor horseman. I couldn't catch up with Grossinger. He sped along his wild course. I bent every effort. Evil Chance! The artillery was holding morning practice near by. The thunder of cannon drowned our cries so that they could not be heard from a distance. Grossinger was thrown. Before me I could see the crowd draw back. The circle opened to my vision. I saw a gleam of steel glitter in the rising sun—ah God, it was the gleam of the headsman's sword!—I charged up only to hear the moans of the bystanders. "Pardon, pardon!" shouted Grossinger like a madman as he lunged with the waving veil into the circle, but the headsman held out toward him the bleeding head of fair Annie, that smiled at him dolefully. Then he cried out:

"God have mercy on me!" and fell over the corpse. "Kill me! Kill me, you people. I have betrayed her. I am the murderer!"

An avenging fury seized the crowd. The women and maidens surged up, tore him from the corpse and spurned him with their feet, but he did nothing to defend himself. The guard could not hold the angry crowd in check. A shout was raised: "The duke, the duke!" He came up in an open carriage, a youth with hat deep over his face, wrapped in a cloak, sat beside him. The crowd dragged Grossinger to where the duke was. "Jesus, my brother!" the youthful officer exclaimed from the carriage in the most feminine tones. The duke, embarrassed, bade him be still and sprang from the carriage. The youth was about to follow when the duke pushed him back not too gently. But the disguise was lifted; it was the sister of Count Grossinger clothed as an officer. The duke commanded that the maltreated, bleeding, fainting Grossinger be placed in his carriage. The sister threw all caution to the winds, she cast her cloak over him. There she stood in woman's apparel. The duke was clearly taken aback; but he soon collected himself and ordered the carriage immediately to turn back, taking the countess and her brother to her dwelling. This had somewhat quelled the rage of the crowd. Then the duke said to the officer in command in a loud voice: "The Countess Grossinger saw her brother gallop past her house to bring the pardon. She wished to be present at this glad event. As I drove by, bent on the same mission, she stood at her window and begged me to take her into my carriage. I could not refuse the dear child. In order to prevent any stir, she quickly donned a hat and a cloak of her brother; now, surprised by an unfortunate accident, she has put on the whole matter the appearance of a romantic scandal. But, lieutenant, were you not able to protect the unfortunate Count Grossinger from the crowd? It is indeed a misfortune that he was thrown, and came too late, but that is scarcely his fault. See to it that the count's assailants are taken and properly punished."

Barely had the duke finished when a general outcry arose: "He is a villain; he is the seducer, the murderer of fair Annie. He confessed to it himself, the wretch, the low-down fellow!"

When the accusations came pouring in from all sides and were confirmed by the pastor, the officer, and the officials, the duke was so thoroughly aroused that he kept repeating: "Revolting, revolting, oh, the miserable fellow!"

Now the duke, pale as a ghost, stepped into the circle to look at the corpse of fair Annie. Upon the green turf she lay, clad in a white dress trimmed with black ribbon. The old woman, who was completely oblivious of all that was going on around her, had laid the head to the body and had covered the terrible cleavage with her apron. She was now engaged in folding fair Annie's hands over the Bible which the pastor of the little city had given her. The golden wreath she bound upon the severed head, and pinned to the lifeless bosom the rose that Grossinger had presented to her in the night, little knowing for whom it might be.

When the duke saw what the old woman had done he spoke: "Ill-fated Annie! Disgraceful seducer, you arrived too late!—Poor old mother, you alone have remained faithful to her 'til death." Now as his eyes fell upon me he remarked: "You told me of a last will of Corporal Casper. Have you it here?" I turned then to the old woman: "Poor mother, let me have Casper's brief-case, the duke wants to read his last will."

The old woman, whose attention up to this point had been riveted upon what she was doing, said sullenly: "You're here too? You might just as well have staid home. Have you the petition? It's too late now. No, I wasn't able to give the poor child the last comfort, that she and Casper should rest in an honorable grave. Ah, I lied to her when I said it had been granted. No, she wouldn't believe me."

Here the duke interrupted: "You did not lie to her, good mother. My messenger did all in his power. The fall of the horse must here bear the blame. She shall have honorable burial beside her mother and Casper, who was a brave fellow. The pastor shall preach a funeral-sermon for them both on the text: 'To God alone be honor!' Casper shall be buried as a corporal, his company shall shoot three times into his grave, and the sword of the corrupter Grossinger shall be laid on his coffin."

After these words he took Grossinger's sword, that with the veil was still lying on the gound, removed the veil, covered Annie with it and said: "This ill-fated veil, that should have brought her pardon, from my heart shall restore her honor. She has died in honor and been pardoned; as token of this it shall be buried with her."

Then he handed the sword to the officer with the remark: "To-day at review I shall give you my further orders in regard to the burial of the lancer and this poor girl."

Now he read aloud Casper's last words in a voice choked with emotion. The old grandmother clasped his feet, her eyes filled with tears of joy as though she had been immeasurably blessed. The duke spoke: "Contain yourself, mother! You shall have a pension until the end of your days. A monument shall be raised to the memory of your grandson and Annie." Then he ordered the pastor to take the old woman and the coffin, in which the body was laid, to his dwelling, and later escort her home, where she should have full charge of the burial. As his adjutant arrived in the meantime with horses, he said to me in parting: "Give your name to my officer, later I'll send for you. You have shown a splendid charitable zeal." The adjutant took down my name and bowed graciously. As the duke galloped off toward the city, he took with him the blessings of the crowd. The body of fair Annie and the good old grandmother were brought to the house of the pastor, and in the following night he took her back home. The next evening the officer with Grossinger's sword and a squadron of lancers arrived. Then the just Casper, with Grossinger's sword on his bier and the corporal's patent, was buried with fair Annie beside the grave of his mother. I too was there to escort the old mother, who seemed childish for joy, but said little. As the lancers fired the third salute into the grave she fell back dead in my arms. Beside her kin she lies buried. God grant them all a blessed resurrection!

> There, far in front, their feet shall go,
> Where blesséd angels sit in row,

Where, newly come, God waits them there,
A beauteous rainbow round His chair.
There souls by God shall now be tried,
When Heaven's doors shall open wide.

When I returned to the captial, I learned that Count Grossinger was dead. He had poisoned himself. On my desk I found a letter from him which read:

"I owe you much. You revealed my disgrace, which long had been eating out my heart. Well did I know that song of the old woman. Annie had told it to me many and many a time. She was an exceptionally noble being. I was a base criminal—I had given her a written promise of marriage—she burned it. She was in service in the home of an old aunt of mine. Melancholy often seized her. Through certain medicinal preparations of a magic content, I ensnared her soul.—God have mercy on me!—You have saved my sister's honor too.—The duke loves her.—I stood high in his favor.—This tragedy has stirred him to the depths.—God help me.—I have taken poison.

JOSEPH, COUNT GROSSINGER."

Fair Annie's apron, to which the head of Jürge, the huntsman, clung at the beheading, has been preserved in the ducal museum. It is rumored that the duke will elevate the sister of Count Grossinger to a princess with the name, *Voile de Grace,* in English, Veil of Mercy, and make her his wife. At the coming review in the neighborhood of D____ the monument over the graves of the two ill-fated victims to honor is to be unveiled and dedicated in the church-yard of the village. The duke and the princess will be there in person. He is exceptionally pleased with the design of this monument. The duke and the princess together, it is said, worked out the theme. It sets forth the true and the false honor. Both figures are deeply bowed, one on either side of a cross, Justice with high-swung sword on the one hand and Mercy on the other casting a veil. Some find in the head of Justice a similarity to the duke, in the head of Mercy a likeness to the princess.

THE CREMONA VIOLIN[1]

Ernst Theodor Amadeus Hoffmann

(1776-1822)

Councillor Krespel was one of the strangest, oddest men
I ever met in my life. When I went to live in H—— for a
time the whole town was full of talk about him, as he happened to be just then in the midst of one of the very craziest
of his schemes. Krespel had the reputation of being both a
clever, learned lawyer and a skilful diplomatist. One of the
reigning princes of Germany—not, however, one of the most
powerful—had appealed to him for assistance in drawing up
a brief, which he was desirous of presenting at the Imperial
Court with the view of furthering his legitimate claims upon
a certain strip of territory. The project was crowned with the
happiest success; and as Krespel had once complained that
he could never find a dwelling sufficiently comfortable to
suit him, the prince, to reward him for his efforts, undertook
to defray the cost of building a house which Krespel might
erect just as he pleased. Moreover, the prince was willing to
purchase any site that he should fancy. This offer, however,
the Councillor would not accept; he insisted that the house
should be built in his garden, situated in a very beautiful
neighborhood outside the town-walls. So he bought all
kinds of materials and had them carted out. Then he might
have been seen day after day, attired in his curious garments
(which he had made himself according to certain fixed rules
of his own), slacking the lime, riddling the sand, packing up
the bricks and stones in regular heaps, and so on. All this he
did without once consulting an architect or thinking about

[1] Translated by J. T. Beally. Reprinted by permission of Charles
Scribner's Sons from *Weird Tales*.

a plan. One fine day, however, he went to an experienced builder of the town and requested him to be in his garden at daybreak the next morning, with all his journeymen and apprentices, and a large body of laborers, etc., to build him his house. Naturally the builder asked for the architect's plan, and was not a little astonished when Krespel replied that none was needed, and that things would turn out all right in the end, just as he wanted them. Next morning, when the builder and his men came to the place, they found a trench drawn out in the shape of an exact square; and Krespel said, "Here's where you must lay the foundations; then carry up the walls until I say they are high enough." "Without windows and doors, and without partition walls?" broke in the builder, as if alarmed at Krespel's mad folly. "Do what I tell you, my dear sir," replied the Councillor quite calmly; "leave the rest to me; it will be all right." It was only the promise of high pay that could induce the builder to proceed with the ridiculous building; but none has ever been erected under merrier circumstances. As there was an abundant supply of food and drink, the workmen never left their work; and amidst their continuous laughter the four walls were run up with incredible quickness, until one day Krespel cried, "Stop!" Then the workmen, laying down trowel and hammer, came down from the scaffoldings and gathered round Krespel in a circle, whilst every laughing face was asking, "Well, and what now?" "Make way!" cried Krespel; and then running to one end of the garden, he strode slowly towards the square of brickwork. When he came close to the wall he shook his head in a dissatisfied manner, ran to the other end of the garden, again strode slowly towards the brickwork square, and proceeded to act as before. These tactics he pursued several times, until at length, running his sharp nose hard against the wall, he cried, "Come here, come here, men! break me a door in here! Here's where I want a door made!" He gave the exact dimensions in feet and inches, and they did as he bid them. Then he stepped inside the structure, and smiled with satisfaction as the builder remarked that the walls were just the height of a good two-storeyed house. Krespel walked thoughtfully backwards and forwards across the space within, the bricklayers behind him with hammers and picks, and wherever he cried, "Make a window here, six feet high by four feet broad!" "There a little window, three feet by two!" a hole was made in a trice.

It was at this stage of the proceedings that I came to H——; and it was highly amusing to see how hundreds of people stood round about the garden and raised a loud shout whenever the stones flew out and a new window appeared where nobody had for a moment expected it. And in the same manner Krespel proceeded with the building and fitting of the rest of the house, and with all the work necessary to that end; everything had to be done on the spot in accordance with the instructions which the Councillor gave from time to time. However, the absurdity of the whole business, the growing conviction that things would in the end turn out better than might have been expected, but above all, Krespel's generosity—which indeed cost him nothing—kept them all in good humor. Thus were the difficulties overcome which necessarily arose out of this eccentric way of building, and in a short time there was a completely finished house, its outside, indeed, presenting a most extraordinary appearance, no two windows, etc., being alike, but on the other hand the interior arrangements suggested a peculiar feeling of comfort. All who entered the house bore witness to the truth of this; and I too experienced it myself when I was taken in by Krespel after I had become more intimate with him. For hitherto I had not exchanged a word with this eccentric man; his building had occupied him so much that he had not even once been to Professor M——'s to dinner, as he was in the habit of doing on Tuesdays. Indeed, in reply to a special invitation, he sent word that he should not set foot over the threshold before the housewarming of his new building took place. All his friends and acquaintances, therefore, confidently looked forward to a great banquet; but Krespel invited nobody except the masters, journeymen, apprentices, and laborers who had built the house. He entertained them with the choicest viands; bricklayers' apprentices devoured partridge pies regardless of consequences; young joiners polished off roast pheasants with the greatest success; whilst hungry laborers helped themselves for once to the choicest morsels of *truffes fricassées*. In the evening their wives and daughters came, and there was a great ball. After waltzing a short while with the wives of the masters, Krespel sat down amongst the town musicians, took a violin in his hand, and led the orchestra until daylight.

On the Tuesday after this festival, which exhibited Councillor Krespel in the character of a friend of the people, I at length saw him appear, to my joy, at Professor M——'s. Anything more strange and fantastic than Krespel's behavior it would be impossible to find. He was so stiff and awkward in his movements, that he looked every moment as if he would run up against something or do some damage. But he did not; and the lady of the house seemed to be well aware that he would not, for she did not grow a shade paler when he rushed with heavy steps round a table crowded with beautiful cups, or when he manœuvred near a large mirror that reached down to the floor, or even when he seized a flower-pot of beautifully painted porcelain and swung it round in the air as if desirous of making its colors play. Moreover, before dinner he subjected everything in the Professor's room to a most minute examination; he also took down a picture from the wall and hung it up again, standing on one of the cushioned chairs to do so. At the same time he talked a good deal and vehemently; at one time his thoughts kept leaping, as it were, from one subject to another (this was most conspicuous during dinner); at another, he was unable to have done with an idea; seizing upon it again and again, he gave it all sorts of wonderful twists and turns, and couldn't get back into the ordinary track until something else took hold of his fancy. Sometimes his voice was rough and harsh and screeching, and sometimes it was low and drawling and singing; but at no time did it harmonize with what he was talking about. Music was the subject of conversation; the praises of a new composer were being sung, when Krespel, smiling, said in his low, singing tones, "I wish the devil with his pitchfork would hurl that atrocious garbler of music millions of fathoms down to the bottomless pit of hell!" Then he burst out passionately and wildly, "She is an angel of heaven, nothing but pure God-given music!—the paragon and queen of song!"—and tears stood in his eyes. To understand this, we had to go back to a celebrated *artiste,* who had been the subject of conversation an hour before.

Just at this time a roast hare was on the table; I noticed that Krespel carefully removed every particle of meat from the bones on his plate, and was most particular in his inquiries after the hare's feet; these the Professor's little five-year-old daughter now brought to him with a very pretty smile. Besides, the children had cast many friendly glances towards Krespel during dinner; now they rose and drew nearer to him, but not without signs of timorous awe. What's the meaning of that? thought I to myself. Dessert was brought in; then the Councillor took a little box from his pocket in which he had a miniature lathe of steel. This he immediately screwed fast to the table, and turning the bones with incredible skill and rapidity, he made all sorts of little fancy boxes and balls, which the children received with cries of delight. Just as we were rising from table, the Professor's niece asked, "And what is our Antonia doing?" Krespel's face was like that of one who has bitten of a sour orange and wants to look as if it were a sweet one; but this expression soon changed into the likeness of a hideous mask, whilst he laughed behind it with downright, bitter, fierce, and, as it seemed to me, satanic scorn. "Our Antonia? our dear Antonia?" he asked in his drawling, disagreeable singing way. The Professor hastened to intervene; in the reproving glance which he gave his niece I read that she had touched a point likely to stir up unpleasant memories in Krespel's heart. "How are you getting on with your violins?" interposed the Professor in a jovial manner, taking the Councillor by both hands. Then Krespel's countenance cleared up, and with a firm voice he replied, "Splendidly, Professor;

you recollect my telling you of the lucky chance which threw that splendid Amati[1] into my hands. Well, I've only cut it open to-day—not before to-day. I hope Antonia has carefully taken the rest of it to pieces." "Antonia is a good child," remarked the Professor. "Yes, indeed, that she is," cried the Councillor, whisking himself round; then, seizing his hat and stick, he hastily rushed out of the room. I saw in the mirror that tears were standing in his eyes.

As soon as the Councillor was gone, I at once urged the Professor to explain to me what Krespel had to do with violins, and particularly with Antonia. "Well," replied the Professor, "not only is the Councillor a remarkably eccentric fellow altogether, but he practises violin-making in his own crack-brained way." "Violin-making!" I exclaimed, perfectly astonished. "Yes," continued the Professor, "according to the judgment of men who understand the thing, Krespel makes the very best violins that can be found nowadays; formerly he would frequently let other people play on those in which he had been especially successful, but that's been all over and done with now for a long time. As soon as he has finished a violin he plays on it himself for one or two hours, with very remarkable power and with the most exquisite expression, then he hangs it up beside the rest, and never touches it again or suffers anybody else to touch it. If a violin by any of the eminent old masters is hunted up anywhere, the Councillor buys it immediately, no matter what the price. But he plays it as he does his own violins, only once; then he takes it to pieces in order to examine closely its inner structure, and should he fancy he hasn't found exactly what he sought for, he in a pet throws the pieces into a big chest, which is already full of the remains of broken violins." "But who and what is Antonia?" I inquired, hastily and impetuously. "Well, now, that," continued the Professor, —"that is a thing which might very well make me conceive

[1] The Amati were a celebrated family of violin-makers of the sixteenth and seventeenth centuries, belonging to Cremona in Italy. They form the connecting-link between the Brescian school of makers and the greatest of all makers, Stradivarius and Guarnerius.

an unconquerable aversion to the Councillor, were I not convinced that there is some peculiar secret behind it, for he is such a good-natured fellow at bottom as to be sometimes guilty of weakness. When we came to H——, several years ago, he led the life of an anchorite, along with an old housekeeper, in —— Street. Soon, by his oddities, he excited the curiosity of his neighbors; and immediately he became aware of this, he sought and made acquaintances. Not only in my house but everywhere we became so accustomed to him that he grew to be indispensable. In spite of his rude exterior, even the children liked him, without ever proving a nuisance to him; for, notwithstanding all their friendly passages together, they always retained a certain timorous awe of him, which secured him against all over-familiarity. You have to-day had an example of the way in which he wins their hearts by his ready skill in various things. We all took him at first for a crusty old bachelor, and he never contradicted us. After he had been living here some time, he went away, nobody knew where, and returned at the end of some months. The evening following his return his windows were lit up to an unusual extent! This alone was sufficient to arouse his neighbors' attention, and they soon heard the surpassingly beautiful voice of a female singing to the accompaniment of a piano. Then the music of a violin was heard chiming in and entering upon a keen ardent contest with the voice. They knew at once that the player was the Councillor. I myself mixed in the large crowd which had gathered in front of his house to listen to this extraordinary concert; and I must confess that, besides this voice and the peculiar, deep, soul-stirring impression which the execution made upon me, the singing of the most celebrated *artistes* whom I had ever heard seemed to me feeble and void of expression. Until then I had had no conception of such long-sustained notes, of such nightingale trills, of such undulations of musical sound, of such swelling up to the strength of organ-notes, of such dying away to the faintest whisper. There was not one whom the sweet witchery did not enthral; and when the singer ceased, nothing but soft sighs broke the impressive silence. Somewhere about midnight the Councillor was heard talking violently, and another male voice seemed, to judge from the tones, to be reproaching him, whilst at intervals the broken words of a sobbing girl could be detected. The Councillor continued to shout with increasing violence, until he fell into that drawling, singing way that you know. He was interrupted by a loud scream from the girl, and then all was as still as death. Suddenly a loud racket was heard on the stairs; a young man rushed out sobbing, threw himself into a post-chaise which stood below, and drove rapidly away. The next day the Councillor was very cheerful, and nobody had the courage to question him about the events of the previous night. But on inquiring of the housekeeper, we gathered that the Councillor had brought home with him an extraordinarily pretty young lady whom he called Antonia, and she it was who had sung so beautifully. A young man also had come along with them; he had treated Antonia very tenderly, and must evidently have been her betrothed. But he, since the Councillor peremptorily insisted on it, had had to go away again in a hurry. What the relations between Antonia and the Councillor are has remained a secret, but this much is certain, that he tyrannizes over the poor girl in the most hateful fashion. He watches her as Doctor Bartholo watches his ward in the *Barber of Seville;* she hardly dare show herself at the window; and if, yielding now and again to her earnest entreaties, he takes her into society, he follows her with Argus' eyes, and will on no account suffer a musical note to be sounded, far less let Antonia sing—indeed, she is not permitted to sing in his own house. Antonia's singing on that memorable night has, therefore, come to be regarded by the townspeople in the light of a tradition of some marvellous wonder that suffices to stir the heart and the fancy; and even those who did not hear it often exclaim, whenever any other singer attempts to display her powers in the place, 'What sort of wretched squeaking do you call that? Nobody but Antonia knows how to sing.' "

Having a singular weakness for such fantastic histories, I found it necessary, as may easily be imagined, to make

Antonia's acquaintance. I had myself often enough heard the stories about her singing, but had never imagined that that exquisite *artiste* was living in the place, held a captive in the bonds of this eccentric Krespel like the victim of a tyrannous sorcerer. On the following night I heard in my dreams Antonia's marvellous voice, and as she besought me in the most touching manner in a glorious *adagio* movement (ridiculously enough, it seemed to me as if I had composed it myself) to save her—I soon resolved, like a second Astolpho,[1] to penetrate into Krespel's house, as if into another Alcina's magic castle, and deliver the queen of song from her ignominious fetters.

It all came about in a different way from what I had expected; I had seen the Councillor scarcely more than two or three times, and eagerly discussed with him the best method of constructing violins, when he invited me to call and see him. I did so; and he showed me his treasure of violins. There were fully thirty of them hanging up in a closet; one amongst them bore conspicuously all the marks of great antiquity (a carved lion's head, etc.), and, hung up higher than the rest, and surmounted by a crown of flowers, it seemed to exercise a queenly supremacy over them. "This violin," said Krespel, on my making some inquiry relative to it, "this violin is a very remarkable and curious specimen of the work of some unknown master, probably of Tartini's[2] age. I am perfectly convinced that there is something especially exceptional in its inner construction, and that, if I took it to pieces, a secret would be revealed to me which I have long been seeking to discover, but—laugh at me if you

[1] A reference to Ariosto's *Orlando Furioso*. Astolpho, an English cousin of Orlando, was a great boaster, but generous, courteous, gay, and remarkably handsome; he was carried to Alcina's island on the back of a whale.

[2] Giuseppe Tartini, born in 1692, died in 1770, was one of the most celebrated violinists of the eighteenth century, and the discoverer (in 1714) of "resultant tones," or "Tartini's tones," as they are frequently called. Most of his life was spent at Padua. He did much to advance the art of the violinist, both by his compositions for that instrument, as well as by his treatise on its capabilities.

like—this senseless thing which only gives signs of life and sound as I make it, often speaks to me in a strange way. The first time I played upon it I somehow fancied that I was only the magnetizer who has the power of moving his subject to reveal of his own accord in words the visions of his inner nature. Don't go away with the belief that I am such a fool as to attach even the slightest importance to such fantastic notions, and yet it's certainly strange that I could never prevail upon myself to cut open that dumb lifeless thing there. I am very pleased now that I have not cut it open, for since Antonia has been with me I sometimes play to her upon this violin. For Antonia is fond of it—very fond of it." As the Councillor uttered these words with visible signs of emotion, I felt encouraged to hazard the question, "Will you not play it to me, Councillor?" Krespel made a wry face, and falling into his drawling, singing way, said, "No, my good sir!" and that was an end of the matter. Then I had to look at all sorts of rare curiosities, the greater part of them childish trifles; at last thrusting his arm into a chest, he brought out a folded piece of paper, which he pressed into my hand, adding solemnly, "You are a lover of art; take this present as a priceless memento, which you must value at all times above everything else." Therewith he took me by the shoulders and gently pushed me towards the door, embracing me on the threshold. That is to say, I was, in a manner of speaking, virtually kicked out of doors. Unfolding the paper, I found a piece of a first string of a violin about an eighth of an inch in length, with the words, "A piece of the treble string with which the late Mr. Stamitz[1] strung his violin for the last concert at which he ever played."

This summary dismissal at mention of Antonia's name led me to infer that I should never see her; but I was mistaken, for on my second visit to the Councillor's I found her in his room, assisting him to put a violin together. At first sight Antonia did not make a strong impression; but soon I found

[1] This was the name of a well-known musical family from Bohemia. Karl Stamitz is the one here possibly meant, since he died about eighteen or twenty years previous to the publication of this tale.

it impossible to tear my glance away from her blue eyes, her sweet rosy lips, her uncommonly graceful, lovely form. She was very pale; but a shrewd remark or a merry sally would call up a winning smile on her face and suffuse her cheeks with a deep burning flush, which, however, soon faded away to a faint rosy glow. My conversation with her was quite unconstrained, and yet I saw nothing whatever of the Arguslike watchings on Krespel's part which the Professor had imputed to him; on the contrary, his behavior moved along the customary lines, nay, he even seemed to approve of my conversation with Antonia. So I often stepped in to see the Councillor; and as we became accustomed to each other's society, a singular feeling of ease, taking possession of our little circle of three, filled our hearts with happiness. I still continued to derive exquisite enjoyment from the Councillor's strange crotchets and oddities; but it was of course Antonia's irresistible charms alone which attracted me, and led me to put up with a good deal which I should otherwise, in the frame of mind in which I then was, have impatiently shunned. For it only too often happened that in the Councillor's characteristic extravagance there was mingled much that was dull and tiresome; and it was in a special degree irritating to me that, as often as I turned the conversation upon music, and particularly upon singing, he was sure to interrupt me, with that sardonic smile upon his face and those repulsive singing tones of his, by some remark of a quite opposite tendency, very often of a commonplace character. From the great distress which at such times Antonia's glances betrayed, I perceived that he only did it to deprive me of a pretext for calling upon her for a song. But I didn't relinquish my design. The hindrances which the Councillor threw in my way only strengthened my resolution to overcome them; I *must* hear Antonia sing if I was not to pine away in reveries and dim aspirations for want of hearing her.

One evening Krespel was in an uncommonly good humor; he had been taking an old Cremona violin to pieces, and had discovered that the sound-post was fixed half a line more obliquely than usual—an important discovery!—one of incalculable advantage in the practical work of making violins! I succeeded in setting him off at full speed on his hobby of the true art of violin-playing. Mention of the way in which the old masters picked up their dexterity in execution from really great singers (which was what Krespel happened just then to be expatiating upon) naturally paved the way for the remark that now the practice was the exact opposite of this, the vocal score erroneously following the affected and abrupt transitions and rapid scaling of the instrumentalists. "What is more nonsensical," I cried, leaping from my chair, running to the piano, and opening it quickly—"what is more nonsensical than such an execrable style as this, which, far from being music, is much more like the noise of peas rolling across the floor?" At the same time I sang several of the modern *fermatas,* which rush up and down and hum like a well-spun peg-top, striking a few villainous chords by way of accompaniment. Krespel laughed outrageously and screamed: "Ha! ha! methinks I hear our German-Italians or our Italian-Germans struggling with an aria from Pucitta,[1] or Portogallo,[2] or some other *Maestro di capella,* or rather *schiavo d'un primo uomo.*"[3] Now, thought I, now's the time; so turning to Antonia, I remarked, "Antonia knows nothing of such singing as that, I believe?" At the same time I struck up one of old Leonardo Leo's[4] beautiful soul-stirring songs. Then Antonia's cheeks glowed; heavenly radiance sparkled in her eyes, which grew full of reawakened inspiration; she hastened to the piano; she opened her lips; but at that very

[1] Vincenzo Puccitta (1778-1861) was an Italian opera composer, whose music "shows great facility, but no invention." He also wrote several songs.

[2] Il Portogallo was the Italian sobriquet of a Portuguese musician named Marcos Antonio da Fonseca (1762-1830). He lived alternately in Italy and Portugal, and wrote several operas.

[3] Literally, "The slave of a *primo uomo,*" *primo uomo* being the masculine form corresponding to *prima donna,* that is, a singer of hero's parts in operatic music. At one time also female parts were sung and acted by men or boys.

[4] Leonardo Leo, the chief Neapolitan representative of Italian music in the first part of the eighteenth century, and author of more than forty operas and nearly one hundred compositions for the Church.

moment Krespel pushed her away, grasped me by the shoulders, and with a shriek that rose up to a tenor pitch, cried, "My son—my son—my son!" And then he immediately went on, singing very softly, and grasping my hand with a bow that was the height of politeness, "In very truth, my esteemed and honorable student-friend, in very truth, it would be a violation of the codes of social intercourse, as well as of all good manners, were I to express aloud and in a stirring way my wish that here, on this very spot, the devil from hell would softly break your neck with his burning claws, and so in a sense make short work of you; but, setting that aside, you must acknowledge, my dearest friend, that it is rapidly growing dark, and there are no lamps burning to-night, so that, even though I did not kick you downstairs at once, your darling limbs might still run a risk of suffering damage. Go home by all means; and cherish a kind remembrance of your faithful friend, if it should happen that you never—pray, understand me—if you should never see him in his own house again." Therewith he embraced me, and, still keeping fast hold of me, turned with me slowly towards the door, so that I could not get another single look at Antonia. Of course it is plain enough that in my position I couldn't thrash the Councillor, though that is what he really deserved. The Professor enjoyed a good laugh at my expense, and assured me that I had ruined for ever all hopes of retaining the Councillor's friendship. Antonia was too dear to me, I might say too holy, for me to go and play the part of the languishing lover and stand gazing up at her window, or to fill the role of the lovesick adventurer. Completely upset, I went away from H——; but, as is usual in such cases, the brilliant colors of the picture of my fancy faded, and the recollection of Antonia, as well as of Antonia's singing (which I had never heard), often fell upon my heart like a soft faint trembling light, comforting me.

Two years afterwards I received an appointment in B——, and set out on a journey to the south of Germany. The towers of H—— rose before me in the red glow of the evening; the nearer I came the more was I oppressed by an

indescribable feeling of the most agonizing distress; it lay
upon me like a heavy burden; I could not breathe; I was
obliged to get out of my carriage into the open air. But my
anguish continued to increase until it became actual physical
pain. Soon I seemed to hear the strains of a solemn chorale
floating in the air; the sounds continued to grow more distinct; I realized the fact that they were men's voices chanting
a church chorale. "What's that? what's that?" I cried, a burning stab darting as it were through my breast. "Don't you
see?" replied the coachman, who was driving along beside
me, "why, don't you see? they're burying somebody up there
in the churchyard." And indeed we were near the church-
yard; I saw a circle of men clothed in black standing round
a grave, which was about to be closed. Tears started to my
eyes; I somehow fancied they were burying there all the
joy and all the happiness of life. Moving on rapidly down
the hill, I was no longer able to see into the churchyard;
the chorale came to an end, and I perceived not far distant
from the gate some of the mourners returning from the
funeral. The Professor, with his niece on his arm, both in
deep mourning, went close past me without noticing me.
The young lady had her handkerchief pressed close to her
eyes, and was weeping bitterly. In the frame of mind in
which I then was I could not possibly go into the town, so I
sent on my servant with the carriage to the hotel where I
usually put up, whilst I took a turn in the familiar neighborhood to get rid of a mood that was possibly only due to
physical causes, such as heating on the journey, etc. On
arriving at a well-known avenue, which leads to a pleasure
resort, I came upon a most extraordinary spectacle. Councillor Krespel was being conducted by two mourners, from
whom he appeared to be endeavoring to make his escape by
all sorts of strange twists and turns. As usual, he was dressed
in his own curious home-made gray coat; but from his little
cocked-hat, which he wore perched over one ear in military
fashion, a long narrow ribbon of black crape fluttered backwards and forwards in the wind. Around his waist he had
buckled a black sword-belt; but instead of a sword he had

stuck a long fiddle-bow into it. A creepy shudder ran through my limbs: "He's insane," I thought, as I slowly followed them. The Councillor's companions led him as far as his house, where he embraced them, laughing loudly. They left him; and then his glance fell upon me, for I now stood near him. He stared at me fixedly for some time; then he cried in a hollow voice, "Welcome, my student friend! you also understand it!" Therewith he took me by the arm and pulled me into the house, up the steps, into the room where the violins hung. They were all draped in black crape; the violin of the old master was missing; in its place was a cypress wreath. I knew what had happened. "Antonia! Antonia!" I cried, in inconsolable grief. The Councillor, with his arms crossed on his breast, stood beside me, as if turned into stone. I pointed to the cypress wreath. "When she died," said he, in a very hoarse solemn voice, "when she died, the sound-post of that violin broke into pieces with a ringing crack, and the sound-board was split from end to end. The faithful instrument could only live with her and in her; it lies beside her in the coffin, it has been buried with her." Deeply agitated, I sank down upon a chair, whilst the Councillor began to sing a gay song in a husky voice; it was truly horrible to see him hopping about on one foot, and the crape ribbons (he still had his hat on) flying about the room and up to the violins hanging on the walls. Indeed, I could not repress a loud cry that rose to my lips when, on the Councillor making an abrupt turn, the crape came all over me; I fancied he wanted to envelop me in it and drag me down into the horrible dark depths of insanity. Suddenly he stood still and addressed me in his singing way, "My son! my son! why do you call out? Have you espied the angel of death? That always precedes the ceremony." Stepping into the middle of the room, he took the violin-bow out of his sword-belt, and, holding it over his head with both hands, broke it into a thousand pieces. Then, with a loud laugh, he cried, "Now you imagine my sentence is pronounced, don't you, my son? but it's nothing of the kind—not at all! not at all! Now I'm free—free—free—hurrah! I'm free! Now I shall make no more

violins—no more violins—hurrah! no more violins!" This he
sang to a horrible mirthful tune, again spinning round on
one foot. Perfectly aghast, I was making the best of my way
to the door, when he held me fast, saying quite calmly,
"Stay, my student friend, pray don't think from this outbreak of grief, which is torturing me as if with the agonies
of death, that I am insane; I only do it because a short time
ago I had a dressing-gown made in which I wanted to look
like Fate or like God!" The Councillor then went on with a
medley of silly and awful rubbish, until he fell down utterly
exhausted; I called up the old housekeeper, and was very
pleased to find myself in the open air again.

I never doubted for a moment that Krespel had become
insane; the Professor, however, asserted the contrary. "There
are men," he remarked, "from whom nature or a special
destiny has taken away the cover behind which the mad
folly of the rest of us runs its course unobserved. They are
like thin-skinned insects, which, as we watch the restless
play of their muscles, seem to be misshapen, while nevertheless everything soon comes back into its proper form
again. All that remains thought with us passes over with
Krespel into action. That bitter scorn which is so often wrapped in the doings and dealings of the earth, Krespel gives
vent to in outrageous gestures and agile caprioles. But these
are his lightning conductor. What comes up out of the earth
he gives again to the earth, but what is divine, that he keeps;
and so I believe that his inner consciousness, in spite of the
apparent madness which springs from it to the surface, is
as right as a trivet. To be sure, Antonia's sudden death
grieves him sore, but I warrant that to-morrow will see him
going along in his old jog-trot way as usual." And the Professor's prediction was almost literally filled. Next day the
Councillor appeared to be just as he formerly was, only he
averred that he would never make another violin, nor yet
ever play on another. And, as I learned later, he kept his
word.

Hints which the Professor let fall confirmed my own private conviction that the so carefully guarded secret of the
Councillor's relations to Antonia, nay, that even her death,

was a crime which must weigh heavily upon him, a crime that could not be atoned for. I determined that I would not leave H—— without taxing him with the offence which I conceived him to be guilty of; I determined to shake his heart down to its very roots, and so compel him to make open confession of the terrible deed. The more I reflected upon the matter, the clearer it grew in my own mind that Krespel must be a villain, and in the same proportion did my intended reproach, which assumed of itself the form of a real rhetorical masterpiece, wax more fiery and more impressive. Thus equipped and mightily incensed, I hurried to his house. I found him with a calm smiling countenance making playthings. "How can peace," I burst out—"how can peace find lodgment even for a single moment in your breast, so long as the memory of your horrible deed preys like a serpent upon you?" He gazed at me in amazement, and laid his chisel aside. "What do you mean, my dear sir?" he asked; "pray take a seat." But my indignation chafing me more and more, I went on to accuse him directly of having murdered Antonia, and to threaten him with eternal vengeance.

Further, as a newly established lawyer, full of my profession, I went so far as to give him to understand that I would leave no stone unturned to get a clue to the business, and so deliver him here in this world into the hands of an earthly judge. I must confess that I was considerably disconcerted when, at the conclusion of my violent and pompous harangue, the Councillor, without answering so much as a single word, calmly fixed his eyes upon me as though expecting me to go on again. And this I did indeed attempt to do, but it sounded so ill-founded and so stupid as well that I soon grew silent again. Krespel gloated over my embarrassment, whilst a malicious ironical smile flitted across his face. Then he grew very grave, and addressed me in solemn tones. "Young man, no doubt you think I am foolish, insane; that I can pardon you, since we are both confined in the same madhouse; and you only blame me for deluding myself with the idea that I am God the Father because you imagine yourself to be God the Son. But how do you dare desire to insinuate

yourself into the secrets and lay bare the hidden motives of
a life that is strange to you and that must continue so? She
has gone and the mystery is solved." He ceased speaking,
rose, and traversed the room backwards and forwards several times. I ventured to ask for an explanation; he fixed his
eyes upon me, grasped me by the hand, and led me to the
window, which he threw wide open. Propping himself upon
his arms, he leaned out, and, looking down into the garden,
told me the history of his life. When he finished I left him,
touched and ashamed.

In a few words, his relations with Antonia began in the
following way. Twenty years before, the Councillor had
been led into Italy by his engrossing passion of hunting up
and buying the best violins of the old masters. At that time
he had not yet begun to make them himself, and so of course
he had not begun to take to pieces those which he bought.
In Venice he heard the celebrated singer Angela ——i, who
at that time was playing with splendid success as *prima
donna* at St. Benedict's Theatre. His enthusiasm was awakened, not only for her art—which Signora Angela had indeed
brought to a high pitch of perfection—but for her angelic
beauty as well. He sought her acquaintance; and in spite
of his rugged manners he succeeded in winning her heart,
principally through his bold and yet at the same time masterly violin-playing. Close intimacy led in a few weeks to
marriage, which, however, was kept a secret, because Angela was unwilling to sever her connection with the theatre,
neither did she wish to part with her professional name,
that by which she was celebrated, nor to add to it the cacoph-
onous "Krespel." With the most extravagant irony he described to me what a strange life of worry and torture Angela led him as soon as she became his wife. Krespel was of
opinion that more capriciousness and waywardness were
concentrated in Angela's little person than in all the rest of
the *prima donnas* in the world put together. If he now and
again presumed to stand up in his own defence, she let
loose a whole army of abbots, musical composers, and students upon him, who, ignorant of his true connection with
Angela, soundly rated him as a most intolerable, ungallant

lover for not submitting to all the Signora's caprices. It was after one of these stormy scenes that Krespel fled to Angela's country seat to try and forget in playing fantasias on his Cremona violin the annoyances of the day. But he had not been there long before the Signora, who had followed hard after him, stepped into the room. She was in an affectionate humor; she embraced her husband, overwhelmed him with sweet and languishing glances, and rested her pretty head on his shoulder. But Krespel, carried away into the world of music, continued to play on until the walls echoed again; thus he chanced to touch the Signora somewhat ungently with his arm and the fiddle-bow. She leapt back full of fury, shrieking that he was a "German brute," snatched the violin from his hands, and dashed it into a thousand pieces on the marble table. Krespel stood like a statue of stone before her; but then, as if awakening out of a dream, he seized her with the strength of a giant and threw her out of the window of her own house, and, without troubling himself about anything more, fled back to Venice—to Germany. It was not, however, until some time had elapsed that he had a clear recollection of what he had done; although he knew that the window was scarcely five feet from the ground, and although he knew that, under the circumstances, he simply had to throw the Signora out of the window, he yet felt troubled by a painful sense of uneasiness particularly so since she had imparted to him in no ambiguous terms an interesting secret as to her condition. He hardly dared to make inquiries; and he was not a little surprised about eight months afterwards at receiving a tender letter from his beloved wife, in which she made not the slightest allusion to what had taken place in her country house, only adding to the intelligence that she had been safely delivered of a sweet little daughter the heartfelt prayer that her dear husband and now a happy father would come to Venice at once. That, however, Krespel did not do; rather he appealed to a confidential friend for a more circumstantial account of the details, and learned that the Signora had alighted upon the soft grass as lightly as a bird, and that the sole consequences of the fall or shock had been psychic. That is to say, after Krespel's action

she had become completely altered; she never showed a trace
of caprice, of her former freaks, or of her teasing habits; and
the composer who wrote for the next carnival was the happiest fellow under the sun, since the Signora was willing to
sing his music without the scores and hundreds of changes
which she at other times had insisted upon. "To be sure,"
added his friend, "there was every reason for preserving the
secret of Angela's cure, else every day would see lady
singers flying through windows." The Councillor was not
a little excited at this news; he engaged horses; he took his
seat in the carriage. "Stop!" he cried suddenly. "Why, there's
not a shadow of doubt," he murmured to himself, "that as
soon as Angela sets eyes upon me again, the evil spirit will
recover his power and once more take possession of her. And
since I have already thrown her out of the window, what
could I do if a similar case were to occur again? What would
there be left for me to do?" He got out of the carriage, and
wrote an affectionate letter to his wife, making graceful allusion to her tenderness in especially dwelling upon the fact
that his tiny daughter had, like him, a little mole behind the
ear, and—remained in Germany. Now ensued an active correspondence betwen them. Assurances of unchanged affection—invitations—laments over the absence of the beloved
one—thwarted wishes—hopes, etc.—flew back and forth between Venice and H——, from H—— to Venice. At length
Angela came to Germany, and, as is well known, sang with
brilliant success as *prima donna* at the great theatre in
F——. Despite the fact that she was no longer young, she
won all hearts by the irresistible charm of her splendid singing. At that time she had not lost her voice in the least degree. Meanwhile, the child Antonia had been growing up;
and her mother never tired of writing to tell her father how
she was developing into a singer of the first rank. Krespel's
friends in F—— also confirmed this intelligence, and urged
him to come for once to F—— to see and admire this uncom-
mon sight of two such glorious singers. They had not the
slightest suspicion of the close relations in which Krespel
stood to the pair. Willingly would he have seen with his own
eyes the daughter who occupied so large a place in his

heart, and who moreover often appeared to him in his
dreams; but as often as he thought upon his wife he felt
very uncomfortable, and so he remained at home amongst
his broken violins.

There was a certain promising young composer, B—— of
F——, who was found to have suddenly disappeared, no
body know where. This young man fell so deeply in love
with Antonia that, as she returned his love, he earnestly be
sought her mother to consent to an immediate union, sanctified as it would further be by art. Angela had nothing to
urge against his suit; and the Councillor the more readily
gave his consent that the young composer's productions had
found favor before his rigorous critical judgment. Krespel
was expecting to hear of the consummation of the marriage,
when he received instead a black sealed envelope addressed in a strange hand. Doctor R—— conveyed to the
Councillor the sad intelligence that Angela had fallen seriously ill in consequence of a cold caught at the theatre, and
that during the night immediately preceding what was to
have been Antonia's wedding-day, she had died. To him,
the Doctor, Angela had disclosed the fact that she was Krespel's wife, and that Antonia was his daughter; he, Krespel,
had better hasten therefore to take charge of the orphan.
Notwithstanding that the Councillor was a good deal upset
by this news of Angela's death, he soon began to feel that
an antipathetic, disturbing influence had departed out of
his life, and that now for the first time he could begin to
breathe freely. The very same day he set out for F——. You
could not credit how heartrending was the Councillor's description of the moment when he first saw Antonia. Even in
the fantastic oddities of his expression there was such a marvellous power of description that I am unable to give even
so much as a faint indication of it. Antonia inherited all her
mother's amiability and all her mother's charms, but not
the repellent reverse of the medal. There was no chronic
moral ulcer, which might break out from time to time.
Antonia's betrothed put in an appearance, whilst Antonia
herself, fathoming with happy instinct the deeper-lying
character of her wonderful father, sang one of old Padre

Martini's[1] motets, which, she knew, Krespel in the heyday of
his courtship had never grown tired of hearing her mother
sing. The tears ran in streams down Krespel's cheeks; even
Angela he had never heard sing like that. Antonia's voice was
of a very remarkable and altogether peculiar timbre: at one
time it was like the singing of an Aeolian harp, at another like
the warbled gush of the nightingale. It seemed as if there
was not room for such notes in the human breast. Antonia,
blushing with joy and happiness, sang on and on—all her
most beautiful songs, B—— playing between whiles as only
enthusiasm that is intoxicated with delight can play. Krespel
was at first transported with rapture, then he grew thoughtful—still—absorbed in reflection. At length he leapt to his
feet, pressed Antonia to his heart, and begged her in a low
husky voice, "Sing no more if you love me—my heart is
bursting—I fear—I fear—don't sing again."

"No!" remarked the Councillor next day to Doctor R——,
"when, as she sang, her blushes gathered into two dark red
spots on her pale cheeks, I knew it had nothing to do with
your nonsensical family likenesses, I knew it was what I
dreaded." The Doctor, whose countenance had shown signs
of deep distress from the very beginning of the conversation, replied, "Whether it arises from a too early taxing of
her powers of song, or whether the fault is Nature's—
enough, Antonia labors under an organic failure in the
chest which gives to her voice its wonderful power and its
singular timbre, a power that I might almost say transcends
the limits of human capabilities of song. But it bears the announcement of her early death; for, if she continues to sing,
I wouldn't give her at the most more than six months longer
to live." Krespel's heart was lacerated as if by the stabs of
hundreds of knives. It was as though his life had been for
the first time overshadowed by a beautiful tree full of the
most magnificent blossoms, and now it was to be sawn to

[1] Giambattista Martini, more commonly called Padre Martini, of
Bologna, formed an influential school of music there in the latter half
of the eighteenth century. He wrote vocal and instrumental pieces both
for the church and for the theatre. He was also a learned historian of
music. He has the merit of having discerned and encouraged the genius
of Mozart when, a boy of fourteen, he visited Bologna in 1770.

pieces at the roots, so that it could not grow green and blossom any more. His resolution was taken. He told Antonia all; he put the alternatives before her—whether she would follow her betrothed and yield to his and the world's seductions, but with the certainty of dying early, or whether she would spread round her father in his old days that joy and peace which had hitherto been unknown to him, and so secure a long life. She threw herself sobbing into his arms, and he, knowing the heartrending trial that was before her, did not press for a more explicit declaration. He talked the matter over with her betrothed; but, notwithstanding that the latter averred that no note should ever cross Antonia's lips, the Councillor was only too well aware that even B—— could not resist the temptation of hearing her sing, at any rate arias of his own composition. And the world, the musical public, even though acquainted with the nature of the singer's affliction, would certainly not relinquish its claims to hear her, for in cases where pleasure is concerned people of this class are very selfish and cruel. The Councillor disappeared from F—— along with Antonia, and came to H——. B—— was in despair when he learned that they had gone. He set out on their track, overtook them, and arrived at H—— at the same time that they did. "Let me see him only once, and then die!" entreated Antonia. "Die! die!" cried Krespel, wild with anger, an icy shudder running through him. His daughter, the only creature in the wide world who had awakened in him the springs of unknown joy, who alone had reconciled him to life, tore herself away from his heart, and he—he suffered the terrible trial to take place. B—— sat down to the piano; Antonia sang; Krespel fiddled away merrily, until the two red spots showed themselves on Antonia's cheeks. Then he bade her stop; and as B—— was taking leave of his betrothed, she suddenly fell to the floor with a loud scream. "I thought," continued Krespel in his narration, "I thought that she was, as I had anticipated, really dead; but as I had prepared myself for the worst, my calmness did not leave me, nor my self-command desert me. I grasped B——, who stood like a silly sheep in his dismay, by the shoulders, and said (here the Councillor fell into his singing tone), 'Now that you, my estimable pianoforte-player, have, as you wished and desired, really murdered your betrothed, you may quietly take your departure; at least have the goodness to make yourself scarce before I run my bright dagger through your heart. My daughter, who, as you see, is rather pale, could very well do with some color from your precious blood. Make haste and run, for I might also hurl a nimble knife or two after you.' I must, I suppose, have looked rather formidable as I uttered these words, for, with a cry of the greatest terror, B—— tore himself loose from my grasp, rushed out of the room, and down the steps." Directly after B—— was gone, when the Councillor tried to lift up his daughter, who lay unconscious on the floor, she opened her eyes with a deep sigh, but soon closed them again as if about to die. Then Krespel's grief found vent aloud, and would not be comforted. The doctor, whom the old housekeeper had called in, pronounced Antonia's case a somewhat serious but by no means dangerous attack; and she did indeed recover more quickly than her father had dared to hope. She now clung to him with the most confiding childlike affection; she entered into his favorite hobbies—into his mad schemes and whims. She helped him take old violins to pieces and glue new ones together. "I won't sing again any more, but live for you," she often said, sweetly smiling upon him, after she had been asked to sing and had refused. Such appeals, however, the Councillor was anxious to spare her as much as possible; therefore it was that he was unwilling to take her into society, and solicitously shunned all music. He well understood how painful it must be for her to forego altogether the exercise of that art which she had brought to such a pitch of perfection. When the Councillor bought the wonderful violin that he had buried with Antonia, and was about to take it to pieces, she met him with such sadness in her face and asked softly, "What! this as well?" By a power, which he could not explain, he felt impelled to leave this particular instrument unbroken, and to play upon it. Scarcely had he drawn the first few notes from it than Antonia cried aloud with joy, "Why, that's me!—now I shall sing again." And, in truth, there was something remarkably striking about the clear, silvery, bell-like tones of the violin; they seemed to have been engendered in the human soul. Krespel's heart was deeply moved; he played, too, better than ever. As he ran up and down the scale, playing bold passages with consummate power and expression, she clapped her hands together and cried with delight, "I did that well! I did that well."

From this time onwards her life was filled with peace and cheerfulness. She often said to the Councillor, "I should like to sing something, father." Then Krespel would take his violin down from the wall and play her most beautiful songs, and her heart was glad and happy. Shortly before my arrival in H——, the Councillor was awakened one night and fancied that he heard somebody playing the piano in the adjoining room; he soon made out distinctly that B—— was flourishing on the instrument in his usual style. He wished to get up, but felt himself held down as if by a dead weight, and lying as if fettered in iron bonds; he was utterly unable to move an inch. Then Antonia's voice was heard singing low and soft; soon, however, it began to rise and rise in volume until it became an ear-splitting *fortissimo;* and at length she passed over into a powerfully impressive song which B—— had once composed for her in the devotional style of the old masters. Krespel described his condition as being incomprehensible, for terrible anguish was mingled with a delight he had never experienced before. All at once he was surrounded by a dazzling brightness, in which he beheld B—— and Antonia locked in a close embrace, and gazing at each other in a rapture of ecstasy. The music of the song and of the pianoforte accompanying it went on without any visible signs that Antonia sang or that B—— touched the instrument. Then the Councillor fell into a sort of dead faint, whilst the images vanished away. On awakening he still felt the terrible anguish of his dream. He rushed into Antonia's room. She lay on the sofa, her eyes closed, a sweet angelic smile on her face, her hands devoutly folded, and looking as if asleep and dreaming of the joys and raptures of heaven. But she was—dead.

THE JEWS' BEECH TREE[1]

ANNETTE VON DROSTE-HÜLSHOFF

(1797-1848)

FREDERICK MERGEL, born in 1738, was the son of a so-called landowner of the lower class in the village of B., a village which, badly built and smoky though it might be, yet attracted the attention of all travellers by the extremely picturesque beauty of its situation in a green and wooded valley of an important and historically famous mountain range. The province to which it belonged was in those days one of those secluded corners of the globe, without factories or trade, without highways, where a strange face still caused a sensation, and to travel thirty miles, even for the people of position, was a matter which raised them to the rank of Ulysses—in short, a spot like so many others in Germany with the failings and virtues, the originality and narrowness which thrive only in such surroundings.

Owing to very simple and often inadequate laws, the ideas of the inhabitants about right and wrong had got into disorder, or rather, a second system of laws had grown up—the law of public opinion, of custom firmly established by time. The landowners, who were responsible for the dispensing of justice, punished and rewarded according to their own ideas, which were in most cases honest: the people did what seemed to them practicable, and, stretching the point a little, pleased them; and only the loser sometimes thought of turning up old and dusty documents. It is difficult to look at that period impartially; since it disappeared it has been either arrogantly censured or stupidly

---

[1] Translated by E. M. Bennett. Reprinted by permission of the Oxford University Press from *Selected German Short Stories*.

praised, for those who lived in it are dazzled by precious memories, and the later-born do not understand it. But this at least can be asserted: that habit was weaker, integrity firmer, wrong-doing more frequent, unscrupulousness rarer. For he who acts according to his convictions, however faulty they may be, can never be quite lost, but nothing is more soul-destroying than having to obey laws which one feels in one's heart to be wrong.

A race of people more restless and adventurous than their neighbours was the reason why many things in the little province of which we are speaking appeared in more glaring colours than in other places under the same circumstances. Crimes were daily committed in the forest, and he who got a broken head in the fighting which constantly occurred had to see to the binding up of it himself. But as most of the wealth of the province consisted in the large and productive forests, these were naturally sharply guarded; not so much in a lawful manner as by constantly renewed attempts to overcome violence and cunning by the same weapons.

The village of B. was considered the most arrogant, cunning, and audacious village in the whole principality. Its position amidst the deep and lofty loneliness of the forest began early to nourish the inborn obstinacy of the people. The proximity of a river which flowed into the sea, and was large enough to bear decked boats which could carry the timber for ship-building safely and easily out of the country, was to a great extent responsible for encouraging the natural audacity of the people, and the fact that the whole neighbourhood teemed with forest-rangers only acted as an incentive, as the frequent clashes between rangers and peasants generally ended in a victory for the peasants. Thirty, forty wagons would drive out at the same time on a fine moonlight night, with twice as many men of all ages, from half-grown boys to the seventy-year-old mayor, who led the company with the same proud consciousness with which he took his seat in the court room. Those who remained behind heard with indifference the gradually lessening noise of the wheels in the defiles, and went off to sleep again. An occasional shot, a feeble scream would sometimes cause a young wife or sweetheart to start up in alarm; but nobody else took any notice of it. At the earliest sign of dawn the company returned as silently as they had gone out, their faces glowing like bronze, here and there a head bound up, but of that no notice was taken; and a few hours later the whole neighbourhood knew of the ill luck of one or more rangers, carried out of the wood, beaten, blinded with snuff, and incapable for a time of doing their work.

In this district Frederick Mergel was born, in a house which, in the proud possession of a chimney and a few panes of glass in the window, showed the pretensions of its builder, and in its present decayed state showed the miserable circumstances of its present owner. What had been a railing round courtyard and garden had become a neglected fence, the roof was ruinous, other people's cattle were pastured on the meadow, other people's corn grew in the field beyond the courtyard, and in the garden, with the exception of a few woody rose-bushes left over from better times, more weeds grew than flowers. True, ill luck had been to a certain extent the cause of all this; but there had been also a great deal of lack of organization and bad management. Frederick's father, old Hermann Mergel, had as a bachelor been a so-called good drinker, that is, one who drank himself into the gutter on Sundays and holidays, and behaved himself well on other days. So he found no obstacles put in the way of his courtship of a pretty and well-to-do girl. The wedding was a merry one. Mergel was not too drunk, and the bride's parents went happily home that evening; but on the following Sunday the young wife, covered with blood, was seen to run screaming through the village to her old home, leaving behind her all her good clothes and new belongings. That caused great scandal and annoyance to Mergel, who needed comfort more than ever. By the afternoon no pane of glass in his windows remained intact, and late that night he was still lying across his doorstep, at intervals trying to lift a broken bottle to his lips, and cutting hands and face miserably in the attempt. His young wife stayed with her parents and very soon pined away and died. Whether it was remorse or shame by which Mergel was now overcome, it remains certain that from that time on he was looked upon as completely demoralized.

The household went to pieces, the maids caused trouble and scandal: and so the years passed. Mergel remained a taciturn and at last rather poor widower, until he suddenly let it be known that he was about to marry again. The fact itself was unexpected, but the personality of the bride made it an even greater wonder. Margaret Semmler was an honest, respectable, middle-aged person, who had been in her youth a village beauty. She was still a clever and capable housewife and not penniless; so that nobody could understand what made her contemplate such a step. Probably her reason can be found in her shrewd and conscious self-sufficiency. It is reported that on the evening before the wedding she said: "A wife who allows her husband to ill-treat her is either stupid or not worth much: if I have a bad time you can say the fault is mine." The result unfortunately showed that she had overestimated her power. At first she made a great impression on her husband; when he had had too much to drink he either kept away from the house or crept up to the loft, but after a while the yoke became too irksome, and he was soon seen to reel across the lane into the house, and from inside came the sound of his wild uproar while Margaret hastily closed doors and windows. On one such occasion—this time not a Sunday—she was seen to rush out of doors without cap or neckerchief, her hair hanging wildly round her head, and throw herself down beside a bed of herbs, where she began to grub up the earth with her hands; then glancing anxiously around her she picked a bunch of herbs and returned slowly towards the house, but went into the loft instead of the house. The rumour spread that on that day Mergel first hit her, but no word of that ever passed her lips. The second year of this unhappy marriage was marked, one cannot say gladdened.

by the birth of a son, for Margaret cried bitterly when the child was handed to her. But in spite of all the sorrows of his mother, Frederick was a healthy, pretty child, and throve in the good air. The father loved him very much, and never came home without bringing him a bit of cake, or something of that sort, and people even thought he had improved since the birth of his child; at least the noise in the house was much less.

Frederick was nine years old. It was the feast of the Epiphany, a raw, stormy winter night. Hermann Mergel had gone to a wedding, and had started off betimes as the bride's house was three-quarters of a mile away. Although he had promised to return in the evening, Frau Mergel did not expect him, more especially as a heavy snowfall had begun at sunset. Towards ten o'clock she raked together the ashes in the fireplace and prepared for bed. Frederick stood beside her, already half undressed, listening to the howl of the wind and the rattling of the garret window.

"Mother, isn't father coming to-night?" he asked.

"No, child, to-morrow." "But why not, mother? he promised to." "Ah, God, if only he would do what he promised! Now get on, and finish undressing."

They were hardly in bed when a gust of wind came which threatened to carry away the house. The bed shook, and there was a rustling as of goblins in the chimney. "Mother, somebody is knocking." "Quiet, Fritz, that is only the wind shaking that loose board in the gable." "No, mother, at the door!" "It isn't shut; the latch is broken. Go to sleep, don't make me lose the miserable bit of rest I can get." "But if father comes?" The mother turned angrily in bed. "The devil will keep him fast enough!" "Where is the devil, mother?" "You wait, fidget! he is standing outside the door, and will fetch you, if you aren't quiet."

Frederick was quiet; he listened for a little while longer and then fell asleep. After a few hours he woke again. The wind had shifted and was now hissing like a snake through the cracks in the window into his ear. His shoulder was stiff; he crept deeper under the quilt and lay quite still with fright. After a time he noticed that his mother was not sleeping either. He heard her crying, and in between, "Ave Maria!" and "Pray for us poor sinners!" The beads of the rosary touched his face. An involuntary sigh escaped him. "Frederick, are you awake?" "Yes, mother." "Child, pray a little— you know part of the Lord's Prayer—that God may protect us from danger by water and fire."

Frederick thought about the devil and wondered what he looked like. The multifarious noises and uproars in the house seemed strange to him. He thought there must be something alive both inside and out. "Listen, mother, I am sure there are people knocking." "Ah, no, child, but there is not one of the old boards in the house which is not clattering." "Listen, can't you hear? Some one called! do listen!"

The mother raised herself in bed; the howl of the storm lessened for an instant. One could distinctly hear knocking on the shutters, and voices, "Margaret, Mistress Margaret, hullo, open the door!" Margaret uttered a loud cry: "They are bringing that swine again."

The rosary fell to the floor, clothes were hastily thrown on. She went over to the hearth, and shortly afterwards Frederick heard her crossing the floor with defiant step. Margaret did not come back, but there was a great deal of murmuring of strange voices in the kitchen. Twice a strange man entered the bedchamber and appeared to be looking anxiously for something. Suddenly a lamp was brought in and two men came in leading Margaret. She was white as chalk and her eyes were closed. Frederick thought she must be dead; he began to scream fearfully, whereupon somebody gave him a box on the ears which quietened him, and little by little he began to understand from the talk of the people round him that his uncle Franz Semmler and Hülsmeyer had found his father lying dead in the woods and that he now lay in the kitchen.

As soon as Margaret regained consciousness she was anxious to get rid of the strangers. Her brother stayed with her, and Frederick, obliged to stay in bed under threat of punishment, heard all night long the crackling of the

kitchen fire and a noise as of things being pushed backwards and forwards and brushed. Little was said, and that
very quietly, but at times sighs reached the boy that, young
as he was, cut him to the quick. Once he heard his uncle say,
"Margaret, don't take that so much to heart; we will both
have three masses said, and at Easter we will go on pilgrimage to the Virgin at Werl."

When the corpse was carried out two days later Margaret
sat by the hearth, hiding her face in her apron. After a few
minutes, when it was all quiet, she murmured to herself,
"Ten years, ten crosses. We have carried them together, and
now I am alone!" Then louder: "Fritz, come here!"

Frederick approached her timidly; with her black ribbons and troubled looks his mother seemed to him a sinister
figure. "Fritz," she said, "will you be a good boy, and make
me happy, or are you going to be naughty, a liar, a drunkard, and a thief?" "Mother, Hülsmeyer steals." "Hülsmeyer?
nonsense! who told you such a wicked story?" "He thrashed
Aaron the other day, and took six groschen from him." "If he
took the money from Aaron, you may be sure the accursed
Jew had swindled him of it before. Hülsmeyer is a decent,
proper man, and the Jews are all rogues." "But mother,
Brandes said he stole wood and venison as well." "Child,
Brandes is a ranger." "Mother, are rangers liars?"

Margaret was silent awhile, then she said, "Listen, Fritz,
the Almighty lets the trees grow wild, and the deer move
from one estate to another; they cannot belong to anybody.
But you don't understand that yet; now go to the outhouse
and fetch some twigs."

Frederick had seen his father lying blue and horrible on
the straw. But he never said anything about it and apparently did not like to think of it. The memory of his father
had left in him a mixture of terror and tenderness, and as
nothing binds so much as love and care for a being against
whom all others seem to have hardened their hearts, so with
Frederick this feeling grew with the years, increased by the
feeling of the neglect on the part of others. As long as he was
a child he was very unhappy if his dead father was spoken

of unkindly, and that was a sorrow which the delicacy of the neighbours did not spare him. In that district it is believed that a person who dies by an accident cannot rest in his grave. Old Mergel became the Breder Wood ghost; he led drunkards like a Jack-o'-lantern till they fell into the ditch; the shepherd boys, when they crouched over the fire at night and the owls called around them, heard a voice saying in broken tones but quite clearly, "Now hearken, fine Lizzie," and an unauthorized wood-cutter who had fallen asleep under a spreading oak and been overtaken by darkness, had on waking seen old Mergel's swollen, blue face watching him through the branches. Frederick had to hear a great many such stories from the other boys; and he cried, struck out with his fists and once even with a knife, and in return was pitiably thrashed. After that he always drove his mother's cows alone to the further end of the valley, where he would lie in the same position in the grass for hours, plucking handfuls of thyme out of the ground.

He was twelve years old when a younger brother of his mother, who had not crossed her doorstep since she had married so foolishly, came on a visit from his home in Breder.

Simon Semmler was a restless little man, with fish-like eyes, and in fact his whole face was like a pike's, a gloomy person, in whom bragging taciturnity and affected sincerity were equally mixed; who would like to have been thought an enlightened person, but who was really considered a disagreeable, quarrelsome fellow, out of whose way everybody was glad to keep as he got older, for with age dull people generally increase their demands as their usefulness decreases.

Nevertheless poor Margaret was glad to see him, for he was now her only living relative.

"Simon, is it you?" she asked, and trembled so much that she had to hold on to her chair. "Have you come to see how I am getting on, and my dirty boy?" Simon looked at her earnestly and then gave her his hand: "You have grown old, Margaret!" Margaret sighed. "Fate has often been cruel to me." "Yes, girl, a late marriage is always regretted! Now you

are old, and the child still small. There is a time for everything. But when an old house catches fire, no water is any
use." A flame, blood-red, spread over Margaret's care-worn
face.

"But I hear that your boy is a knowing little chap and very
bright," went on Simon. "Well, more or less, and yet honest."
"Hm, once somebody stole a cow, and his name was Honest
also. But he is quiet and thoughtful, isn't he? and does not
run about with the other boys?" "He is a strange child," said
Margaret as though to herself, "and that is not good." Simon
laughed aloud: "Your boy is scared because the others have
several times given him a good thrashing. He'll return that
to them yet. Hülsmeyer came to see me a short time ago, and
he said the boy was like a deer."

What mother's heart does not rejoice when she hears her
child praised? Margaret had never felt so pleased, for every
one said her boy was spiteful and taciturn. Tears came into
her eyes. "Yes, God be praised, he has straight limbs." "What
does he look like?" continued Simon. "He has a great deal
from you, Simon, a great deal." Simon laughed. "Ho, he must
be a fine fellow, I grow handsomer every day. They say he is
not doing much at school. You let him herd the cows? That's
just as well. Only half of what the master says is true. But
where does he go with the cows? Telengrund? Koderholz?
Teutoburger Wald? by night and day?" "The whole night
through: but why do you ask that?"

Simon appeared not to have heard this last question; he
put his head out of the door. "Ha, here comes the fellow! His
father's son! he swings his arm just as your husband did.
And just look, actually the boy has my fair hair!"

A stealthy, proud smile crossed the mother's face: her
Frederick's blond curls and Simon's red bristles! Without
answering she broke a twig from the hedge and went to
meet her son, apparently to help him with a lazy cow, but
really to whisper a few quick, half-threatening words to
him; for she knew his stubborn nature, and Simon's manner
seemed to her to-day more intimidating than ever. But
everything went off better than she expected; Frederick was

neither stubborn nor cheeky, but rather somewhat foolish and very anxious to please his uncle. So it came about that after half an hour's talk Simon put forward the suggestion of adopting the boy, whom he did not want to take right away from his mother, but whom he wanted to have with him for a great part of the time, and whom in the end he would make his heir, which he would be in any case. Margaret allowed him to explain how great the advantage and how small the renunciation would be. She knew better what a loss to a sickly widow a twelve-year-old son whom she had brought up almost to take the place of a daughter could be. But she was silent and agreed to everything. Only she begged her brother to be strict, but not hard with the boy.

"He is a good boy," she said, "but I am a solitary woman; my son is not like one who has been ruled by a father's hand." Simon nodded his head slyly: "You leave that to me, we shall get on quite well together, and do you know what? let the boy come with me now. I have to fetch two sacks from the mill; the smaller will be just the right size for him, and like that he will learn to help me. Come along, Fritz, put on your wooden shoes." And soon Margaret was watching them striding away, Simon in front, his head well forward, and the tails of his red coat waving like flames behind him. He had almost the look of a fiery man atoning for the theft of sacks; Frederick followed him, straight and tall for his age, with fine, almost noble features, and long fair hair which was in better order than was to be expected from the rest of his appearance, otherwise ragged, sunburnt, and with a sort of raw melancholy in his looks. But a certain family likeness was not to be denied, and as Frederick slowly followed his guide, his gaze fixed firmly upon the man whose strange appearance attracted him, one had instinctively to think of some one watching with troubled attention his own future picure in a magic mirror.

Now the two neared that part of the Teutoburger Wood where Breder Wood comes down the sides of the hill and makes a very dark patch. So far very little had been said. Simon seemed meditative, the boy absent-minded, and both

were panting under the weight of their sacks. Suddenly
Simon asked: "Do you like brandy?" The child did not answer. "I asked you if you like brandy? does your mother
sometimes give you some to drink?" "Mother has none herself," said Frederick. "Ah, so much the better!—do you know
this wood in front of us?" "That is Breder Wood." "And do
you know what happened in there?" Frederick remained
silent. In the meantime they drew nearer to the gloomy
ravine.

"Does your mother still pray so much?" went on Simon.
"Yes, every evening, two rosaries." "Oh! and you pray with
her?" The boy laughed, half embarrassed, but with a sly
look sideways. "Mother says one rosary before supper, and I
am not home with the cows then, and the other in bed, and
then I am asleep." "Oh, ho, comrade!" These last few words
were said under the shade of a wide-spreading beech-tree
which overhung the entrance to the ravine. By this time it
was quite dark; the moon was in its first quarter, but its feeble light only served to give a strange appearance to those
things which it reached through an occasional thinning of the
trees. Frederick kept close behind his uncle; his uncle walked
quickly, and if anybody had been there to look at him, they
would have noticed an expression of extreme, but strange
rather than fearful, attention. So the two marched vigorously
forwards, Simon with the firm tread of an experienced
walker, Frederick unsteadily and as though in a dream. It
seemed to him that everything moved in the separate moon-
beams, and the trees swayed, first together and then apart.
His steps were made unsteady by the roots of trees and slippery places where the ground was damp; once or twice he
nearly fell. At last the darkness seemed less, and the two
entered a fairly large clearing. Here the moon shone clear
and showed that but a short while earlier the axe had been
used unmercifully. Everywhere stood stumps, many several
feet high, just as they had been most convenient to cut. The
proscribed work must have been interrupted, for a beech-
tree in full leaf lay right across the path, its branches stretching high above it and its leaves moving gently in the night
wind. Simon stopped for a moment and looked attentively at

the fallen tree. In the middle of the clearing stood an old oak, broader than it was tall; a pale ray of light which fell through the branches upon its trunk showed that it was hollow, a fact which had probably saved it from the general disturbance. Here Simon suddenly gripped the boy's hand.

"Frederick, do you know that tree? That is the broad oak." Frederick shuddered and clung tightly to his uncle's hand. "Look," went on Simon, "this is where your uncle Franz and Hülsmeyer found your father, when quite drunken, and without penance or extreme unction he went to the devil." "Uncle, uncle," panted Frederick. "You aren't afraid? You devil of a boy, you are pinching my arm, let me go!" He tried to shake off the boy, "Your father was a good sort, anyway; God won't be so particular. I loved him as though he were my own brother." Frederick loosed his grip of his uncle's arm; both went on silently until the rest of the wood was behind them and they came in sight of the village of Breder with its mud huts and the few better houses, Simon's amongst them, of bricks.

The next evening Margaret sat for an hour in front of her house and waited for her boy. It had been the first night the boy had ever spent away from her, and still Frederick did not come. She was annoyed and anxious, yet knew that she had no grounds to be either. The clock in the church tower struck seven, and the cattle returned home; he was still not there, and she had to get up and look after her cows.

When she returned to the dark kitchen Frederick was standing on the hearth; he was bending down and warming his hands at the flames. The firelight played over his features and gave him an unpleasant look of thinness and nervous twitching. Margaret stopped short in the doorway her child looked so strangely altered.

"Frederick, how is your uncle?" The boy murmured a few unintelligible words, and pressed closer to the wall. "Frederick, have you lost your tongue? Child, say something, you know quite well that I don't hear well with the right ear." The child raised his voice and began to stammer so badly that Margaret could not understand anything.

"What is that you say? a greeting from Master Semmler?

back again? where? the cows are already home. Wretched
boy, I can't understand you. Wait, let me see if you still have
a tongue in your mouth!" She moved a few steps nearer him.
The child looked up at her with the sad eyes of a half-grown
dog learning tricks, and in his terror began to stamp his feet
and rub his back against the wall.

Margaret stood still, her look grew anxious. The boy appeared to her to have fallen together, even his clothes were
not the same, no, that was not her child! and yet—"Frederick,
Frederick!" she called.

In the bedroom a cupboard door banged, and the boy
she called stepped forward, in one hand a so-called wooden
violin, that is an old wooden shoe spanned with three or
four old violin-strings, in the other a bow worthy of his instrument. He went straight up to his wretched double with an
air of conscious dignity and independence that showed up
the difference between the two otherwise amazingly similar
boys.

"There, John," he said, and with a patronizing expression
gave him the work of art; "there is the violin I promised you.
My playtime is over, I must earn money now." John threw
another shy glance at Margaret, then slowly stretched out
his hand until he held the proffered gift tight, and hid it
under his wretched jacket.

Margaret stood quite still and let the children alone. Her
thoughts had taken another, a very serious turn, and she
looked uneasily from one to the other. The strange boy had
turned back and was bending again over the fire with an
expression of momentary comfort which bordered on simplicity. In Frederick's face the play of expression changed
continually, but self-seeking was more obvious than kindness, and his eye in its almost glassy clearness certainly
showed for the first time that expression of unbridled ambition and propensity to braggadocio, which appeared later
as so strong a motive in most of his dealings.

His mother's voice roused him from thoughts which were
as new as they were pleasant.

She was sitting at her spinning-wheel again.

"Frederick," she said hesitatingly, "tell me—" and stopped. Frederick looked up, and as she said no more, turned back to his protégé. "No, listen," and then more quietly: "what boy is that? what is his name?" Frederick answered equally quietly: "That is uncle's pigherd, who has a message for Hülsmeyer. Uncle has given me a pair of shoes and a drill vest, and the boy carried them here for me, that is why I promised him the violin; he is only a poor boy; he is called John." "Well?" said Margaret. "What do you want, mother?" "What else is he called?" "Yes, oh, nothing else—or, wait— yes: Nobody, John Nobody. He has no father," he added more quietly.

Margaret rose and went into the bedroom. When she came back after a short time her face wore a hard, morose expression. "Now Frederick," she said, "let the boy go on his errand. Boy, what are you putting into the ashes? have you nothing to do at home?"

The boy pulled himself together so hastily that his limbs got in the way, and his wood violin was within a hair's breadth of falling into the fire.

"Wait, John," said Frederick proudly; "I will give you half my slice of bread and butter: it is too much for me, mother always cuts right across the loaf."

"Don't," said Margaret; "he is going home."

"Yes, but he won't get anything there; Uncle Simon eats at seven o'clock." Margaret turned to the boy: "Won't somebody keep something for you? Tell me, who looks after you?" "Nobody," stammered the child. "Nobody?" she echoed, "there, take it, take it!" she added hastily; "you are called Nobody, and nobody looks after you! That is a shame! And now go! Frederick, don't go with him, do you hear? don't go together through the village." "I am only going to get wood from the shed," answered Frederick. When both boys had gone, Margaret threw herself down on a chair and beat her hands together with an expression of the deepest misery. Her face was white as a cloth. "A broken oath, a broken oath!" she groaned. "Simon, Simon, how will you face your God?"

She sat for a while, motionless with tightly pressed lips, as though completely absent in mind. Frederick stood in front of her and had already spoken twice to her. "What is it? what do you want?" she cried starting up. "I have brought you money," he said, more astonished than frightened. "Money, where?" She moved and the small coins fell with a clink to the floor. Frederick picked them up. "Money from Uncle Simon, because I have helped him with some work. I can earn money for myself now." "Money from Simon? throw it away, away! no, give it to the poor. But no, keep it," she whispered almost inaudibly; "we are poor ourselves, who knows if we shall manage without begging?"

"I am to go to uncle again on Monday and help him with the sowing." "You go again to him? no, no, never again." She threw her arms passionately round her child. "Yes," she added, a stream of tears pouring down her hollow cheeks, "go, he is my only brother, and the shame is great! But remember God, and do not forget your daily prayer!"

Margaret laid her face against the wall, and wept aloud. She had had many heavy burdens to bear, her husband's wicked treatment, still heavier his death, and it had been a bitter hour when she had had to give over the last piece of ground to a creditor as usufruct, and her plough stood idle before her door. But never before had she felt like this; yet, after she had wept throughout the whole evening, and lain awake a whole night, she decided that her brother Simon could not be so wicked, the child could not be his, resemblance meant nothing. She herself, forty years earlier, had lost a little sister who had looked exactly like the strange pedlar. What things one believed when one had so little, and through unbelief was likely to lose that little!

From that time on Frederick was rarely at home. All the varmer feelings of which Simon was capable he seemed to expend on his nephew; at least he missed him very much, and was always sending messages, when any domestic matter kept the boy too long with his mother. The boy was completely changed; the dreaminess had quite gone, he grew more decided, began to pay attention to his appear-

ance, and soon became known as a handsome, active youth.
His uncle, who had always some new projects on hand,
undertook amongst other things important public works, for
example, road building, in which Frederick was reckoned
his best workman, and in everything his right hand; for
though he was not yet fully developed, there were few who
could compete with him in endurance. Margaret had till
yet only loved her son, now she began to be proud of him,
and even to feel a sort of esteem for him, as she watched the
youth developing without any assistance from her, even
without her advice, which she, like most people, considered
priceless, and she therefore could not rate high enough the
talent which was able to manage without it.

In his eighteenth year Frederick had already won a considerable name for himself amongst the youth of the village
as the result of a bet by the terms of which he carried on his
back for two miles without putting it down a wild boar
which he had killed. In the meantime participation in the
glory which he won was the only advantage which came to
Margaret from these propitious circumstances, for Frederick
spent more and more on his appearance, and at last began
to find it hard to bear when, owing to want of money, he had
to play second fiddle to any other of the village youths.
Added to that all his energy was given over to outside gains;
at home, quite in contrast to his previous reputation, every
continuous occupation seemed troublesome to him, he preferred to undertake a difficult but short job, which soon
allowed him to go back to his earlier post as cowherd. But
this was an unsuitable occupation for his age, and drew a
great deal of ridicule upon him; ridicule which he soon
silenced by a few sharp reprimands with his fist. So one was
soon accustomed to seeing him first decked out and happy
as the young elegant and leader of the village youth; then
as a ragged cowherd, solitary and dreamy, slinking along
behind the cows, or lying face downwards in a clearing in
the woods, apparently quite aimlessly stripping the moss off
the tree-trunks.

About this time the sleepy laws were to a certain extent

shaken up by a band of forest trespassers who, under the name of the Blue Blouses, so far outdid their predecessors in cunning and insolence that it was too much for even the most long-suffering. Quite contrary to the usual state of affairs, when it was easy to point out the leaders of the business, it was now impossible, in spite of the greatest vigilance, to discover one single individual. They took their name from the identical dress which they wore to make it more difficult for them to be recognized in case a ranger should catch sight of one of them disappearing into the undergrowth. They ravaged everything like the palmer worm; whole stretches of forest would be felled in a night and carried away, so that the next morning nothing was there but chips and untidy heaps of the top wood; and the fact that the cart-tracks never led to a village, but always to the river and back again, showed that they were working under the protection, and probably with the aid, of the shipowners. The band must have had very clever spies, for the rangers might watch in vain for weeks; but in that night, no matter whether stormy or bright moonlight, when they gave up in need of rest, the destruction began again. The strange thing was that the people in the neighbourhood seemed to know as little about it as the rangers themselves.

It could be said with certainty of some villages that they did not belong to the Blue Blouses, but no village could be seriously suspected since the most suspicious of them all, the village of B., was cleared. A coincidence was responsible for this, a wedding, at which the whole village had caroused through the night, while at the same time the Blue Blouses had carried out one of their most notable expeditions.

The damage in the forests was becoming so great that the measures taken against it were increased to a hitherto unknown rigour; the forests were patrolled day and night, farm servants and men servants were armed and detailed to help the rangers. But the result was slight, and the watchers had often hardly left one end of the forest when the Blue Blouses entered at the other. This state of things lasted more than a year, watchers and thieves, thieves and watchers, like sun and moon, alternately in possession of the ground and never meeting.

It was in July 1756, at 3 o'clock in the morning; the moon was high in the heavens, but its brightness was beginning to wane, and a narrow yellow stripe was already showing in the east, edging the horizon and closing the entrance to a ravine like a golden band. Frederick lay in the grass, in his usual position, carving a willow stick whose knotty end he was trying to shape into an animal. He looked overtired, yawned, and sometimes rested his head against a weathered tree-stump, while his eyes, duskier than the horizon, strayed over the young growth which nearly hid the entrance to the place where he lay. Once or twice his eyes brightened and took their characteristic glassy expression, but he immediately shut them again, and yawned and stretched himself in the manner of lazy cowherds. His dog lay a short distance from him close to the cows, which, untroubled by the forest rules, were browsing as much on the young green of the trees as on the grass, and blowing contentedly in the fresh morning air.

From time to time a dull, crashing noise came from the woods; the sound, which recurred at intervals of five to eight minutes, lasted but a moment and was followed by a long echo from the hill-sides. Frederick took no notice of it; only occasionally, when the noise was particularly loud or continuous, he raised his head and his gaze wandered slowly over the different paths which led into the clearing.

It was already getting light; the birds began to twitter and the dew to rise from the ground. Frederick had slipped down from his tree-stump and was lying, his arms folded above his head, staring into the softly increasing morning light. Suddenly he started up; something passed over his face like a flash; he listened for a few seconds, his body bent forward like a hunting dog on the scent. Then he hastily put two fingers into his mouth and whistled shrilly and continuously. "Fidel, you miserable creature!" He threw a stone

and hit the flanks of the quiet dog, which wakened from
sleep, first snapped round, then howling, went to seek comfort from the spot whence the evil had come.

At that moment the branches of a near-by thicket were
parted almost noiselessly and there stepped out a man in a
green coat with a silver escutcheon on the sleeve, carrying
his gun cocked. His eyes wandered quickly over the clearing
and then rested with particular keenness on the boy. He
stepped forward, made a sign towards the thicket, and gradually seven or eight men appeared all wearing similar uniform, hunting-knives in their belts and their guns cocked.

"Frederick, what was that?" said the first. "I wanted the
wretched animal to obey at once. For all he cares the cows
can graze the ears off my head." "The beast saw us," said
another.

"To-morrow you'll go a journey with a stone tied round
your neck," went on Frederick, and threw another stone at
the dog." "Frederick, don't pretend to be so big a fool! you
know me, and you understand me as well." A look which
worked at once accompanied these words. "Herr Brandes,
think of my mother!" "That is what I am doing. Haven't you
heard anything in the woods?" "In the woods?" The boy cast
a rapid glance at the ranger's face. "Your wood-cutters, but
nothing else." "My wood-cutters!"

The ranger's already dark complexion became darker
yet. "How many of them are there, and where are they
working?" "Where you sent them; I don't know." Brandes
turned to his companions. "Go on, I will follow you."

When they had all disappeared one after the other into
the undergrowth, Brandes went close to the boy: "Frederick,"
he said in a tone of repressed fury, "my patience is at an end;
I would like to beat you like a dog, and you are not worth
anything else. You scum, without a tile to your roof. You will
soon, praise be to God, have reached beggary, and your
mother, the old witch, shan't get even a mouldy crust when
she comes begging at my door. But first I'll see you both
living in misery." Frederick clutched convulsively at a
branch. He was deadly pale, and his eyes like balls of crys-

tal seemed to be on the point of shooting out of his head.
But only for an instant. Then a complete, almost sleepy
peace came over him again. "Sir," he said firmly, with an almost soft tone in his voice, "you have said something for
which you are not responsible, and I perhaps also. Let us
wipe it out, and now I will tell you what you want to know.
If those wood-cutters are not there by your orders, then it
must be the Blue Blouses; for no wagon has come from the
village, the path is just in front of me; and there were four
wagons. I have not seen them but I heard them driving up
the ravine." He hesitated a moment.

"Can you say that I ever cut down a tree in your district?
that I ever felled any tree anywhere except by order? Think
whether you can."

An embarrassed murmur was the only answer of the ranger, who, like most rough men, easily repented. He turned
brusquely away and strode towards the bushes. "No, sir,"
cried Frederick, "if you want to join the other rangers, they
went up there past the beech-tree." "By the beech?" said
Brandes doubtfully, "no, over there towards Mester Wood."
"I tell you, by the beech; the strap of Henry's gun got hung
up on that crooked branch; I saw it."

The ranger took the path which had been pointed out
to him.

All this time Frederick had not altered his position; half
lying, his arm flung round a withered branch, he watched
unmoved, as the ranger glided, with the careful stride of his
calling, as noiselessly as a lynx entering a hen-roost, through
the bushes which almost overgrew the footpath. Here a
branch fell to behind him, there another; the outline of his
figure disappeared little by little. There was a flash through
the leaves. It was a button on his coat; at last he was gone.
During this gradual disappearance, Frederick's face lost
its expression of unconcern and grew agitated. Did he perhaps regret not having bound the ranger to silence regarding
what he had told him? He moved a few steps forward, then
stopped. "It is too late," he murmured, and picked up his
hat. There was a slight noise in the thicket not twenty paces

from him; it was the ranger sharpening his flint. Frederick listened. "No," he said at last decisively, and collecting his things together began to drive his cattle hastily down the ravine.

At midday Margaret sat by the fire and made tea. Frederick had come home ill, he complained of severe headache, and in reply to her anxious inquiries had told how the ranger had annoyed him, had in fact related the whole of the foregoing affair with the exception of one small item which he found it better to keep to himself. Margaret looked silently and sadly into the boiling water. She was used to hearing her son complain, but to-day he seemed more exhausted than ever before. Was he going to be ill? She sighed deeply and dropped the log of wood which she had just picked up.

"Mother," called Frederick from the bedroom. "What do you want?" "Was that a shot?" "Ah, no, I don't know what you mean." "It must be the throbbing in my head," he replied. A neighbour came in and related some insignificant gossip to which Margaret listened unmoved. Then she went.

"Mother," called Frederick. Margaret went to him. "What was she talking about?" "Oh, nothing, lies, gossip!" Frederick raised himself on his elbow. "About Grete Siemers: you know that old story; and there is nothing in it." Frederick lay down again. "I will try to sleep," he said.

Margaret sat by the fire; she was spinning, and her thoughts were not pleasant. In the village a clock struck half past twelve; the door opened and the magistrate's clerk came in.

"Good day, Frau Mergel," he said; "can you give me a drink of milk? I have just come from M." When Frau Mergel brought him what he desired, he asked, "Where is Frederick?" She was just busy fetching a plate, and missed his question. He drank slowly and in short gulps. "Do you know," he said at last, "that the Blue Blouses have laid a stretch of wood as bare as my hand again to-night?" "Oh, dear, dear!" she said unconcernedly. "The rascals ruin everything," went on the clerk; "if only they spared the young trees; but oak saplings not as thick as my arm, not even large enough for a rudder post! It seems as though they are as anxious to damage things for other people as to make profit for themselves."

"It is a pity," said Margaret. The clerk had finished his drink but made no move to go. He seemed to have something on his conscience. "Haven't you heard anything about Brandes?" he asked suddenly. "Nothing, he never comes into this house." "Then you don't know what has happened to him?" "No, what?" asked Margaret anxiously. "He is dead!" "Dead!" she cried, "what, dead? In God's name! he passed here only this morning with his gun slung across his back!" "He is dead," repeated the clerk, gazing sharply at her, "killed by the Blue Blouses. A quarter of an hour ago his body was brought back to the village."

Margaret beat her hands together, "God in Heaven, do not judge him! he did not know what he did!" "Him!" cried the clerk, "the accursed murderer do you mean?" From the bedroom came loud groans. Margaret rushed in and the clerk followed her. Frederick sat upright in bed, his face hidden in his hands, groaning like a dying man. "Frederick, what is it?" asked his mother. "What is it?" echoed the clerk. "Oh my head, my head!" he moaned. "What is the matter with him?" "God knows," she replied, "he brought the cows home before four o'clock because he felt so ill. Frederick, Frederick, tell me, shall I fetch the doctor?" "No, no," he whined, "it is nothing, it will soon be better."

He lay back; his face twitched convulsively with pain; then the colour returned to it. "Go," he said dully; "I must sleep, then it will be over."

"Frau Mergel," said the clerk earnestly; "is it certain that Frederick came home at four o'clock and did not go out again?" She stared at him. "Ask any child in the street. And go out again?—would to God he could!" "Did he say nothing about Brandes?" "Yes, in God's name, that Brandes abused him in the woods, and threw his poverty in his face, the ruffian! But God forgive me, he is dead! Go!" she added angrily, "have you come to insult honest poeple? Go!" She turned back to her son, the clerk went. "Frederick, what does it mean?" she asked, "did you hear? terrible, terrible, without confession or absolution!"

"Mother, mother, for God's sake let me sleep; I can't bear any more!"

At this moment John Nobody entered the bedroom; thin and tall like a hop-pole, but ragged and frightened just as he had been five years before. His face was even paler than usual. "Frederick," he said, "you are to come to uncle at once, he needs you; at once!" Frederick turned to the wall. "I am not coming," he said roughly, "I am ill." "But you must come," croaked John, "he said I must bring you."

Frederick laughed scornfully, "I'd like to see that!" "Leave him in peace," said Margaret, "he cannot, you can see for yourself." She went out for a few moments; when she returned, Frederick was already dressed. "What are you thinking of?" she said, "you cannot, you shall not go." "What must be, can be," he answered, and was already out of the house with John. "Ah, God," sighed the mother, "when our children are young, they trample our laps, when they are older, our hearts!"

The legal inquiry had begun, the deed was clear as daylight; but all signs of the murderer were so slight that, although everything pointed to the Blue Blouses, it was not possible to get beyond surmise. One clue seemed to give some light, though there were reasons why little notice was taken of it. The absence of the lord of the manor had made it necessary that the magistrate's clerk should begin proceedings himself. He sat at the table; the room was crowded with peasants, some just curious, others from whom it was hoped, failing actual witnesses, to get some information. Cowherds who had been out with their cattle that night, labourers working in near-by fields, they all stood firm and upright, hands in pockets, a silent declaration as it were that they had no intention of interfering.

Eight rangers were examined. Their evidence agreed exactly: Brandes had ordered them to meet him on the evening of the tenth to make a round of inspection, as he had received intelligence that the Blue Blouses would be out; but he had only spoken vaguely about it. At two in the morning they started and had come across many signs of destruction which had angered the head ranger very much; otherwise all was quiet. About four o'clock Brandes said: "We have been hoaxed, let us go home." As they turned back along the Bremerberg, and at the same time the wind shifted, they heard distinctly the sound of the axe in Mester Wood, and from the rapidity of the blows realized that the Blue Blouses were at work. They had consulted together whether with so small a number it was advisable to try an attack on the daring band, and then without coming to any decision had moved nearer to the sounds. Then followed the meeting with Frederick. Further: after Brandes had sent them on without definite orders, they crept forward for a while, and then, as they noticed that the noise, which had come from a great distance, had now ceased completely, they had stopped to wait for their leader. The delay had annoyed them, and after about ten minutes they had moved on to the scene of destruction. All was over, there was no sound in the forest, of twenty felled trees eight were still there, the others had already been removed. They could not understand how this had been managed as there were no signs of cart tracks.

And owing to the dryness of the season and the fact that the ground was covered with pine needles it had been impossible to distinguish any footprints, though the ground all around had been stamped hard. Deciding that it was useless to wait there for their leader, they had hurried to the other side of the wood in the hope of catching some glimpse of the miscreants. Here on the edge of the wood one of them had got entangled in the blackberry-bushes, and looking back to free himself had caught sight of something glittering in the undergrowth; it was the buckle on Brandes's belt, and he himself was lying in the undergrowth, his right hand on the barrel of his gun, the other clenched, and his head split open by the blow of an axe.

Such was the evidence of the rangers; now it was the turn of the peasants. Many asserted that at four o'clock they were busy at home or elsewhere, and they were all settled, trustworthy people. The court had to be satisfied with their negative evidence.

Frederick was called. He was quite unconcerned, and neither anxious nor impudent when he entered. The inquiry lasted a fairly long time, and a number of subtle questions were put to him; but he answered them all openly and precisely; and told of his encounter with the ranger fairly accurately, except the end, which he thought better to keep to himself. His alibi for the time of the murder was easily established.

The ranger had been murdered at the edge of the Mester Wood: more than three-quarters of an hour's walk from the ravine in which he had talked to Frederick at four o'clock, and from which the latter had driven his herd into the village ten minutes later. Everybody had seen this; all the peasants were sure of it and hastened to say so; he had spoken to this one, nodded to that.

The clerk sat there angry and perplexed. Suddenly he put his hand behind him and thrust something glittering before Frederick's eyes. "To whom does this belong?" Frederick sprang back. "Oh, God, I thought you were going to smash my skull." His eyes passed rapidly over the deadly weapon and seemed to hang for a moment on a splintered corner of the handle. "I do not know," he said firmly. It was the axe which had been found firmly embedded in the ranger's skull. "Look at it carefully," went on the clerk. Frederick took it in his hands, looked at it, turned it over, looked again. "It is just an axe like any other," he said then, and laid it unconcernedly on the table. A bloodstain was visible; he appeared to shudder, but he repeated very definitely, "I do not know it." The clerk sighed his displeasure. He knew of nothing more, and he had hoped by surprise to make some discovery. Nothing remained but to close the inquiry.

To those who are perhaps anxious to hear the result of this affair, I can only say that the mystery was never cleared up, though many further inquiries were held. The stir caused by this affair, and the tightening up of the precautions against the forest thieves which followed, seemed to have caused the Blue Blouses to lose their courage; from that time onward they disappeared, and although later many forest thieves were caught, there was never any reason for connecting them with the infamous band. Twenty years later the axe was still lying, a useless *corpus delicti*, in the archives, where it is probably still lying with its spots of rust. In a work of fiction it would not be right to impose thus upon the reader's curiosity. But all this really happened; I can add nothing to it nor take away.

The following Sunday Frederick got up very early to go to confession. It was the feast of the Assumption of the Virgin, and the priest was already in the confessional before daybreak.

After he had dressed himself in the dark, he went as noiselessly as possible out of the tiny cubicle which was given up to him in Simon's house.

His prayer-book must be lying on the sill in the kitchen, and he hoped to find it by the help of the weak moonlight; it was not there. He looked round for it, and shrank back in alarm; in the doorway stood Simon, almost undressed; his thin figure, his dishevelled hair and the ghastly whiteness of his face in the moonlight gave him a horribly changed appearance. "Is he walking in his sleep?" thought Frederick, and remained motionless. "Frederick, where are you going?" whispered the old man. "Uncle, is it you? I am going to confession." "I thought so; go, for God's sake, but confess like a good Christian." "I will," said Frederick. "Think of the ten commandments; thou shalt not bear witness against thy neighbour." "False witness." "No, none at all, you have been badly taught; he who accuses another in the confessional is unworthy to receive the sacrament."

Both were silent. "Uncle, what makes you say that?" asked Frederick at last; "your conscience is not clear, you have lied to me." "I? how?" "Where is your axe?" "My axe? In the loft." "Have you made a new handle for it? Where is the old one?" "You can find that by daylight in the wood house."

"Go," he added, contemptuously, "I thought you were a

man; but you are just an old woman, who thinks the house is on fire directly the stove smokes. Listen," he went on, "if I know more of the affair than this door-post, then may I be for ever accursed. I had been at home a long time," he added. Frederick stood there anxious and doubting. He would have given much to see his uncle's face, but while they whispered together the sky had become overcast.

"I have been very guilty," sighed Frederick, "in sending him the wrong way—though—I did not expect this—no, certainly not. Uncle, I have to thank you for a heavy load on my conscience." "Oh, go and confess," whispered Simon with quaking voice, "profane the sacrament with tale-bearing, and set poor people a spy on their trail, who will soon find the way to snatch the miserable crusts of bread from their teeth, even though he dares not speak—go!"

Frederick stood undecided: he heard a slight sound; the clouds drifted away, the moonlight fell again on the door of the kitchen: it was shut. That morning Frederick did not go to confession.

The impression which this encounter made on Frederick unfortunately was soon erased. Who doubts that Simon did all he could to guide his adopted son along the path he himself was going? And Frederick had attributes which made this only too easy: thoughtlessness, excitability, and above all an unbounded arrogance that did not always disdain pretence, and then staked all to make that pretence real, in order to avoid being shamed. By nature he was not ignoble, but he accustomed himself to prefer inner shame to outer disgrace. One can only say he got into the habit of showing off while his mother starved.

This unhappy change in his character was the work of several years, during which it was noticeable that Margaret grew more and more silent regarding her son, and sank slowly into a state of such complete demoralization as one would not have thought possible. She became suspicious, careless, even untidy, and many people thought that her head had suffered. Frederick became noisier and noisier; he never missed any festival or wedding, and as a very touchy sense of honour would not allow him to overlook the secret disapproval of those around him, he was continually prepared not only to bid defiance to public opinion, but also to lead it in the way he thought it should go. He was outwardly tidy, sober, and apparently faithful, but cunning, boastful, and often brutal, a being in whom nobody could take pleasure, least of 'all his mother, and who yet, owing to his dreaded audacity and still more dreaded malice, had won for himself a certain ascendancy in the village that was the more acknowledged as it grew more obvious that his real capabilities were not known. Only one youth in the village, Wilm Hülsmeyer, dared by knowledge of his strength and good circumstances to oppose him; and as he was quicker with his tongue than Frederick, and always knew how to turn defeat into a joke, he was the only one whom Frederick was not very willing to meet.

Four years had passed; it was October; the mild autumn of 1760, which filled every barn with corn and every cellar with wine, had flooded this corner of the earth with its riches also, and there was more drunkenness to be seen and more brawling and foolish pranks to be heard of than ever before. Amusement and pleasure reigned everywhere; holidays came into fashion, and whoever had a few pence to spare, wanted a wife at once, to-day to help him eat, to-morrow to help him starve. There was a hearty wedding in the village, at which the guests had more to look forward to than an out-of-tune fiddle, a glass of spirits, and the good humour they brought themselves. Everybody had been busy since dawn; in front of every house clothes were hung out to air, and the village looked the whole day like a jumble sale. As many outsiders were expected everybody was anxious to help to uphold the honour of the village.

It was seven o'clock in the evening, and the fun at its height; everywhere rejoicing and laughter, the low rooms full to suffocation with red, blue, and yellow figures, like a pound into which too big a herd has been driven. There was dancing on the threshing-floor, at least, those who had succeeded in getting two feet of room turned round and round on it and tried to make up by shouting what failed in movement. The orchestra was brilliant; the first fiddle, a recognized artist, overpowered the second and a large bass viol with three strings which were scraped ad libitum by amateurs; a super-abundance of spirits and coffee; all the guests streaming with sweat; in fact a wonderful fête.

Frederick, in a new blue coat, strutted about like a cock and asserted his rights as a beau. When the gentry arrived he was sitting behind the bass viol and played the deepest note with vigour and much feeling.

"John," he cried, peremptorily, and his protégé appeared from the dance-floor, where he had been attempting to swing his clumsy legs and shout with the rest. Frederick handed him the bow, gave him to understand his wishes with a proud movement of the head, and went back to the dance. "Now, merrily, musicians: Papen van Istrup!" The favourite dance was played, and Frederick leapt about in front of the gentry, so violently that the cows below drew back their horns and raised a noise of rattling chains and loud moos. His fair hair went up and down a head above the others, like a pike turning over and over in the water; all round were heard the shouts of the maidens he desired to honour by thrusting his long fair hair in their face with a quick movement of the head.

"That's enough!" he cried at last, and moved, the sweat dropping from him, over to the sideboard; "hurrah for our good master and all his family, and all the most noble princes and princesses, and who won't drink with me, I'll box his ears till he hears the angels singing!" A loud cheer greeted this gallant toast. Frederick made a bow—"No offence, ladies and gentlemen; we are only ignorant peasants!"

At this moment a tumult arose at the other end of the floor, shrieks, scolding, laughter, all together. "Butter thief! butter thief!" cried a few children, and there appeared, or rather was pushed forward, John Nobody, his head lowered, doing his utmost to reach the entrance. "What is it? What are you doing with our John?" cried Frederick peremptorily.

"You'll know that soon enough," croaked an old woman in a kitchen apron, with a dish-cloth in her hand. Shame! John, the poor creature, who had to put up with the worst of everything at home, had tried to lay in a pound of butter for the hard times ahead, and forgetting that he had wrapped it into his handkerchief and put it in his pocket, he had gone close to the kitchen fire, and now the fat was running ignominiously down his coat-tails.

General uproar; the maidens sprang aside, afraid of getting greasy, or pushed the delinquent on. Others made way out of pity or prudence. But Frederick stepped forward, "Scamp!" he cried, and gave his patient protégé several slaps in the face; then he pushed him to the door and gave him a vigorous kick to help him on his way. He came back depressed, his dignity was hurt, the general laughter cut him to the heart, and though he tried by vigorous shouting to set things going again he was not successful. He was just about to take refuge behind the bass viol again; but first one supreme effort—he drew out his silver watch, in those days a rare and costly ornament. "It is nearly ten," he said. "Now for the Bride's Minuet! I will play."

"A wonderful watch," said the swineherd, and thrust forward his face in reverent curiosity.

"What did it cost?" cried Wilm Hülsmeyer, Frederick's rival. "Do you want to pay for it?" asked Frederick. "Have you paid for it?" answered Wilm. Frederick threw him a haughty glance and picked up the bow in silent majesty. "Well, well," said Hülsmeyer, "one has heard of such things, you know; Fray Ebel had a beautiful watch too, until Aaron the Jew took it from him again." Frederick did not answer, but signed proudly to the first violin, and they began to play with all their might.

In the meantime the gentry had gone into the bedroom where the neighbours were binding the white scarf round the head of the bride as a sign of her new standing. The poor young thing cried bitterly, partly because it was the custom, partly from real depression. She was to take her place at the head of a muddled household, under the eyes of a surly old

man, whom she was expected to love. He stood beside her,
not in the least like the bridegroom of the Psalms who coming out of his chamber rejoiceth as a strong man to run a
race. "You have wept enough now," he said peevishly, "remember you are not expected to make me happy, I shall
make you happy!" She looked up at him submissively and
appeared to think he was right. The business was finished;
the young wife had drunk to her husband, some young wags
had looked through the tripod to see that the veil sat
straight, and everybody was pushing their way back to the
dancing-floor, whence came unceasing laughter and noise.
Frederick was no longer there. A great and unbearable insult had been offered him, for the Jew Aaron, a butcher and,
when occasion offered, second-hand dealer, from the next
town, had suddenly arrived, and after a short but unsatis-
factory private talk had dunned him before everybody for
the payment of ten talers due since the previous Easter for
his silver watch. Frederick had gone away like a ruined man,
the Jew following him and crying, "Oh alas! why did I not
listen to sensible people! They told me a hundred times
that you had all your possessions on your back, and no bread
in the cupboard!" The place shook with laughter; many had
followed into the yard. "Seize the Jew! weigh him against a
pig!" shouted some; others had become serious. "Frederick
looked as white as a sheet," said one old woman, and the
crowd parted as the gentry's carriage drove out of the yard.
On the way home Baron von S. was very depressed, the
usual result when his desire for popularity had caused him
to attend such a festivity. He looked morosely out of the
carriage. "What figures are those?" He pointed to two dark
shadows running in front of the carriage like ostriches. They
disappeared into the castle. "A pair from our own stall!" he
sighed. Arrived at home, he found the entire entrance hall
filled with servants gathered round two of the farm hands
who had sunk down pale and breathless on the stairs. They
declared that they had been followed by old Mergel's
ghost as they returned home through Breder Wood. First
there was a rustling and snapping above them; then high

in the air a clapping sound like two sticks beaten together; then suddenly a piercing scream, and quite distinctly the words, "Alas, my poor soul!" from high above them. One of them declared that he had seen glowing eyes shining through the branches, and both had run as fast as their legs would carry them.

"Rubbish," said the master crossly, and went into his room to change his clothes. The next morning the fountain in the garden would not play, and it was discovered that somebody had damaged a pipe, apparently in looking for the head of a horse which long years before had been buried there, and which was considered a sure safeguard against witches and ghosts. "Hm," said the master, "what rogues don't steal, fools spoil."

Three days later a fearful storm raged. It was midnight, but nobody in the castle had gone to bed. The master stood at the window and looked anxiously out into the darkness across his fields. Leaves and twigs blew past the window-panes; at times a tile fell and was smashed to pieces in the courtyard. "Terrible weather," said Baron von S. His wife looked nervous. "Are you certain that the fire is safe?" she said; "Grete, go and make quite sure, put it quite out! Let us read the Gospel of St. John." They all knelt down, and the housewife began to read:

"In the beginning was the Word, and the Word was with God, and the Word was God."—A terrible peal of thunder— they all started up; then a frightful scream and tumult on the stairs. "In God's name, is the house on fire?" cried Frau von S. and sank down with her face on the seat of her chair. The door was flung open and in rushed the wife of Aaron the Jew, white as death, her hair hanging wildly round her, dripping with rain. She threw herself on her knees before the master. "Justice!" she cried, "Justice! my husband has been murdered!" and fell in a dead faint.

It was only too true, and the inquiry which followed showed that Aaron the Jew had been killed by a single blow on the temple with a blunt instrument, probably a cudgel. Except the blue mark on the left temple there was no wound. The evidence of the Jewess and her servant, Samuel, was this: Three days before, Aaron had gone out in the afternoon to buy cattle, and had said that he would probably be away all night as there were several people in the villages of B. and S. whom he wanted to call on to collect money long owing. In that case he would spend the night with Salomon the butcher at B. When he did not return the next day his wife was very worried, and on the third day at three o'clock in the afternoon, accompanied by her servant and her dog, she had set out to look for him. Nobody knew anything of him at Salomon's, he had not been there at all. Then she went to all the peasants with whom she knew Aaron had business.

Only two of them had seen him, and both on the day on which he had left home. By this time it was growing late. Driven by terrible anxiety the woman turned homewards with some faint hope that her husband might be already there. In Breder Wood they were overtaken by the storm and had sought shelter under a great beech-tree on the hill-side; the dog had behaved strangely, and at last, in spite of every attempt to coax him back, had disappeared into the wood. Suddenly by a flash of lightning the woman saw something white lying beside her on the ground. It was her husband's staff, and almost at the same moment the dog burst through the undergrowth carrying something in his mouth; it was her husband's shoe. It was not long before they found the body of the Jew in a ditch, covered with dead leaves.

This was the account which the servant gave, backed up intermittently by the woman; the terrible tension had less-ened, and she seemed to be half crazy or rather stupid. "An eye for an eye, a tooth for a tooth," she said at intervals.

The same night orders were sent to the watchmen to arrest Frederick. No accusation was necessary, for the Baron S. had himself been an eyewitness of a scene which was bound to throw the deepest suspicion on him; added to that there was the ghost story of that evening, the clash of sticks in Breder Wood, the cry from the height. As the clerk was just

then absent, Herr von S. dealt with the affair more quickly
than would otherwise have happened. Nevertheless dawn
was beginning to appear before the watchmen had managed, as noiselessly as possible, to surround poor Margaret's
house. The Baron himself knocked; hardly a moment passed
before the door was opened and Margaret appeared, fully
clothed. Herr von S. was startled, he hardly recognized her,
she looked so pale and stony. "Where is Frederick?" he asked
with unsteady voice.

"Seek him," she replied, and sat down on a chair. The
Baron hesitated an instant longer.

"Come in, come in!" he said then, brusquely; "what are we
waiting for?" They entered Frederick's room. He was not
there, but the bed was still warm. They went up into the
loft, down into the cellar, prodded the hay, looked behind
every barrel, and even into the oven: he was not there. Some
went into the garden, looked behind the fence and up into
the apple-trees: he was not to be found.

"Got away!" said the master, with very mixed feelings; the
sight of the old woman had affected him very much. "Give
me the key to that box!" Margaret did not answer. "Give me
the key!" repeated the master, and then noticed that it was
sticking in the lock. The contents of the box were emptied
out: the fugitive's best clothes, and his mother's poor finery,
then two shrouds with black ribbons, one for a man and one
for a woman. Baron von S. was deeply touched. Right at the
bottom of the box lay the silver watch, and a few letters in
a very clear hand, one signed by a man who was under
strong suspicion of being connected with the Blue Blouses.
The Baron took them with him to look through, and they
all left the house, Margaret all the time giving no other
sign of life than an incessant biting of the lips and twitching
of the eyelids.

When he reached the castle the Baron found his clerk
there. The latter had reached home the previous evening,
and declared that, as his master had not sent for him, he had
slept through the whole affair.

"You are always too late," said the Baron angrily. "Wasn't

there a single old woman in the village to tell the story to your maid? and why did nobody call you?" "Sir," replied Kapp, "certainly Anne Marie heard of the affair an hour before I did; but she knew that Your Excellency was managing the business yourself, and also," he added in a plaintive tone, "I was dead tired." "Pretty police!" murmured the master, "all the old women in the village know all about everything which should be kept absolutely secret." Then he added vehemently: "He must be a silly fool of a criminal who manages to get caught!"

Both were silent awhile. "My coachman lost his way in the darkness," began the clerk presently; "we had to halt over an hour in the wood, it was an awful storm; I thought the wind would blow the carriage over. At last, when the rain ceased, we drove on, straight ahead, unable to see a hand before our face. Then the coachman said, 'If only we don't get too near the quarry!' I was terrified myself; I ordered a halt and struck a light that at least I might have the comfort of my pipe. Suddenly we heard, nearly perpendicularly below us, the clock strike. Your Excellency can imagine what I felt like. I jumped out of the carriage, for one can trust one's own legs but not those of a horse. So I stood, in mud and rain, without daring to move, until, thank God, daylight shortly began to appear. And where were we? Close to Heerser Cliff, and the tower of Heerser church was just below us. Another twenty steps and we should all have been killed." "That was certainly no joke," said the Baron, half appeased.

He had in the meantime looked through the papers he had brought with him. They were dunning letters about borrowed money, mostly from money-lenders. "I did not think," he murmured, "that the Mergels were in so deeply." "Yes, and that it must all be exposed," added Kapp, "that will be a bitter pill for Margaret to swallow." "Ah, good God! she isn't thinking of that now!" With these words the master got up and left the room with Kapp in order to view the body. The investigation was short, the verdict, death by violence, the probable murderer fled; the proof against him certainly strong, but not demonstrable without personal confession, his flight very suspicious. So the judicial proceedings were closed for lack of evidence.

The Jews of the neighbourhood had shown great interest; the widow's house was always full of mourners and counsellors.

No one could remember having seen so many Jews in L.

Much embittered by the murder of their fellow believer, they spared neither trouble nor money to find the murderer. It was known that one of them offered to one of his customers, whose debt ran into hundreds, and whom he thought a particularly astute person, to cancel his entire debt if he would help to get Mergel arrested; for the belief was widespread amongst the Jews that the murderer had only escaped with the help of good friends, and was probably still in the neighbourhood. But when nothing was any use, and the judicial proceedings were declared closed, on the following morning there appeared at the castle a number of the most respected Jews to arrange a deal with the master. Their object was the beech-tree under which Aaron's stick was found and where the murder had probably taken place. "Do you want to cut it down? Now in full leaf?" asked the master.

"No, Your Excellency, it must stand, summer and winter, as long as a chip of it remains." "But if I cut down that wood, then it will damage the new growth." "We are prepared to give much more than the ordinary price." They offered 200 talers. The deal was closed, and all the rangers strongly enjoined on no account to damage the Jews' Beech.

In the evening a procession of at least sixty Jews, their Rabbis at the head, all silent and with downcast eyes, was seen to make its way to Breder Wood.

They remained more than an hour in the wood, and then came solemnly and silently back, through the village of B. to the Zellerfelde, where they separated, each going his own way.

The next morning a Jewish inscription was found cut into the trunk with an axe.

And where was Frederick? Gone, without doubt, far enough to be out of reach of the short arm of so weak a police. He had soon been forgotten. Simon rarely spoke of him, and then badly; the Jewess comforted herself and took another husband. Only poor Margaret remained unconsoled.

Some six months later the Baron read aloud to his clerk a letter which he had just received. "Strange, strange!" he said. "Think, Kapp, Mergel was perhaps not guilty of murder. Here is a letter from the presiding judge at P. 'Le vrai n'est pas toujours vraisemblable'; I have often noticed that in my calling, and again quite recently. Do you know that your faithful Frederick Mergel was perhaps as innocent of murdering the Jew as you or I? Unfortunately there is no proof, but the likelihood is great. A member of the Schlemming Band (who by the way are nearly all under lock and key) named Moses, said at the last trial that he repented of nothing so much as the murder of a fellow believer, Aaron, whom he had killed in a wood, and then found only sixpence on the body. Unfortunately the court adjourned then for lunch, and while we were at table, the dog of a Jew hung himself with one of his own garters. What do you say to that? Aaron is certainly a common Jewish name, &c."

"What do you say to that?" repeated the Baron, "and why did the silly fellow run away?"

The clerk thought the matter over. "Well, it might have been because of an affair in the wood which we have just been investigating. Isn't there a saying, a 'wicked man runs away from his own shadow'? Mergel's conscience was black enough without that extra spot."

And that was all. Frederick gone, disappeared, and—John Nobody, the poor, unnoticed John, disappeared at the same time.

A long time passed, twenty-eight years, almost the half of a lifetime: the Baron had grown old and grey, his good-natured assistant Kapp was long in his grave. Men, animals, plants had been born, grown up, died; only the castle remained the same, grey and distinguished, looking down upon the huts which resembled old, suffering people, just about to fall down but still standing.

It was Christmas Eve, 1788.

Deep snow lay in the defiles, a good twelve foot high, and the bitter wind froze the windows of the warm rooms. It was nearly midnight, but pale lights shone out everywhere above the snow, and in every house the inhabitants were kneeling to welcome the beginning of Christmas Day by prayer, as is the custom in all Catholic countries, or was, at least, in those days. From Breder Wood a figure emerged and began to make its way slowly towards the village; the wayfarer seemed very weak or ill; he groaned heavily, and dragged himself with great trouble through the snow.

Halfway down the hill-side he stood still, leaned upon his staff, and gazed steadfastly at the lights. It was so quiet everywhere, so dead and cold; one was reminded of will-o'-the-wisps in churchyards. The clock in the church tower struck twelve, the last stroke faded slowly away and in the nearest house quiet singing began, swelling from house to house through the whole village:

> A child so dear
> Is born to us to-day
> Of a Virgin pure
> That joy be ours alway.
> And had that child not been born
> Then were we all together forlorn,
> Salvation is for all.
> O, Jesus Christ, my own dear love,
> Who came as man from heaven above,
> Redeem thou us from hell!

The man on the hill-side had fallen on his knees and tried with trembling voice to join in; but nothing came but loud sobs, and heavy, hot tears fell in the snow. The second verse began; he murmured the words; then the third and the fourth. The carol was ended, and the lights in the houses began to move. Then the man got up wearily and crept slowly down into the village. He crept past several houses, then he stopped in front of a door and knocked gently.

"What is that?" said a woman's voice within; "the door is rattling and there is no wind." He knocked louder—"In God's name let a poor half-frozen man in, who comes from Turkish slavery!"—Whispering in the kitchen. "Go to the inn," said another voice, "the fifth house from here." "For the mercy of God, let me in, I have no money."

After some hesitation the door was opened, and a man with a lamp looked out. "Come in," he said at last, "you won't cut our throats."

In the kitchen, beside the man, there were a middle-aged woman, an old woman, and five children. They all crowded round the new-comer, and surveyed him with shy curiosity. A wretched figure! With wry neck and crooked back, the whole figure broken and wasted; long, snow-white hair hung round his face, which had the drawn expression of one who has suffered much and long. The woman went silently to the fire and added fresh fuel. "We can't give you a bed," she said, "but I will lay some fresh straw for you here; you must do the best you can with that." "May God reward you," answered the stranger, "I am used to much worse." The returned wanderer was recognized as John Nobody, and he confirmed the fact that he was the same John who had once fled with Frederick Mergel.

The next day the village was full of the adventures of the long-missing man.

Everybody wanted to see the man who had come back from Turkey, and they were almost astonished that he looked like other men. The young people had certainly no remembrance of him, but the older ones recognized him quite easily, pitiably changed though he was.

"John, John, how grey you are!" said one old woman. "And how did you get a wry neck?" "From wood and water carrying as a slave," he replied.

"And what happened to Mergel? Surely you both went away together?"

"Certainly, but I don't know where he is; we got separated. When you think of him, say a prayer for him," he added, "he will need it."

People inquired why Frederick had fled when he had

not killed the Jew after all. "Not?" said John, and listened eagerly while they related what the Baron had told them in order to clear Frederick's name. "Then it was all for nothing," he said thoughtfully, "all for nothing, all that suffering!" He sighed deeply, and began to ask about many things. Simon was long dead, but first he had been reduced to complete poverty, through lawsuits and bad debtors whom he dared not bring to justice because the business between them would not stand the light of day.

He had finally been reduced to begging, and had died on the straw in a stranger's shed. Margaret had lived longer, but completely imbecile.

The villagers had got tired of helping her, as she allowed everything they gave her to be ruined; but that is the way of people, to neglect the most helpless, those who are always in need of help because they cannot help themselves. Nevertheless she had never been in actual need; the people at the castle looked after her, sending her some dinner every day, and when her wretched condition became complete emaciation, they sent her medical help. The son of the swineherd who on that ill-fated evening had admired Frederick's silver watch now lived in her house. "All gone, all dead!" sighed John.

In the evening as it grew dark and the moon rose, he was seen moving about the churchyard; he did not pray by any grave, did not even go close to any, but he seemed to stare fixedly at certain ones from a distance. There he was found by Brandes, the ranger, the son of the murdered man, who had been sent by his master to fetch him to the castle.

On entering the living room he looked shyly round, as though dazzled by the light, and then at the Baron, who sat huddled up in an armchair, but still with the bright eyes, and still wearing a little red cap on his head as twenty-eight years before; beside him sat his wife, also grown old, very old.

"Now, John," said the Baron, "give me a good account of all your adventures. But," he looked at him through his glasses, "they did make a wreck of you in Turkey."

John began: how Mergel had called him away from the

fire at night, and said he must go away with him. "But why did the silly boy run away? You know that he was innocent?" John looked down: "I don't really know, but I think it was because of trouble in the woods. Simon had so many things on hand; nobody said anything to me about them, but I think things were not all as they should be." "What did Frederick tell you?" "Nothing but that we must get away, they were after us. So we ran as far as Heerser; there it was still dark, and we hid behind the big crucifix in the churchyard till it grew lighter, because we were afraid of the stone-quarries at Zellerfelde; and when we had sat there awhile we suddenly heard snorting and stamping above us, and saw long rays of light in the air right above Heerser church tower. We jumped up and ran as fast as we could, straight ahead, and when daylight came we actually found ourselves on the road to P."

John shuddered at the remembrance, and the Baron though of the dead Kapp and his adventure on the Heerser Cliff.

"Strange," he laughed, "you were so near one another! but go on!"

John related how they reached P. and were lucky enough to get over the frontier.

From there they had begged their way as wandering artisans as far as Freiburg in Breisgau. "I had my bread-bag," he said, "and Frederick a small bundle, so people believed us." In Freiburg they had been recruited by the Austrians; he had not been wanted, but Frederick insisted that he be taken as well. So he began his training. "We stayed in Freiburg that winter," he went on, "and it was not too bad, even for me, for Frederick often remembered me and helped me when I did anything stupid. In the spring we marched away to Hungary, and in the autumn the war with Turkey began. I do not know much about it, for I was taken prisoner in the first engagement, and since then have been for twenty-six years a Turkish slave!" "Dear God, that is dreadful," said the Baron's wife.—"Bad enough, for the Turks treated us Christians like dogs; the worst was that the hard work took away my strength; also I grew older, and yet was expected to do as much as in earlier days."

He was silent awhile.

"Yes," he said then, "it was more than human strength or patience could stand; I could not go on. From there I got aboard a Dutch ship." "How did you manage to do that?" asked the Baron. "They fished me out of the Bosporus," answered John. The Baron looked at him with surprise and raised a warning finger; but John went on with his story.

"On the ship things were not much better. There was an outbreak of scurvy; those who were not absolutely helpless had to work beyond their strength, and the power of the ship's rope was as great as that of the Turkish whip.

"At last," he said, "when we reached Amsterdam, Holland, I was allowed to go free because I was of no use, and the merchant to whom the ship belonged took pity on me and wanted to give me a job as a porter. But"—he shook his head —"I preferred to beg my way back here." "That was silly enough," said the Baron. "Oh, sir, I have spent my life amongst Turks and heretics, might I not at least lay my bones in a Catholic churchyard?" The Baron drew out his purse, "There John, now go, but come again soon. You must tell me all in greater detail; to-day it was rather confused.

"You are still very tired?" "Very tired," answered John, "and," here he pointed to his forehead, "my thoughts are sometimes so strange, I don't quite know what it is." "I know, from old days," said the Baron. "Now go. Hülsmeyer will put you up to-night; come again to-morrow."

Baron von S. felt the deepest sympathy for the poor creature; by the next day it had been arranged where he could be lodged; he was to have his food at the castle, and clothes could also be found. "Sir," said John, "I can still do some work; I can make wooden spoons, and you can use me to carry messages."

Baron von S. shook his head pityingly. "You won't manage that very well." "Oh, yes, sir, when I am once in the way of it—I can't go quickly, but I shall get there, and it won't be as bitter to me as one might think." "Well," said the Baron, doubtfully, "would you like to try? Here is a letter to be taken to P. There is no particular hurry."

The next day John took possession of a small room in the house of a widow in the village.

He carved spoons, had his meals at the castle, and went errands for the Baron. On the whole things went well with him; his master was kind and often talked with him about Turkey, the Austrian service, and the sea.

"John could tell wonderful stories," he said to his wife, "if he were not so weak-minded." "Rather melancholy than weak-minded," she replied, "I am always afraid he will go mad." "Oh, nonsense," answered the Baron, "he was always half-witted; half-wits never go mad."

Some time later John took an unusually long time on one of his errands. The good Frau von S. was very worried about him and was just sending out to search for him when he was heard stumbling up the stairs.

"You have been a long time, John," she said, "I thought you must have got lost in Breder Wood."

"I came through the pine wood."

"That is a long way round; why didn't you come through Breder Wood?"

He looked up sadly: "I was told that the wood had been cut down, and now there are many side paths there so I was afraid of not finding my way out again. I am getting old and silly," he added slowly. "Did you see," said Frau von S. later to her husband, "what a strange look there was in his eyes? I tell you, Ernst, he will come to a sad end."

September was drawing near. The fields were bare, the leaves began to fall, and many began to feel that the scissors were nearing the thread of their lives. John also seemed to be suffering under the influence of the approaching equinox: those who saw him in those days said he looked noticeably troubled, and talked to himself incessantly, a thing which he had done but seldom. Finally he failed to return home one night. It was thought that perhaps the Baron had sent him rather far; the second night he did not return, on the third day his landlady grew anxious. She went to the castle and made inquiries. "God forbid," said the Baron, "I know nothing of him; but call the hunters at once and William the ranger! If the poor cripple has only fallen into a dry ditch he would be unable to get out again. Who knows if he has not perhaps broken one of his bent legs. Take the dogs," he called to the departing hunters, "and look carefully in the ditches, and in the stone-quarry," he added louder.

The hunters returned several hours later; they had found no sign of John. The Baron was very troubled: "When I think that he might be lying like a stone, and unable to help himself! But he may still be alive; a man can live for three days without food." He set out himself to search; questions were asked at every house, horns were blown everywhere, the dogs were urged on to seek—all in vain! A child had seen him sitting at the edge of Breder Wood, carving a spoon; "but he cut it right in two," said the little girl. That was two days earlier. In the afternoon there was another clue; again a child, who had seen him on the opposite side of Breder Wood, sitting with his face on his knees, as though asleep. That was yesterday. It seemed as though he had wandered about all the time in Breder Wood.

"If only this wretched undergrowth were not so thick! One cannot get through it," said the Baron. The dogs were driven into the young growth; they blew and shouted and at last returned dissatisfied home, when they had convinced themselves that the whole wood had been searched. "Go on! go on!" begged Frau von S., "rather a few unnecessary steps than something missed." The Baron was almost as anxious as she was. His uneasiness even drove him to John's lodging, though he was certain of not finding him there. He had the room opened. The bed was unmade, just as he had left it, his best coat, which Frau von S. had had made out of an old coat of her husband's, hung behind the door: on the table were a bowl, six new wooden spoons, and a box.

The Baron opened it; it contained five groschen neatly wrapped in paper, and four silver waistcoat buttons; the Baron looked at them carefully. "A souvenir of Mergel," he murmured, and went out, for he felt quite cramped in the stuffy little room.

The search went on until it was quite certain that John was no longer in the district, at least not alive.

So for the second time he had disappeared: would he ever be found again—perhaps in years to come his bones in some dry ditch? There was little hope of seeing him again alive, and certainly not after another twenty-eight years.

One morning a fortnight later young Brandes was returning through Breder Wood from that part of the forest under his charge. It was, for the time of year, an exceptionally hot day; the air shimmered, no birds were singing, only the ravens croaked in a bored manner from the branches, and held their beaks open towards the wind. Brandes was very tired. First he took off his cap, which was heated through by the sun, then he put it on again. Both ways it was unbearable. Forcing his way through the knee-high undergrowth was difficult. No tree near except the Jews' Beech. Towards that he pushed his way and dropped tired out in the mossy shade beneath it. The coolness was so pleasant to his limbs that he closed his eyes.

"Disgusting toadstools!" he murmured, half asleep. In that district there are certain juicy toadstools which stand for a few days, then rot and give forth an unsupportable stench. Brandes thought he noticed some of these near him; he turned from side to side but did not want to get up; his dog, in the meantime, was very restless, scratched at the trunk of the tree, and barked up into the branches. "What is it, Bello? a cat?" murmured Brandes. He half opened his eyes and saw the Jewish inscription just above him, much overgrown, but still quite recognizable. He shut his eyes again; the dog continued to bark, and finally pushed his cold muzzle into his master's face.

"Leave me in peace! what is the matter?" At that instant Brandes, lying on his back, looked up into the branches overhead, and with one movement sprang to his feet and fled like one possessed into the undergrowth.

He was deadly pale when he reached the castle: a man

was hanging in the Jews' Beech; he had seen the legs hanging right above his face. "And you did not cut him down, you ass?" shouted the Baron.

"Sir," croaked Brandes, "if Your Excellency had been there, you would have known that the man was no longer alive. I thought at first it was the toadstools!" Nevertheless the Baron urged them to hasten and went out with them.

They reached the beech. "I see nothing," said the Baron. "You must come here, here, on this spot!" So that was it: the Baron recognized his own old shoes.

"God, it is John!—Put up the ladder! so—now down!—careful, careful, don't let him fall!—Dear heaven, the worms have begun! But undo the noose, and the cravat." A broad scar was visible; the Baron started back.

"My God!" he said; he bent again over the corpse, looked at the scar very carefully, and then remained silent, deeply shaken.

Then he turned to the ranger: "It is not right that the innocent should suffer for the guilty; tell everybody: this"—he pointed to the corpse—"was Frederick Mergel."

The body was buried in the carrion pit. In their main details these events really occurred in September of the year 1788.

The Jewish inscription on the tree ran:

"When thou approachest this place, thou shalt do to thyself what thou didst do to me."

GODS IN EXILE[1]

HEINRICH HEINE

(1797-1856)

I MEAN to tell of that metamorphosis into demons which
the Greek and Roman gods underwent when Christianity
achieved supreme control of the world. The superstition of
the people ascribed to those gods a real but cursed existence, coinciding entirely in this respect with the teaching of
the Church. The latter by no means declared the ancient
gods to be myths, inventions of falsehood and error, as did
the philosophers, but held them to be evil spirits, who,
through the victory of Christ, had been hurled from the
summit of their power, and now dragged along their miserable existences in the obscurity of dismantled temples or
in enchanted groves, and by their diabolic arts, through
lust and beauty, particularly through dancing and singing,
lured to apostasy unsteadfast Christians who had lost their
way in the forest . . . I will remind the reader that the per-
plexities into which the poor old gods fell at the time of the
final triumph of Christendom—that is, in the third century
—offer striking analogies to former sorrowful events in their
god-lives; for they found themselves plunged into the same
sad predicament in which they had once before been
placed in that most ancient time, in that revolutionary
epoch when the Titans broke loose from their confinement
in Orcus and, piling Pelion on Ossa, scaled high Olympus.
At that time the poor gods were compelled to flee ignominiously and conceal themselves under various disguises on
earth. Most of them repaired to Egypt, where, as is well
known, for greater safety, they assumed the forms of ani-

[1] Translated by M. Fleishman.

mals. And in a like manner, when the true Lord of the universe planted the banner of the cross on the heavenly heights, and those iconoclastic zealots, the black band of monks, hunted down the gods with fire and malediction and razed their temples, then these unfortunate heathen divinities were again compelled to take to flight, seeking safety under the most varied disguises and in the most retired hiding-places. Many of these poor refugees, deprived of shelter and ambrosia, were now forced to work at some plebeian trade in order to earn a livelihood. Under these circumstances several, whose shrines had been confiscated, became wood-choppers and day-laborers in Germany, and were compelled to drink beer instead of nectar. It appears that Apollo was reduced to this dire plight, and stooped so low as to accept service with cattle-breeders, and as once before he had tended the cows of Admetus, so now he lived as a shepherd in Lower Austria. Here, however, he aroused suspicion through the marvelous sweetness of his singing, and, being recognized by a learned monk as one of the ancient magic-working heathen gods, he was delivered over to the ecclesiastical courts. On the rack he confessed that he was the god Apollo. Before his execution he begged that he might be permitted for the last time to play the zither and sing to its accompaniment. But he played so touchingly and sang so enchantingly, and was so handsome in face and form, that all the women wept; and many of them indeed afterwards sickened. After some lapse of time, it was decided to remove his body from the grave under the impression that he was a vampire, and impale it upon a stake, this being an approved domestic remedy certain to effect the cure of the sick women; but the grave was found empty.

I have but little to communicate concerning the fate of Mars, the ancient god of war. I am not disinclined to believe that during the feudal ages he availed himself of the then prevailing doctrine that might makes right. Lank Schimmelpennig, nephew of the executioner of Münster, once met Mars at Bologna, and conversed with him. Shortly before he had served as a peasant under Froudsberg, and was present at the storming of Rome. Bitter thoughts must have filled his breast when he saw his ancient, favorite city, and the temples wherein he and his brother gods had been so revered, now ignominiously laid waste.

Better than either Mars or Apollo fared the god Bacchus at the great stampede, and the legends relate the following: —In Tyrol there are very large lakes, surrounded by magnificent trees that are mirrored in the blue waters. Trees and water murmur so that one experiences strange feelings of awe when one wanders there alone. On the bank of such a lake stood the hut of a young fisherman, who lived by fishing, and who also acted as ferryman to any travelers who wished to cross the lake. He had a large boat, that was fastened to the trunk of an old tree not far from his dwelling. Here he lived quite alone. Once, about the time of the autumnal equinox, towards midnight, he heard a knocking at his window, and on opening the door he saw three monks, with their heads deeply muffled in their cowls, who seemed to be in great haste. One of them hurriedly asked him for the boat, promising to return it within a few hours. The monks were three, and the fisherman could not hesitate; so he unfastened the boat, and when they had embarked and departed, he went back to his hut and lay down. He was young, and soon fell asleep; but in a few hours he was awakened by the returning monks. When he went out to them, one of them pressed a silver coin into his hand, and then all three hastened away. The fisherman went to look at his boat, which he found made fast. Then he shivered, but not from the night-air. A peculiarly chilling sensation had passed through his limbs, and his heart seemed almost frozen, when the monk who paid the fare touched his hand; the monk's fingers were cold as ice. For some days the fisherman could not forget this circumstance; but youth will soon shake off mysterious influences, and the fisherman thought no more of the occurrence until the following year, when, again just at the time of the autumnal equinoxes, towards midnight, there was a knocking at the window of the hut, and again the three cowled monks appeared, and again demanded the boat. The fisherman delivered up the boat with less anxiety this time, but when after a few hours they returned, and one of the monks again hastily pressed a coin into his hand, he again shuddered at the touch of the icy cold fingers. This happened every year at the same time and in the same manner. At last, as the seventh year drew near, an irresistible desire seized on the fisherman to learn, at all costs, the secret that was hidden under these three cowls. He piled a mass of nets into the boat, so as to form a hiding-place into which he could slip while the monks were preparing to embark. The somber expected travelers came at the accustomed time, and the fisherman succeeded in hiding himself under the nets unobserved. To his astonishment, the voyage lasted but a short time, whereas it usually took him over an hour to reach the opposite shore; and greater yet was his surprise when here, in a locality with which he had been quite familiar, he beheld a wide forest-glade which he had never before seen, and which was covered with flowers that, to him, were of quite strange kind. Innumerable lamps hung from the trees, and vases filled with blazing rosin stood on high pedestals; the moon, too, was so bright that the fisherman could see all that took place, as distinctly as if it had been mid-day. There were many hundreds of young men and young women, most of them beautiful as pictures, although their faces were all as white as marble, and this circumstance, together with their garments, which consisted of white, very white tunics with purple borders, girt up, gave them the appearance of moving statues. The women wore on their heads wreaths of vine leaves, either natural or wrought of gold and silver, and their hair was partly plaited over the brow into the shape of a crown, and partly fell in wild locks on their necks. The young men also wore wreaths of vine-leaves. Both men and women swinging in their hands golden staffs covered with vine leaves, hastened joyously to greet the newcomers One of the latter threw aside his cowl, revealing an impertinent fellow of middle age, with a repulsive, libidinous face, and pointed goat-ears, and scandalously extravagant sex·

uality. The second monk also threw aside his cowl, and there came to view a big-bellied fellow, not less naked, whose bald pate the mischievous women crowned with a wreath of roses. The faces of the two monks, like those of the rest of the assemblage, were white as snow. White as snow also was the face of the third monk, who laughingly brushed the cowl from his head. As he unbound the girdle of his robe, and with a gesture of disgust flung off from him the pious and dirty garment, together with crucifix and rosary, lo! there stood, robed in a tunic brilliant as a diamond, a marvelously beautiful youth with a form of noble symmetry, save that there was something feminine in the rounded hips and the slender waist. His delicately curved lips, also, and soft, mobile features gave him a somewhat feminine appearance; but his face expressed also a certain daring, almost reckless heroism. The women caressed him with wild enthusiasm, placed an ivy-wreath upon his head, and threw a magnificent leopard-skin over his shoulders. At this moment came swiftly dashing along, drawn by two lions, a golden two-wheeled triumphal chariot. Majestically, yet with a merry glance, the youth leaped on the chariot, guiding the wild steeds with purple reins. At the right of the chariot strode one of his uncassocked companions, whose lewd gestures and unseemly form delighted the beholders, while his comrade, with the bald pate and fat paunch, whom the merry women had placed on an ass, rode at the left of the chariot, carrying in his hand a golden drinking-cup, which was constantly refilled with wine. On moved the chariot, and behind it whirled the romping, dancing, vine-crowned men and women. At the head of the triumphal procession marched the orchestra; the pretty, chubby-cheeked youth, playing the double flute; then the nymph with the high-girt tunic, striking the jingling tambourine with her knuckles; then the equally gracious beauty, with the triangle; then the goat-footed trumpeters, with handsome but lascivious faces, who blew their fanfares on curious sea-shells and fantastically shaped horns; then the lute players.

But, dear reader, I forgot that you are a most cultured and well-informed reader, and have long since observed that I have been describing a Bacchanalia and a feast of Dionysus. You have often seen on ancient bas-reliefs, or in the engravings of archæological works, pictures of the triumphal processions held in honor of the god Bacchus; and surely, with your cultivated and classic tastes, you would not be frightened even if at dead of night, in the depths of a lonely forest, the lonely specters of such a Bacchanalian procession, together with the customary tipsy *personnel,* should appear bodily before your eyes. At the most you would only give way to a slight voluptuous shudder, an æsthetic awe, at sight of this pale assemblage of graceful phantoms, who have risen from their monumental sarcophagi, or from their hiding-places amid the ruins of ancient temples, to perform once more their ancient, joyous, divine service; once more, with sport and merry-making, to celebrate the triumphal march of the divine liberator, the Savior of the senses; to dance once more the merry dance of paganism, the *can-can* of the antique world—to dance it without any hypocritical disguise, without fear of the interference of the police of a spiritualistic morality, with the wild abandonment of the old days, shouting, exulting, rapturous. Evoe Bacche!

But alas, dear reader, the poor fisherman was not, like yourself, versed in mythology; he had never made archæological studies; and terror and fear seized upon him when he beheld the Triumphator and his two wonderful acolytes emerge from their monks' garb. He shuddered at the immodest gestures and leaps of the Bacchantes, Fauns, and Satyrs, who, with their goats' feet and horns, seemed to him peculiarly diabolical, and he regarded the whole assemblage as a congress of specters and demons, who were seeking by their mysterious rites to bring ruin on all Christians. His hair stood on end at sight of the reckless impossible posture of a Mænad, who, with flowing hair and head thrown back, only balanced herself by the weight of her thyrsus. His own brain seemed to reel as he saw the Corybantes in mad frenzy wounding their own bodies with short swords, seeking voluptuousness in pain itself. The soft and tender, yet so terrible, tones of the music seemed to penetrate to his very soul, like a burning, consuming, excruciating flame. But when he saw that defamed Egyptian symbol of exaggerated size and crowned with flowers, borne upon a tall pole by an unashamed woman, then sight and hearing forsook the poor fisherman—and he darted back to the boat, and crept under the nets, with chattering teeth and trembling limbs, as though Satan already held him fast by the foot. Soon after, the three monks also returned to the boat and shoved off. When they had disembarked at the original starting-place, the fisherman managed to escape unobserved from his hiding-place, so that they supposed he had merely been behind the willows awaiting their return. One of the monks, as usual, with icy-cold fingers pressed the fare into the fisherman's hand, then all three hurried away.

For the salvation of his own soul, which he believed to be endangered, and also to guard other good Christians from ruin, the fisherman held it his duty to communicate a full account of the mysterious occurrence to the Church authorities; and as the superior of a neighboring Franciscan monastery was in great repute as a learned exorcist, the fisherman determined to go to him without delay. The rising sun found him on his way to the monastery, where, with modest demeanor, he soon stood before his excellency the superior, who received him seated in an easy-chair in the library, and with hood drawn closely over his face, listened meditatively while the fisherman told his tale of horror. When the recital was finished, the superior raised his head, and as the hood fell back, the fisherman saw, to his dismay, that his excellency was one of the three monks who annually sailed over the lake—the very one, indeed, whom he had the previous night seen as a heathen demon riding in the golden chariot drawn by lions. It was the same marble-white face, the same regular, beautiful features, the same mouth with its delicately curved lips. And these lips now wore a kindly smile, and from that mouth now issued the gracious and melodious words, "Beloved son in Christ, we willingly believe that you have spent the night in company of the god Bacchus. Your fantastic ghost story gives ample proof of that. Not that we would say aught unpleasant of this god: at times he is undoubtedly a care-dispeller, and gladdens the heart of man. But he is very dangerous for those who cannot bear much; and to this class you seem to belong. We advise you to partake in future very sparingly of the golden juice of the grape, and not again to trouble the spiritual authorities with the fantasies of a drunken brain. Concerning this last vision of yours, you had better keep a very quiet tongue in your head; otherwise the secular arm of our beadle shall measure out to you twenty-five lashes. And now, beloved son in Christ, go to the kitchen, where brother butler and brother cook will set before you a slight repast."

With this, the reverend father bestowed the customary benediction on the fisherman, and when the latter, bewildered, took himself off to the kitchen and suddenly came face to face with brother cook and brother butler, he almost fell to the earth in affright, for they were the same monks who had accompanied the superior on his midnight excursions across the lake. He recognized one by his fat paunch and bald head, and the other by his lascivious grin and goat-ears. But he held his tongue, and only in later years did he relate his strange story.

Several old chronicles which contain similar legends locate the scene near the city of Speyer, on the Rhine.

Along the coast of East Friesland an analogous tradition is found, in which the ancient conception of the transportation of the dead to the realm of Hades, which underlies all those legends, is most distinctly seen. It is true that none of them contain any mention of Charon, the steersman of the boat: this old fellow seems to have entirely disappeared from folk-lore, and is to be met with only in puppet-shows. But a far more notable mythological personage is to be recognized in the so-called forwarding agent, or dispatcher, who makes arrangements for the transportation of the dead, and pays the customary passage-money into the hands of the boatman; the latter is generally a common fisherman, who officiates as Charon. Notwithstanding his quaint disguise, the true name of this dispatcher may readily be guessed, and I shall therefore relate the legend as faithfully as possible.

The shores of East Friesland that border on the North Sea abound with bays, which are used as harbors, and are called fiords. On the farthest projecting promontory of land generally stands the solitary hut of some fisherman, who here lives, peaceful and contented, with his family. Here nature wears a sad and melancholy aspect. Not even the chirping of a bird is to be heard, only now and then the shrill screech of a sea-gull flying up from its nest among the sand-hills, that announces the coming storm. The monotonous plashings of the restless sea harmonize with the somber, shifting shadows of the passing clouds. Even the human inhabitants do not sing here, and on these melancholy coasts the strain of a *volkslied* is never heard. The people who live here are an earnest, honest, matter-of-fact race, proud of their bold spirit and of the liberties which they have inherited from their ancestors. Such a people are not imaginative, and are little given to metaphysical speculations. Fishing is their principal support, added to which is an occasional pittance of passage-money for transporting some traveler to one of the adjacent islands.

It is said that at a certain period of the year, just at midday, when the fisherman and his family are seated at table eating their noonday meal, a traveler enters and asks the master of the house to vouchsafe him an audience for a few minutes to speak with him on a matter of business. The fisherman, after vainly inviting the stranger to partake of the meal, grants his request, and they both step aside to a little table. I shall not describe the personal appearance of the stranger in detail, after the tedious manner of novelwriters: a brief enumeration of the salient points will suffice. He is a little man, advanced in years but well preserved.

He is, so to say, a youthful graybeard: plump, but not corpulent; cheeks ruddy as an apple; small eyes, which blink merrily and continually, and on his powdered little head is set a three-cornered little hat. Under his flaming yellow cloak, with its many collars, he wears the old-fashioned dress of a well-to-do Dutch merchant, such as we see depicted in old portraits—namely, a short silk coat of a parrot-green color, a vest embroidered with flowers, short black trousers, striped stockings, and shoes ornamented with buckles. The latter are so brightly polished that it is hard to understand how the wearer could trudge afoot through the slimy mud of the coast and yet keep them so clean. His voice is a thin, asthmatic treble, sometimes inclining to be rather lachrymose; but the address and bearing of the little man are as grave and measured as beseem a Dutch merchant. This gravity, however, appears to be more assumed than natural, and is in marked contrast with the searching, roving, swift-darting glances of the eye, and with the ill-repressed fidgetiness of the legs and arms. That the stranger is a Dutch merchant is evidenced not only by his apparel, but also by the mercantile exactitude and caution with which he endeavors to effect as favorable a bargain as possible for his employers. He is, as he says, a forwarding agent, and has received from some of his mercantile friends a commission to transport a certain number of souls, as many as can find room in an ordinary boat, from the coast of East Friesland to the White Island. In fulfillment of this commission, he adds, he wishes to know if the fisherman will this night convey in his boat the aforesaid cargo to the aforesaid island; in which case he is authorized to pay the passage money in advance, confidently hoping that, in Christian fairness, the fisherman will make his price very moderate. The Dutch merchant (which term is, in fact, a pleonasm, since every Dutchman is a merchant) makes this proposition with the utmost nonchalance, as if it referred to a cargo of cheeses, and not to the souls of the dead. The fisherman is startled at the word "souls," and a cold chill creeps down his back, for he immediately comprehends that the souls of the dead are here meant, and that the stranger is none other than the phantom Dutchman, who has already entrusted several of his fellow-fishermen with the transportation of the souls of the dead, and paid them well for it, too.

These East Frieslanders are, as I have already remarked, a brave, healthy, practical people; in them is lacking that morbid imagination which makes us so impressionable to the ghostly and supernatural. Our fisherman's weird dismay lasts but a moment; suppressing the uncanny sensation that is stealing over him, he soon regains his composure, and, intent on securing as high a sum as possible, he assumes an air of supreme indifference. But after a little chaffering the two come to an understanding, and shake hands to seal the bargain. The Dutchman draws forth a dirty leather pouch, filled entirely with little silver pennies of the smallest denomination ever coined in Holland, and in these tiny coins counts out the whole amount of the fare. With instructions to the fisherman to be ready with his boat at the appointed place about the midnight hour when the moon becomes visible, the Dutchman takes leave of the whole family, and, declining their repeated invitations to dine, the grave little figure, dignified as ever, trips lightly away.

At the time agreed upon the fisherman appears at the appointed place. At first the boat is rocked lightly to and fro by the waves; but by the time the full moon has risen above the horizon the fisherman notices that his bark is less easily swayed, and so it gradually sinks deeper and deeper in the stream, until finally the water comes within a hand's-breadth of the boat's bow. This circumstance apprises him that his passengers, the souls, are now aboard, and he pushes off from shore with his cargo. Although he strains his eyes to the utmost, he can distinguish nothing but a few vapory streaks that seem to be swayed hither and thither, and to intermingle with one another, but assume no definite forms. Listen intently as he may, he hears nothing but an indescribably faint chirping and rustling. Only now and then a sea-gull with a shrill scream flies swiftly over his head; or near him a fish leaps up from out the stream, and for a moment stares at him with a vacuous look. The night-winds sigh, and the sea-breezes grow more chilly. Everywhere only water, moonlight, and silence! and silent as all around him is the fisherman, who finally reaches the White Island and moors his boat. He sees no one on the strand, but he hears a shrill, asthmatic, wheezy, lachrymose voice, which he recognizes as that of the Dutchman. The latter seems to be reading off a list of proper names, with a peculiar, monotonous intonation, as if rehearsing a roll-call. Among the names are some which are known to the fisherman as belonging to persons who have died that year. During the reading of the list, the boat is evidently being gradually lightened of its load, and as soon as the last name is called it rises suddenly and floats free, although but a moment before it was deeply imbedded in the sand of the sea-shore. To the fisherman this is a token that his cargo has been properly delivered, and he calmly rows back to his wife and child, to his beloved home on the fiord.

. . . Notwithstanding this clever disguise, I have ventured to guess who the important mythological personage is that figures in this tradition. It is none other than the god Mercury, Hermes Psychopompos, the whilom conductor of the dead to Hades. Verily, under that shabby yellow cloak and prosaic tradesman's figure is concealed the youthful and most accomplished god of heathendom, the cunning son of Maia. On his little three-cornered hat not the slightest tuft of a feather is to be seen which might remind the beholder of the winged cap, and the clumsy shoes with steel buckles fail to give the least hint of the winged sandals. This grave and heavy Dutch lead is quite different from the mobile quicksilver, from which the god derived his very name. But the contrast is so exceedingly striking as to betray the god's design, which is the more effectually to disguise himself. Perhaps this mask was not chosen out of mere caprice. Mercury was, as you know, the patron god of thieves and merchants, and, in all probability, in choosing a disguise that should conceal him, and a trade by which to earn his livelihood, he took into consideration his talents and his antecedents.

. . . And thus it came to pass that the shrewdest and most cunning of the gods became a merchant, and, to adapt himself most thoroughly to his role, became the *ne plus ultra* of merchants—a Dutch merchant. His long practice in the olden time as Psychopompos, as conveyor of the dead to Hades, marks him out as particularly fitted to conduct the transportation of the souls of the dead to the White Island, in the manner just described.

The White Island is occasionally also called Brea, or Britannia. Does this perhaps refer to White Albion, to the chalky cliffs of the English coast? It would be a very humorous idea if England was designated as the land of the dead, as the Plutonian realm, as hell. In such a form, in truth, England has appeared to many a stranger.

In my essay on the Faust legend I discussed at full length the popular superstition concerning Pluto and his dominion. I showed how the old realm of shadows became hell, and how its old gloomy ruler became more and more diabolical. Neither Pluto, god of the nether regions, nor his brother, Neptune, god of the sea, emigrated like the other gods. Even after the final triumph of Christendom they remained in their domains, their respective elements. No matter what silly fables concerning him were invented here above on earth, old Pluto sat by his Proserpine, warm and cozy down below.

Neptune suffered less from calumny than his brother Pluto, and neither church-bell chimes nor organ-strains could offend his ears in the depths of old ocean, where he sat peacefully by the side of his white-bosomed wife, Dame Amphitrite, surrounded by his court of dripping nereids and tritons. Only now and then, when a young sailor crossed the equator, he would dart up from the briny deep, in his hand brandishing the trident, his head crowned with seaweed, and his flowing, silvery beard reaching down to the navel. Then he would confer on the neophyte the terrible sea-water baptism, accompanying it with a long unctuous

harangue, interspersed with coarse sailor jests, to the great
delight of the jolly tars. The harangue was frequently interrupted by the spitting of amber quids of chewed tobacco,
which Neptune so freely scattered around him. A friend,
who gave me a detailed description of the manner in which
such a sea-miracle is performed, assured me that the very
sailors that laughed most heartily at the droll antics of Neptune never for a moment doubted the existence of such a
god, and sometimes when in great danger they even prayed
to him.

Neptune, as we have seen, remained monarch of the wa-
tery realm; and Pluto, notwithstanding his metamorphosis
into Satan, still continued to be prince of the lower regions.
They fared better than did their brother Jupiter, who, after
the overthrow of their father, Saturn, became ruler of
heaven, and as sovereign of the universe resided at Olympus,
where, surrounded by his merry troop of gods, goddesses,
and nymphs-of-honor, he carried on his ambrosial rule of
joy. But when the great catastrophe occurred—when the
rule of the cross, that symbol of suffering, was proclaimed
—then the great Kronides fled, and disappeared amid the
tumults and confusion of the transmigration of races. All
traces of him were lost, and I have in vain consulted old
chronicles and old women: none could give me the least
information concerning his fate. With the same purpose in
view, I have ransacked many libraries, where I was shown
the magnificent codices ornamented with gold and precious
stones, true odalisques in the harem of science. To the
learned eunuchs who, with such affability, unlocked for me
those brilliant treasures, I here return the customary thanks.
It appears as if no popular tradition of a medieval Jupiter
exists; and all that I could gather concerning him consists of
a story told me by my friend, Niels Andersen.

. . . The events that I am about to relate, said Niels Andersen, occurred on an island, the exact situation of which I
cannot tell. Since its discovery no one has been able again
to reach it, being prevented by the immense icebergs that
tower like a high wall around the island, and seldom, prob-

ably, permit a near approach. Only the crew of a Russian whaling-vessel, which a storm had driven so far to the north ever trod its soil; and since then over a hundred years have elapsed. When the sailors had, by means of a small boat, effected a landing, they found the island to be wild and desolate. Sadly waved the blades of tall sedgy grass over the quicksands; here and there grew a few stunted fir-trees, or barren shrubs. They saw a multitude of rabbits springing around, on which account they named it the Island of Rabbits. Only one miserable hut gave evidence that a human being dwelt there. As the sailors entered the hut they saw an old, very old man, wretchedly clad in a garment of rabbit skins rudely stitched together. He was seated in a stone chair in front of the hearth, trying to warm his emaciated hands and trembling knees by the flaring brushwood fire. At his right side stood an immense bird, evidently an eagle, but which had been roughly treated by time, and shorn of all its plumage save the long bristly quills of its wings, that gave it a highly grotesque, and, at the same time, hideous appearance. At the old man's left, squatted on the earth, was an extraordinarily large hairless goat, which seemed to be very old; although full milky udders, with fresh, rosy nipples, hung at its belly.

Among the sailors were several Greeks, one of whom, not thinking that his words would be understood by the aged inhabitant of the hut, remarked in the Greek language to a comrade, "This old fellow is either a specter or an evil demon." But at these words the old man suddenly rose from his seat, and to their great surprise the sailors beheld a stately figure, which, in spite of its advanced age, raised itself erect with commanding, yes, with king-like dignity, his head almost touching the rafters. The features, too, although rugged and weather-beaten, showed traces of original beauty, they were so noble and well-proportioned. A few silvery locks fell over his brow, which was furrowed by pride and age. His eyes had a dim and fixed look, but occasionally they would still gleam piercingly; and from his mouth were heard in the melodious and sonorous words of the ancient Greek language, "You are mistaken, young man; I am neither a specter nor an evil demon; I am an unhappy old man, who once knew better days. But who are ye?"

The sailors explained the accident which had befallen them, and then inquired concerning the island. The information, however, was very meager. The old man told them that since time immemorial he had inhabited this island, whose bulwark of ice served him as a secure asylum against his inexorable foes. He subsisted principally by catching rabbits, and every year, when the floating icebergs had settled, a few bands of savages crossed over on sleds, and to them he sold rabbit-skins, receiving in exchange various articles of indispensable necessity. The whales, which sometimes came swimming close to the island, were his favorite company. But it gave him pleasure to hear again his native tongue, for he too was a Greek. He entreated his countrymen to give him an account of the present condition of Greece. That the cross had been torn down from the battlements of Grecian cities apparently caused the old man a malicious satisfaction; but it did not altogether please him when he heard that the crescent had been planted there instead. It was strange that none of the sailors knew the names of the cities concerning which the old man inquired, and which, as he assured them, had flourished in his time. In like manner the names of the present cities and villages in Greece, which were mentioned by the sailors, were unknown to him; at this the old man would shake his head sadly, and the sailors looked at one another perplexed. They noticed that he knew exactly all the localities and geographical peculiarities of Greece; and he described so accurately and vividly the bays, the peninsulas, the mountain-ridges, even the knolls and most trifling rocky elevations, that his ignorance of these localities was all the more surprising. With especial interest, with a certain anxiety even, he questioned them concerning an ancient temple, which in his time, he assured them, had been the most beautiful in all Greece; but none of his hearers knew the name, which he pronounced with a loving tenderness. But finally, when the old man had again described the site of the temple, with the utmost particularity, a young sailor recognized the place by the description.

The village wherein he was born, said the young man, was situated hard by, and when a boy he had often tended his father's swine at the very place where there had been found ruins of an ancient structure, indicating a magnificent grandeur in the past. Now, only a few large marble pillars remained standing; some were plain, unadorned columns, others were surmounted by the square stones of a gable. From the cracks of the masonry the blooming honeysuckle vines and red bell-flowers trailed downwards. Other pillars —among the number some of rose-colored marble—lay shattered on the ground, and the costly marble head-pieces, ornamented with beautiful sculpture, representing foliage and flowers, were overgrown by rank creepers and grasses. Half buried in the earth lay huge marble blocks, some of which were squares, such as were used for the walls; others were three-cornered slabs for roof-pieces. Over them waved a large, wild fig-tree, which had grown up out of the ruins. Under the shadow of that tree, continued the young man, he had passed whole hours in examining the strange figures carved on the large marble blocks; they seemed to be pictorial representations of all sorts of sports and combats, and were very pleasing to look at, but, alas! much injured by exposure, and overgrown with moss and ivy. His father, whom he had questioned in regard to the mysterious signification of these pillars and sculptures, told him that these were the ruins of an ancient pagan temple, and had once been the abode of a wicked heathen god, who had here wantoned in lewd debauchery, incest, and unnatural vices. Notwithstanding this, the unenlightened heathen were accustomed to slaughter in his honor a hundred oxen at a time, and the hollowed marble block into which was gathered the blood of the sacrifices was yet in existence. It was, in fact, the very trough which they were in the habit of using as a receptacle for refuse wherewith to feed the swine.

So spoke the young sailor. But the old man heaved a sigh

that betrayed the most terrible anguish. Tottering, he sank into his stone chair, covered his face with his hands, and wept like a child. The great, gaunt bird, with a shrill screech, flapped its immense wings, and menaced the strangers with claws and beak. The old goat licked its master's hands, and bleated mournfully as in consolation.

At this strange sight, an uncanny terror seized upon the sailors: they hurriedly left the hut, and were glad when they could no longer hear the sobbing of the old man, the screaming of the bird, and the bleating of the goat. When they were safely on board the boat, they narrated their adventure. Among the crew was a learned Russian, professor of philosophy at the university of Kazan; and he declared the matter to be highly important. With his forefinger held knowingly to the side of his nose, he assured the sailors that the old man of the island was undoubtedly the ancient god Jupiter, son of Saturn and Rhea. The bird at his side was clearly the eagle that once carried in its claws the terrible thunderbolts. And the old goat was, in all probability, none other than Althea, Jupiter's old nurse, who had suckled him in Crete, and now in exile again nourished him with her milk.

This is the story as told to me by Niels Andersen; and I must confess that it filled my soul with a profound melancholy. Decay is secretly undermining all that is great in the universe, and the gods themselves must finally succumb to the same miserable destiny. The iron law of fate so wills it, and even the greatest of the immortals must submissively bow his head. He of whom Homer sang, and whom Phidias sculptured in gold and ivory, he at whose glance earth trembled, he, the lover of Leda, Alcmena, Semele, Danaë, Callisto, Io, Leto, Europa, etc.—even he is compelled to hide himself behind the icebergs of the North Pole, and in order to prolong his wretched existence must deal in rabbit-skins, like a shabby Savoyard!

I do not doubt that there are people who will derive a malicious pleasure from such a spectacle. They are, perhaps, the descendants of these unfortunate oxen who, in hecatombs, were slaughtered on the altars of Jupiter. Rejoice!

avenged is the blood of your ancestors, those poor martyrs of superstition. But we, who have no hereditary grudge rankling in us, we are touched at the sight of fallen greatness, and withhold not our holiest compassion . . .

IMMENSEE[1]

Theodor W. Storm

(1817-1888)

The Old Man

One afternoon in the late autumn a well-dressed old man was walking slowly down the street. He appeared to be returning home from a walk, for his buckle-shoes, which followed a fashion long since out of date, were covered with dust.

Under his arm he carried a long, gold-headed cane; his dark eyes, in which the whole of his long-lost youth seemed to have centered, and which contrasted strangely with his snow-white hair, gazed calmly on the sights around him or peered into the town below as it lay before him, bathed in the haze of sunset.

He appeared to be almost a stranger, for of the passers-by only a few greeted him, although many a one involuntarily was compelled to gaze into those grave eyes.

At last he halted before a high, gabled house, cast one more glance out toward the town, and then passed into the hall. At the sound of the door-bell some one in the room within drew aside the green curtain from a small window that looked out on to the hall, and the face of an old woman was seen behind it. The man made a sign to her with his cane.

"No light yet!" he said in a slightly southern accent, and the housekeeper let the curtain fall again.

The old man now passed through the broad hall, through an inner hall, wherein against the walls stood huge oaken

[1] Translated by C. W. Bell.

chests bearing porcelain vases; then through the door opposite he entered a small lobby, from which a narrow staircase led to the upper rooms at the back of the house. He climbed the stairs slowly, unlocked a door at the top, and landed in a room of medium size.

It was a comfortable, quiet retreat. One of the walls was lined with cupboards and bookcases; on the other hung pictures of men and places; on a table with a green cover lay a number of open books, and before the table stood a massive armchair with a red velvet cushion.

After the old man had placed his hat and stick in a corner, he sat down in the armchair and, folding his hands, seemed to be taking his rest after his walk. While he sat thus, it was growing gradually darker; and before long a moonbeam came streaming through the window-panes and upon the pictures on the wall; and as the bright band of light passed slowly onward the old man followed it involuntarily with his eyes.

Now it reached a little picture in a simple black frame. "Elisabeth!" said the old man softly; and as he uttered the word, time had changed: *he was young again*.

THE CHILDREN

Before very long the dainty form of a little maiden advanced toward him. Her name was Elisabeth, and she might have been five years old. He himself was twice that age. Round her neck she wore a red silk kerchief which was very becoming to her brown eyes.

"Reinhard!" she cried, "we have a holiday, a holiday! No school the whole day and none to-morrow either!"

Reinhard was carrying his slate under his arm, but he flung it behind the front door, and then both the children ran through the house into the garden and through the garden gate out into the meadow. The unexpected holiday came to them at a most happily opportune moment.

It was in the meadow that Reinhard, with Elisabeth's help, had built a house out of sods of grass. They meant to live in it during the summer evenings; but it still wanted a bench. He set to work at once; nails, hammer, and the necessary boards were already to hand.

While he was thus engaged, Elisabeth went along the dyke, gathering the ring-shaped seeds of the wild mallow in her apron, with the object of making herself chains and necklaces out of them; so that when Reinhard had at last finished his bench in spite of many a crookedly hammered nail, and came out into the sunlight again, she was already wandering far away at the other end of the meadow.

"Elisabeth!" he called, "Elisabeth!" and then she came, her hair streaming behind her.

"Come here," he said; "our house is finished now. Why, you have got quite hot! Come in, and let us sit on the new bench. I will tell you a story."

So they both went in and sat down on the new bench. Elisabeth took the little seed-rings out of her apron and strung them on long threads. Reinhard began his tale: "There were once upon a time three spinning-women . . ."[1]

"Oh!" said Elisabeth, "I know that off by heart; you really must not always tell me the same story."

Accordingly Reinhard had to give up the story of the three spinning-women and tell instead the story of the poor man who was cast into the den of lions.

"It was now night," he said, "black night, you know, and the lions were asleep. But every now and then they would yawn in their sleep and shoot out their red tongues. And then the man would shudder and think it was morning. All at once a bright light fell all about him, and when he looked up an angel was standing before him. The angel beckoned to him with his hand and then went straight into the rocks.

Elisabeth had been listening attentively. "An angel?" she said. "Had he wings, then?"

"It is only a story," answered Reinhard; "there are no angels, you know."

"Oh, fie! Reinhard!" she said, staring him straight in the face.

He looked at her with a frown, and she asked him hesi-

[1] The beginning of one of the best known of Grimm's fairy tales

tatingly: "Well, why do they always say there are? Mother, and Aunt, and at school as well?"

"I don't know," he answered.

"But tell me," said Elisabeth, "are there no lions either?"

"Lions? Are there lions? In India, yes. The heathen priests harness them to their carriages, and drive about the desert with them. When I'm big, I mean to go out there myself. It is thousands of times more beautiful in that country than it is here at home; there's no winter at all there. And you must come with me. Will you?"

"Yes," said Elisabeth; "but Mother must come with us, and your mother as well."

"No," said Reinhard, "they will be too old then, and cannot come with us."

"But I mayn't go by myself."

"Oh but you may right enough; you will then really be my wife, and the others will have no say in the matter."

"But Mother will cry!"

"We shall come back again, of course," said Reinhard impetuously. "Now just tell me straight out, will you go with me? If not, I will go all alone, and then I shall never come back again."

The little girl came very near to crying. "Please don't look so angry," said she; "I will go to India with you."

Reinhard seized both her hands with frantic glee, and rushed out with her into the meadow.

"To India, to India!" he sang, and swung her round and round, so that her little red kerchief was whirled from off her neck. Then he suddenly let her go and said solemnly:

"Nothing will come of it, I'm sure; you haven't the pluck."

"Elisabeth! Reinhard!" some one was now calling from the garden gate. "Here we are!" the children answered, and raced home hand in hand.

IN THE WOODS

So the children lived together. She was often too quiet for him, and he was often too headstrong for her, but for all that they stuck to one another. They spent nearly all their leisure hours together: in winter in their mothers' tiny rooms, during the summer in wood and field.

Once when Elisabeth was scolded by the teacher in Reinhard's hearing, he angrily banged his slate upon the table in order to turn upon himself the master's wrath. This failed to attract attention.

But Reinhard paid no further attention to the geography lessons, and instead he composed a long poem, in which he compared himself to a young eagle, the schoolmaster to a gray crow, and Elisabeth to a white dove; the eagle vowed vengeance on the gray crow, as soon as his wings had grown.

Tears stood in the young poet's eyes: he felt very proud of himself. When he reached home he contrived to get hold of a little parchment-bound volume with a lot of blank pages in it; and on the first pages he elaborately wrote out his first poem.

Soon after this he went to another school. Here he made many new friendships among boys of his own age, but this did not interrupt his comings and goings with Elisabeth. Of the stories which he had formerly told her over and over again he now began to write down the ones which she had liked best, and in doing so the fancy often took him to weave in something of his own thoughts; yet, for some reason he could not understand, he could never manage it.

So he wrote them down exactly as he had heard them himself. Then he handed them over to Elisabeth, who kept them carefully in a drawer of her writing-desk, and now and again of an evening when he was present it afforded him agreeable satisfaction to hear her reading aloud to her mother these little tales out of the notebooks in which he had written them.

Seven years had gone by. Reinhard was to leave the town in order to proceed to his higher education. Elisabeth could not bring herself to think that there would now be a time to be passed entirely without Reinhard. She was delighted when he told her one day that he would continue to write out stories for her as before; he would send them to her ir the letters to his mother, and then she would have to write back to him and tell him how she liked them.

The day of departure was approaching, but ere it came a good deal more poetry found its way into the parchment-bound volume. This was the one secret he kept from Elisabeth, although she herself had inspired the whole book and most of the songs which gradually had filled up almost half of the blank pages.

It was the month of June, and Reinhard was to start on the following day. It was proposed to spend one more festive day together, and therefore a picnic was arranged for a rather large party of friends in an adjacent forest.

It was an hour's drive along the road to the edge of the wood, and there the company took down the provision baskets from the carriages and walked the rest of the way. The road lay first of all through a pine grove, where it was cool and darksome, and the ground was all strewed with pine needles.

After half an hour's walk they passed out of the gloom of the pine trees into a bright fresh beech wood. Here everything was light and green; every here and there a sunbeam burst through the leafy branches, and high above their heads a squirrel was leaping from branch to branch.

The party came to a halt at a certain spot, over which the topmost branches of ancient beech trees interwove a transparent canopy of leaves. Elisabeth's mother opened one of the baskets, and an old gentleman constituted himself quartermaster.

"Round me, all of you young people," he cried, "and attend carefully to what I have to say to you. For lunch each one of you will now get two dry rolls; the butter has been left behind at home. The extras every one must find for himself. There are plenty of strawberries in the wood—that is, for any one who knows where to find them. Unless you are sharp, you'll have to eat dry bread; that's the way of the world all over. Do you understand what I say?"

"Yes, yes," cried the young folks.

"Yes, but look here," said the old gentleman, "I have not

done yet. We old folks have done enough roaming about in our time, and therefore we will stay at home now, here, I mean, under these wide-spreading trees, and we'll peel the potatoes and make a fire and lay the table, and by twelve o'clock the eggs shall be boiled.

"In return for all this you will be owing us half of your strawberries, so that we may also be able to serve some dessert. So off you go now, east and west, and mind be honest."

The young folks cast many a roguish glance at one another.

"Wait," cried the old gentleman once again. "I suppose I need not tell you this, that whoever finds none need not produce any; but take particular note of this, that he will get nothing out of us old folks either. Now you have had enough good advice for to-day; and if you gather strawberries to match you will get on very well for the present at any rate."

The young people were of the same opinion, and pairing off in couples set out on their quest.

"Come along, Elisabeth," said Reinhard. "I know where there is a clump of strawberry bushes; you shan't eat dry bread."

Elisabeth tied the green ribbons of her straw hat together and hung it on her arm. "Come on, then," she said, "the basket is ready."

Off into the wood they went, on and on; on through moist shady glens, where everything was so peaceful, except for the cry of the falcon flying unseen in the heavens far above their heads; on again through the thick brushwood, so thick that Reinhard must needs go on ahead to make a track, here snapping off a branch, there bending aside a trailing vine. But ere long he heard Elisabeth behind him calling out his name. He turned round.

"Reinhard!" she called, "do wait for me! Reinhard!"

He could not see her, but at length he caught sight of her some way off struggling with the undergrowth, her dainty head just peeping out over the tops of the ferns. So back he went once more and brought her out from the tangled mass of briar and brake into an open space where blue butterflies fluttered among the solitary wood blossoms.

Reinhard brushed the damp hair away from her heated face, and would have tied the straw hat upon her head, but she refused; yet at his earnest request she consented after all.

"But where are your strawberries?" she asked at length, standing still and drawing a deep breath.

"They were here," he said, "but the toads have got here before us, or the martens, or perhaps the fairies."

"Yes," said Elisabeth, "the leaves are still here; but not a word about fairies in this place. Come along, I'm not a bit tired yet; let us look farther on."

In front of them ran a little brook, and on the far side the wood began again. Reinhard raised Elisabeth in his arms and carried her over. After a while they emerged from the shady foliage and stood in a wide clearing.

"There must be strawberries here," said the girl, "it all smells so sweet."

They searched about the sunny spot, but they found none. "No," said Reinhard, "it is only the smell of the heather."

Everywhere was a confusion of raspberry-bushes and holly, and the air was filled with a strong smell of heather, patches of which alternated with the short grass over these open spaces.

"How lonely it is here!" said Elisabeth: "I wonder where the others are?"

Reinhard had never thought of getting back.

"Wait a bit," he said, holding his hand aloft; "where is the wind coming from?" But wind there was none.

"Listen!" said Elisabeth; "I think I heard them talking. Just give a call in that direction."

Reinhard hollowed his hand and shouted: "Come here!"

"Here!" was echoed back.

"They answered," cried Elisabeth, clapping her hands.

"No, that was nothing; it was only the echo."

Elisabeth seized Reinhard's hand. "I'm frightened!" she said.

"Oh! no, you must not be frightened. It is lovely here. Sit

down there in the shade among the long grass. Let us rest awhile: we'll find the others soon enough."

Elisabeth sat down under the overhanging branch of a beech and listened intently in every direction. Reinhard sat a few paces off on a tree stump, and gazed over at her in silence.

The sun was just above their heads, shining with the full glare of midday heat. Tiny, gold-flecked, steel-blue flies poised in the air with vibrating wings. Their ears caught a gentle humming and buzzing all round them, and far away in the wood were heard now and again the tap-tap of the wood-pecker and the screech of other birds.

"Listen," said Elisabeth, "I hear a bell."

"Where?" asked Reinhard.

"Behind us. Do you hear it? It is striking twelve o'clock."

"Then the town lies behind us, and if we go straight through in this direction we are bound to fall in with the others."

So they started on their homeward way; they had given up looking for strawberries, for Elisabeth had become tired. And at last there rang out from among the trees the laughing voices of the picnic party; then they saw too a white cloth spread gleaming on the ground; it was the luncheon-table and on it were strawberries enough and to spare.

The old gentleman had a table-napkin tucked in his button-hole and was continuing his moral sermon to the young folks and vigorously carving a joint of roast meat.

"Here come the stragglers," cried the young people when they saw Reinhard and Elisabeth advancing among the trees.

"This way," shouted the old gentleman. "Empty your handkerchiefs, upside down with your hats! Now show us what you have found."

"Only hunger and thirst," said Reinhard.

"If that's all," replied the old man, lifting up and showing them the bowl full of fruit, "you must keep what you've got. You remember the agreement: nothing here for lazybones to eat."

But in the end he was prevailed on to relent; the banquet

proceeded, and a thrush in a juniper bush provided the music.

So the day passed. But Reinhard had, after all, found something, and though it was not strawberries yet it was something that had grown in the wood. When he got home this is what he wrote in his old parchment-bound volume:

> Out on the hillside yonder
>   The wind to rest is laid;
> Under the drooping branches
>   There sits the little maid.
>
> She sits among the wild thyme,
>   She sits in the fragrant air;
> The blue flies hum around her,
>   Bright wings flash everywhere.
>
> And through the silent woodland
>   She peers with watchful eyen,
> While on her hazel ringlets
>   Sparkles the glad sunshine.
>
> And afar, far off the cuckooo
>   Laughs out his song. I ween
> Hers are the bright, the golden
>   Eyes of the woodland queen.

So she was not only his little sweetheart, but was also the expression of all that was lovely and wonderful in his opening life.

By the Roadside the Child Stood

The time is Christmas Eve. Before the close of the afternoon Reinhard and some other students were sitting together at an old oak table in the Ratskeller. The lamps on the wall were lighted, for down here in the basement it was already growing dark; but there was only a thin sprinkling of customers present, and the waiters were leaning idly up against the pillars let into the walls.

In a corner of the vaulted room sat a fiddler and a fine-featured gypsy-girl with a zither; their instruments lay in

their laps, and they seemed to be looking about them with an
air of indifference.

A champagne cork popped off at the table occupied by
the students. "Drink, my gypsy darling!" cried a young man
of aristocratic appearance, holding out to the girl a glass
full of wine.

"I don't care about it," she said, without altering her position.

"Well, then, give us a song," cried the young nobleman,
and threw a silver coin into her lap. The girl slowly ran her
fingers through her black hair while the fiddler whispered
in her ear. But she threw back her head, and rested her chin
on her zither.

"For him," she said, "I'm not going to play."

Reinhard leapt up with his glass in his hand and stood in
front of her.

"What do you want?" she asked defiantly.

"To have a look at your eyes."

"What have my eyes to do with you?"

Reinhard's glance flashed down on her.

"I *know* they are false."

She laid her cheek in the palm of her hand and gave him a
searching look. Reinhard raised his glass to his mouth.

"Here's to your beautiful, wicked eyes!" he said, and
drank.

She laughed and tossed her head.

"Give it here," she said, and fastening her black eyes on
his, she slowly drank what was left in the glass. Then she
struck a chord and sang in a deep, passionate voice:

> To-day, to-day thou think'st me
>   Fairest maid of all;
> To-morrow, ah! then beauty
>   Fadeth past recall.
> While the hour remaineth,
>   Thou art yet mine own;
> Then when death shall claim me,
>   I must die alone.

While the fiddler struck up an allegro finale, a new arrival joined the group.

"I went to call for you, Reinhard," he said. "You had already gone out, but Santa Claus had paid you a visit."

"Santa Claus?" said Reinhard. "Santa Claus never comes to me now."

"Oh, yes, he does! The whole of your room smelt of Christmas tree and ginger cakes."

Reinhard dropped the glass out of his hand and seized his cap.

"Well, what are you going to do now?" asked the girl.

"I'll be back in a minute."

She frowned. "Stay," she said gently, casting an amorous glance at him.

Reinhard hesitated. "I can't," he said.

She laughingly gave him a tap with the toe of her shoe and said: "Go away, then, you good-for-nothing; you are one as bad as the other, all good-for-nothings." And as she turned away from him, Reinhard went slowly up the steps of the Ratskeller.

Outside in the street deep twilight had set in; he felt the cool winter air blowing on his heated brow. From some window every here and there fell the bright gleam of a Christmas tree all lighted up, now and then was heard from within some room the sound of little pipes and tin trumpets mingled with the merry din of children's voices.

Crowds of beggar children were going from house to house or climbing up on to the railings of the front steps, trying to catch a glimpse through the window of a splendor that was denied to them. Sometimes too a door would suddenly be flung open, and scolding voices would drive a whole swarm of these little visitors away out into the dark street. In the vestibule of yet another house they were singing an old Christmas carol, and little girls' clear voices were heard among the rest.

But Reinhard heard not; he passed quickly by them all,

out of one street into another. When he reached his lodging
it had grown almost quite dark; he stumbled up the stairs
and so gained his apartment.

A sweet fragrance greeted him; it reminded him of home;
it was the smell of the parlor in his mother's house at Christmas time. With trembling hand he lit his lamp; and there
lay a mighty parcel on the table. When he opened it, out
fell the familiar ginger cakes. On some of them were the
initial letters of his name written in sprinkles of sugar; no
one but Elisabeth could have done that.

Next came to view a little parcel containing neatly embroidered linen, handkerchiefs and cuffs; and finally letters
from his mother and Elisabeth. Reinhard opened Elisabeth's
letter first, and this is what she wrote:

"The pretty sugared letters will no doubt tell you who
helped with the cakes. The same person also embroidered
the cuffs for you. We shall have a very quiet time at home
this Christmas Eve. Mother always puts her spinning-wheel
away in the corner as early as half-past nine. It is so very
lonesome this winter now that you are not here.

"And now, too, the linnet you made me a present of died
last Sunday. It made me cry a good deal, though I am sure
I looked after it well.

"It always used to sing of an afternoon when the sun
shone on its cage. You remember how often mother would
hang a piece of cloth over the cage in order to keep it quiet
when it sang so lustily.

"Thus our room is now quieter than ever, except that your
old friend Eric now drops in to see us occasionally. You told
us once that he was just like his brown top-coat. I can't help
thinking of it every time he comes in at the door, and it is
really too funny; but don't tell mother, it might easily make
her angry.

"Guess what I am giving your mother for a Christmas
present! You can't guess! Well, it is myself! Eric is making
a drawing of me in black chalk; I have had to give him
three sittings, each time for a whole hour.

"I simply loathed the idea of a stranger getting to know my face so well. Nor did I wish it, but mother pressed me, and said it would very much please dear Frau Werner.

"But you are not keeping your word, Reinhard. You haven't sent me any stories. I have often complained to your mother about it, but she always says you now have more to do than to attend to such childish things. But I don't believe it; there's something else perhaps."

After this Reinhard read his mother's letter, and when he had read them both and slowly folded them up again and put them away, he was overcome with an irresistible feeling of homesickness. For a long while he walked up and down his room, talking softly to himself, and then, under his breath, he murmured:

> I have err'd from the straight path,
>   Bewilder'd I roam;
> By the roadside the child stands
>   And beckons me home.

Then he went to his desk, took out some money, and stepped down into the street again. During all this while it had become quieter out there; the lights on the Christmas trees had burnt out, the processions of children had come to an end. The wind was sweeping through the deserted streets; old and young alike were sitting together at home in family parties; the second period of Christmas Eve celebrations had begun.

As Reinhard drew near the Ratskeller he heard from below the scraping of the fiddle and the singing of the zither girl. The restaurant door-bell tinkled and a dark form staggered up the broad dimly-lighted stair.

Reinhard drew aside into the shadow of the houses and then passed swiftly by. After a while he reached the well-lighted shop of a jeweler, and after buying a little cross studded with red corals, he returned by the same way he had come.

Not far from his lodgings he caught sight of a little girl,

dressed in miserable rags, standing before a tall door, in a vain attempt to open it.

"Shall I help you?" he said.

The child gave no answer, but let go the massive door-handle. Reinhard had soon opened the door.

"No," he said; "they might drive you out again. Come along with me, and I'll give you some Christmas cake."

He then closed the door again and gave his hand to the little girl, who walked along with him in silence to his lodgings.

On going out he had left the light burning.

"Here are some cakes for you," he said, pouring half of his whole stock into her apron, though he gave none that bore the sugar letters.

"Now, off you go home, and give your mother some of them too."

The child cast a shy look up at him; she seemed unaccustomed to such kindness and unable to say anything in reply. Reinhard opened the door, and lighted her way, and then the little thing like a bird flew downstairs with her cakes and out of the house.

Reinhard poked the fire in the stove, set the dusty inkstand on the table, and then sat down and wrote and wrote letters the whole night long to his mother and Elisabeth.

The remainder of the Christmas cakes lay untouched by his side, but he had buttoned on Elisabeth's cuffs, and odd they looked on his shaggy coat of undyed wool. And there he was still sitting when the winter sun cast its light on the frosted window-panes, and showed him a pale, grave face reflected in the looking-glass.

HOME

When the Easter vacation came Reinhard journeyed home. On the morning after his arrival he went to see Elisabeth.

"How tall you've grown!" he said, as the pretty, slender

girl advanced with a smile to meet him. She blushed, but made no reply; he had taken her hand in his own in greeting, and she tried to draw it gently away. He looked at her doubtingly, for never had she done that before; but now it was as if some strange thing was coming between them.

The same feeling remained, too, after he had been at home for some time and came to see her constantly day after day. When they sat alone together there ensued pauses in the conversation which distressed him, and which he anxiously did his best to avoid. In order to have a definite occupation during the holidays, he began to give Elisabeth some instruction in botany, in which he himself had been keenly interested during the early months of his university career.

Elisabeth, who was wont to follow him in all things and was, moreover, very quick to learn, willingly entered into the proposal. So now several times in the week they made excursions into the fields or the moors, and if by midday they brought home their green field-box full of plants and flowers, Reinhard would come again later in the day and share with Elisabeth what they had collected in common.

With this same object in view, he entered the room one afternoon while Elisabeth was standing by the window and sticking some fresh chickweed in a gilded birdcage which he had not seen in the place before. In the cage was a canary, which was flapping its wings and shrilly chirruping as it pecked at Elisabeth's fingers. Previously to this Reinhard's bird had hung in that spot.

"Has my poor linnet changed into a goldfinch after its death?" he asked jovially.

"Linnets are not accustomed to do any such thing," said Elisabeth's mother, who sat spinning in her armchair. "Your friend Eric sent it this noon from his estate as a present for Elisabeth."

"What estate?"

"Why, don't you know?"

"Know what?"

"That a month ago Eric took over his father's second estate by the Immensee."[1]

---

[1] i.e. the "Lake of the Bees."

"But you have never said a word to me about it."

"Well," said the mother, "you haven't yet made a single word of inquiry after your friend. He is a very nice, sensible young man."

The mother went out of the room to make the coffee. Elisabeth had her back turned to Reinhard, and was still busy with the making of her little chickweed bower.

"Please, just a little longer," she said. "I'll be done in a minute."

As Reinhard did not answer, contrary to his wont, she turned round and faced him. In his eyes there was a sudden expression of trouble which she had never observed before in them.

"What is the matter with you, Reinhard?" she said, drawing nearer to him.

"With me?" he said, his thoughts far away and his eyes resting dreamily on hers.

"You look so sad."

"Elisabeth," he said, "I cannot bear that yellow bird."

She looked at him in astonishment, without understanding his meaning. "You are so strange," she said.

He took both her hands in his, and she let him keep them there. Her mother came back into the room shortly after; and after they had drunk their coffee she sat down at her spinning-wheel, while Reinhard and Elisabeth went off into the next room to arrange their plants.

Stamens were counted, leaves and blossoms carefully opened out, and two specimens of each sort were laid to dry betwen the pages of a large folio volume.

All was calm and still this sunny afternoon; the only sounds to be heard were the hum of the mother's spinning-wheel in the next room, and now and then the subdued voice of Reinhard, as he named the orders of the families of the plants, and corrected Elisabeth's awkward pronunciation of the Latin names.

"I am still short of that lily of the valley which I didn't get last time," said she, after the whole collection had been classified and arranged.

Reinhard pulled a little white vellum volume from his

pocket. "Here is a spray of the lily of the valley for you," he said, taking out a half-pressed bloom.

When Elisabeth saw the pages all covered with writing, she asked: "Have you been writing stories again?"

"These aren't stories," he answered, handing her the book.

The contents were all poems, and the majority of them at most filled one page. Elisabeth turned over the leaves one after another; she appeared to be reading the titles only. "When she was scolded by the teacher." "When they lost their way in the woods." "An Easter story." "On her writing to me for the first time." Thus ran most of the titles.

Reinhard fixed his eyes on her with a searching look, and as she kept turning over the leaves he saw that a gentle blush arose and gradually mantled over the whole of her sweet face. He would fain have looked into her eyes, but Elisabeth did not look up, and finally laid the book down before him without a word.

"Don't give it back like that," he said.

She took a brown spray out of the tin case. "I will put your favorite flower inside," she said, giving back the book into his hands.

At length came the last day of the vacation and the morning of his departure. At her own request Elisabeth received permission from her mother to accompany her friend to the stage-coach, which had its station a few streets from their house.

When they passed out of the front door Reinhard gave her his arm, and thus he walked in silence side by side with the slender maiden. The nearer they came to their destination the more he felt as if he had something he must say to her before he bade her a long farewell, something on which all that was worthy and all that was sweet in his future life depended, and yet he could not formulate the saving word. In his anguish, he walked slower and slower.

"You'll be too late," she said; "it has already struck ten by St. Mary's clock."

But he did not quicken his pace for all that. At last he stammered out:

"Elisabeth, you will not see me again for two whole years. Shall I be as dear to you as ever when I come back?"

She nodded, and looked affectionately into his face.

"I stood up for you," she said, after a pause.

"Me? And against whom had you to stand up for me?"

"Against my mother. We were talking about you a long time yesterday evening after you left. She thought you were not so nice now as you once were."

Reinhard held his peace for a moment: then he took her hand in his, and looking gravely into her childish eyes, he said:

"I am still just as nice as I ever was; I would have you firmly believe that. Do you believe it, Elisabeth?"

"Yes," she said.

He freed her hand and quickly walked with her through the last street. The nearer he felt the time of parting approach, the happier became the look on his face; he went almost too quickly for her.

"What is the matter with you, Reinhard?" she asked.

"I have a secret, a beautiful secret," said Reinhard, looking at her with a light in his eyes. "When I come back again in two years' time, then you shall know it."

Meanwhile they had reached the stage-coach; they were only just in time. Once more Reinhard took her hand. "Farewell!" he said, "farewell, Elisabeth! Do not forget!"

She shook her head. "Farewell," she said. Reinhard climbed up into the coach and the horses started. As the coach rumbled round the corner of the street he saw her dear form once more as she slowly wended her way home.

A Letter

Nearly two years later Reinhard was sitting by lamplight with his books and papers around him, expecting a friend with whom he used to study in common. Some one came upstairs. "Come in." It was the landlady. "A letter for you, Herr Werner," and she went away.

Reinhard had never written to Elisabeth since his visit

home, and he had received no letter from her. Nor was this one from her; it was in his mother's handwriting.

Reinhard broke the seal and read, and ere long he came to this paragraph:

"At your time of life, my dear boy, nearly every year still brings its own peculiar experience; for youth is apt to turn everything to the best account. At home, too, things have changed very much, and all this will, I fear, cause you much pain at first, if my understanding of you is at all correct.

"Yesterday Eric was at last accepted by Elisabeth, after having twice proposed in vain during the last three months. She had never been able to make up her mind to it, but now in the end she has done so. To my mind she is still far too young. The wedding is to take place soon, and her mother means to go away with them."

IMMENSEE

Again years have passed. One warm afternoon in spring a young man, whose sunburnt face was the picture of health, was walking along a shady road through the wood leading down to the valley below.

His grave dark eyes looked intently into the distance, as though he was expecting to find every moment some change in the monotony of the road, a change, however, which seemed reluctant to come about. At length he saw a cart slowly coming up from below.

"Hullo! my friend," shouted the traveler to the farmer, who was walking by the side of the cart, "is this the right road to Immensee?"

"Yes, straight on," answered the man, touching his slouch hat.

"Is it still far off?"

"You are close to the place, sir. In less time than it takes to smoke half a pipe of tobacco you'll be at the lake side, and the manor is hard by."

The farmer passed on, while the other quickened his pace as he went along under the trees. After a quarter of an hour's walk the shade to the left of him suddenly came to an end; the road led along a steep slope from which the ancient oaks growing below hardly reared their topmost branches.

Away over their crests opened out a broad, sunny landscape. Far below lay the peaceful, dark-blue lake, almost entirely surrounded by green sun-lit woods, save where on one spot they divided and afforded an extensive view until it closed in the distant blue mountains.

Straight opposite, in the middle of all this forest verdure, there lay a patch of white, like driven snow. This was an expanse of blossoming fruit-trees, and out of them, up on the high lake shore, rose the manor-house, shining white with tiles of red. A stork flew up from the chimney, and circled slowly above the waters.

"Immensee!" exclaimed the traveler.

It almost seemed as if he had now reached the end of his journey, for he stood motionless, looking out over the tops of the trees at his feet, and gazing at the farther shore, where the reflection of the manor-house floated, rocking gently, on the bosom of the water. Then he suddenly started on his way again.

His road now led almost steeply down the mountainside, so that the trees that had once stood below him again gave him their shade, but at the same time cut off from him the view of the lake, which only now and then peeped out between the gaps in the branches.

Soon the way went gently upwards again, and to left and right the woods disappeared, yielding place to vine-clad hills stretching along the pathway; while on either side stood fruit-trees in blossom, filled with the hum of the bees as they busily pried into the blossoms. A tall man wearing a brown overcoat advanced to meet the traveler. When he had almost come up to him, he waved his cap and cried out in a loud voice:

"Welcome, welcome, brother Reinhard! Welcome to my Immensee estate!"

"God's greeting to you, Eric, and thank you for your welcome," replied the other.

By this time they had come up close to one another, and clasped hands.

"And is it really you?" said Eric, when he at last got a near sight of the grave face of his old school-fellow.

"It is I right enough, Eric, and I recognize you too; only you almost look cheerier than you ever did before."

At these words a glad smile made Eric's plain features all the more cheerful.

"Yes, brother Reinhard," he said, as he once more held out his hand to him, "but since those days, you see, I have won the great prize; but you know that well enough."

Then he rubbed his hands and cried cheerily, "This *will* be a surprise! You are the last person she expects to see."

"A surprise?" asked Reinhard. "For whom, pray?"

"Why, for Elisabeth."

"Elisabeth! You haven't told her a word about my visit?"

"Not a word, brother Reinhard; she has no thought of you, nor her mother either. I invited you entirely on the quiet, in order that the pleasure might be all the greater. You know I always had little quiet schemes of my own."

Reinhard turned thoughtful; he seemed to breathe more heavily the nearer they approached the house.

On the left side of the road the vineyards came to an end, and gave place to an extensive kitchen-garden, which reached almost as far as the lake-shore. The stork had meanwhile come to earth and was striding solemnly between the vegetable beds.

"Hullo!" cried Eric, clapping his hands together, "if that long-legged Egyptian isn't stealing my short pea-sticks again!"

The bird slowly rose and flew on to the roof of a new building, which ran along the end of the kitchen-garden, and whose walls were covered with the branches of the peach and apricot trees that were trained over them.

"That's the distillery," said Eric. "I built it only two years ago. My late father had the farm buildings rebuilt; the dwelling-house was built as far back as my grandfather's time. So we go ever forward a little bit at a time."

Talking thus they came to a wide, open space, enclosed

at the sides by farm-buildings, and in the rear by the manor-house, the two wings of which were connected by a high garden wall. Behind this wall ran dark hedges of yew trees, while here and there syringa trees trailed their blossoming branches over into the courtyard.

Men with faces scorched by the sun and heated with toil were walking over the open space and gave a greeting to the two friends, while Eric called out to one or another of them some order or question about their day's work.

By this time they had reached the house. They entered a high, cool vestibule, at the far end of which they turned to the left into a somewhat darker passage.

Here Eric opened a door and they passed into a spacious room that opened into a garden. The heavy mass of leafage that covered the opposite windows filled this room at either end with a green twilight, while between the windows two lofty wide-open folding-doors let in the full glow of spring sunshine, and afforded a view into a garden, laid out with circular flower-beds and steep hedgerows and divided by a straight, broad path, along which the eye roamed out on to the lake and away over the woods growing on the opposite shore.

As the two friends entered, a breath of wind bore in upon them a perfect stream of fragrance.

On a terrace in front of the door leading to the garden sat a girlish figure dressed in white. She rose and came to meet the two friends as they entered, but half-way she stood stock-still as if rooted to the spot and stared at the stranger. With a smile he held out his hand to her.

"Reinhard!" she cried. "Reinhard! Oh! is it you? It is such a long time since we have seen each other."

"Yes, a long time," he said, and not a word more could he utter; for on hearing her voice he felt a keen, physical pain at his heart, and as he looked up to her, there she stood before him, the same slight, graceful figure to whom he had said farewell years ago in the town where he was born.

Eric had stood back by the door, with joy beaming from his eyes.

"Now, then, Elisabeth," he said, "isn't he really the very

last person in the world you would have expected to see?"

Elisabeth looked at him with the eyes of a sister. "You are so kind, Eric," she said.

He took her slender hand caressingly in his. "And now that we have him," he said, "we shall not be in a hurry to let him go. He has been so long away abroad, we will try to make him feel at home again. Just see how foreign-looking he has become, and what a distinguished appearance he has!"

Elisabeth shyly scanned Reinhard's face. "The time that we have been separated is enough to account for that," she said.

At this moment in at the door came her mother, key basket on arm.

"Herr Werner!" she cried, when she caught sight of Reinhard; "ah! you are as dearly welcome as you are unexpected."

And so the conversation went smoothly on with questions and answers. The ladies sat over their work, and while Reinhard enjoyed the refreshment that had been prepared for him, Eric had lighted his huge meerschaum pipe and sat smoking and conversing by his side.

Next day Reinhard had to go out with him to see the fields, the vineyards, the hop-garden, the distillery. It was all well appointed; the people who were working on the land or at the vats all had a healthy and contented look.

For dinner the family assembled in the room that opened into the garden, and the day was spent more or less in company just according to the leisure of the host and hostess. Only during the hours preceding the evening meal, as also during the early hours of the forenoon, did Reinhard stay working in his own room.

For some years past, whenever he could come across them, he had been collecting the rhymes and songs that form part of the life of the people, and now set about arranging his treasure, and wherever possible increasing it by means of fresh records from the immediate neighborhood.

Elisabeth was at all times gentle and kind. Eric's constant attentions she received with an almost humble gratitude, and Reinhard thought at whiles that the gay, cheerful child of bygone days had given promise of a somewhat less sedate womanhood.

Ever since the second day of his visit he had been wont of an evening to take a walk along the shore of the lake. The road led along close under the garden. At the end of the latter, on a projecting mound, there was a bench under some tall birch trees. Elisabeth's mother had christened it the Evening Bench, because the spot faced westward, and was mostly used at that time of the day in order to enjoy a view of the sunset.

One evening Reinhard was returning from his walk along this road when he was overtaken by the rain. He sought shelter under one of the linden trees that grew by the water-side, but the heavy drops were soon pelting through the leaves. Wet through as he was he resigned himself to his fate and slowly continued his homeward way.

It was almost dark; the rain fell faster and faster. As he drew near to the Evening Bench he fancied he could make out the figure of a woman dressed in white standing among the gleaming birch tree trunks. She stood motionless, and, as far as he could make out on approaching nearer, with her face turned in his direction, as if she was expecting some one.

He thought it was Elisabeth. But when he quickened his pace in order that he might catch up to her and then return together with her through the garden into the house, she turned slowly away and disappeared among the dark side-paths.

He could not understand it; he was almost angry with Elisabeth, and yet he doubted whether it had really been she. He was, however, shy of questioning her about it—nay, he even avoided going into the garden-room on his return to the house for fear he should happen to see Elisabeth enter through the garden-door.

By my Mother's Hard Decree

Some days later, as evening was already closing in, the family was, as usual at this time of the day, sitting all to-

gether in their garden-room. The doors stood wide open, and
the sun had already sunk behind the woods on the far side
of the lake.

Reinhard was invited to read some folk-songs which had
been sent to him that afternoon by a friend who lived away
in the country. He went up to his room and soon returned
with a roll of papers which seemed to consist of detached
neatly written pages.

So they all sat down to the table, Elisabeth beside Reinhard. "We shall read them at random," said the latter, "I have
not yet looked through them myself."

Elisabeth unrolled the manuscript. "Here's some music,"
she said, "you must sing it, Reinhard."

To begin with he read some Tyrolese ditties, and as he
read on he would now and then hum one or other of the
lively melodies. A general feeling of cheeriness pervaded the
little party. "And who, pray, made all these pretty songs?"
asked Elisabeth.

"Oh," said Eric, "you can tell that by listening to the
rubbishy things—tailors' apprentices and barbers and such-
like merry folk."

Reinhard said: "They are not made; they grow, they drop
from the clouds, they float over the land like gossamer,
hither and thither, and are sung in a thousand places at the
same time. We discover in these songs our very inmost
activities and sufferings: it is as if we all had helped to write
them."

He took up another sheet: "I stood on the mountain
height . . ."

"I know that one," cried Elisabeth; "begin it, do, Reinhard,
and I will help you out."

So they sang that famous melody, which is so mysterious
that one can hardly believe that it was ever conceived by
the heart of man, Elisabeth with her slightly clouded con-
tralto taking the second part to the young man's tenor.

The mother meanwhile sat busy with her needlework,
while Eric listened attentively, with one hand clasped in the
other. The song finished, Reinhard laid the sheet on one side

in silence. Up from the lake-shore came through the evening calm the tinkle of the cattle bells; they were all listening without knowing why, and presently they heard a boy's clear voice singing:

> I stood on the mountain height
> And viewed the deep valley beneath . . .

Reinhard smiled. "Do you hear that now? So it passes from mouth to mouth."

"It is often sung in these parts," said Elisabeth.

"Yes," said Eric, "it is Casper the herdsman; he is driving the heifers home."

They listened a while longer until the tinkle of the bells died away behind the farm buildings. "These melodies are as old as the world," said Reinhard; "they slumber in the depths of the forest; God knows who discovered them."

He drew forth a fresh sheet.

It had now grown darker; a crimson evening glow lay like foam over the woods in the farther side of the lake. Reinhard unrolled the sheet, Elisabeth caught one side of it in her hand, and they both examined it together. Then Reinhard read:

> By my mother's hard decree
> Another's wife I needs must be;
> Him on whom my heart was set,
> Him, alas! I must forget;
> My heart protesting, but not free.
>
> Bitterly did I complain
> That my mother brought me pain.
> What mine honor might have been,
> That is turned to deadly sin.
> Can I ever hope again?
>
> For my pride what can I show,
> And my joy, save grief and woe?
> Ah! could I undo what's done,
> O'er the moor scorched by the sun
> Beggerwise I'd gladly go.

During the reading of this Reinhard had felt an imperceptible quivering of the paper; and when he came to an end Elisabeth gently pushed her chair back and passed silently out into the garden. Her mother followed her with a look. Eric made as if to go after, but the mother said: "Elisabeth has one or two little things to do outside," so he remained where he was.

But out of doors the evening brooded darker and darker over garden and lake. Moths whirred past the open doors through which the fragrance of flower and bush floated in increasingly; up from the water came the croak of the frogs, under the windows a nightingale commenced his song answered by another from within the depths of the garden; the moon appeared over the tree-tops.

Reinhard looked for a little while longer at the spot where Elisabeth's sweet form had been lost to sight in the thick-foliaged garden paths, and then he rolled up his manuscript, bade his friends good-night and passed through the house down to the water.

The woods stood silent and cast their dark shadow far out over the lake, while the center was bathed in the haze of a pale moonlight. Now and then a gentle rustle trembled through the trees, though wind there was none: it was but the breath of summer night.

Reinhard continued along the shore. A stone's throw from the land he perceived a white water-lily. All at once he was seized with the desire to see it quiet close, so he threw off his clothes and entered the water. It was quite shallow; sharp stones and water plants cut his feet, and yet he could not reach water deep enough for him to swim in.

Then suddenly he stepped out of his depth: the waters swirled above him, and it was some time before he rose to the surface again. He struck out with hands and feet and swam about in a circle until he had made quite sure from what point he had entered the water. And soon too he saw the lily again floating lonely among the large, gleaming leaves.

He swam slowly out, lifting every now and then his arms out of the water so that the drops trickled down and sparkled in the moonlight. Yet the distance between him and the flower showed no signs of diminishing, while the shore, as he glanced back at it, showed behind him in a hazy mist that ever deepened. But he refused to give up the venture and vigorously continued swimming in the same direction.

At length he had come so near the flower that he was able clearly to distinguish the silvery leaves in the moonlight; but at the same time he felt himself entangled in a net formed by the smooth stems of the water plants which swayed up from the bottom and wound themselves round his naked limbs.

The unfamiliar water was black all round about him, and behind him he heard the sound of a fish leaping. Suddenly such an uncanny feeling overpowered him in the midst of this strange element that with might and main he tore asunder the network of plants and swam back to land in breathless haste. And when from the shore he looked back upon the lake, there floated the lily on the bosom of the darkling water as far away and as lonely as before.

He dressed and slowly wended his way home. As he passed out of the garden into the room he discovered Eric and the mother busied with preparations for a short journey which had to be undertaken for business purposes on the morrow.

"Wherever have you been so late in the dark?" the mother called out to him.

"I?" he answered; "oh, I wanted to pay a call on the water-lily, but I failed."

"That's beyond the comprehension of any man," said Eric. "What on earth had you to do with the water-lily?"

"Oh, I used to be friends with the lily once," said Reinhard; "but that was long ago."

ELISABETH

The following afternoon Reinhard and Elisabeth went for a walk on the farther side of the lake, strolling at times through the woodland, at other times along the shore where it jutted out into the water. Elisabeth had received injunctions from Eric, during the absence of himself and her mother, to show Reinhard the prettiest views in the immediate neighborhood, particularly the view toward the farm itself from the other side of the lake. So now they proceeded from one point to another.

At last Elisabeth got tired and sat down in the shade of some overhanging branches. Reinhard stood opposite to her, leaning against a tree trunk; and as he heard the cuckoo calling farther back in the woods, it suddenly struck him that all this had happened once before. He looked at her and with an odd smile asked:

"Shall we look for strawberries?"

"It isn't strawberry time," she said.

"No, but it will soon be here."

Elisabeth shook her head in silence; then she rose and the two strolled on together. And as they wandered side by side, his eyes ever and again were bent toward her; for she walked gracefully and her step was light. He often unconsciously fell back a pace in order that he might feast his eyes on a full view of her.

So they came to an open space overgrown with heather where the view extended far over the country-side. Reinhard bent down and plucked a bloom from one of the little plants that grew at his feet. When he looked up again there was an expression of deep pain on his face.

"Do you know this flower?" he asked.

She gave him a questioning look. "It is an erica. I have often gathered them in the woods."

"I have an old book at home," he said; "I once used to write in it all sorts of songs and rhymes, but that is all over and done with long since. Between its leaves also there is an erica, but it is only a faded one. Do you know who gave it me?"

She nodded without saying a word; but she cast down her eyes and fixed them on the bloom which he held in his hand. For a long time they stood thus. When she raised her eyes on him again he saw that they were brimming over with tears.

"Elisabeth," he said, "beyond yonder blue hills lies our youth. What has become of it?"

Nothing more was spoken. They walked dumbly by each other's side down to the lake. The air was sultry; to westward dark clouds were rising. "There's going to be a storm," said Elisabeth, hastening her steps. Reinhard nodded in silence, and together they rapidly sped along the shore till they reached their boat.

On the way across Elisabeth rested her hand on the gunwale of the boat. As he rowed Reinhard glanced along at her, but she gazed past him into the distance. And so his glance fell downward and rested on her hand, and the white hand betrayed to him what her lips had failed to reveal.

It revealed those fine traces of secret pain that so readily mark a woman's fair hands, when they lie at nights folded across an aching heart. And as Elisabeth felt his glance resting on her hand she let it slip gently over the gunwale into the water.

On arriving at the farm they fell in with a scissors grinder's cart standing in front of the manor-house. A man with black, loosely-flowing hair was busily plying his wheel and humming a gypsy melody between his teeth, while a dog that was harnessed to the cart lay panting hard by. On the threshold stood a girl dressed in rags, with features of faded beauty, and with outstretched hand she asked alms of Elisabeth.

Reinhard thrust his hand into his pocket, but Elisabeth was before him, and hastily emptied the entire contents of her purse into the beggar's open palm. Then she turned quickly away, and Reinhard heard her go sobbing up the stairs.

He would fain have detained her, but he changed his mind and remained at the foot of the stairs. The beggar girl was still standing at the doorway, motionless, and holding in her hand the money she had received.

"What more do you want?" asked Reinhard.

She gave a sudden start: "I want nothing more," she said; then, turning her head toward him and staring at him with wild eyes, she passed slowly out of the door. He uttered a name, but she heard him not; with drooping head, with arms folded over her breast, she walked down across the farmyard:

> Then when death shall claim me,
>   I must die alone.

An old song surged in Reinhard's ears, he gasped for breath; a little while only, and then he turned away and went up to his chamber.

He sat down to work, but his thoughts were far afield. After an hour's vain attempt he descended to the parlor. Nobody was in it, only cool, green twilight; on Elisabeth's work-table lay a red ribbon which she had worn round her neck during the afternoon. He took it up in his hand, but it hurt him, and he laid it down again.

He could find no rest. He walked down to the lake and untied the boat. He rowed over the water and trod once again all the paths which he and Elisabeth had paced together but a short hour ago. When he got back home it was dark. At the farm he met the coachman, who was about to turn the carriage horses out into the pasture; the travelers had just returned.

As he came into the entrance hall he heard Eric pacing up and down the garden-room. He did not go in to him; he stood still for a moment, and then softly climbed the stairs and so to his own room. Here he sat in the armchair by the window. He made himself believe that he was listening to the nightingale's throbbing music in the garden hedges below, but what he heard was the throbbing of his own heart. Downstairs in the house every one went to bed, the night-hours passed, but he paid no heed.

For hours he sat thus, till at last he rose and leaned out of the open window. The dew was dripping among the leaves, the nightingale had ceased to trill. By degrees the deep blue of the darksome sky was chased away by a faint yellow gleam that came from the east; a fresh wind rose and brushed Reinhard's heated brow; the early lark soared triumphant up into the sky.

Reinhard suddenly turned and stepped up to the table. He groped about for a pencil and when he had found one he sat down and wrote a few lines on a sheet of white paper. Having finished his writing he took up hat and stick, and leaving the paper behind him, carefully opened the door and descended to the vestibule.

The morning twilight yet brooded in every corner; the big house-cat stretched its limbs on the straw mat and arched its back against Reinhard's hand, which he unthinkingly held out to it. Outside in the garden the sparrows were already chirping their patter from among the branches, and giving notice to all that the night was now past.

Then within the house he heard a door open on the upper floor; some one came downstairs, and on looking up he saw Elisabeth standing before him. She laid her hand upon his arm, her lips moved, but not a word did he hear.

Presently she said: "You will never come back. I know it; do not deny it; you will never come back."

"No, never," he said.

She let her hand fall from his arm and said no more. He crossed the hall to the door, then turned once more. She was standing motionless on the same spot and looking at him with lifeless eyes. He advanced one step and opened his arms toward her; then, with a violent effort, he turned away and so passed out of the door.

Outside the world lay bathed in morning light, the drops of pearly dew caught on the spiders' webs glistened in the first rays of the rising sun. He never looked back; he walked rapidly onward; behind him the peaceful farmstead gradually disappeared from view as out in front of him rose the great wide world.

THE OLD MAN

The moon had ceased to shine in through the window-panes, and it had grown quite dark; but the old man still sat in his armchair with folded hands and gazed before him into the emptiness of the room.

Gradually the murky darkness around him dissolved away

before his eyes and changed into a broad dark lake; one black wave after another went rolling on farther and farther, and on the last one, so far away as to be almost beyond the reach of the old man's vision, floated lonely among its broad leaves a white water-lily.

The door opened, and a bright glare of light filled the room.

"I am glad that you have come, Bridget," said the old man. "Set the lamp upon the table."

Then he drew his chair up to the table, took one of the open books and buried himself in studies to which he had once applied all the strength of his youth.

THE NAUGHTY SAINT VITALIS[1]

GOTTFRIED KELLER

(1819-1890)

At the beginning of the eighth century there lived in
Alexandria of Egypt an extraordinary monk, by name Vitalis, who had made it his particular task to reclaim the souls
of lost women from the ways of sin and lead them back to
virtue. But the method which he pursued was so peculiar,
and the fondness, nay enthusiasm with which he unceasingly
prosecuted his ends, was alloyed with such remarkable self-
abasement and simulation, that the like was scarcely ever
known in the world.

He kept an exact roll of all those wantons on a neat slip of
parchment, and, whenever he discovered a new quarry in
the city or its environs, he immediately noted her name and
dwelling on it; so that the frivolous young patricians of
Alexandria could have found no better guide than the indus-
trious Vitalis, had he been disposed to harbor less saintly
aims. As it was, the monk wormed out much news and information for his business from his sly conversations with
them; but he never suffered the scamps to pick up any information of the sort from him.

He carried this directory in his cowl, rolled up in a silver
case, and drew it out repeatedly to add a newly-discovered
light name, or to run over those already inscribed, count
them, and reckon which of the occupants should have her
turn next.

Then he would seek her hurriedly and half ashamed, and
say hastily, "Keep the night after to-morrow for me, and
promise no one else!" When he entered the house at the

1 Translated by Martin Wyness.

appointed time, he would leave the fair one standing, and
betake him to the farthest corner of the room, fall on his
knees, and pray fervently and at the pitch of his voice all
night long for the occupant of the house. In the early morning he would leave her, and charge her strictly not to tell
any one what had passed between them.

So he went on for a good while, and got himself into very
ill odor indeed. For while in secret, behind the closed doors
of the wantons, he alarmed and touched many a lost woman
by his fiery words of thunder and the fervent sweetness of
his murmured prayers, so that she came to herself and began
to lead a holy life; in the public eye, on the contrary, he
appeared to have laid himself out of set purpose to merit
the reputation of a vicious and sinful monk, who wallowed
gleefully in all the debaucheries of the world, and flaunted
his religious habit as a banner of shame.

If he found himself of an evening at dusk in respectable
company, he would exclaim abruptly, "Oh, what am I
about? I had almost forgotten that the brunette Doris is
waiting for me, the little dear! The deuce! I must be off, or
she will be vexed!"

If any one reproached him, he would cry out as if incensed, "Do you think that I am a stone? Do you imagine
that God did not create a little woman for a monk?" If any
one said, "Father, you would be better to lay aside your
frock and marry, so as not to offend others," he would answer, "Let them be offended if they choose, and run their
heads against a wall! Who is my judge?"

All this he used to say with great vehemence and all the
address of an actor, like one who defends a bad cause with
a multitude of bold words.

And he would go off and quarrel with the other suitors
before the girls' doors. He would even come to blows with
them, and administered many a rude buffet when they said,
"Away with the monk! Does the cleric mean to dispute the
ground with us? Get out, bald-pate!"

But he was so obstinate and persistent that in most cases
he got the better of them, and slipped into the house before
they knew where they were.

When he returned to his cell in the gray of the morning, he would cast himself down before the Mother of God, to whose sole honor and praise he undertook those adventures and drew down on himself the world's blame; and, did he succeed in bringing back some lost lamb and placing her in some holy convent, he felt more blissful in the presence of Heaven's Queen than if he had converted a thousand heathen. For this was his very remarkable taste, to endure the martyrdom of appearing in the eye of the world as an unclean profligate, while all the time Our Undefiled Lady in Heaven was well aware that he had never touched a woman, and that he wore an invisible crown of white roses on his much-maligned head.

Once he heard of a peculiarly dangerous person, who by her beauty and unusual charms had occasioned much trouble, and even bloodshed, inasmuch as a ferocious military dandy laid siege to her door, and struck down all who attempted to dispute her possession with him. Vitalis immediately proposed the attack and conquest of this hell. He did not wait to write the fair sinner's name in his list, but went straight off to the notorious house, and at the door, sure enough, encountered the soldier, who was stalking along, clad in scarlet, and with a javelin in his hand.

"Dodge aside, monkling!" he shouted contemptuously to the pious Vitalis. "How dare you come sneaking about my lion's den? Heaven is your place; the world is ours!"

"Heaven and earth and all that therein is," said Vitalis, "belong to the Lord, and to his merry servants! Pack, you gaudy lout, and let me go where I choose."

The warrior wrathfully raised the shaft of his javelin to bring it down on the monk's pate; but he suddenly pulled out a peaceful olive-branch from beneath his frock, parried the blow, and smote the bully so roughly on the crown that he well-nigh lost his senses, after which the fighting cleric gave him several raps on the muzzle, until the soldier, completely dumbfounded, made off cursing.

Thereupon Vitalis forced his way triumphantly into the house, where, at the head of a narrow staircase, the woman stood with a light in her hand, listening to the noise and shouting. She was an uncommonly fine figure of a woman, with beautiful, strong but rather defiant, features, about which her reddish hair floated in abundant loose waves, like a lion's mane.

She looked down contemptuously on Vitalis as he ascended, and said, "Where are you going?" "To you, my dove!" he answered. "Have you never head of the tender monk Vitalis, the jolly Vitalis?" But she answered harshly, as she blocked the staircase with her powerful figure, "Have you money, monk?" Disconcerted, he said, "Monks do not carry money about with them." "Then trot off," she said, "or I'll have you beaten out of the house with firebrands!"

Vitalis scratched his head, completely nonplussed, for he had never reckoned on this happening. The creatures whom he had hitherto converted had naturally thought no more of the price of iniquity, and those whom he failed to convert contented themselves with hard words in compensation for the precious time which he had made them lose. But here he could get no footing inside to begin his pious work; and yet there was something hugely attractive in the prospect of breaking in this red-haired daughter of Satan; for large and beautiful figures of men and women always mislead the judgment, so that we attribute greater qualities to them than they really possess. In desperation he searched through his frock, and came upon the silver case, which was adorned with an amethyst of some value. "I have nothing but this," he said; "let me in for it!" She took the case, examined it carefully, then bade him come with her. Arrived at her bedchamber, he did not favor her with another glance; but knelt down in a corner after his custom, and began to pray aloud.

The harlot, who believed that from force of habit the holy man meant to begin his worldly performance with prayer, broke into uncontrollable laughter, and sat down on her couch to look at him, for his behavior amused her monstrously. But as the business never came to an end, and was beginning to weary her, she bared her shoulders immodestly, went up to him, clasped him in her strong, white arms,

and pressed the good Vitalis with his shorn and tonsured
head so roughly against her breast that he was like to choke,
and began to gasp as if the flames of purgatory had taken
hold of him. But it did not last long; he began to kick out in
all directions like a young horse in a smithy, until he freed
himself from the hellish embrace. Then he took the long
cord which he wore about his waist, and caught hold of the
woman, to bind her hands behind her back, and have peace
from her. He had to wrestle hard with her before he succeeded in tying her up. He bound her feet together as well,
and threw the whole bundle with a mighty heave upon the
bed; after which he betook himself to his corner again, and
continued his prayers as if nothing had happened.

The captive lioness at first turned about angrily and restlessly, endeavoring to release herself, and uttered a hundred
curses. Then she became quieter as the monk never ceased
to pray, to preach, to adjure her, and towards morning she
uttered manifest sighs, which, as it seemed, were soon followed by contrite sobbing. In short, when the sun rose, she
was lying like a Magadalene at his feet, released from her
bonds, and bedewing the hem of his garment with tears.
With dignity, yet with gladness, Vitalis stroked her head,
and promised to pay her another visit as soon as it was dark,
to inform her in what convent he had found a penitent's
cell for her. Then he left, not forgetting first to impress upon her that she was to say nothing in the meantime about
her conversion, but only tell any one who might inquire,
that he had been very merry with her.

But judge of his surprise, when he reappeared at the appointed time, and found the door shut fast, and the female
freshly bedizened in all her glory looking out of the window.
"What do you want, priest?" she cried down. And in
astonishment he answered in an undertone, "What does this
mean, my lamb? Put away those sinful baubles, and let
me in to prepare you for your penance." "You want me,
you naughty monk?" she said with a smile, as if she had misunderstood him. "Have you money, or money's worth,
about you?" Vitalis stared up open-mouthed, then shook the

door desperately; but it remained shut as fast as ever, and the woman too disappeared from the window.

At last the laughter and imprecations of the passers-by drove the apparently depraved and shameless monk away from the door of the house of ill fame. But his thought and endeavor ran entirely upon making his way into the house again, and finding some means or other to overcome the devil by which the woman was possessed.

Absorbed in such thoughts, he turned his steps to a church, where, instead of praying, he thought over ways and means by which he might contrive to gain access to the lost woman. While thus engaged, his eye fell upon the box in which the charitable offerings were kept, and scarcely was the church deserted (it had become dark), when he burst the box violently open with his fist, poured the contents, which consisted of a lot of small silver coins, into his tucked-up frock, and hastened faster than any lover to the sinful woman's abode.

A foppish admirer was about to slip in at the opening door. Vitalis seized him from behind by his perfumed locks, flung him into the street, slammed the door in his face as he sprang in himself, and in another instant found himself once again in the presence of the disreputable person, who glared at him with flaming eyes when he appeared instead of her expected admirer. But Vitalis promptly poured the stolen money out on the table, saying, "Is that enough for to-night?" Without a word, but carefully, she counted the sum, said, "It is enough!" and put it away.

Now they confronted each other in the strangest fashion. Biting her lips to restrain a laugh, she looked at him with a simulated air of utter ignorance; while the monk scrutinized her with undecided and anxious glances, not knowing how he should begin to bring her to book. But when she suddenly proceeded to alluring gestures, and made to stroke his dark, glossy beard, the storm of his saintly character broke out in all its fury, he struck her hand indignantly away, and flung her upon the couch so that it shook. Then kneeling upon her, and grasping her hands, unaffected by her charms, he began to speak home to her in such fashion that at last her obduracy seemed to soften.

She desisted from her violent struggles to free herself. Copious tears flowed over her strong and lovely features, and, when at length the zealous man of God released her, and stood erect beside her sinful couch, the great form lay upon it with weary, relaxed limbs, as if broken by repentance and remorse, sobbing and turning her tear-dimmed eyes upon him, as if in astonishment at her unwilling transformation.

Then the tempest of his eloquent wrath changed likewise to tender emotion and deep sympathy. In his heart he gave praise to his Heavenly protectress, in whose honor this hardest of all his victories had been gained; and now his words of forgiveness and consolation flowed like the mild breath of spring over the broken ice of her heart.

More delighted than if he had enjoyed the sweetest favors of love, he hastened thence, not to snatch a brief slumber on his hard bed, but to throw himself down before the Virgin's altar, and pray for the poor repentant soul until the day had fully dawned. Then he vowed not to close an eye until the strayed lamb was finally safe within the shelter of the convent-walls.

The morning was scarcely astir when he was again on the way to her house. But he saw approaching at the same moment from the other end of the street the fierce warrior, who, after a riotous night, had taken it into his half-drunken head to wind up with a fresh conquest of the harlot.

Vitalis was the nearer to the unhallowed door, and he sprang nimbly forward to reach it. Thereupon the other hurled his spear at him, which buried itself just beside the monk's head in the door so that its shaft quivered. But, before it had ceased quivering, the monk wrenched it out of the wood with all his force, faced the infuriated soldier as he sprang towards him brandishing a naked sword, and quick as lightning drove the spear through his breast. The man sank in a heap, dead, and Vitalis was almost instantly seized and bound by a troop of soldiers, who were returning from the night-watch and had seen his deed, and he was led away to jail.

In genuine anguish he looked back to the house, where he could no longer accomplish his good work. The watch thought that he was simply deploring his evil star which had balked him of his wicked purpose, and treated the apparently incorrigible monk to blows and hard words until he was safely in ward.

He had to lie there for many days, and was several times brought before the judge. True, he was at length discharged without punishment, seeing that he had killed the man in self-defense. But nevertheless he came out of the affair with the reputation of a homicide, and every one cried out that now, surely, they must unfrock him. But Bishop Joannes, who was then chief at Alexandria, must have had some inkling of the real state of affairs, or else have cherished some deeper design; for he declined to expel the disreputable monk from the clergy, and ordered that for the present he was to be allowed to continue his extraordinary career.

He lost no time in returning to the converted sinner, who in the interval had gone back to her old ways, and would not admit the horrified and distressed Vitalis until he had appropriated another object of value and brought it to her. She repented and converted a third, and likewise a fourth and fifth time, for she found these conversions more lucrative than anything else, and moreover the evil spirit in her found an infernal satisfaction in mocking the poor monk with an endless variety of devices and inventions.

As for him, he now became a veritable martyr inwardly and outwardly; for, the more cruelly he was deceived, the more he felt compelled to exert himself, and it seemed to him as if his own eternal welfare depended on the reformation of this one person. He was already a homicide, a violator of churches, a thief; but he would rather have cut off his hand than part with the least portion of his reputation as a profligate; and, though all this became harder and harder for his heart to bear, he strove all the more eagerly to maintain his wicked exterior in the world's eye by means of frivolous speech. For this was the special form of martyrdom which he had elected. All the same, he became pale and thin, and began to flit about like a shadow on the wall, though always with a laughing face.

Now over against that house of torment dwelt a rich Greek merchant who had an only daughter called Iole, who could do what she liked, and consequently never knew what to do with herself all the livelong day. For her father, who was retired from business, studied Plato, and when tired of him he would compose neat epigrams on the ancient engraved gems of which he had a large collection; but Iole, when she had laid aside her music, could think of no outlet for her lively fancies, and would peep out restlessly at the sky and at the distance, from every peep-hole she found.

So it came about that she discovered the monk's coming and going in the street, and ascertained how matters stood with the notorious cleric. Startled and shy, she peeped at him from her safe concealment, and could not help commiserating his handsome form and manly appearance. When she learned from one of her maids, who was intimate with a maid of the wicked strumpet, how Vitalis was being deceived by her, and what was the real truth about him, she was amazed beyond measure, and, far from respecting his martrydom, was overcome by a strange indignation, and considered this sort of holiness little conducive to the honor of her sex. She dreamed and puzzled over it a while, and became always the more displeased, while, at the same time, her partiality for the monk increased and conflicted with her wrath.

All of a sudden she resolved that if the Virgin Mary had not sense enough to lead the erring monk back to more respectable ways, she would undertake the task herself, and lend the Virgin a hand in the business, little dreaming that she was the unwitting instrument of the Queen of Heaven, who had now begun to intervene. Forthwith she went to her father, and complained bitterly to him of the unseemly proximity of the lady of pleasure, and adjured him to employ his wealth in getting her out of the way immediately, at any price.

In obedience to her directions, the old gentleman addressed himself to the person, and offered her a certain sum for her house, on condition that she handed it over at once, and left the neighborhood entirely. She desired nothing better; and that same forenoon she had disappeared from the quarter, while the old merchant was sitting once more over his Plato and had dismissed the whole affair from his mind.

Not so Iole, who was in the utmost eagerness to rid the house from top to bottom of every trace of its former occupant. When it was all swept and garnished, she had it fumigated with rare spices so that the fragrant clouds poured out from all the windows.

Then she furnished the empty room with nothing but a carpet, a rose-bush, and a lamp, and, as soon as her father, who went to bed with the sun, was asleep, she went across, with a wreath of roses adorning her hair, and took her seat alone on the outspread carpet, while two trusty old servants kept watch at the door.

They turned away several night-revelers, but, whenever they saw Vitalis approach, they hid themselves and allowed him to pass in unhindered by the open door. With many sighs, he climbed the stair, full of fear lest he should see himself made a fool of once again, full of hope that he might be freed at last from this burden by the genuine repentance of a creature who was hindering him from rescuing so many other souls. But judge of his astonishment, when he entered the room, and found it stripped of all the wild red lioness's trumpery, and instead of her a sweet and tender form sitting on the carpet with the rose-bush opposite her on the floor.

"Where is the wretched creature who used to live here?" he exclaimed, looking about him in wonder, and finally letting his eyes rest on the lovely apparition which he saw before him.

"She has gone out into the Desert," answered Iole, without looking up. "There she means to live as an anchorite and do penance. It came upon her suddenly this morning, and broke her like a straw, and her conscience is awakened at last. She cried out for a certain priest Vitalis, who could have helped her. But the spirit which had entered into her would not suffer her to wait. The fool gathered all her possessions together, sold them, and gave the money to the poor, then went off hot-foot with a hair-cloth shift, and shorn hair, and a staff in her hand, the way of the Desert."

"Glory to thee, O Lord, and praise to thy Gracious Mother!" cried Vitalis, his hands folded in glad devotion, while a burden as of stone fell from his heart. But at the same time he looked more narrowly at the maiden with her rose-wreath, and said, "Why do you call her a fool? and who are you? and where do you come from? and what are you about?"

At that the lovely Iole cast her dark eyes to the ground lower than ever. She hung her head, and a bright flush of modesty spread over her face, for she thought shame of herself for the sad things she was going to say before a man.

"I am an outcast orphan, who have neither father nor mother. This lamp and carpet and rose-bush are the last remnants of my inheritance, and I have settled in this house with them to take up the life which my predecessor here has abandoned."

"Ah, so you would——!" the monk exclaimed, and clapped his hands. "Just see how busy the Devil is! And this innocent creature says the thing as indifferently as if I were not Vitalis! Now, my kitten, how do you mean to do? Just tell me!"

"I mean to devote myself to love and serve the men as long as this rose lives!" she said, pointing hastily at the flower-pot. Still, she could hardly get the words out, and almost sank on the floor for shame, so deeply did she droop her head. This natural modesty served the little rogue well; for it convinced the monk that he had to do this time with a childish innocent, who was possessed by the Devil and was on the point of jumping plump into the abyss. He caressed his beard in satisfaction at having arrived on the scene so opportunely for once, and, to enjoy his satisfaction still longer, he said slowly and jestingly, "Then afterwards, my dove?"

"Afterwards I will go, a poor lost soul, to Hell where beauteous Dame Venus is; or perhaps, if I meet a good preacher, I may even enter a convent later on, and do penance!"

"Better and better!" he cried. "That is an orderly plan of campaign, indeed, and not badly thought out. For, so far as the preacher is concerned, he is here now, he is standing before you, you black-eyed Devil's tit-bit! And the convent is all ready rigged up for you, like a mousetrap, only you'll go into it without having sinned, do you see? Without having sinned in anything but the pretty intention, which after all may make a very toothsome bone of repentance for you to gnaw all your days, and may serve your turn. For without it, you little witch, you would be too comical and light-hearted for a real penitent! But now!" he continued seriously, "first off with the roses, and then listen attentively!"

"No!" answered Iole, somewhat more pertly. "I will listen first, and then see whether I'll take off the roses. Now that I have once overcome my womanly feelings, mere words will not suffice to restrain me until I know the sin. And, without sin, I can know nothing about repentance. I give you this to think over before you begin your efforts. But still I am willing to hear you."

Then Vitalis began the finest exhortation he had ever delivered. The maiden listened good-naturedly and attentively, and the sight of her had, unknown to him, a considerable influence on his choice of language; for the beauty and daintiness of the prospective convert were themselves enough to evoke a lofty eloquence. But, as she was not the least bit in earnest about the project which she had so outrageously advertised, the monk's oration could not have any very serious effect upon her. On the contrary, a charming laugh flitted about her mouth, and, when he had concluded, and expectantly wiped the sweat from his brow, Iole said, "I am only half moved by your words, and cannot decide to give up my project; for I am only too curious to know what it is like to live in sin and pleasure!"

Vitalis stood as if petrified, and could not get so much as one word out. It was the first time that his powers of conversion had failed so roundly. Sighing and thoughtful, he paced up and down the room, and took another look at the little candidate for Hell. The power of the Devil seemed to have combined in some bewildering fashion with the power of innocence to thwart him. But he was all the more passionately anxious to overcome them.

"I do not leave this place until you repent," he cried at length, "not though I should spend three days and three nights here!"

"That would only make me more obstinate," responded Iole. "But I will take time to think, and will hear you again to-morrow night. The day will soon be dawning now. Go your way. Meantime I promise to do nothing in the matter, and to remain in my present condition; in return for which you must promise on no account to mention me to anybody, and to come here only under cover of darkness."

"So be it!" exclaimed Vitalis, and took his departure, while Iole slipped quickly back into her father's house.

She did not sleep long, and awaited the coming evening with impatience. For the monk, now that he had been so close to her throughout the night, pleased her better than he had done at a distance. She saw now what a fire of enthusiasm glowed in his eyes, and how resolute all his movements were, despite his monkish garments. And when she represented to herself his self-abnegation, his perseverance in the course he had once chosen, she could not help wishing that those good qualities were utilized to her own pleasure and profit, in the shape of a cherished and faithful husband. Her project, accordingly, was to make a brave martyr into a still better husband.

The next night she found Vitalis at her carpet in good time, and he continued his exertions on behalf of her virtue with undiminished zeal. He had to stand all the time, except when he knelt to pray. Iole, on the contrary, made herself comfortable. She laid herself back on the carpet, clasped her hands behind her head, and kept her half-closed eyes steadily fixed upon the monk as he stood and preached. Sometimes she closed them as if overcome by drowsiness, and, as soon as Vitalis saw this, he pushed her with his foot to waken her. But this harsh measure always turned out milder than he intended; for, as soon as his foot neared the maiden's slender side, it spontaneously moderated its force, and touched her tender ribs quite gently; not to mention that a most unusual sensation ran along the whole length of the monk, a sensation which he had never before experienced in the slightest degree from any of the numerous fair sinners with whom he had had to deal.

As morning approached, Iole nodded more and more frequently, till at last Vitalis exclaimed indignantly, "Child, you are not listening! I can't keep you awake. You are utterly sunk in sloth!"

"Not so!" she said, as she suddenly opened her eyes, and a sweet smile flitted across her face, as if the approaching day were already reflected in it. "I have been paying attention; I am beginning to hate that wretched sin, which is all the more repulsive to me that it causes you vexation, dear monk; for nothing could be pleasing to me that is displeasing to you."

"Really?" he queried, full of joy. "So I have really succeeded? Come away to the convent at once, that we may make sure of you. This time we'll strike while the iron's hot."

"You do not understand me aright," Iole answered, and, blushing, cast her eyes again to the ground. "I am enamored of you, and have conceived a tender inclination towards you!"

For a moment, Vitalis felt as if a hand had smitten his heart; yet he did not feel that it caused him pain. Paralyzed, he opened wide his mouth and eyes, and stood stock-still.

But Iole, blushing redder than ever, went on to say gently and softly, "You must now lecture me and charm away this new mischief from me, in order to deliver me entirely from the malady, and I hope you may succeed!"

Vitalis, without saying a word, turned tail and ran out of the house. Instead of seeking his bed, he rushed out into the silvery gray morning, and debated whether he should leave this dangerous young woman to her fate and have done with her, or should endeavor to cast out this latest whim also, which appeared to be the most reprehensible of all her notions, and not altogether without danger to himself. But a wrathful flush of shame flew to his head at the thought that anything of the sort could be perilous for him. Then again it occurred to him that the Devil might have set a snare for him, in which case it were best to avoid it betimes. But to become a deserter in the face of such a wisp of a temptress! And supposing the poor creature were in earnest, and could be cured of her latest unseemly delusion by a few rough words? In short, Vitalis could not settle within himself, all the more that at the bottom of his heart a dim wave was beginning to cause the skiff of his reason to be unsteady.

In his perplexity he slipped into a little chapel where a beautiful ancient marble statue of the goddess Juno had recently been set up with a golden nimbus as an image of the Virgin Mary, so as not to waste such a gift of divine art. He cast himself down before this Mary, and laid his doubts fervently before her, and prayed his patroness for a token. If she nodded, he would complete Iole's conversion; if she shook her head, he would desist.

But the image left him in the most cruel uncertainty, and did neither one thing nor the other; it neither nodded nor shook its head. Only when the red gleam of some flying morning clouds passed over the marble, its face seemed to smile most propitiously; whether it was that the ancient goddess, as guardian deity of connubial love and chastity, was giving a sign, so that the new one could not refrain from smiling at her adorer's troubles; for both were women at heart, and such are always tickled when a love-affair is in train. But Vitalis knew nothing of all this. On the contrary, the beauty of the expression raised his courage amazingly, and, still more remarkable to relate, the statue appeared to assume the features of the blushing Iole, who was challenging him to expel her love of him from her mind.

Meantime, at the same hour, Iole's father was strolling beneath the cypresses of his garden. He had acquired some very fine new gems, the engraving on which had brought him out of bed at that early hour. He was handling them rapturously, and making them play in the beams of the rising sun. There was a dark amethyst, on which Luna drove her car through the heavens, unwitting that Love was squatted behind her, while flying Cupids called to her the Greek for "Whip behind!" A handsome onyx showed Minerva lost in meditation, holding Love on her knee, who was busy polishing her breast-plate with his hand to see his own reflection.

And lastly, on a cornelian, Love, in the form of a salamander, was tumbling about in a vestal fire and throwing its guardian virgins into perplexity and alarm.

These scenes tempted the old man to compose some distichs, and he was considering which he should attack first when his daughter Iole came through the garden, pale and unslept. Anxious and surprised, he called her to him and inquired what had robbed her of her slumbers. But, before she could answer, he began to show her his gems and explain them to her.

At that she heaved a deep sigh and said, "Ah, if all those great powers, Chastity herself, Wisdom, and Religion, could not defend themselves against Love, how is a poor insignificant creature like me to fortify herself against him?"

The old gentleman was not a little astonished at these words. "What do I hear?" he said. "Is it that the dart of mighty Eros has smitten thee?"

"It has pierced me to the heart," she responded, "and, if I am not in possession of the man whom I love within a day and a night, I shall be the bride of Death!"

Although her father was accustomed to let her have her own way in everything she desired, this haste was rather too violent for him, and he recommended repose and reflection to his daughter. But she had no lack of the latter, and she employed it so well that the old man exclaimed, "So I must discharge the most unpleasant of all a father's duties, I must go to your choice, to your man, and lead him by the nose up to the best that I can call mine, and beg him to be so kind as to take possession? Here is a tidy little woman, my dear sir! I pray you, don't despise her! I had much rather give you a box or two on the ear, but my little daughter will die, so I must be civil! So be graciously pleased, for Heaven's sake, to taste the pasty which is offered you. It has been well baked, and will fairly melt in your mouth!"

"All that is spared us," said Iole, "for, if you will only allow me, I hope to bring him to it that he will come himself and ask for my hand."

"And what if this man, whom I know nothing of, turns out to be a wastrel and a good-for-nothing?"

"Then let him be driven away with scorn! But he is a saint!"

"Then run away, and leave me to the Muses," said the good old man.

When evening came, the night did not follow the dusk so promptly as Vitalis appeared at Iole's heels in the familiar house. But he had never entered the house in the same fashion as now. His heart beat, and he was forced to feel what it meant to see again a person who had played such a trump. It was another Vitalis than the one who had descended in the early morning, who now came up the steps, although he himself was the most unconscious of the fact; for the poor converter of frail women and monk of evil renown had never learned the difference between the smile of a harlot and that of an honorable woman.

Yet he came with the best of intentions, and with the old purpose of driving all the idle notions out of the little monster's head for good and all. Only he had a vague idea that once his task was accomplished he might be permitted a pause in his martyr activity; all at once he began to be very tired of it.

But it was determined that some new surprise should always await him in that enchanted dwelling. When he entered the room, he found it beautifully decorated, and furnished with all usual furniture. A delicate, insidious odor of flowers pervaded the room, and was in keeping with a certain modest worldliness. On a snow-white couch, not a fold out of place in its silk coverings, sat Iole, splendidly arrayed, in sweet troubled melancholy, like an angel in meditation. Under the trim pleats of her robe her bosom heaved like the foam on a milking pail, and, though the white arms, which she folded beneath her breast, shone so fair, yet all those charms looked so lawful and permissible in the order of things that Vitalis's accustomed eloquence stuck in his throat.

"You are amazed, my pretty monk," began Iole, "to find all this show and finery here! Know that this is the farewell which I mean to take of the world, and, at the same time, I will lay aside the inclination which, unfortunately, I cannot help feeling for you. But you must help me to this end to the best of your ability, and after the fashion that I have devised and request of you. I mean that when you address me in these garments and as a cleric it is always the same. The bearing of a churchman fails to convince me, for I belong to the world. I cannot be cured of love by a monk, who is unacquainted with love, and does not know what he is talking about. If you really mean to afford me rest and put me on the way to Heaven, go into that closet, where you will find secular clothes laid out ready for you. Exchange your monk's clothes there for them, array yourself like a man of the world, then seat yourself beside me to partake of a little repast with me, and in such worldly externals exert all your acuteness and understanding to wean me from you and incline me to piety."

Vitalis made no reply, but bethought himself a while. Then he decided to end all his difficulties at one stroke, and to put the devil of this world to flight with his own weapons by acceding to Iole's eccentric proposal.

So he actually betook himself into an adjoining closet, where a couple of servants awaited him with splendid garments of purple and fine linen. Scarcely had he put them on, when he looked a good head taller, and it was with a noble mien that he strode back to Iole, who could not take her eyes off him, and clapped her hands for joy.

Now, however, a real miracle and a strange transformation was wrought on the monk. For scarcely had he sat down in his worldly array beside the charming woman, when the immediate past was blown away like a dream from his mind, and he forgot all about his purpose. Instead of speaking so much as a word, he listened eagerly to what was said by Iole, who had taken possession of his hand and begun to tell him her true story, who she was, where she lived, and how it was her most heart-felt desire that he should give over his strange manner of life, and ask her father for her hand, so that he might become a good husband, well-pleasing to God. She also said many wonderful things in the most beautiful words about the history of a happy and chaste love, but concluded with a sigh that she saw well how hopeless her desire was, and that he was now at liberty to argue her out of all those ideas, but not before he had fortified himself duly for his task with meat and drink.

Then at her signal the servants set drinking-vessels on the table together with a basket of cakes and fruits. Iole mixed a goblet of wine for the silent Vitalis, and affectionately handed him something to eat, so that he felt quite at home, and was reminded of his childhood, when as a little boy he was tenderly fed by his mother. He ate and drank, and, when he had done so, it seemed to him as if he might now venture to rest from his long, weary toil, and lo! our Vitalis leant his head to one side, towards Iole, and without more ado fell asleep, and lay till sunrise.

When he awoke, he was alone, and no one was to be seen or heard. He sprang up hastily, and was horrified at the splendid garment in which he was dressed. He rushed madly through the house from top to bottom, seeking for his monk's frock. But not the smallest trace of it could he find, until he chanced to see a little heap of cinders and ashes, on which a sleeve of his priest's dress was lying half consumed, whereupon he rightly concluded that there it had been solemnly burned.

Next he put his head out cautiously, first at one, then at another of the windows which looked on to the street, drawing it in every time that any one approached. At last he flung himself down upon the silken couch as comfortable and at ease as if he had never lain on a monk's hard bed. Then he roused himself, put his dress straight, and stole in high excitement to the street-door. There he still hesitated a moment; but suddenly he flung it wide open, and went out into the world a magnificent and imposing figure. No one recognized him; every one took him for some fine gentleman from abroad, who was enjoying a few gay days at Alexandria.

He looked neither to right nor left, else he would have seen Iole on her house-top. So he went straight back to his convent, where, however, all the monks and their superior had just resolved to expel him from their fellowship; for the measure of his iniquities was now full, and he contributed only to the scandal and disgrace of the Church. The sight of him, actually coming among them in his worldly gallant's attire, knocked the bottom out of the tub of their patience; they drenched him and doused him with water from all sides, and drove him with crosses, besoms, pitchforks and kitchen-ladles out of the convent.

Once on a time this rough handling would have been the height of felicity to him, and a triumph of his martyrdom. True, he laughed inwardly even now, but for a somewhat different reason. He took one more stroll round about the city-walls, and let his red cloak wave in the wind. A fine breeze from the Holy Land blew across the sparkling sea; but Vitalis was becoming more and more worldly-minded. Suddenly he retraced his steps into the bustling streets of the city, sought the house where Iole dwelt, and did what she wished.

He now made as excellent and complete a layman and husband as he had been a martyr. The Church, however, when she understood the real facts of the case, was inconsolable over the loss of such a saint, and made every endeavor to recall the fugitive to her bosom. But Iole held him fast and gave it to be understood that he was in very good hands with her.

PLAUTUS IN THE CONVENT[1]

CONRAD FERDINAND MEYER

(1825-1908)

To enjoy the cool of evening after a hot summer day a company of cultivated Florentines had assembled, in front of a pavilion in the Medici gardens, about Cosimo de' Medici, the "father of his country." The dusk crept by slow degrees over a gorgeous but delicately shaded, cloudless sky above the group of temperate revelers, in which a sharp-featured, gray-haired man was conspicuous, whose eloquent lips held the listening circle spellbound. The expression of his animated countenance was a strange mixture: over the serene brow and the smiling corners of the mouth lay the shadow of a sad experience.

When a pause ensued, Cosimo, with the shrewd eyes in an ill-favored face, spoke out and said, "Poggio, my friend, I have lately been browsing again in the little volume of your *Facetiæ*. To be sure, I know it by heart, and this I could not but regret, since I was now able to take pleasure only in the happy turns of a supple style, without the former sensation either of curiosity or of surprise. Fastidious as you are, it is impossible that you should not have excluded from the authorized edition of the book one or another of your droll and amiable pleasantries, whether because it was too spicy, or because it was not spicy enough. Try to recollect. Favor these friends, who will understand the most veiled allusion and excuse the boldest jest, with a *Facetia inedita*. Telling your story and sipping your wine"—he pointed to the goblet—"you will forget your sorrow."

The fresh grief to which Cosimo alluded, as to a matter

[1] Translated by William Guild Howard.

of common report about town, had befallen the venerable
Poggio—present secretary of the Florentine Republic, past
secretary to five popes, formerly a cleric and latterly a family man—at the hands of one of his sons, of whom all were
brilliantly endowed and all worthless. This miscreant had
disgraced the gray hairs of his father by an act which came
close to theft and robbery, and which, moreover, imposed
upon the thrifty Poggio, his bondsman, a serious financial
sacrifice.

After a little reflection the old man replied, "Those and
similar pleasantries which are to your liking, friend Cosimo,
comport, like flowery wreaths, only with brown locks, and
sound ill from the lips of a toothless graybeard." Smiling,
he displayed a fine row of white teeth. "And," he sighed,
"only with reluctance do I return to these youthful fri-
volities, harmless as in themselves they may be, now that I
behold my open-mindedness and my easy-going philosophy
of life degenerate in my son—I know not by what uncanny
law of increase—into intolerable impudence, even into
profligacy."

"Poggio, you are preaching!" interposed a youth. "You,
who have given back to the world the comedies of Plautus!"

"Thank you for your warning, Romolo!" cried the unhappy father, collecting himself; for, as a good companion,
he too thought it improper to burden the guests with his
domestic troubles. "Thank you for reminding me. *The Discovery of Plautus* is the *Facetia* with which, indulgent
friends, I will entertain you today."

"Call it rather *The Rape of Plautus*," interrupted a
scoffer.

But Poggio, without deigning to look at him, continued,
"May it please you, friends, and at the same time demonstrate how unjust is the reproach with which the envious
pursue me, that in a dishonorable, reprehensible way I
have appropriated to myself those classics of which they
cannot deny I am the discoverer—that, to put it bluntly, I
have stolen them. Nothing is farther from the truth."

A smile went about the circle, in which Poggio at first

gravely declined to join, but in which finally he also participated; for as one who knew human nature he was aware that even the falsest prejudices can be uprooted only with difficulty.

"My *Facetia*," he said, with a parody of the inclusive summary usually prefixed to an Italian short-story, "has to do with two crosses, a heavy and a light one, and with two barbarian nuns, a novice and an abbess."

"Fit for the gods, Poggio," a neighbor interrupted him, "like those simple-minded German vestals with whom, in your admirable letters from abroad, you peopled as with naiads the healing springs along the Limmat—by the nine muses, the best thing you have written! That letter circulated in a thousand copies all over Italy."

"I exaggerated, knowing your taste," said Poggio jocosely. "At any rate, Ippolito, you, as a lover of simple-mindedness, will delight in my barbarian nun. And so I begin."

In those days, illustrious Cosimo, when we were lopping off the superfluous heads of our holy church, lately become a hydra, I found myself in Constance and actively devoted myself to the magnificent business of an ecumenical council. My leisure time, however, I divided between contemplation of the stimulating spectacle which had crowded upon the narrow stage of a German imperial city the piety, science, and statecraft of the century, with its popes, heretics, mountebanks, and courtesans, and the occasional search for manuscripts in the neighboring monasteries.

Following up various clues and trails, I came to the supposition, amounting to certainty, that in a nearby convent there was a Plautus in the hands of the barbarian nuns, having strayed thither as a legacy or as a pledge from some impoverished Benedictine abbey. A Plautus! Imagine, illustrious patron, what that meant at a time when our curiosity was being so unbearably goaded by the few fragments then extant of the great Roman comedian. That I could not sleep you may well believe, Cosimo—you who share and encourage my enthusiasm for the relics of a greater world which has declined and fallen. Would that I had left everything in the lurch and had hastened to the spot where an immortal, instead of delighting the world, lay moldering in ignoble obscurity! But those were the days when the election of a new pope occupied the minds of all men and the Holy Spirit was beginning to turn the attention of the assembled fathers to the merits and virtues of Otto Colonna; though this is not to say that the daily and hourly running about of his adherents and servants, of whom I was one, had thereby become any the less necessary.

Thus it happened that an inferior and dishonest searcher, unfortunately a fellow-countryman of ours, in whose presence I had, in the joy of my heart, indiscreetly mentioned the possibility of so great a discovery, anticipated me, and—blunderer that he was—instead of getting the classic by fair means or foul, aroused the suspicion of the abbess of the convent in which it lay buried in dust, and directed her attention to the treasure which she unwittingly possessed.

Finally I got a free hand and, in spite of the impending papal election, mounted a sturdy mule, leaving orders that a messenger should be dispatched to me upon the occurrence of the great event. My mule-driver was a Rhætian who had come to Constance in the retinue of the Bishop of Chur, and his name was Hans of Splügen. He had unhesitatingly accepted my first offer and we had agreed upon an incredibly low sum.

A thousand pleasantries passed through my mind. The blue ether, the summer air tempered by a cool, almost cold breath from the north, the inexpensive trip, the difficulties of the papal election happily overcome, the supreme satisfaction awaiting me in the discovery of a classic—these heavenly benefits disposed me to infinite good-humor, and I heard the muses and the angels sing. My companion, on the contrary, Hans of Splügen, abandoned himself, as it seemed, to the most melancholy reflections.

Happy myself, I benevolently sought to make him happy also, or at least to cheer him up, and I gave him all sorts of riddles—mostly from biblical history, which is familiar to the people. "Do you know," I asked, "the manner in which the prince of the apostles was freed from his chains?" And I received the answer that he had seen the miracle depicted in the church of the Apostles at Tosana. "Listen, Hänsel," I continued. "The angel said unto Peter, 'Bind on thy sandals and follow me.' And they went, Peter not knowing that it was an angel, past the first and the second ward, through the gate and along a street. And forthwith the companion departed and then Peter said, 'Now I know of a surety that an angel hath led me.' From what circumstance, Hänsel, did this sudden knowledge, this incontrovertible certainty come to him? Tell me that, if you can guess it." Hans thought a while and then shook the curly locks of his hard head. "Listen, Hänsel," I said, "I will answer the question. From this circumstance Peter recognized the angel, that he asked no gratuity for his services. Such is not the way of this world. That is the way only of the heavenly beings!"

But one ought not to jest with the people. Hänsel suspected in this joke, born of nothing, a purpose or an allusion.

"It is true, sir, that I am conducting you for almost nothing, and that, though I am not an angel, I shall ask you for no gratuity. Know, then, that I also on my own account am drawn to Monasterlingen"—he mentioned the name of the nunnery which was the goal of our expedition—"where tomorrow Gertrude will wind the rope girdle about her hips, and her blond hair will be shorn from her head."

Tears rolled down the sunburnt face of the hardy youth who, I may add—perhaps there was a drop of Roman blood in his veins—possessed much natural dignity of speech and action. "By Cupid's bow," I exclaimed, "an unhappy lover!" and bade him tell me his story, which proved to be simple but by no means easy to understand.

Hänsel had, he said, come with his bishop to Constance, and being without employment, had sought work in the neighborhood as a carpenter. He had found it on some buildings in process of erection for the nunnery, and had made the acquaintance of Gertrude, who lived nearby. They had learned to like each other and found favor in each others's sight. Gladly and often they had sat together—"in all decency and honor," said he, "for she is a good girl." Then suddenly she had withdrawn from him, without detriment to their love, but peradventure as though a strictly limited time had elapsed; and he had heard for certain that she intended to take the veil. Tomorrow she was to be invested, and he had in mind to attend this ceremony, in order to have the testimony of his own eyes to the fact that an honest and by no means impulsive girl could, for no conceivable reason, leave a man whom she confessedly loved, to become a nun—to embrace duties for which Gertrude, a natural woman and full of life, was as unsuited as she could possibly be, and for which, to judge from her own expressions, she had no desire, but rather recoiled from them with horror and dread.

"It is unexplainable," the melancholy Rhætian concluded; and added that through the mercy of heaven his wicked stepmother had recently died, on whose acount he had left his father's house; so that this and the arms of his aged father were again open to receive him. His love, accordingly, would now find a warm nest awaiting her; but she was incomprehensibly determined to nestle in a cell.

At the close of this speech Hänsel relapsed into his dark brooding and obstinate silence, which he interrupted only to answer my question concerning the kind of woman the abbess was. He said she was an ugly little person, but an excellent manager who had restored and rehabilitated from slovenliness the economic administration of the convent. She came from Abbatis Cella and people called her simply "Brigittchen of Trogen."

Finally the convent appeared above the sky-line of monotonous vineyards. Hänsel now asked me to leave him behind at an inn by the roadside, since he wished to see Gertrude only once more—at her investiture. I nodded assent and dismounted from the mule, in order to stroll at leisure toward the not distant convent.

There they were having a merry time. On the lawn of the convent yard an indistinguishable great object was being sold at auction or exhibited for some other purpose. A rough soldier, with his helmet on his head, blew from time to time a discordant trumpet, perhaps a piece of booty, perhaps an ecclesiastical instrument. About the abbess, with her nuns, and the questionable herald in a patched doublet and tattered hose, whose bare toes peered forth from his worn-out boots, laity and an aggregation of monks formed a motley group in the most free and easy attitudes. Among the peasants stood here and there a nobleman—in Turgovia, as this German district is called, there is an overabundance of such small and petty crested fowl—but minstrels, gypsies, vagabonds, strumpets, and rabble of every sort, attracted thither by the Council, also mingled in the strange circle. One after another, they stepped forth and tried the weight of the object in which, upon nearer approach, I recognized a gigantic old horrible cross. It seemed to be extraordinarily heavy; for after a short while it began to sway back and forth in the wearying hands of even the strongest bearer; it threatened to fall, and would have come crashing down if other hands and shoulders had not tumultuously put themselves under the ponderous beams. Shouts and laughter accompanied the scandalous performance. To complete the ignoble scene, the boorish abbess danced about like one possessed upon the freshly mown lawn, inspired by the worth of her relic—the meaning of this country fair began to dawn upon me—and probably also inspirited by the convent wine which, without cups and without ceremony, passed in huge wooden buckets from lip to lip.

"By the tresses of the Virgin Mother!" shrieked the impious jade, "not a man of you, not even the stoutest, can lift and carry this cross of our blessed Duchess Amalaswinta; but tomorrow our Gertrude will toss it like a shuttle-cock. I only hope the mortal creature will not grow vain! To God alone the glory, says Brigittchen. People, the miracle is a thousand years old and to this day is brand new. It has always worked, and upon my word it shall go off tomorrow without a hitch." Manifestly the excellent abbess had had a drop too much in the course of this heavenly day.

Comparing these comical doings with similar events that I have witnessed in my own blessed country, I began to understand them and to estimate them at their true value—just as, an hour later, with fuller knowledge of the facts, I definitely solved the problem; but the trend of my thoughts was suddenly and unpleasantly interrupted by a shrill call of the clownish woman in the white cowl, with the flushed face, the blinking, crafty eyes, the scarcely discoverable pug-nose, and the bestial mouth gaping at an enormous distance below it.

"Hi, there, Italian scribe!" she yelled at me. I was on this day clad in a simple traveling costume and carry the evidence of my classical origin in my countenance. "Come a bit nearer and let me see you lift the cross of the blessed Amalaswinta!"

All eyes were turned in expectation of amusement at me, people made way for me, and with rude jolts in the Swiss fashion shoved me forward. I excused myself on the ground, well known to you, my friends, of the shortness and weakness of my arms.—The narrator raised his arms enough to reveal the fact.

Then the shameless woman, looking me over, cried out, "Your fingers are all the longer for it, you smooth customer!" —and in fact, by the daily practice of writing, my fingers have become developed and pliant. The crowd of bystanders burst into a boisterous laugh, incomprehensible to me, but offensive, and I charged the abbess with it. In vexation I turned away, went around the corner of the church nearby, and finding the main portal open, I entered. The noble round arch of the windows and ceiling, instead of the new-fangled pointed arch and the foolish French filigree, restored my soul to peace and composure. Slowly I strode forward the length of the nave, attracted by a piece of sculpture which, lighted from above, stood forth in impressive solidity from the religious dimness and seemed, in its way, to be a thing of beauty. I went up to it and was not disappointed. The statuary consisted of two figures united by a cross, and this cross completely resembled in size and proportions the one exhibited on the lawn, whichever may have been imitated from the other. A powerful woman crowned with thorns was carrying it almost level in brawny arms and on her mighty shoulder, and yet was sinking beneath its weight, as was shown by her knees, roughly outlined on her gown. By the side and in front of this tottering giantess a smaller figure, with a little crown upon her lovely head, mercifully placed her more delicate shoulder under the unbearable burden. The old master had purposely—or more probably from lack of artistic resources—treated the forms and garments only in the rough, reserving his cunning and the ardor of his soul for the faces, which expressed despair and mercy.

Taken with the charm of this expression, I stepped backward to get a better light. Lo and behold, there knelt before me on the other side of the group a maiden, presumably a native, a peasant girl of the vicinity, almost as powerfully built as the sculptured duchess, and with the hood of her white cowl thrown back over heavy braids of blond hair and a sturdy neck unused to concealment.

She arose; for absorbed in meditation, she had not sooner become aware of my presence than I of hers; brushed away a flood of tears from her eyes, and made a move as if to depart. She was to all appearances a novice.

I detained her and asked her to explain the statue to me. I was one of the foreign fathers at the Council, I told her in my broken German. This information did not seem to make much impression upon her. She related to me in a simple way that the image represented an ancient queen or duchess, the founder of this convent, who, taking the vow here, had wished to proceed to the investiture, her head crowned with thorns and her shoulder laden with the cross. "They say," continued the girl doubtfully, "that she was a great sinner, heavy laden with guilt for the murder of her husband, but of such high station that secular justice could not reach her. Then God touched her heart and she fell into great distress, despairing of the salvation of her soul!" After a long and bitter atonement, craving a sign that she was forgiven, she had caused this great, heavy cross to be built, which the strongest man of her time was hardly able to lift alone; and she too would have succumbed beneath its weight, had not the Mother of God in visible form mercifully assisted her to bear it, placing her ambrosial shoulder beside the earthly one.

These words the blond German did not use, but simpler ones, indeed so crude and uncouth that they could not be translated from a barbarian speech into our cultivated Tuscan without becoming boorish and grotesque; and that, my lords, would in turn be inappropriate to the expression of large-mindedness in the defiant blue eyes and the bold but shapely features of the girl whom I then saw before me.

"The story is credible!" I said to myself; for this feat by a barbarian queen seemed to me befitting the times and the customs of the dark close of the first millennium. "It might be true!"

"It is true!" Gertrude asserted curtly and vehemently, with a gloomy glance of conviction at the statuary, and again made a move as if to depart; but I detained her for the second time, with the question whether she were the Gertrude of whom my guide of today, Hans of Splügen, had told me. She replied in the affirmative, unabashed, not even embarrassed, and a smile like a wandering light spread slowly from the firm corners of her mouth over her brown face, now beginning to grow pale in the convent air.

Then she reflected and said, "I knew that he would come to my investiture, and I can have no objection. Seeing my tresses fall will help him to forget me. Since you happen to be here, reverend father, I will make a request of you. If the man returns with you to Constance, reveal to him the cause of my refusal to be his wife after"—and she blushed, though almost imperceptibly—"after I had been friendly with him in all honor, according to the custom of our country. More than once I have been on the point of telling him the story, but I bit my lip; for it is a secret compact between the Mother of God and myself, and secrets should not be disclosed. To you, however, who are versed in secrets of the soul, I can confide the compact without betrayal. You shall then acquaint Hans with as much of it as is fitting and to you seems meet. It is only that he may not deem me fickle and ungrateful, and remember me as such.

"This is how it is with me. When I was a mere child—I was ten years old and had already lost my father—mother was taken with a grave and hopeless sickness, and fear came upon me, lest I be left alone in the world. Out of this fear, and out of love for my mother, I dedicated myself to the Virgin Mary for my twentieth year, if she would preserve my mother's life until then, or nearly then. She did so, and mother lived until last Corpus Christi day, when she peacefully died, just at the time when Hans had work as a carpenter in the convent; so that he it was who made mother's coffin. Since I was now alone in the world, what wonder is it that I fell in love with him? He is honest and thrifty, as the Italians are for the most part; 'modest and discreet,' as they say on the other side of the mountains. Moreover, we could converse in two languages; for my father, who was a strong and courageous man, had repeatedly accompanied a puny, timid tradesman, not without profit, over the mountains, and had brought home a few bits of Italian from the other side. If now Hans called me *cara bambina,* I returned the compliment by calling him *poverello,* and both ring true, though I will find no fault with the words of endearment usual in our country, when they are honestly meant.

"But it was at this time also that I was due to keep my vow, and every ringing of the Angelus reminded me of it.

"On the other hand, thoughts came into my mind and whispered to me such things as 'The vow of an innocent child who does not know the difference between man and woman could have no power to bind you,' or 'Kind as she is, the Virgin Mother would likely have granted you your mother's life of her own mercy and as a free gift.' But I said in reply, 'A bargain is a bargain,' and 'Honesty is the best policy!' She has kept her part of the agreement, and I will keep mine. Without truth and faith the world cannot endure. What did my father say, who is no more? 'I would keep my word with the devil,' said he, 'not to mention the Lord our God!'

"Hear now, reverend father, what I think and believe. Since the Virgin Mother bore the cross for the queen, she has, recruiting her convent, from time immemorial helped all novices without distinction to bear it. It has become a habit with her; she does it unconsciously. With my own eyes I, a nine-year-old child, saw how Lieschen of Wein-felden, a sickly creature who took the veil here, carried the ponderous cross as if in sport on her drooping shoulder.

"Now I shall say to the Virgin, 'If thou wilt have me, take me!—although I—if thou wert Gertrude and I were the Mother of God—should perhaps not take a child at its word. But no matter: a bargain is a bargain!—only with this dif-ference: the duchess, burdened with sins, felt relieved and happy in the convent; it will be pain and sorrow for me. If thou bearest the cross for me, lighten my heart also; else there will be trouble, Mother of God! If thou canst not lighten my heart, then let me a thousand times rather to my shame and before the eyes of all the people plunge down and fall flat upon the floor!"

As I watched these laboring thoughts slowly draw deep furrows in Gertrude's young brow I smiled and suggested cunningly, "An adroit and clever girl could extricate herself from the difficulty by stumbling!" Then fire flashed from her blue eyes. "Do you think, sir, I shall cheat?" she exclaimed wrathfully. "So help me God the Father, the Son, and the Holy Ghost in my last hour, as I will honestly bear the cross with all the strength and sinews of these my arms!" And she raised her arms convulsively, as though she were already carrying the cross, so that the sleeves of her cowl and smock fell far back. Then I, as the Florentine that I am, beheld the slender, powerful, feminine arms with artistic delight. She observed me, frowned, and indignantly turned her back upon me.

After she had gone I seated myself in a confessional, rested upon my elbow, and meditated—verily not upon the barbarian maiden, but upon the Roman classic. Suddenly my heart rejoiced and I cried out exultantly, "Thanks, ye immortal gods. A darling of the comic muse is restored to the world! Plautus is won!"

Friends, a conspiracy of circumstances guaranteed me this success.

I know not, Cosimo, what your views are on the subject of miracles. I myself am a tolerable believer, neither superstitious nor presumptuous; for I cannot endure those absolutists who, when an inexplicable fact has gathered an atmosphere of superstition about it, either summarily believe or just as summarily reject the whole phenomenon—moon and corona—without investigation and without distinction.

The marvel and the fraud, both I believed I had here discovered.

The heavy cross was genuine, and a magnificent sinner, a barbarian woman, might have lifted it with the superhuman strength of despair and fervor. But this deed had not been repeated; on the contrary, it had for centuries been imitated by jugglery. Who was guilty of the fraud? Was it mistaken piety? Calculating avarice? The answer to these questions lay hidden in the darkness of the times. But so much was certain: the horrible cross, black with age, which was exhibited to the people, and the one which had been borne by a succession of simple or compliant novices—and only lately by the feeble and wily Lieschen of Weinfelden at her investiture—were two distinct pieces of wood; and all the while that the heavy one was being shown and weighed on the lawn, a light counterfeit was carefully locked up in some secret place within the convent, in order on the morrow to change places with the true one and deceive the eyes of the people.

The existence of a counterfeit cross, of which I was as much convinced as of my own existence, afforded me one weapon. A recent event afforded me another weapon.

Three dethroned popes and two heretics burned at the stake did not suffice to reform the church; the commissions of the Council were busied, one with this, the other with that abuse to be corrected. One of the commissions, of which

the most Christian doctor Gerson and the stern Pierre d'Ailly
were members and I for the time being was secretary, sought
to restore discipline in the nunneries. Counterfeit miracles,
dangerous in the unreliable hands of women, and the evil
books read by the sisters came up for discussion. Be it said
in passing: these matters were treated by the two Frenchmen with a degree of pedantry simply incomprehensible to
us Italians, without the suggestion of a jest, howsoever
readily one might have found the humor of the situation.
Enough! The fact of these discussions formed the warp, sinful participation in a fraudulent miracle the woof of my
fabric, and the net was woven which unexpectedly I cast
over the head of the abbess.

Slowly I mounted the steps of the choir and from there
turned to the right into the likewise lofty and boldly vaulted
sacristy, in which, designated by self-glorifying inscriptions,
the empty spot appeared where the heavy cross usually
leaned against the wall, and whither it was destined presently to return from the convent lawn. Two small portals
led into two side rooms. One proved to be locked. Opening
the other, I stood in a room dimly lighted by a circular window obscured with cobwebs. Behold, it contained the convent library huddled together upon a few worm-eaten
shelves.

My whole being throbbed with excitement, as though I
were a youthful lover entering the chamber of Lydia or
Glycera. With trembling hands and shaking knees I drew
near to the parchments; and if I had found the Umbrian's
comedies among them, I should have covered them with
insatiable kisses.

But alas! I turned the leaves of naught but rituals and
liturgies, the sacred contents of which gave cold comfort to
my disappointment. No manuscript of Plautus! The report
had been true. Instead of finding the buried treasure, a
stupid collector had, by clumsy importunity, caused it to
sink into unfathomable depths. I came upon—as my only
booty—a dust-covered copy of the *Confessions of St. Aug-
ustine,* and as I have always been fond of the subtle little

volume, I mechanically thrust it into my pocket, thus providing myself, according to my habit, with reading matter
for the evening. Lo, like a bolt of lightning from a clear sky,
my little abbess, who had had the cross dragged back to the
sacristy and, without my having noticed her in the all-
absorbing keenness of my desire and my disappointment, had
trailed me through the open door into the library—like a bolt
of lightning, I say, the little woman, cursing and railing,
descended upon me; nay more, she groped with unseemly
searching about my toga and brought to light again the
church father reposing in my bosom.

"Mannikin," she shrieked, "I saw at once by your long
nose that you are one of those Italian martens which of late
have been sniffing around after books in our convents. But I
tell you there is a difference between a befuddled monk of
St. Gall and a nimble woman of Appenzell. I know," she continued with a smirk, "what bacon draws the cats. They are
watching for an opportunity to seize the buffoon's book
which we have stored up here. No one of us knew what was
in it until the other day an Italian scamp came to venerate
our most holy relics and then tried to carry off the jester
under his long priestly gown,"—she pointed to mine. "But I
said to myself, 'Brigittchen of Trogen, don't be swindled!
The pigskin must be worth its weight in gold, since the Italian
risks his neck for it.' For in our country, man, we say, 'He
who steals a rope's worth shall hang by the rope!' Brigittchen, who is up to snuff, privately consults a learned friend,
a man without guile, the priest of Diessenhofen, who is fond
of our humble wine and at times plays merry pranks upon
our sisters. After he had examined the odd scrolls, yellow
with age, he exclaimed, 'Odsnigs, Lady Abbess, you can get
something for that! You can build your convent a barn and
a winepress! Take the book, my good woman, hide it under
your pillow, lie with the podex—so it is called—beneath you,
and by the crown of the Virgin stay there until an honest
purchaser presents himself!' And so Brigittchen did, though
she has lain somewhat uncomfortably ever since."

I suppressed a smile at the Umbrian's resting-place, to

which the three judges of the lower world may have consigned him for his sins, and, assuming the dignity which I possess when circumstances call for it, I reproved her with a stern glance.

"Abbess," I said in a solemn tone, "you do not know who I am. Before you stands an emissary of the Council, one of the fathers assembled in Constance, one of the holy men commissioned to reform the nunneries." And I unfolded a splendidly engrossed bill of innkeeper's charges; for I was inspired by the nearness of the comic poet in hiding.

"In the name," I read, "and by authority of the seventeenth ecumenical council! Let no Christian vestal sully her hands with one of those works dangerous to good morals, whether composed in Latin or in one of the vulgar tongues, whereof the invention hath corrupted the souls of . . . Pious Mother Superior, I may not offend your chaste ears by reading the names of these reprobates. . . .

"Counterfeit miracles, traditional or once performed, we prosecute with inexorable severity. If intentional fraud can be proved, the guilty woman—though she were the abbess—shall without exception atone for the sacrilege by death in the flames."

The abbess became as white as a ghost. But with admirable presence of mind the hypocrite immediately recovered her composure.

"Glory and honor to God!" she cried, "for finally setting His holy church in order!" And with an ingratiating smirk she fetched from a corner of the bookcase a daintily bound little volume. "This," she said, "an Italian cardinal, our guest, left behind for us. He used to read himself to sleep with it after dinner. The priest of Diessenhofen, who examined it, pronounced the opinion that it was the grossest and most damnable thing that had been conceived since the invention of the alphabet—and that too by a cleric. Pious father, I confide this abomination to your keeping. Free me from its contagion!" And she handed over to me—my *Facetiæ!*

Although this surprise was probably due to the malicious

mischief-making of chance rather than of the Mother Superior, I felt hurt and indignant. I began to hate the little abbess. For our writings are our own flesh and blood, and I flattered myself that in mine I walk demurely, offending neither the modest muses nor the infallible church.

"It is well," I said. "I only wish you might be found guiltless in the second and more essential point! To the assembled people you have, in the neighborhood and under the very eyes of the Council," I remarked reproachfully, "promised a miracle with so much vulgar advertising that you cannot now withhold the performance. I do not know whether that was wise. Do not marvel, abbess, that your miracle is going to be put to the test! You have invited your own doom!"

The woman's knees knocked together and her eyes wandered. "Follow me," I said sternly, "and let us inspect the instruments of the miracle!"

She followed in dismay and we entered the sacristy, to which the genuine cross had returned, and with its rifts and cracks and gigantic shadow in the spacious dimness of the noble room was resting as mightily on the wall as if only today a despairing great sinner had seized it and had sunk to her knees under its weight, touching the stone pavement with her forehead at the moment when the Queen of Heaven appeared and succored her. I tried to raise it, but could not lift it an inch. All the more ridiculous did the outrage appear, of replacing this crushing burden with a bauble. I turned resolutely toward the high narrow door behind which I suspected the latter to be.

"The key, abbess," I commanded. The little woman stared at me with eyes of horror, but boldly answered, "Lost, my lord bishop, more than ten years ago."

"Woman," I rejoined with terrible seriousness, "your life is at stake! Yonder dwells a retainer of my friend the count of Doccaburgo. Thither I shall send or go for help. If there be found here a counterfeit copy of the real cross, of lighter weight, you shall be consumed by flames of fire, you sinner, like the heretic Huss, and not less guilty than he!"

There was a moment of silence. Then the woman—I know not whether with chattering teeth or with gnashing of teeth —drew forth an antique key with complicated wards and opened the door. The result was flattering—my intelligence had not deceived me. There against the wall of the high, chimney-like room leaned a black cross with rifts and cracks, which I at once grasped and in my feeble arms lifted without difficulty. In every one of its bumps and hollows, in all details the counterfeit conformed to the model of the genuine cross, and even for a sharp eye was indistinguishable from it—only that it was ten times lighter. Whether it was hollowed out or constructed of cork or some other light material, the rush and tumble of events never permitted me to ascertain.

I admired the perfection of the imitation and the thought dawned upon me that only a great artist, only an Italian could have brought this to pass; and, enthusiastic as I am for the fame of my native land, I exclaimed, "Perfect! Masterly!"—verily, extolling not the fraud, but the art expended upon it.

With a grin, the brazen woman, who had watched me attentively, shook her finger at me and said, "Crafty joker, you have outwitted me, and I know what there will be to pay! Take your jester, whom I will fetch at once, under your arm, keep your own counsel, and God be with you on your way!" Whenever, on one of the seven hills of Rome, two augurs met and, according to an ancient saying, smiled knowingly at each other, the play of features was surely more delicate than the gross laugh which distorted the face of my abbess and was translatable into the cynical words, "We all know where Bartolo gets his wine. We are rogues all together, and no one needs to put on airs."

But meanwhile I was pondering over a punishment for the worthless woman.

Then in the silence that had suddenly ensued we heard a tripping, a whispering and tittering in the adjacent choir and surmised that we were being watched by the idle and inquisitive nuns. "By my precious maidenhood," the woman implored me, "let us go, my lord bishop! Not for the wealth of the world would I have my nuns find me here with you; for you are a handsome man and my sisters' tongues are as sharp as scissors and knives!" This scruple seemed to me well founded. I bade her depart and take her nuns with her.

After a while I too left the sacristy. But I only carefully closed the door of the room in which the sham cross was concealed, without turning the key. This I drew out, put it beneath my cloak, and let it slip into a crevice between two stalls in the choir, where, for all I know, it may still repose to this very day. I did this, however, with no definite plan, but prompted by some whispering god or goddess.

When I sat in the low-studded prioress's room, alone with my abbess and an odor of sanctity, I experienced such a longing for the innocent play of the muse and such a repugnance for the twists and turns of entrapped mendacity that I determined to make short work of the matter. The Mother Superior had to confess to me how she had been initiated into the hoary swindle, and I closed the incident with few pretorian edicts. She confessed that her predecessor in office had, when at the point of death, called her and the father confessor into secret conference, and that both had commended the inherited sham miracle to her fostering care as the economic salvation of the convent. The confessor, she volubly related, had been inexhaustible in praise of the venerable age of the fraud, its deep meaning, and instructiveness. Better and more convincingly than any sermon, he said, the phantom miracle symbolized to the people the initial difficulty and the subsequent ease of a godly life. This symbolism had so turned the head of the poor woman that in one and the same breath she affirmed that she had committed no wrong and that as a child she too had once been honest.

"I will spare you for the sake of our Mother Church, upon which the flame of your burning at the stake would cast a false light"—with these words I cut short her rustic logic, and curtly commanded her to give the counterfeit cross to the flames after the loudly trumpeted miracle had been performed once more—from motives of prudence I did not venture to prevent this—but to deliver the Plautus without delay.

Scolding and reviling me, the abbess obeyed. She submitted to the decrees of the Council of Constance as they were formulated by me, not indeed with the foreknowledge of the assembled fathers, but certainly in their spirit and in conformity to their intention.

When Brigittchen, growling like a bear, brought me the codex—I had fled to a comfortable room in the visitors' quarters situated next the wall that encircled the convent—I forced her ill-bred ladyship out of the apartment and locked myself in with the Umbrian's comic characters. Not a sound disturbed me there, except the refrain of a children's song which some peasant girls were singing in the meadow beneath my window, and this made my solitude only the more enjoyable.

After a while, to be sure, the Mother Superior, highly excited, made a great pother outside, and with desperate fists pounded upon the heavy bolted oaken door, demanding the key to the open room of the counterfeit cross. I gave her, with my regrets, the brief and veritable information that it was not in my hands, paid no further attention to her, and, myself in the seventh heaven of delight, let the miserable woman wail and groan like a soul in Purgatory. But I reveled as one bidden to a wedding feast.

A classic author newly come to light—not an obscure thinker, nor a sublime poet—no, that which lies nearest at hand and eternally fascinates, the wide, wide world, the pulse of life, the hilarious market-places of Rome and Athens, wit, altercation, and equivocation, the passions, the effrontery of human nature in the extenuating exaggeration of the comic mirror. While I devoured one piece I was already keeping hungry watch over the next.

I had finished the witty *Amphitruo,* the *Aulularia* with the incomparable figure of the miser lay open before me—but I stopped and leaned back in my chair; for my eyes pained me. Twilight and darkness were coming on. The girls in the

meadow outside had for at least a quarter of an hour inde-
fatigably repeated the silly ditty,

> "Adam, he had seven sons . . . "

Now they mischievously struck up a new refrain, and
with droll resoluteness they sang,

> "To the convent I'll not go,
> I'll not be a nun, no, no!"

I leaned out in order to catch sight of these little foes of
celibacy and take pleasure in the contemplation of their
innocence. But their game was in no wise an innocent one.
Nudging each other with their elbows, and exchanging
knowing glances, they sang, not without invidiousness and
malice, up at a grated window, behind which they supposed
Gertrude to be. Or was she already kneeling in the sacristy
yonder, under the pale glimmer of the ever-burning light,
according to the custom of those about to take the veil, who
pass in prayer the night before their marriage to heaven?
But what was that to me? I lighted the lamp and began to
read the comedy of the Pot.

Not until my lamp burned out and the letters swam before
my weary eyes did I throw myself down upon my couch and
fall into a restless slumber. Soon the comic characters were
again hovering about me. Here a soldier boasted with high-
sounding words, there the drunken youth caressed his sweetheart, who with a graceful turn of her head met his kisses
half way. Then, without warning, there stood in the midst
of the merry antique rabble a broad-shouldered, barefoot
barbarian maiden girdled with a rope, brought like a slave
to the mart, staring at me, as it seemed, with reproachful
and threatening eyes that gleamed forth from beneath her
gloomy brow.

I was frightened and awoke with a start. The morning
dawned. On account of the summer sultriness I had left one
half of the little window open, and from the adjacent choir
of the convent chapel I heard a monotonous orison that

passed over into a smothered groan and then into a violent
outcry.

Interrupting himself, the narrator turned to a grave man
who sat over against him and, in spite of the summer heat,
had after the manner of the ancients draped the folds of his
mantle about him. "My learned and far-famed friend," said
he, "my great philosopher, tell me, I beseech you, what is
conscience?"

"Is it a universal attribute? By no means. We have all
known men who had none, and, to mention only one, our
holy father, John XXIII., whom we dethroned at Constance,
had no conscience, but on the contrary, such a happy heart,
such a cheerful, I had almost said childlike spirit, that in the
midst of his evil deeds no spectre disturbed his slumbers and
he awoke every morning more serene than he had lain down
the day before. When at the castle of Gottlieben, where he
was confined, I unfolded the scroll of complaints against
him and with hesitant voice and flushed face read to him
the sum of his sins—ten times greater than the number attached to his papal name, *scelera horrenda, abominanda*—
he picked up a pen and to while away the time adorned a
St. Barbara in his breviary with a moustache.

"No, conscience is no universal attribute, and even among
us, who have a conscience, it appears as a Proteus, in changing forms. In your humble servant, for example, it awakes
every time that it can embody itself in an image or in a tone.
When recently I was a guest at the court of one of those
petty tyrants with whom our fortunate Italy swarms, and
on that balmy evening sat to wine and music with fair
women on an airy balcony that jutted out from the tower of
the castle over a bottomless pool of cool water, I heard a
sigh from below. It was the voice of a prisoner. Banished
was my joy, and I could remain there no longer. It troubled
my conscience to enjoy life, kissing, drinking, and laughing
so near to misery."

In the same manner I could not now endure the cry of a
woman in despair so close at hand. I threw a cloak about

me and stole through the dim cloister to the choir, saying to myself that while I was reading Plautus a change must have come over Gertrude: on the threshold of a decision she must have come to the incontrovertible conviction that she should surely perish in this community, in the nothingness— or worse, the corruption of the convent, confined as she should be together with the common herd, despising it and hated in her turn.

In the portal of the sacristy I stopped to listen, and saw Gertrude wringing her hands before the genuine, heavy cross. Believe me, they were bleeding, and I daresay her knees were bleeding too; for she had been upon her knees in prayer the whole night long; her voice was hoarse, and her converse with God, after her heart had sunk within her and no new words came to her lips, was convulsive and brutish, like a dying effort.

"Mary, Mother of God," she cried, "have mercy on me! Let me fall beneath the weight of thy cross; it is too heavy for me! I shudder at the thought of a cell!" And she made a motion as if she were snatching or uncoiling a serpent from about her body; and then, in a paroxysm of anguish, even suppressing her shame, she exclaimed, "What befits me is sun and cloud, sickle and scythe, husband and child . . ."

In the midst of this misery I could not restrain a smile at this human confession made to the Blessed Virgin; but the smile died on my lips. Gertrude had suddenly jumped to her feet and fixed her great eyes, weirdly staring from out her blanched face, upon a spot in the wall which was marred by I know not what red stain.

"Mary, Mother of God, have mercy on me!" she cried again. "My limbs cannot abide in the cell and I shall strike my head against the ceiling. Let me sink under the weight of thy cross; it is too heavy for me! But if thou shouldst make it light upon my shoulder without being able to make light my heart, then beware"—and she stared at the uncanny spot —"lest some morning they find me lying with a crushed head at the foot of the wall!" Infinite compassion seized me—

and not compassion alone, but anxious apprehension also.

Exhausted, Gertrude had seated herself upon a chest which contained some sacred relic, and was plaiting her blond hair which, during her wrestling with God, had loosened itself from the braids. At the same time she sang to herself half sadly, half playfully, not in her robust alto, but in a high-pitched child's voice not her own,

> "To the convent I must run,
> Must be a poor, unhappy nun . . ."

paraphrasing that refrain with which the peasant children had derided her.

This was madness, which sought to waylay her and slip with her into the cell. But Optimus Maximus availed himself of me as the instrument of his will and bade me save Gertrude at any cost.

Now I, too, addressed myself in unfeigned piety to that virgin goddess whom the ancients adored as Pallas Athena and whom we call Mary. "Whoever thou art," I prayed with uplifted hands, "Wisdom, as some say, Mercy, as others affirm—it is all one; Wisdom doth not record the vow of an inexperienced child, nor will Mercy hold an adult woman bound by the foolish promise of an infant. With a smile of clemency thou wilt annul this empty bond. It is thy cause I plead, goddess. Be gracious unto me!"

Since I had given the abbess, who feared treachery, my word that I should have no further speech with Gertrude, I determined after the manner of the ancients with three symbolical actions to bring the truth home to the novice, so manifestly that even the slow wits of a peasant girl could grasp it.

Paying no attention to Gertrude, I stepped up to the cross. "When I wish to recognize an object that I have once seen, I put my mark on it," I said pedantically; and drawing my sharp dagger, forged by our famous fellow-citizen, Pantaleone Ubbriaco the cutler, I cut a chip of some size out from under the head and the cross-beam, as it were the arm-pit of the cross.

Secondly, I took five measured steps. Then I burst out laughing and began with expressive gesticulation, "That porter in the hall at Constance cut a comical figure when my luggage arrived! He surveyed the biggest piece there was, an enormous box, rolled his sleeves above his elbows, spat upon his hands—the rude fellow—and, straining every muscle for a supreme effort, raised the trifling burden of an empty chest with ease to his deluded shoulder. Ha! Ha! Ha!"

Thirdly and lastly, I placed myself in mock solemnity between the real cross and the sham cross in its unlocked abiding place, and repeatedly pointing this way and that, I oracularly murmured, "Truth in the air, falsehood in there!" —presto! and I clapped my hands, "Falsehood i' the air, truth is in there!"

Out of the corner of my eye I looked over at the novice sitting in the twilight, in order to gather from the facial expression of the young barbarian the effect of these three oracles upon her. I perceived the tension of disquieting meditation and the first flicker of blazing wrath.

Then I repaired to my room, cautiously, as I had gone forth from it, threw myself without undressing upon my couch, and enjoyed the sweet slumber of a good conscience until aroused by the hum of the multitude proceeding to the convent and by the clangor of the festal bells above my head.

When I again entered the sacristy, Gertrude, deathly pale, as though she were being led to the scaffold, was just returning from a procession to a neighboring chapel, a traditional requirement no doubt instituted to give opportunity for the fraudulent exchange of crosses. The adornment of the bride of heaven began. In the group of psalm-singing nuns the novice girded herself with the coarse, thrice-knotted rope and slowly removed the shoes from her sinewy but well-shapen feet. Now they presented to her the crown of thorns. This, by contrast to the symbolical counterfeit cross, was a wreath of hard, real thorns, bristling with sharp points. Gertrude seized it eagerly and pressed it with voluptuous cruelty so firmly upon her head that the warm rain of her young blood spurted forth and in heavy drops ran down her innocent brow. Sublime wrath, a present judgment of the righteous God, gleamed destruction in the blue eyes of the peasant girl; so that the nuns began to recoil from her in fear. Six of their number, whom the abbess had presumably initiated into the pious fraud, now laid the sham cross upon her honest shoulder, with clumsy grimaces, as though they were hardly able to lift the bauble, and with such stupid hypocrisy that I verily believed I saw the truth of God in the thorny crown, openly honored and glorified by human untruthfulness, but secretly reviled.

Now everything developed with the swiftness of a thunderstorm. Gertrude cast a quick glance at the place where on the genuine cross my dagger had cut a deep mark, and found the false one unscarred. Contemptuously she let the light cross glide from her shoulder, without clasping it in her arms. Then with a shriek of derisive laughter she seized it again, and triumphantly smote it to pieces upon the stone pavement. And with a bound she stood before the door of the room in which the real, the heavy cross was concealed, opened the door, found and lifted the cross, shouted wildly for joy, as though she had discovered a treasure, raised the cross unaided to her shoulder, embraced it exultantly with her valiant arms, and turned with her burden slowly toward the choir where, as upon an open stage, she was to appear before the multitude. Breathlessly waiting, nobility, clergy, peasantry, a whole people, crowded the spacious nave of the church. Lamenting, reproving, threatening, imploring, the abbess with her nuns threw herself in the way.

But she, with gleaming eyes lifted up to heaven, cried out, "Now, Mother of God, do thou conclude this business honestly!" And then with a loud voice, "Make way!"—like a workman carrying a piece of timber through a press of people.

All gave way before her and she entered the choir, where, with a vicar of the bishop at their head, the rural clergy awaited her. All eyes were focussed upon the heavy-laden shoulder and the blood-besprinkled countenance. But the true cross proved too heavy for Gertrude and no goddess made it lighter. She strode with panting bosom, ever more bent and more slowly, as though her bare feet were implanted and rooted in the floor. She stumbled a little, recovered her balance, stumbled again, sank down upon her left knee, then upon her right, and endeavored with all her might to rise again. It was in vain. Now her left hand let go the cross and, stretched forward to reach the floor, supported for a moment the weight of her entire body. Then the arm bent at the elbow and doubled up. The head with its crown of thorns fell forward heavily and struck the stone pavement with a thud. Over the body of the exhausted victim the cross rolled ponderously, released by the right hand only after Gertrude had been stunned by the fall.

That was bloody truth, not the illusion of jugglery. One sigh rose from the breasts of a thousand witnesses.

The horrified nuns drew Gertrude forth from beneath the cross and lifted her to her feet. She had swooned in her fall, but consciousness soon returned to the sturdy maiden. She passed her hand over her forehead. Her eye fell upon the cross which had overwhelmed her. A smile of thanks flitted across her face, to the goddess whose help had not been forthcoming. Then with heavenly humor she spoke the roguish words, "Thou dost not wish me, Virgin pure! Then another will have me!"

Still wearing the crown of thorns, without appearing to feel the bloody pricks, she now set her foot upon the first of the steps that led from the choir down into the nave. At the same time her eyes wandered searchingly about the congregation, and found him, whom they sought for. A profound silence ensued. "Hans of Splügen," Gertrude began in clear and audible tones, "wilt thou take me for thy wedded wife?" "Indeed, I will, with joy a thousandfold. Come down and see!" answered a happy and convincing masculine voice from the back of the nave.

She did so and descended calmly, but radiant with joy, one step after another, once more the simple peasant, who no doubt was glad soon to forget the affecting spectacle that in her despair she had given the multitude, now that her modest human desire was granted and she was permitted to return to the every-day sphere of her humble existence. Laugh at me, if you will, Cosimo; I was disappointed. For a short space the peasant girl had appeared to my excited senses as the incarnation of a higher being, as a demonic creature, as Truth exultantly unmasking Falsehood. But "What is truth?" asked Pilate.

Pondering this and following Gertrude from the choir down into the nave, I was plucked in the sleeve by my messenger, who informed me of the sudden election of Otto Colonna to the papacy by enthusiastic acclamation, and of sundry remarkable circumstances.

When I looked up again, Gertrude had vanished. But the excited multitude was shouting and clamoring with divided opinion. From yonder group of men the words resounded, "Hag! Witch!" They meant the abbess. Here women's voices shrilled, "Sinner! Impudent hussy!" That was Gertrude. Whether the former surmised the pious fraud, or the latter believed the miracle to be desecrated by Gertrude's worldliness—no matter; in either case the spell of the relic was broken and the career of the miracle closed.

Coarsely reviled by the people, the valiant Brigittchen began to retort in kind, and the dumbfounded faces of the attending priests showed a complete scale of expressions from sly complicity down to the most incorruptible stupidity.

I felt my dignity as a cleric and put an end to the abomination. Mounting the pulpit, I solemnly announced to assembled Christendom, *"Habemus pontificem Dominum Othonem Colonna!"* and struck up a resounding *Te Deum*, in which first the chorus of nuns and then the entire congregation lustily joined. After the hymn had been sung, nobles and peasants hastened to mount their horses or to set out afoot on the way to Constance, where, after the *triregnum* had come to an end, the blessing conveyed to the city and to the world must be trebly strong.

I, for my part, slipped back into the cloister in order with all secrecy to get the Plautus that was in my room. Going furtively away again, with the codex under my arm, I happened upon the abbess who, economical as she was, was carefully carrying the pieces of the sham cross in a great basket to the kitchen. I congratulated her upon the *dénouement*. But Brigittchen believed herself swindled and yelled at me in fury, "Go to the devil, you two Italian scoundrels," meaning, so far as I could judge, the Umbrian Marcus Accius Plautus and the Tuscan Poggio Bracciolini, your fellow-citizen. A pretty blond boy, another curly-head, whom Hans of Splügen, before his departure with Gertrude, had thoughtfully engaged for me, then led out my mule, which carried me back to Constance.

Plaudite amici! My story is at an end. When the Council of Constance, which lasted longer than this little narrative, was likewise at an end, I returned with my gracious master, His Holiness Martin V., over the mountains, and found as our host and hostess in the inn at Splügen, to the north of the dangerous pass, Hänsel and Gertrude in health and prosperity—she not in a stifling cell but in a wind-swept rocky valley, with a child at her breast and the conjugal cross resting lightly upon her shoulder.

"Let this *Facetia inedita,* illustrious Cosimo, be a not unwelcome supplement to the codex of Plautus which at this hour I present to you, or rather to our native land, whose Father you are, and to learning, to which your halls with their store of treasures are always open.

"It was my intention to bequeath the unique manuscript to you, lest, as a living donor, I should invite the tenfold greater recompense with which you are wont in your incorrigible generosity to reward every gift presented to you in homage. But who knows—Poggio sighed resignedly—whether my sons would respect my last will?"

Cosimo replied amiably, "I thank you for both, your Plautus and your *Facetia*. Without a scruple you lived this and accomplished it, young as you then were. As a mature man you have recounted it to us in the wisdom of your years. This toast"—he lifted a noble bowl enclasped by a laughing satyr—"I pledge to my honest Poggio and his blond barbarian maiden!"

They drank and laughed. Then the conversation passed quickly from Plautus to the thousand discovered treasures and unrolled parchments of antiquity, and to the greatness of the century.

FLAGMAN THIEL[1]

GERHART HAUPTMANN

(1862-1946)

I

EVERY Sunday Thiel, the flagman, was to be seen sitting in a pew in the church at Neu Zittau. If he was absent, you might be sure he was on Sunday duty or else—as happened twice in the course of ten years—at home ill in bed. Once a great lump of coal from the tender of a passing locomotive had struck his leg and sent him rolling into the ditch at the bottom of the embankment. The second time the trouble was a wine bottle that had come flying from an express and had hit him in the middle of his chest. Nothing but these two mishaps had ever succeeded in keeping Thiel from church the instant he was off duty.

The first five years he had had to come alone to Neu Zittau from Schön-Schornstein, a small collection of homes on the Spree. Then, one fine day, he appeared in the company of a delicate, sickly looking woman. The people thought she ill suited his herculean build. And on a later Sunday afternoon, at the altar of the church, he solemnly gave her his hand and pledged his troth.

So, for two years, the delicate young creature sat beside him in the pew. For two years her fine, hollow-cheeked face bent over the ancient hymnal beside his weather-tanned face.

And suddenly the flagman was to be seen sitting alone, as of old.

[1] Translated by Adele S. Seltzer. Copyright, 1933, by The Modern Library, Inc.

On one of the preceding weekdays the bell had tolled for the dead. That was all.

Scarcely any change, so the people declared, was to be observed in the flagman. The brass buttons of his clean Sunday uniform were as brightly polished as before, his red hair as sleekly pomaded and as neatly parted, military fashion. Only he held his broad, hairy neck a little bent, and sang more eagerly, and listened to the sermon more devoutly. The general opinion was that his wife's death had not hit him very hard. A view that was strengthened when in the course of the year he married again. The second wife was a strong, stout milkmaid from Altegrund.

Even the pastor felt free to express his doubts when Thiel came to announce his engagement.

"So soon again? You really want to marry so soon again?"

"I can't keep my house running, sir, with the wife who's gone."

"To be sure. But I mean—aren't you in a bit of a hurry?"

"It's on account of the boy."

Thiel's wife had died in childbirth. The boy had lived and been named Tobias.

"Yes, yes, to be sure, the boy," said the pastor, with a gesture clearly revealing that he had not thought of the infant until that moment. "That throws a different light on the matter. What have you been doing with him until now while you are at work?"

Thiel explained that he left Tobias in the care of an old woman. Once she had nearly let him get burned, and another time had let him roll from her lap to the floor. Fortunately the child had not been badly hurt—only a big surface bruise. Such a state of things could not continue, the flagman said, especially as the child, being delicate, required particular attention. For that reason and also because he had sworn to his wife on her deathbed that he would always take exceedingly good care of the child, he had decided to marry again.

The people found absolutely nothing to cavil with in the

new couple that now visited the church regularly on Sundays. The milkmaid seemed to have been made for the flagman. She was but a few inches shorter than he and exceeded him in girth, while her features were just as coarsely molded as his, though, in contrast, they lacked soul.

If Thiel had cherished the desire for an inveterate worker and paragon of a housewife in his second wife, then his hopes were surprisingly fulfilled. However, without knowing it, he had purchased three other qualities, too, a hard, domineering disposition, quarrelsomeness, and brutal passion.

Within half a year the whole place knew who was lord and master in the flagman's little house. Thiel became the object of general pity. It was a piece of good luck for the "creature," the exercised husbands said, that she had got such a gentle lamb as Thiel for a husband. With other men she wouldn't come off so easy, she'd receive some hard knocks. An animal like that had to be managed—with blows, if need be—a good sound thrashing to make her behave herself.

But Thiel, despite his sinewy arms, was not the man to thrash his wife. What got the people so annoyed seemed to cause him no perturbation. As a rule, he let his wife's endless sermonizings pass without a word, and when he did occasionally make a response, the slow drag of his speech and the quiet coolness of his tone contrasted oddly with her high-pitched bawling.

The outside world seemed scarcely to touch him. It was as though he carried something within him that heavily overbalanced all of the evil it brought by good.

Nevertheless, for all his phlegm, there were occasions on which he would not allow things to pass—when little Toby was concerned. Then his childlike goodness, his yieldingness took on a dash of determination that even so untamed a temperament as Lena's did not dare to oppose.

The moments, however, in which he revealed this side of his character became rarer and rarer, and finally ceased completely. During the first year of his marriage he had shown a certain suffering resistance to Lena's tyranny. In the second year this also ceased completely. After a quarrel he no longer left for his work with his earlier indifference in case he had not previously placated her. Often he ever stooped to beg her to be kind again. His solitary post in the heart of the Brandenburg pine forest was no longer, as it had been, the place where he would rather be than anywhere else on earth. The quiet devout thoughts of his dead wife were crossed by thoughts of the living wife. It was not with repugnance, as in the first months of his marriage, that he trod the homeward way, but often with passionate haste, after having counted the hours and minutes till the time of his release.

He who had been united to his first wife by a more spiritual love fell into his second wife's grip through the power of crude impulses. He became almost wholly dependent upon her.

At times he experienced pangs of conscience at this turn, and resorted to a number of unusual devices to bring about a change. For one thing, he declared his hut and his beat to be holy ground, dedicated exclusively to the shades of the dead. And he actually succeeded by all sorts of pretexts in preventing Lena from accompanying him there. He hoped he should always be able to keep her off. The very number of his hut and the direction in which it lay were still unknown to her.

Thus, by conscientiously dividing the time at his disposal between the living and the dead, Thiel actually succeeded in soothing his conscience.

Often, to be sure, especially in moments of solitary devotion, when he felt the tie between him and his dead wife deeply and warmly, he beheld his present condition in the light of truth, and he experienced disgust.

If he was doing day duty, his spiritual intercourse with her was limited to dear recollections of their life together. But in the dark, when a snowstorm raged among the pines and along the embankment, his hut at midnight, by the light of his lantern, became a chapel.

With a faded photograph of the departed before him on the table, and the hymnal and the Bible turned open, he alternately read and sang the whole night long, interrupted only at intervals by the trains rushing past. He would attain a state of ecstasy in which he had visions of his wife standing there in person.

In its remoteness this post, which Thiel had held for ten years, contributed to the intensification of his mystic inclinations. To the north, east, south and west, it was separated by a walk of at least three quarters of an hour from the nearest habitation. It lay in the very heart of the forest. But there was a grade crossing there, and Thiel's duty was to lower and raise the gates.

In the summer days passed, in the winter weeks without a single person except other railroad workers setting foot on Thiel's beat. Almost the only changes in the solitude came from the weather and the periodic mutations of the seasons. It was not difficult to recall the events—besides the two mishaps to his body—that had broken into the regular course of the hours of service.

Four years previous the imperial special bearing the Kaiser to Breslau had gone dashing by. Once on a winter's night an express had run over a stag. And once on a hot summer's day, as Thiel was making an inspection of his beat, he had found a corked bottle of wine. It was scorching hot to the touch, and Thiel had esteemed its contents because when he uncorked it a geyser spouted out, showing that the stuff was well fermented. Thiel had laid the bottle on the edge of a pond in the woods to cool off. Somehow it had disappeared from the spot, and even after the passage of years Thiel never thought of that bottle without a pang of regret.

A bit of diversion was provided by a spring behind the hut. From time to time men at work on the road bed or on the telegraph lines came for a drink, and stayed, of course, to talk a while. Sometimes the forest ranger would also come when he was thirsty.

Tobias developed slowly. It was not until he was two years old that he learned to walk and talk. For his father he displayed unusual affection, and as he grew more understanding Thiel's old love for his child was re-awakened. Accordingly Lena's love for the child decreased, turning into unmistakable dislike when the next year a baby boy was born to her, too.

After that bad times began for Tobias. In his father's absence he was particularly made to suffer. He had to dedicate his feeble powers unrewarded to the service of the little cry-baby. He became more and more exhausted. His head grew too large round, and his fiery red hair, with the chalky face beneath, on top of his wretched little body, made an unlovely and pitiful impression. When the backward mite was seen dragging himself down to the Spree with his baby brother bursting with health in his arms, curses were muttered behind the windows of the cottages. But no one ever ventured to utter the curses in the open.

Thiel, who was most of all concerned, seemed to have no eyes for what was going on, and refused to understand the hints of well-meaning neighbors.

II

Once Thiel returned from night duty at seven o'clock of a June morning. Directly Lena had greeted him, she burst into her usual complaining.

A few weeks before notice had been given that they could no longer cultivate the piece of land which they rented for planting potatoes for their own use, and no other land had been found to replace it. Though everything pertaining to the land was part of Lena's duty, Thiel none the less had to listen to a hundred iterations that he would be to blame if they had to buy ten sacks of potatoes for dear money. Thiel merely muttered a word or two. Paying slight attention to

Lena's tirade, he went straight over to Tobias's bed, which he shared with the boy on nights when he was off duty.

He sat down and watched the sleeping child with an anxious expression on his good face. For a while he contented himself with chasing away the persistent flies, then he woke him up. A touching joy lighted up the boy's blue, deep-set eyes. He snatched for his father's hand, and a pitiful smile drew the corners of his mouth. Thiel helped him put on his few bits of clothing. Suddenly a shadow chased across his face. He noticed that his son's right cheek was slightly swollen and bore finger marks designed white on red.

At breakfast Lena brought up the same subject again, pursuing it with even more vigor. Thiel cut her off by telling her that the railroad inspector had given him for nothing the use of a stretch of land alongside the tracks not far from his hut, probably because it was too distant for the inspector to use for himself.

Lena was incredulous, then gradually her doubts melted away and she became noticeably good-humored. How big was the lot? How good was the soil? She plied him with questions. And when she learned that there were actually two dwarf fruit trees on the land, she fairly lost her head. At length the questions were all asked, and as the shopkeeper's bell, which could be heard in every house in the place, kept ringing incessantly, Lena ran forth to ferret out the latest news.

While she remained in the dark shop crowded with wares, Thiel occupied himself at home with Tobias, who sat on his knee playing with pine cones that his father had brought from the woods.

"What do you want to be when you grow up?" asked Thiel. The stereotyped question was invariably answered by the equally stereotyped reply, "Railroad inspector." It was not asked in fun. The flagman's dreams actually soared so high. It was in all seriousness that he cherished the hope that with God's help Tobias would become something extraordinary. The instant "railroad inspector" left the child's bloodless lips, Thiel's face brightened, fairly radiated bliss.

"Go play now, Tobias," he said soon afterward, lighting his pipe with a shaving kindled at the hearth fire. The boy showing shy pleasure went out.

Thiel undressed and got into bed. For a long while he lay staring up at the low, cracked ceiling. Finally he fell asleep and woke up shortly before twelve o'clock. While Lena in her noisy fashion prepared the midday meal, he dressed and went out on the street to fetch Tobias, whom he found scratching plaster out of a hole in the wall and stuffing it into his mouth. Thiel led him by the hand past the eight houses that constituted the hamlet down to the Spree. The stream lay dark and glassy between sparsely foliaged poplars. Thiel sat down on a block of granite close to the water's edge.

Every fair day the villagers were accustomed to see him on this spot. The children were devoted to him. They called him Father Thiel. He taught them games that he remembered from his own childhood, reserving, however, the best of his memories for Tobias. He whittled him arrows that flew farther than those of the other boys, he carved him willow pipes, and even deigned to sing ditties in his rusty bass, and tap the beat with the horn handle of his knife against the bark of a tree.

The people thought him silly. They blamed him. They could not understand how he could go to so much trouble for the little brats. Though they should have been richly content, seeing that the children were well taken care of when in his charge. Besides, Thiel did more than play with them. He took up serious things, too. He heard the older ones recite their lessons, helped them study their Bible and hymn verses, and spelled out c-a-t and d-o-g with the younger ones.

After the midday meal Thiel rested again a while, drank a cup of coffee, and began to prepare for work. It took him a lot of time, as for everything he did. Each move had been regulated for years. The objects carefully spread out on the walnut dresser went into his various pockets always in the same order—knife, notebook, comb, a horse's tooth, an old watch in a case, and a small book wrapped in red paper. The last was handled with especial care. During the night it lay under Thiel's pillow, and by day was carried in his breast pocket. On a label pasted on the cover was written in Thiel's awkward yet flourishing hand, "Savings Account of Tobias Thiel."

The clock on the wall with the long pendulum and sickly yellow face indicated a quarter to five when Thiel left. A small boat, his own property, ferried him across the Spree. Arrived at the further side, he stood still a moment and listened back in the direction he had come from. Then he turned into a broad path through the woods and within a few moments reached the depths of the deep-booming pine forest, its mass of needles like a dark green undulating sea.

The moist layers of needles and moss made a carpet as inaudible to the tread as felt. Thiel made his way without looking up, now past the rusty brown columns of the older trees, now between the thickly enmeshed younger growth, and farther on across broad stretches of nursery, over-shadowed by a few tall slim pines for the protection of the young saplings. A transparent bluish haze rising from the earth laden with mingled fragrances blurred the forms of the trees. A heavy, drab sky hung low over the tops. Flocks of cawing crows seemed to bathe in the gray of the atmosphere. Black puddles filled the depressions in the path and cast a still drearier reflection of a dreary nature.

"Fearful weather," thought Thiel when he roused out of deep reflection and looked up.

Suddenly his thoughts were deflected. A dim feeling came to him that he must have forgotten something. And surely enough, when he searched his pockets, he discovered that he had not brought along the sandwich that he required on account of the long hours on duty. For a while he stood undecided. Then turned and hurried back.

In a short while he reached the Spree, rowed himself across in a few powerful strokes, and without delay, perspiring from every pore, ascended the gradual slope of the village street. The shopkeeper's old, mangy poodle lay in the middle of the road. On the tarred board fence around a cottager's yard perched a hooded crow. It spread its feathers, shook itself, nodded, uttered an ear-splitting caw, caw, and with a slapping sound of its wings rose in the air and let the wind drive it in the direction of the forest.

Nothing was to be seen of the villagers—about twenty fishermen and lumbermen with their families.

The stillness was broken—by a high-pitched voice. The flagman involuntarily stopped. A volley of violent, jangling tones assailed his ears. It seemed to come from the open dormer window of a low house that he knew only too well.

Treading as silently as possible, he glided nearer. Now he quite clearly recognized his wife's voice. Only a few steps more, and he could understand almost everything she said.

"You horrid little beast, you! Is the poor baby to scream its belly inside out from hunger? What? Just you wait—just you wait. I'll teach you to mind. You'll never forget."

For a few moments there was silence. Then a sound could be heard like the beating out of clothes. And the next instant another hailstorm of abuse was let loose.

"You miserable little puppy, you! Do you think I'll let my own child die of hunger because of a mean little thing like you?—Shut your mouth!" A slight whimper had been audible. "If you don't shut your mouth, I'll give you something that'll keep you going a whole week."

The whimpering did not subside.

The flagman felt his heart pounding in irregular beats. He began to tremble slightly. His glance fastened on the ground as though his mind were wandering, and again and again his coarse, hard hand went up to his freckled forehead to brush back a dank strand of hair. For a second he was about to give way. He stood shaken by a convulsion that swelled his muscles and drew his fingers into a clenched ball. The convulsion subsided. He was left in a state of dull exhaustion.

With unsteady steps he entered the narrow, brick-paved

vestibule and slowly, wearily mounted the creaking wooden stairs.

"Pugh, pugh, pugh!" You could hear how with every sign of scorn and fury some one spat out three times in succession. "You horrid, mean, sneaking, cowardly, low-down good-for-nothing!" The epithets followed one another in crescendo, the voice that uttered them breaking several times from strain. "You want to hit my boy, do you? You ugly little brat you, don't you dare to hit the poor helpless child on its mouth. What's that? Huh? If I wanted to soil my hands on you, I'd—"

At that moment the door to the living room was opened, and the rest of the sentence remained unspoken on the frightened woman's tongue. She was livid with passion, her lips twitched evilly. Her right hand raised in the air sank and grasped the saucepan with milk in it. She tried to pour some into the baby's bottle, but desisted as the larger part of the milk flowed down the outside of the bottle on to the table. She clutched at various objects without being able to hold them any length of time. Finally she recovered herself sufficiently to address her husband with violence. What did he mean by coming home at this unusual hour? Was he thinking of spying on her? That would be too much. This last was directly followed by the asseveration that she had a clear conscience and need not lower her eyes before any one.

Thiel scarcely heard what she said. He gave a hasty look at Toby, who was crying aloud, and for a few moments he had to restrain forcibly a something dreadful rising within him. Then the old phlegm spread over his taut features, and at the same time a furtive, lustful light came into his eyes. His glance played over his wife's heavy limbs while she with averted face, bustled about still making an effort to be composed. Her full, half-bared breasts swelled with excitement and threatened to burst her corset. Her drawn-up skirts accentuated the width of her broad hips. A force seemed to emanate from the woman, indomitable, inescapable. Thiel felt himself powerless to cope with it. Tightly, like a cobweb, yet firmly as a mesh of steel, it laid itself around him, chaining him down, robbing him of his strength. In this condition he was incapable of saying a word to her, much less a harsh word.

Thus it was that Tobias, bathed in tears, cowering in a corner, saw his father go over to the oven bench without looking round at him, pick up the forgotten sandwich, hold it out to Lena by way of the only explanation, give a short, distraught nod of his head in good-by, and disappear.

III

Thiel made all possible haste back to his solitary post in the woods. Even so he was a quarter of an hour late. The assistant who relieved him, a consumptive, the victim of the unavoidably rapid changes in temperature to which the work subjected one, was waiting prepared to leave on the sanded little platform of the hut, on which the number, black on white, gleamed from a distance between the tree trunks.

The two men shook hands, exchanged a few brief reports, and parted, the one disappearing within the hut, the other taking the continuation of the road by which Thiel had come. His convulsive cough sounded further and further away among the trees, until finally the one human sound in the solitude fell silent.

Thiel as always, after his fashion, set about preparing the small square room for the night. He worked mechanically, his mind occupied with the impression of the past hour.

First he laid his supper on the narrow, brown-painted table beside one of the windows like slits through which the stretch of track could be conveniently viewed. Next he kindled a fire in the small, rusty stove and placed a pot of cold water on top. After that he straightened out his utensils, a shovel, a spade, a wrench and a few other things, and then cleaned his lantern and filled it with fresh oil.

Scarcely were his arrangements completed when the signal rang shrilly, three times, and three times again, to announce that a train from the direction of Breslau was pulling out of the near station. Thiel showed no hurry, allowing a few minutes to pass before emerging from the hut with flag and cartridge case in his hand. And it was with a lazy, dragging shuffle that he walked along the narrow strip of sand to the crossing, about sixty feet away. Though there was scarcely any traffic along the road at that point, still he conscientiously let down and raised the gates before and after the passage of each train.

This operation now concluded, he leaned idly on one of the black-and-white barred anchor-posts.

The tracks cut in a straight line right and left into the green forest stretching beyond the reach of the eye. On each side the mass of needles stood apart to leave, as it were, an avenue free for the reddish-brown graveled embankment. The black tracks running parallel looked like the strands of a huge iron net drawn together to a point on the horizon in the extreme south and north.

The wind had risen, it drove light waves of mist along the edge of the forest into the distance. A humming came from the telegraph poles alongside the tracks. On the wires that stretched from pole to pole like the sustaining cords spun by a huge spider perched swarms of chirping birds. A woodpecker flew with a laugh over Thiel's head. The man did not so much as look up.

The sun hanging from under the edge of vast masses of clouds and about to sink into the dark-green sea of treetops poured streams of purple over the forest. The pillared arcades of the pine trunks on the yon side of the embankment took fire as from within and glowed like metal. The tracks, too, began to glow, turning into the semblance of fiery snakes. They were the first to pale. The glow, leaving the ground, slowly ascended upward, resigning first the bodies of the trees, then the lower tops to the cold light of dissolution. For a while a reddish sheen lingered on the extreme crowns.

Silently and solemnly was the exalted drama enacted.

The flagman still stood at the gates motionless. At length he made a step forward. A dark point on the horizon where the tracks joined, became more than a point. Increasing from second to second it yet seemed to stand still. Then of a sudden it acquired movement, and drew nearer. A vibrating and humming went through the tracks, a rhythmic clang, a muted thunder. It grew louder and louder until at length it sounded not unlike the hoof beats of a storming cavalry regiment. From a distance the air pulsated intermittently with a panting and a blustering. Then suddenly the serenity of the forest snapped. A mad uproar filled the welkin, the tracks curved, the earth shook—a blast of air, a cloud of dust and steam and smoke—and the snorting monster had gone by.

The noises waned as they had waxed. The exhalations thinned away. Shrunken to a point again the train vanished in the distance, and the old solemn hush again settled upon this corner of the forest.

"Minna," whispered the flagman, as if coming out of a dream.

He returned to the hut, where he brewed himself some weak coffee, then sat down, sipping from time to time and all the while staring at a dirty piece of newspaper that he had picked up on his round.

Gradually a curious unrest came upon him. Attributing it to the heat from the stove, he tore off his coat and waistcoat. That proving to be of no help, he got up, took a spade from a corner, and went out to the lot that the inspector had presented to him.

It was a narrow strip of soil, overgrown with weeds. The blossoms on the two fruit trees were like snowy white foam. Thiel calmed down, a quiet content possessed him.

To work now.

The spade cut into the earth with a crunch. The wet clods flew and crumbled as they fell.

For a long while he dug uninterruptedly. Then he paused and said to himself audibly, shaking his head gravely:

"No, no, it won't do. No, it won't do."

The thought had suddenly struck him that Lena would be coming there often to look after the lot, and his accustomed life would be seriously disturbed. At one blow pleasure in the possession of the bit of ground turned into distaste. Hastily, as if he had been about to do wrong, he ripped the spade out of the earth and carried it back to the hut.

Again he sank into gloomy reflections. Almost without knowing why, he could not endure the prospect of Lena's presence for whole days at a stretch while he was on duty. Much as he might try he could not reconcile himself to the idea. It seemed to him he had something valuable to defend, against some one who was attempting to violate his holiest sanctuary. Involuntarily his muscles tautened in a slight cramp, and a short, defiant laugh escaped him.

The sound of his own laughter was alarming. He looked about and lost the thread of his thoughts. Finding it again he went back to the same dismal broodings.

Then suddenly a heavy black curtain was torn apart, his eyes so long befogged had now a clear view. He had the sensation of awakening from a deathlike sleep that had lasted two years. With an incredulous shake of the head he contemplated all the awful things he must have been guilty of in that condition. The long-suffering of his child, which the impressions of the earlier afternoon should only have confirmed, now were clearly revealed to his soul. Pity and penitence overcame him, and also great shame, that all this long while he had lived in disgraceful resignation, never taking the dear, helpless child's part, not even finding the strength to admit how much the child suffered.

From the self-tormenting contemplation of his sins of omission a great tiredness came over him. He fell asleep, bent over the table with his forehead resting on his hand.

For a long while he lay like that, and several times uttered the name Minna in a choked voice.

A rushing and roaring filled his ears, as of great masses

of water. He tore his eyes open and looked about. Darkness enveloped him. His limbs gave way, the sweat of terror oozed from every pore, his pulse beat irregularly, his face was wet with tears.

He wanted to look toward the door, but in the inky darkness did not know which way to turn. He rose reeling. And still terror possessed him. The woods outside boomed like the ocean, the wind drove rain and sleet against the panes. Thiel groped about helplessly. For a moment he felt himself to be drowning. Then suddenly there was a dazzling bluish flare, as of drops of supernatural light falling down into the earth's atmosphere to be instantly extinguished by it.

The moment sufficed to restore the flagman to reason. He fumbled for his lantern and found it. At the same instant the thunder awoke on the farthest edge of the heavens over Brandenburg. At first a dull, restrained rumble, it rolled nearer in surging metallic waves, until overhead it discharged itself in great peals, menacing roars that shook the earth to its foundations.

The window panes clattered. Thiel lighted the lantern, and his first glance after he regained self-control was at the clock. In a bare five minutes the express was due. Thinking he had failed to hear the signal, he made for the crossing as quickly as the dark and the storm permitted. Just as he was letting down the gates the signal rang—the sound was scattered by the wind in all directions.

The pine-trees bent over, their branches scraped against each other with uncanny creakings and squeakings. For a few moments the moon was visible, a pale yellow chalice amid the torn clouds. By its light could be seen the wind's mauling of the black treetops. The foliage of the birches along the embankment waved and fluttered like ghostly horses' tails. Beneath them lay the rails gleaming wet, absorbing the pale moonlight in spots here and there.

Thiel tore the cap from his head. The rain soothed him. It ran down his face mingled with tears.

His brain was in a ferment with confused recollections of

his dream. Tobias seemed to be undergoing maltreatment, and such horrible maltreatment that the mere thought of it stopped his heart. Another vision was clearer, of his dead wife. She had come from somewhere along the railroad tracks. She had looked very ill and was wearing rags for clothes. Without looking round she passed the hut, and then —here his memory became vague—she had great difficulty somehow in proceeding, she even collapsed several times.

Thiel pondered. And then he knew that she was in flight. No doubt of it. Else why those anxious backward glances as she dragged herself forward with her legs giving way under her? Oh, those awful looks of hers!

But there was something that she was carrying, wrapped in cloths, something limp, bloody, pale. And the way she looked down on it reminded him of a past scene.

A dying woman who kept her gaze fixed on her new-born babe with an expression of the deepest pain, intolerable torture. It was an expression he could no more forget than that he had a father and a mother.

Where had she gone? He did not know. But one thing was clear in his soul: she had withdrawn from him, disregarded him, dragged herself further and further away into the dark, stormy night. "Minna, Minna," he had cried, and the sound of his own cry awakened him.

Two round red lights like the staring eyes of a huge monster penetrated the dark. A bloody sheen glided in advance, transforming the drops of rain in its course into drops of blood. A veritable rain of blood seemed to descend from heaven.

Horror fell upon Thiel, mounting and mounting as the train drew nearer. Dream and reality fused into one. He still saw the woman wandering down the tracks. His hand wavered toward the cartridge case, as if to stop the speeding train. Fortunately it was too late. Lights flared before his eyes, the train had rushed past.

The remainder of the night there was little peace for Thiel. He felt a great urgency to be at home, a great longing to see little Toby, from whom, it seemed to him, he had been separated for years. Several times, in his growing anxiety over the child's condition he was tempted to quit duty.

To shorten the hours until his release he determined as soon as day dawned to walk his beat. So, with a cane in one hand and a large iron wrench in the other, he went out into the dirty-gray twilight and stepped along on the spine of a rail, halting every now and then to tighten a bolt with the wrench or to hammer at one of the fish-plates that held the rails together.

The wind and rain had stopped, fragments of a pale blue sky became visible between rifts in the banked clouds. The monotonous tap-tap of his soles on the hard metal and the sleepy drip-drop from the wet trees gradually calmed Thiel.

At six o'clock he was relieved. Without delay he started home.

It was a glorious Sunday morning. The clouds had broken and drifted beyond the horizon. The sun, gleaming like a great blood-red gem, poured veritable masses of light upon the forest. Through the network of the branches the beams shot in sharp straight lines casting a glow upon islets of lacy ferns and here and there turning silvery gray patches on the ground into bits of coral. The tops of the trees, the trunks, the grass shed fire like dew. The world seemed to lie under a deluge of light. And the freshness of the air penetrated to the very core of one's being.

Even in Thiel's brain the fantasies of the night could not but grow pale. And when he entered the room where little Toby was lying in bed with the sun shining on him and more color in his cheeks than usual, they disappeared completely.

To be sure, in the course of the day Lena thought she noticed something odd about him. At church instead of looking in the book he observed her sidewise, and in the middle of the day, when Toby was supposed as usual to carry the baby out on the street, he took it from the boy's arms and laid it in her lap. Otherwise there was nothing conspicuously different about him.

Having no chance to take a nap and as he was to do day

duty that week, he went to bed early, at nine o'clock. Exactly as he was about to fall asleep, his wife told him that she intended to accompany him the next morning to dig the lot and plant potatoes.

Thiel winced. He awoke completely, but kept his eyes shut.

Lena went on. If the potatoes were to amount to anything, she said, it was high time to do the planting. And she would have to take the children along because it would probably occupy her the entire day.

Thiel muttered a few unintelligible words, to which she paid no attention. She had turned her back and by the light of a tallow candle was occupied with unfastening her corset and letting down her skirts. Suddenly, without herself knowing why, she turned round and beheld her husband's ashen face distorted by a play of passions. He had raised himself partly, supporting himself by his hands on the edge of the bed, his burning eyes fastened upon her.

"Thiel!" cried the woman, half in anger, half in fear.

Like a somnambulist who hears his name called, Thiel came out of his daze. He stammered something, threw his head back on the pillow, and pulled the quilt over his ears.

Lena was the first to get up the next morning. She went about noiselessly, making the necessary preparations for the excursion. The baby was put into the perambulator, then Tobias was awakened and dressed. He smiled when he was told where he was going.

When everything was ready and even the coffee was made and set on the table, Thiel awoke. His first sensation on seeing the arrangements was of displeasure. He wanted to protest, but the proper opening refused to frame itself. Besides, what arguments could he advance that would weigh with Lena? And there was his child's little face beaming with joy, growing happier and happier each instant, until Thiel, from the sight of his delight in the approaching excursion, could not think of opposing it.

Nevertheless, on the way through the woods, as he pushed

the baby-carriage with difficulty through the deep soil, Thiel was not free from anxiety.

Tobias gathered flowers and laid them in the carriage. He was happier than almost any time his father had seen him. In his little brown plush cap he hopped about among the ferns and tried, helplessly to be sure, to catch the glassy winged dragonflies that darted above them.

As soon as they reached the spot, Lena made a survey. She threw the sack of seed potatoes on the grassy edge of a small grove of birches, kneeled down, and let the darkish soil run between her fingers.

Thiel watched her eagerly.

"Well," he said, "how is it?"

"Every bit as good as the corner on the Spree."

A burden fell from the flagman. He contentedly scratched the stubble on his face. He had feared she would be dissatisfied.

After hastily devouring a thick slice of bread the woman tossed aside head cloth and jacket, and began to spade up the earth with the speed and endurance of a machine. At regular intervals she straightened up and took several deep breaths. But the pauses were never for long, except when she had to suckle the baby, which she did quickly, with panting, perspiring breasts.

After a while the flagman called to her from the platform in front of the hut:

"I must inspect the beat. I'm taking Tobias with me."

"What!" she screamed back. "Nonsense! Who'll stay with the baby? You'll come here," she shouted still louder.

But the flagman as if not hearing walked off with Toby. For a moment she considered whether she should not run after the two, then desisted because of the loss of time.

Thiel walked down the tracks with his son. The boy was quite excited, everything was so new and strange. Those narrow black rails warmed by the sun—he could not comprehend what they could be meant for. And he kept up an incessant stream of funny questions. What struck him as strangest of all was the resonance of the telegraph poles.

Thiel knew the sound of each pole on his beat so well that with closed eyes he could tell at exactly what spot he stood. And now he stopped several times, holding Tobias by the hand, to listen to the wonderful tones that came from the wood like sonorous chorals from inside a church. The pole at the extreme south end made a particularly full, beautiful sound. It was a mingling of tones that seemed to come without pausing for breath.

Tobias ran round the weathered post to see if he could not through some hole discover the originators of the lovely music. His father listening sank into a devout mood, as in church. He distinguished a voice that reminded him of his dead wife, and fancied it was a choir of blessed spirits, her voice mingling with the others. A deep emotion, a great yearning brought the tears to his eyes.

Tobias asked to be allowed to gather the flowers in the field alongside the tracks. Thiel as always let the child have his way.

Fragments of the blue sky seemed to have dropped on to the meadow, so thickly was it strewn with small, blue blossoms. Like colored pennants the butterflies fluttered and floated among the shining white trunks of the birches. The delicate green foliage gave forth a soft rustle.

Tobias plucked flowers. His father watched him meditatively. Occasionally the flagman raised his eyes and searched between the leaves for a glimpse of the sky, which held the golden sunlight like a huge, spotless bowl.

"Father," said the child, pointing to a brown squirrel which with small scratching sounds was darting up a solitary pine-tree, "father, is that the good Lord?"

"Silly boy," was all that Thiel could find to reply as bits of loosened bark fell from the trunk of the tree to his feet.

Lena was still digging when Thiel and Tobias returned. She had already spaded up half the plot!

The trains passed at intervals. Each time they rushed by Tobias watched with mouth agape. Even his stepmother was amused by the funny faces he made.

The midday meal, consisting of potatoes and a remnant of roast pork, was consumed inside the hut. Lena was in good spirits. Even Thiel seemed ready to resign himself to the inevitable with good grace. While they ate, he entertained his wife by telling her various things connected with his work. Could she, for instance, imagine that there were forty-six screws in one rail, and more like that.

By mealtime the spading had been done, and in the afternoon Lena was going to sow the potatoes. This time, insisting that Tobias must look after the baby, she took him along.

"Watch out!" Thiel called after her, suddenly gripped by concern. "Watch out that he doesn't go too close to the tracks."

A shrug of Lena's shoulders was her only answer.

The signal rang for the Silesian express. Scarcely had Thiel taken his place in readiness at the gates when the approaching rumble became audible. Within a fraction of a minute he could see the train. On it came, the black funnel spitting steam in countless puffs, one chasing upward after the other. There! One—two—three milk-white geysers gushing up straight as candles—the engine whistling. Three times in succession, short, shrill, alarming.

"They're putting on the brakes," Thiel said to himself. "I wonder why."

He stepped out beyond the gates to look down the tracks, mechanically pulling the red flag from its case and holding it straight in front of him.

Good heavens! Had he been blind? God, O God, what was that? There—between the rails.

"Stop!" he screamed with every atom of breath in his lungs.

Too late. A dark mass had gone down under the train and was being tossed between the wheels like a rubber ball.

Only a few seconds more and with a grating and squeaking of the brakes, the train came to a standstill.

Instantly the lonely stretch became a scene of animation. The conductor and brakeman ran along the gravel path beside the tracks back to the rear end. From every window curious faces peered. And then the crowd that had gathered in the rear formed into a cluster, and moved forward.

Thiel panted. He had to hold on to something not to sink to the ground like a slaughtered steer.

How's that? Were they actually waving to him?

"No!"

A scream came from the spot where the accident had occurred, followed by a howling as from an animal. Who was that? Lena? It was not her voice, yet—

A man came hurrying down the tracks.

"Flagman!"

"What's the matter?"

"An accident."

The messenger shrank before the strange expression in the flagman's eyes. His cap hung on the side of his head, his red hair stood straight up.

"He's still alive. Maybe something can be done."

A rattle in the flagman's throat was the only answer.

"Come quickly—quickly."

With a tremendous effort Thiel pulled himself together. His slack muscles tautened, he drew himself to his full height, his face was empty and dead.

He followed the man at a run, oblivious of the pale, frightened faces at the windows. A young woman looked out, a traveling salesman with a fez on his head, a young couple apparently on their honeymoon. What were they to him? The contents of those rattling, thumping boxes on wheels had never concerned him. His ears were filled with Lena's lamentations.

Yellow dots swam before his eyes, countless yellow dots like fireflies. He shrank back, he stood still. From out of the dance of fireflies it came toward him, pale, limp, bloody —a forehead beaten black and blue, blue lips with dark blood trickling from them. Tobias!

Thiel said nothing. His face went a dirty white. He grinned as if out of his senses. At length he bent over, he felt the limp, dead limbs heavy in his arms. The red flag went round them.

He started to leave.

Where?

"To the railroad doctor, to the railroad doctor," came from all sides.

"We'll take him," called the baggage-master, and turned to prepare a couch of coats and books in his car. "Well?"

Thiel made no move to let go of the boy. They urged him. In vain. The baggage-master had a stretcher handed out from the car and ordered a man to remain with the father. Time was precious. The conductor's whistle shrilled. Coins rained from the windows.

Lena raved like a madwoman. "The poor woman," they said in the coaches, "the poor, poor mother."

The conductor whistled several times, the engine blew a signal, sent white clouds hissing up from its cylinders, and stretched its sinews of iron. In a few seconds, the mail express, with floating flags of smoke, was dashing with redoubled speed through the forest.

The flagman, whose mood had altered, laid the half-dead child on the stretcher.

There he lay with his racked tiny body. Every now and then a long wheeze raised the bony chest, which was visible under the tattered shirt. The little arms and legs, broken not only at the joints, assumed the most unnatural positions. The heel of one small foot was twisted to the front, the arms hung over the sides of the stretcher.

Lena kept up a continuous whimper. Every trace of her former insolence had disappeared. Over and over again she repeated a story to exonerate herself.

Thiel seemed not to notice her. With an expression of awful anxiety he kept his eyes riveted on the child.

A hush had fallen, a deadly hush. The tracks rested hot and black on the glaring gravel. The noon had stifled the wind, and the forest stood motionless, as if carved in stone

In muffled voices the two men took counsel. The quickest way to reach Friedrichshagen would be to go back to the neighboring station in the direction of Breslau, because the next train, a fast commutation, did not stop at the station that was nearer to Friedrichshagen.

Thiel seemed to consider if he should go along. At the time there was no one there who understood the duties of the position, so with a mute motion of his head he indicated to his wife that she should take hold of the stretcher. She did not dare to refuse though she was concerned about having to leave the baby behind.

Thiel accompanied the cortège of two to the end of his beat, then stood still and looked after them long. Suddenly he clapped his hand to his forehead with a blow that resounded afar. It might wake him up, he thought. Because this was a dream like the one he had had yesterday. No use. Reeling rather than walking he reached his hut. There he fell face downward on the floor. His cap flew into a corner, his carefully kept watch fell from his pocket, the case sprang open, the glass broke. An iron fist seemed to be clamped on his neck, so tight that he could not move no matter how he moaned and groaned and tried to free himself. His forehead was cold, his throat parched.

The ringing of the signal roused him. Under the influence of those three repeated sounds the attack abated. Thiel could rise and do his duty. To be sure, his feet were heavy as lead, and the stretch of rails circled about him like the spokes of an enormous wheel with his head for its axis. But at least he could stand up a while.

The commutation train approached. Tobias must be in it. The nearer it drew the more the pictures before Thiel's eyes blurred. Finally all he saw was the mutilated boy with the bloody mouth. Then darkness fell.

After a while he awoke from the swoon. He found himself lying in the hot sun close to the gates. He rose, shook the sand from his clothes and spat it from his mouth. His head cleared a bit, he could think more quietly.

In the hut he immediately picked his watch up from the floor and laid it on the table. It was still going. For two hours he counted the seconds, then the minutes, while representing to himself what was happening to Tobias. Now

Lena was arriving with him, now she stood in front of the doctor. The doctor observed the boy and felt him all over, and shook his head.

"Bad, very bad—but perhaps—who can tell?"

He made a more thorough examination.

"No," he then said, "no, it's all over."

"All over, all over," groaned the flagman. But then he drew himself up, raised his unconsciously clenched fist, rolled his eyes to the ceiling, and shouted as if the narrow little room must burst with the sound of his voice. "He must live, he must. I tell you, he must live."

He flung open the door of the hut—the red glow of evening fell through—and ran rather than walked to the gates. Here he stood still seemingly bewildered. Then suddenly spreading his arms he went to the middle of the road-bed, as if to stop something that was coming from the same direction as the commutation. His wide-open eyes made the impression of blindness. While stepping backward to make way for something, a stream of half-intelligible words came from between his gritted teeth.

"Listen. Don't go. Listen, listen. Don't go. Stay here. Give him back to me. He's beaten black and blue. Yes, yes. All right. I'll beat her black and blue, too. Do you hear? Stay. Give him back to me."

Something seemed to move past him, because he turned and made as if to follow.

"Minna, Minna,"—his voice was weepy like a small child's—"Minna, listen. Give him back to me. I will—" He groped in the air as if to catch and hold some one fast. "My little wife—yes, yes—and I'll—and I'll beat her—so she's black and blue, too—I'll beat her, too—with the hatchet—you see?—with the kitchen hatchet—I'll beat her with the kitchen hatchet. And that'll be the end of her. And then—yes, yes—with the hatchet—yes, with the kitchen hatchet—black blood."

Foam gathered on his lips, his glassy eyeballs rolled incessantly.

A gentle breath of the evening blew steadily over the forest, a rosy cloud mass hung in the western sky.

He had followed the invisible something about a hundred paces when he stood still, apparently having lost courage. With fearful dread in his eyes, he stretched out his arms, pleading, adjuring. He strained his eyes, shaded them with his hand, as if to discern the inessential being in the far distance. Finally his head sank, and the tense expression of his face changed into apathy. He turned and dragged himself the way he had come.

The sunlight laid its final glow over the forest, then was extinguished. The trunks of the pines rose among the tops like pale, decayed bones, and the tops weighed upon them like grayish black layers of mold. The hammering of a woodpecker penetrated the silence. Up above one last dilatory pink cloud traversed the steely blue of the sky. The breath of the wind turned dankly cold as if blowing from a cellar.

The flagman shivered. Everything was new and strange. He did not know what he was walking on, or what was about him. A squirrel hopped along the road-bed. Thiel pondered. He had to think of the Lord. But why? "The Lord is hopping along the tracks, the Lord is hopping along the tracks." He said it several times as if to get at something associated with it. He interrupted himself. A ray of illumination fell upon his brain. "Good heavens! That's madness." He forgot everything else and turned upon this new enemy. He tried to order his thoughts. In vain. They'd come and go and ramble away and shoot off at a tangent. He caught himself in the absurdest fancies, and shuddered at the consciousness of his impotence.

The sound of a child crying came from the birch grove near by. It was the signal for madness. Almost against his will he had to hurry to the spot where the baby, whom everybody had neglected, was crying and kicking on the unblanketed floor of its carriage.

What did he mean to do? What had driven him there? The questions were submerged in a whirling eddy of thoughts and emotions.

"The Lord is hopping along the tracks." Now he knew. Tobias—she had murdered him—Lena—the child had been entrusted to her care. "Stepmother! Beast of a mother!" he hissed between clenched teeth. "And her brat lives."

A red mist enveloped his senses. Two baby eyes penetrated through it. He felt something soft, fleshy between his fingers. He heard gurgling, whistling sounds, mingled with hoarse cries that came from he did not know whom.

Then something fell upon his brain like hot drops of sealing wax, and his spirit was cleared as from a cataleptic trance. Aroused to consciousness, he caught the quiver in the air that was the final reverberation of the signal, and in a trice he realized what he had been about to do. His hand relaxed its grip on the throat, under which the infant had writhed and squirmed. It gasped for breath, then began to cough and bawl.

"It's alive. Thank the Lord, it's alive."

He let it lie and hastened to the crossing. Dark clouds of smoke rolled in the distance, the wind drove them to the ground. He distinguished the panting of an engine that sounded like the intermittent, tortured breathing of a giant.

The stretch was shrouded in a cold twilight. But after a while the clouds of smoke parted, and Thiel recognized the train as being the freight that was returning with open empty cars and bringing home the men who had been working on the road-bed during the day. It had ample running time to stop at each station to drop or pick up the men.

Quite a distance from Thiel's hut the brakes began to be put on, and a loud clanking and clanging and rattling and screeching tore the silence before the train came to a standstill with a single shrill, long-drawn whistle.

About fifty men and women were in the different cars. Nearly all of them stood, some of the men with bared heads. There was a mystifying air of solemnity about them. When they caught sight of the flagman, a whispering began among them, and the old men drew their pipes from between their yellow teeth and held them respectfully in their hands. Here and there a woman would turn to blow her nose.

The conductor descended and advanced toward Thiel. The workmen saw him solemnly shake the flagman's hand, and then saw Thiel with slow steps almost military in their stiffness go back to the rear. None of them dared to address him, though they all knew him.

From the rear wagon they were lifting little Toby.

He was dead.

Lena followed. Her face was a bluish white, brown rings underlined her eyes.

Thiel did not so much as cast a glance at her. She, however, was shocked at sight of her husband. His cheeks were hollow, his eyelashes and beard were plastered, his hair, it seemed to her, was gone grayer. Traces of dried tears all over his face. And an unsteady light in his eyes that made her shudder.

The stretcher had been brought back for transporting the body home.

For a while there was gruesome silence. Thiel lost himself in black depths of awful thoughts. Darkness deepened. A herd of deer started to cross the embankment. The stag stood still between the rails and turned his agile neck curiously. The engine whistled. He and the rest of the herd disappeared in a flash.

At the moment that the train was about to start Thiel collapsed. The train stood still, and counsel was held as to what had now best be done. Since every effort they made to bring the flagman back to his senses, proved futile, they decided to let the child's body lie in the hut temporarily, and use the stretcher for conveying the flagman instead. Two men carried the stretcher, Lena followed, pushing the baby carriage, sobbing the whole way, the tears running down her cheeks.

The great purplish ball of the moon shone low between the trunks of the pine-trees. As it rose it paled and diminished in size until finally it hung high in the heavens like a swinging lamp, and cast a pale sheen over the forest, through every chink and cranny of the foliage, painting the faces of the processionists a livid white.

Cautiously but sturdily they made their way through the close second growth, then past broad nurseries with the larger trees scattered among the younger ones. Here the pale light seemed to have collected itself in great dark bowls.

Occasionally a rattle came from the unconscious man's throat, and occasionally he raved. Several times he clenched his fists and tried to raise himself, his eyes all the time remaining closed. Getting him across the Spree was difficult, and a return trip had to be made to fetch Lena and the baby.

As they ascended the slight eminence on which the hamlet was situated, they met a few of the inhabitants, who forthwith spread the news of the misfortune. The whole colony came running.

Among her gossips Lena broke into fresh lamentations.

Thiel was with difficulty carried up the narrow stairway of his home and put to bed. And the men returned immediately to bring little Toby's body back.

Some of the old, experienced people advised cold compresses. Lena carried out their prescription eagerly, properly, dropping cloths into icy cold spring water and renewing them as soon as the unconscious man's burning forehead had heated them. Anxiously she observed his breathing. It seemed to come more regularly and to continue to improve each minute.

However, the day's excitement had told upon her, and she decided to try to get a little sleep. No use! Whether she held her eyes open or shut, she kept seeing the events of the past hours. The baby slept. Contrary to her wont, she had not paid much attention to it. Altogether she had turned into a different person. Not a trace of her former arrogance. The sick man with the colorless face shining with sweat dominated her even in sleep.

A cloud passed, obscuring the moon and throwing the room into complete darkness. Lena heard nothing but her husband's heavy though regular breathing. She felt creepy in the dark and considered whether she should not rise and kindle a light. But as she attempted to get up, a leaden weight on her limbs pulled her back, her lids drooped, she fell asleep.

Some time later the men returning with the boy's body found the front door wide open. Surprised at this, they mounted and found the upstairs door also open. They called the woman by her name. No answer. They struck a match. The flare of it revealed awful havoc.

"Murder, murder!"

Lena lay in her blood, her face unrecognizable, her skull broken open.

"He murdered his wife, he murdered his wife!"

They ran about witless. Neighbors came. One bumped against the cradle.

"Good heavens!" He shrank back, ashen pale, his eyes fixed in a horrified stare. The baby lay with its throat cut.

The flagman had disappeared. The search made for him that night proved fruitless. The next morning, however, the man who replaced him found him on the tracks at the spot where little Toby had been run over, holding the shaggy brown cap in his arm and caressing it as if it were a living thing.

The block signaler, apprised of his discovery, telegraphed for help. Several men tried with kindly inducements to lure Thiel from the tracks. He was not to be budged. The express then due had to be stopped, and it was only by the united efforts of the entire crew and the use of force that the man, who had begun to rave fearfully, could be removed from the railroad. They had to bind him hands and feet, and the policeman summoned to the spot guarded his transportation the whole way to Berlin, where he was examined in the jail and the next day was sent to a free psychopathic ward. He never let go of the shaggy brown cap. He watched over it with jealous tenderness.

A FAREWELL[1]

ARTHUR SCHNITZLER

(1862-1931)

HE had been waiting an hour. His heart beat violently, and now and then he felt as if he had forgotten to breathe; then he drank in long draughts of air, and it did him no good. He ought to have been used to it, for it was always happening, always he was bound to wait an hour, sometimes two, three hours, and often he waited in vain. And it wasn't even possible to reproach her for it. When her husband stayed at home till late, she couldn't get away. Not till he went out dared she rush headlong hither, press one hurried kiss on his lips and then fly off again down the stairs, leaving him alone.

Then, after she was gone, he would fling himself full length on the sofa, utterly exhausted from those terrible hours of waiting; waiting which rendered him incapable of any work, which was gradually working his ruin. It had been going on like this for nearly a quarter of a year—since the end of spring. Every afternoon, from three o'clock onwards found him in his room with blinds let down, unable to set his mind to anything. He hadn't the patience to glance at a book or a newspaper; could not write a letter; could do nothing but smoke cigarettes one after the other, until the room lay buried in a cloud of greyish-blue vapour. The door of the ante-room was always left open; he was quite by himself, for the servant must not be there when she was coming. Then suddenly the bell would ring, and he

[1] Translated by Beatrice Marshall. Reprinted by permission of *The National & English Review*.

would start up in alarm. But if it were only she; if it were really and truly she *at last*. Then all was well! He felt released from a spell, a man once more, and often he almost wept for pure joy that it really was she at last, and that he needn't wait any longer. He would draw her quickly into his room, bolt the door, and the next minute they were in heaven. It was an understood thing that he should wait till the stroke of seven, for later than that there was no chance of her coming. He had told her once that he would never stay in a moment after seven, because waiting made him so nervous. And yet he always stayed in longer, and never went out till after eight had struck.

With a shudder he recalled the days before he had known her. Especially did he think with melancholy regrets of the last summer when all his time was his own; of charming afternoons in the country; of August sea-bathing; oh, how happy and healthy he had been! And he longed to be free, to travel away to some distant place, to be alone. Yet he could not tear himself away, for he worshipped her.

To-day seemed to him the most trying day of all. Yesterday she hadn't come, and he had received no news of her. It would soon be seven o'clock, but the later it grew the less calm he became. He didn't know what to do. The horrible part of it was that he had no means of access to her. The most he could accomplish was to walk up and down a few times outside her house, looking at her windows. He might not go in to her, might not send a message; and there was no one of whom he might ask how she was. For not a soul suspected that they knew each other. Their glowing tenderness was full of unrest and suspicion; every moment they were afraid of being betrayed. That their intimacy was carried on in profoundest secrecy seemed to him beautiful; but it made such days as this all the greater torture. Now it was eight, and she had not come. He had spent the last hour at the door looking out on the corridor. Lights were already being kindled. He went back to his room, dead tired, and threw himself on the sofa. The room was dark and he dozed. In half an hour he got up and decided to go out. His head ached and his legs hurt him, as if he had been running about for hours. He turned in the direction of her house. It almost soothed him to see that every window had its blinds drawn down. From the dining-room and bedroom windows a light shone through the shutters. He walked up and down for half an hour on the opposite pavement, his gaze fixed on the windows. The street was very quiet. Only when some servant girls and the housekeeper appeared in the doorway did he walk quickly away for fear he should be noticed.

That night he slept soundly and well. The next morning he lay in bed late, having told his servant not to disturb him. At ten o'clock there was a ring. The man brought him his breakfast and the morning's post. There was no letter from her. He told himself that as she had not written she would all the more certainly come to him in the afternoon, and he passed the time till three o'clock with something like calmness.

At three, but not a minute sooner, he returned home from lunch. He sat down on a chair in the ante-room to prevent himself running madly to and fro at every sound on the stairs. And yet each time that he heard steps on the entrance floor he was glad, because it gave him fresh hope. But he hoped in vain. Four, five, six, seven struck and she didn't come. Then he tore about his room, making a low moaning, and when he became giddy threw himself on the bed. He was in utter despair; this was more than he could endure. Away, to go away, that would be best. This happiness was too dearly paid for. Or there must be a change . . . he must agree to wait only *one* hour, or at most two. It couldn't go on like this, or it would be fatal to his capacity for work, to his health, aye, and even to his love. He noted that already he was ceasing to think altogether of her; his thoughts revolved as in a nightmare. He sprang from the bed, wrenched open the window, and looked down into the street, into the dusk. Ah! there at the corner; was it she? He thought he recognized her in every woman who went by. He drew back from the window. It was impossible that she could come now. The hour was past. And suddenly he began to think that it was absurd to have settled to wait only these few hours. Perhaps she might have been able to come to him this morning, or at other times, and at once there rose to his lips what he would say the next time they met . . . he whispered it to himself: "The whole day I will stay at home and expect you from early morning till late at night." But directly he had said it he laughed the idea to scorn, and whispered to himself again: "I am going mad; yes, mad, mad, mad!"

And once more he rushed to her house. Everything looked the same as yesterday. Light glimmered through the closed shutters. Again he paced the opposite pavement for half an hour. Again he came away because the housekeeper and some of the servant girls appeared in the doorway. To-day he thought they looked at him, and he was almost convinced that they were talking about him, and saying one to the other, "That is the same gentleman who was walking up and down here at the same time yesterday."

He went and walked about the back streets close by, and and then, when ten sounded from the belfries and the gates were closed, he came and stared up again at the window. A faint ray of light still shone from the bedroom window. He stared like one transfixed. How helpless he was! He could do nothing, ask nothing. The hours that lay before him made him shudder. A night, a morning, a day till three. . . . Yes, till three, and then? Ah, if she didn't come again! He hailed the driver of an empty carriage, and let himself be driven about the deserted, moonlit streets. He remembered their last meeting. . . . No, she had never ceased to love him— that couldn't be. There might have been suspicions awakened in her home. But that, too, was hardly possible. So far, not the slightest rumour of anything had leaked out—and she was so cautious. Then there could be only one reason: she was lying in bed ill; and that was why she could not let

him know. . . . To-morrow she would be up again and send
him a line to allay his anxiety. . . . Yes, but what if she could
not leave her bed for some days, say a week . . . if she were
dangerously ill? . . . No, no, no! Why should she be dangerously ill?

Then suddenly a thought occurred to him that seemed
like a solution. As she must assuredly be ill, there would be
no harm in his sending to inquire after her health. His messenger needn't know who sent him . . . or he needn't catch
the name. . . . Yes, now he had hit on the right course of
action. What a happy thought!

He passed that night and the following day in a calmer
frame of mind. Though no news of her came . . . he felt the
evening would put an end to uncertainty, and he yearned
for her more tenderly than he had done during the last few
days.

He left his house at eight o'clock and engaged a messenger
who didn't know him at a street corner some little way off.
He signed to the man to follow him. Not far from her dwelling he stood still and dispatched the man with an urgent
message.

By the light of the street-lamp he looked at his watch and
paced up and down. The next moment it flashed across his
mind that the husband's suspicion might be aroused; that he
would interview his messenger and insist on being brought
by him to the spot where he waited. He began to overtake
the messenger in a panic; then he slackened his footsteps
and let him disappear into the house. Edward paused, and
had to strain his eyes to keep the door in view. . . . In about
three minutes he saw the man come out again . . . he waited
a minute to see if anyone followed him, but no one came.
Now he hurried up to the man and questioned him eagerly.
How was she? What was the matter?

"The master of the house's compliments," answered his
messenger, "and the lady is not much better. She will have
to remain in bed a few days longer."

"Who told you?"

"A maid. She went into the room and came out again quickly. . . . I believe just at that moment the doctor was there. . . ."

What had the maid said? Two or three times he asked the messenger to repeat the words, till at last he was conscious that he was very little wiser now than he had been before.

Evidently she must be seriously ill. . . . People were inquiring for her openly from many quarters, so that his inquiries had not seemed extraordinary. He might venture again. He ordered the man for the same time to-morrow. She would have to stay in bed a few days longer. That was all he had learned. Of whether she thought of him, or had the least conception of how he was suffering for her sake . . . he knew nothing. Would she guess from whom this last inquiry had come? *He,* the husband, had sent his compliments, not she. . . . Perhaps she was too ill to be told. And what was the matter with her? The names of a hundred diseases flashed through his mind. She would stay in bed probably a few days longer. . . . A few days; it could be nothing very serious then. . . . But that was a *façon de parler.* When his own father was at the point of death, people had said he would not leave his bed for a few days. . . . He found that he was running, for he was in a more frequented street and kept knocking up against the passers-by. Oh, what an eternity it would seem till to-morrow evening. The hours passed, and several times he wondered why it was that he could not realise the illness of his mistress. It seemed almost a sin to take it so calmly. In the afternoon (ah! how long it was since anything had happened in the afternoon!) he read a novel as if there was nothing to be anxious about.

The messenger was at the appointed corner when Edward hurried there in the evening. To-day he instructed the man if possible to open a conversation with the lady's maid, to ascertain what the illness really was. The man was longer away than yesterday, and Edward became uneasy. It was nearly a quarter of an hour before he reappeared. Edward ran to meet him.

"The lady is very bad, they say."

"What?" cried Edward.

"The lady is very bad indeed," the man repeated.

"Who told you? What have they said to you?"

"The maid told me that it is very serious. . . . Three doctors have been to-day, and the master is nearly out of his mind."

"Go on. Tell me more. What is the illness? Haven't you asked? Did I not charge you to—"

"I asked, of course. It's brain typhus; and the lady has been unconscious now for two days."

Edward stood still and looked at the man with a half-dazed expression. Then he asked: "Is that all you can tell me?"

The man began his story all over again, and Edward listened as if every word was news. Then he paid him and went straight back to the street in which her house was. There was no reason why he shouldn't stand there now, as long as he liked. No one troubled about him. Why should anyone? He stood and stared up at the bedroom window, trying to penetrate the panes of glass and the curtains with his gaze, to see into the sick room. Yes! behind those silent windows, there was now not the least doubt, lay someone dangerously ill. He ought to have known it from the first evening. To-day it seemed so natural that this was the cause of her not coming. A carriage drove up to the house, and Edward ran across the road just in time to see a well-known specialist alight and pass through the gates. Edward hung about in the vague hope that when the doctor came out he would be able to gather something from his features. He stood some moments motionless, and then he felt as if the ground were swaying under his feet. Unconsciously he had closed his eyes, and now as he opened them it seemed to him that he had been asleep and dreaming, and now woke refreshed.

That she should be dangerously ill . . . she . . . so young, so fair, and so beloved—again it seemed impossible. "Brain typhus"—the name of the illness flashed across him, and he wasn't sure that he knew exactly what it was. He remembered to have seen it given sometimes in obituary notices as

the cause of death. He began to picture her name and age
in print, and underneath, "Died August 10, of brain typhus."
Oh, no! it was unbelievable, he could not believe it, that in
a few days he would be reading her obituary. . . . The doctor
came out; Edward had almost forgotten him, and he held
his breath. The features of the great physician were grave
and passionless. He called out an address to his coachman,
got into the carriage and drove away. "Why didn't I ask
him?" Edward thought to himself; but the next moment he
was glad that he hadn't. He would only have heard something bad. Now he might still hope on. And suddenly he
tried to imagine what it would be when she came to him for
the first time after her illness. He was astonished at the vivid-
ness of the picture. He even saw that the day would be grey,
and a drizzly rain falling. The cloak would fall from her
shoulders before she was out of the ante-room. She would
throw herself into his arms and only cry and cry, and at last
she would whisper, "Now you have me safely in your arms
once more." Ah! but it would never be; never, never again
would he hold her in his arms. Five days ago she had come
to him for the last time, and he hadn't known it was the last
time, and had let her go. . . .

Again he tore wildly up and down the streets, thoughts
whirling through his head. He longed to lose the power of
thinking. And here he was back at her house. The door was
open, and the lights still shone from the bedroom and dining-
room windows. . . . Edward turned and ran for his life. He
knew that if he had stood there another moment he must
have rushed into the house up the stairs to her—to her bedside . . . to his mistress's bedside . . . and he followed this
train of thought to the end, as was his way. He saw the husband, who had grasped everything, hurry to the patient as
she lay there motionless, shake her by the arm, and hiss in
her ear: "Your lover is here. Your lover has come to see you."
But she didn't hear, for she was dead. . . .

The night passed in troubled dreams, the day in dull
weariness. As early as eleven in the morning he engaged

another messenger, and sent him to inquire. The news that came was: "Condition unchanged."

He lay stretched out the whole afternoon on the sofa, and could not understand himself. He was indifferent to everything, and thought what a delightful relief it was to be so absolutely tired out. He slept a good deal. But he jumped to his feet when it grew dark, feeling all at once that for the first time he saw this perplexing situation clearly. An intense longing for certainty overpowered him—to-day he must speak to the doctor. He hurried to her house. The housekeeper was standing outside. He went up to her, marvelling at his own calmness, and asked casually how her mistress was. The housekeeper answered:

"It's going badly with her. She will never come downstairs again."

"Indeed!" Edward said; and added formally, "That's very sad."

"Of course it's sad," said the woman. "So young and beautiful as she is," and she disappeared through the doorway.

Edward gazed after her. The woman's curiosity had not been aroused concerning him, and the thought struck him that he might now venture into the dwelling itself as he had become such a master at assuming a part.

The doctor's carriage drove up. Edward greeted him as he stepped out of it, and received a courteous response. This suited his purpose; it put him on a footing of acquaintanceship with the great man, and he felt he might question him when he came down. He stood rooted to the spot, and he liked to think that the doctor was with her. What a long time he was . . . at all events, there must be a chance of saving her, else surely he would not stay upstairs so long. Or perhaps it had come to the last agony. . . . Or—but why did he imagine things? . . . it was useless—useless. All might be possible.

Then all at once he thought that he heard the doctor speaking; his words came to him clearly, "This is the crisis." Involuntarily he looked up at the window, which was closed. He considered whether in extraordinary circumstances, when the senses were excited and therefore keenly on the alert, whether then a man's voice could penetrate shut windows, and the words spoken in an ordinary tone could reach someone standing in the street. Distinctly he had heard the words—*heard*, not imagined them. . . . But at that moment the doctor came out at the door. Edward approached him, thinking that he might be taken for a member of the family. Already the unspoken question had been read in his eyes, and the doctor answered with a shake of the head. But that was not enough to satisfy Edward. He spoke. "May I ask, sir, how . . ." The doctor was standing with one foot on the step of the carriage. Again he shook his head. ". . . Her condition is very grave," he said, and looked at the young man. "You are her brother?" . . . "Yes," said Edward.

The doctor regarded him with compassionate interest. Then he sprang into his carriage, nodded to Edward, and was driven away.

Edward looked after the carriage wistfully, as if hope were vanishing with it. Then he went home, talking to himself in a low tone. His sentences were broken, almost delirious, and his teeth chattered.

"What shall I do to-day? . . . Start for the country? No, it is too late—too late. . . . Am I sorry? Yes, of course I am. . . . Am I broken-hearted? No. I can go out for a walk as if nothing at all had happened—nothing at all! I believe I could go to the theatre and sit through a play; or take a country ride. . . . Oh, no, not quite. . . . I only think I could because I am so cut up. It's insane to suppose such things. . . . This is a moment when one can understand without feeling—an exceptional moment. I want to feel nothing—nothing. I'm freezing! I'll go home, home. Some time or other I must have had a similar experience . . . but when—*when?* Perhaps it was in a dream. . . . Or is this a dream? Yes, here I am going home, as if everything was the same as usual . . . the same as usual. But I shall not be able to stay at home; in the middle of the night I shall be running again to the house—her house, my mistress's house, my dying mistress. . . ."

He found himself in his room without remembering how he got up the stairs. He struck a light, and sat down on the sofa.

"I know what it is," he said. "Sorrow is knocking at the door, and I won't let him in. I know that he is standing outside. I can see him through the keyhole. . . . Oh, how stupid! . . . and my mistress is dying—yes, dying . . . dying, dying! . . . Or is there still hope? That accounts for my being so calm. No, there is none. Ah, and the doctor took me for her brother! Suppose I had answered, 'No, I am not her brother, but her lover, her lover. . . .' "

And suddenly he cried aloud, "Oh, God, have mercy!" leapt up, and tore about the room. "I have let him in!" he said. "Sorrow is there! Anna, Anna, my sweet, my own beloved Anna! . . . And I may not come to you. . . . Only *I* may not, just I—the one in all the world to whom you belong. . . . Perhaps she is not unconscious. How can we tell? She may be yearning for me . . . and I can't go to her—dare not go. Or, at the very last when she is being released from all earthly cares, she will whisper, 'Bring him to me. I should like to see him once more. . . . What will he do without me?' "

And he saw the whole scene. Saw himself hurrying up the stairs, being received by her husband and led by him to the dying woman's bed. She smiles at him with her glazing eyes. . . . He bends down, and she embraces him, and just as he raises himself again she breathes her last. . . . And now her husband confronts him and says, "Go away now; later you and I will have something to say to each other." . . . But, no; life was not like that. . . . Yet the most beautiful thing in the world would be to see her once more, to feel really sure that he had been loved by her. . . . He would, he must see her once more—somehow. He could not let her die without seeing her. That would be too horrible. He had not realised before how horrible it would be. But how was it to be managed? It was nearly midnight. Under what pretext could he go to her now? "But do I want an excuse?" he asked himself, "now when death———" Ah, but even when she was dying. What right had he to betray her secret, to sully her memory for her husband and family?

"Ah, but I'll pretend to be mad. I can pretend so easily. . . . What a comic idea. . . . But if I play the *role* to the bitter end, and am shut up in a madhouse for the rest of my life in consequence. Or if she were to get well and declare me to be a lunatic whom she had never known or seen. . . . Oh, my head, my head!"

He flung himself on the bed. He became gradually aware of the darkness and stillness around him, and said to himself that now he would reflect quietly.

"I will see her once more," he said; "that, at any rate, is settled."

And the next minute his brain began to whirl again. He saw himself in a hundred disguises mounting the staircase of her house. First he was the doctor's dresser; then the chemist's assistant, a lackey, a lawyer, a beggar. Finally he saw himself, approaching the dead, as undertaker's apprentice, sitting beside her whom he might not know, helping to wrap her in her shroud and lay her in her coffin. . . .

At dawn he awoke. The window had been left open, and though he had been lying on the bed in his clothes, he shivered. A light rain was falling, and the wind blew a few drops into the room.

"So autumn is here," thought Edward. He got up and looked at the clock, and found that he had been sleeping soundly for five hours. How much might have happened in these hours. He shuddered. Curiously enough, he seemed now quite decided about what he was going to do. He would go himself, with his collar turned up, straight to the front door of the house, and . . . inquire.

First he poured out a glass of cognac, which he didn't drink. Then he went and looked out of the window. How squalid the streets were at this early hour. There were actually people who had to be out by seven o'clock! Well, to-day he was one of them. The doctor's words came back to him: "Very grave." But he hadn't said she would die . . . and yet all the day before he somehow was under the impression that she was already—— Oh, he must be off. . . . He put on his overcoat, took his umbrella, and went into the ante-room. His servant regarded him in amazement.

"I shall be back soon," he said; and went.

His steps were slow and hesitating. Now it came to the point he hated going. What should he say when he got there?

He drew nearer and nearer the house. It looked strange to him at this hour. He felt as if he had never seen it before. He noticed the effect of tired light which the rainy morning cast over the town. On this sort of day people died. . . . If he had thought the last time that Anna had come to him that she was taking leave of him for ever in an ordinary way, he would almost have forgotten her by this time. For it seemed such an eternity since he had seen her last. It was quite uncanny how long it seemed. A rainy morning gave one wrong ideas of time. Oh, God! Edward was worn out and very distraught. He nearly passed the house, the door of which was wide open. A boy with milk-cans came through the gates. Edward got through the gateway calmly enough. Then as he was in the act of mounting the steps, he was seized with a full consciousness of all that had happened, was happening, and was going to happen.

He felt as if he had walked here in his sleep, and was only now waking up. This was the staircase. He had never seen it before. Dim lights burned in sconces on its walls. Now he had come to the first floor, where she lived. He clutched at his heart with both hands before going further——

What did this mean? The folding doors were thrown open. He could see in to the first room, but no one was there. He opened a small side door that led into the kitchen; here, too, there was no one. For a minute he stood irresolute. Then another side door opened, and a servant girl came out on tip-toe without noticing him. Edward addressed her.

"How is she, Mrs.——?" he asked.

The girl looked at him absently. "She died half an hour

ago," was her answer; and she disappeared into the kitchen.

Edward experienced a sensation as if the world around him had suddenly stood still. He felt certain that at this moment no hearts were beating, nobody was walking about, no carriages driving in the streets, no clocks ticking. It was as if the whole of moving creation had stopped to hold its breath. That was death, he thought. Yesterday he hadn't understood what it meant.

"Excuse me." It was a man clad in black who spoke. He was coming towards the ante-room, and Edward blocked the way. With a start, Edward stepped back and let the man pass. He took no further notice of him, and went through, leaving the door between the first room and the adjoining one half open. Edward could now see into the second room. It was nearly dark, because the curtains were drawn, but he could discern two figures rise from a writing-table to greet the newcomer. He heard them whisper together. Then they vanished behind a *portière*. Edward remained stationed at the door, and thought:

"She is lying in there. . . . It is not a week since I held her in my arms. . . . And I may not go in."

He heard voices on the stairs. Two women came up and passed by him. The younger of the two had eyes red from weeping, and was like his mistress. This, of course, was her sister, of whom she had now and then spoken to him. An elderly lady came out to meet them. They embraced, and sobbed softly on each other's breasts. "Half an hour ago. Quite sudden at the end," said the elderly lady, and she couldn't add more, for tears choked her. The three went together through the *portière*. No one took any heed of him.

"I can't stand here," Edward thought. "I'll go away, and come back in an hour."

In a moment he was in the street. The morning's traffic was in full swing. People hurried along, carts and cabs rolled past him. Nothing was standing still after all.

"In another hour," he said to himself. "More friends and relations will have collected there, and I shall not be observed among so many. What a relief it is to know for certain! I feel better than I did yesterday. . . . She is dead. Half an hour ago she died. And yet the knowledge that an hour ago she was still breathing gives one the impression that even now she must in some degree be conscious of existence, that she must know something of which when we are alive we don't have any idea. . . . Perhaps only that intangible moment when we pass from life to death is our poor eternity. . . . Ah, well, now it is all over. No more waiting indoors the whole afternoon. No more waiting for *her*."

And the memory of those hours came back to him and seemed unspeakably beautiful and sacred. Such a few days ago, and they were so happy . . . yes, happy. It had been a sultry, absorbing bliss. Ah! when he heard her feet on the last stair, . . . when she came flying into his arms, . . . when in the dusky room which smelt of flowers and cigarettes they lay speechless and still on the white pillows. . . . All over —over!

He must go away and travel. It was the only thing to be done. Could he ever go into his room again? If he did, he would cry, and do nothing else but cry day and night. . . .

The sight of a *café* reminded him that he had not tasted food since midday yesterday. He went in and breakfasted. When he left the *café* it was past nine o'clock. "Now," he reflected, "I can go back. I must see her just once more. . . . But what right have I there? Will they let me see her? Oh, but I must—yes, I must see my darling dead Anna for the last time. Shall I be allowed in the death chamber? Of course. . . . There will be a crowd of people, and all the doors will be open."

He hurried to the house. As he went in the housekeeper, who was at the front door, greeted him. He kept behind two gentlemen who were also ascending the staircase. Several people were assembled in the ante-rooms. The folding doors were open, and Edward entered. The curtains of one of the windows were drawn back, and let light into the room. The old lady whom he had seen earlier sat in the corner of a red velvet divan, quite overcome. As Edward passed her she looked at him. He paused and held out his hand to her. She nodded, and then buried her face in her handkerchief again. Edward looked round him. The further door, which led into the room beyond, was shut. He turned to a gentleman who stood at the window gazing absently out through a chink in the blinds.

"Where is she?" he inquired.

The other pointed to the closed door on the right. Edward opened it softly. He was dazzled by the flood of light that met his eyes. He was in a small boudoir with white hangings and furniture upholstered in gold and pale blue. No one was there. The door leading into the next room was ajar. He went through it. Now he was in the bedroom.

The shutters were closed, and a lamp was burning. The body lay stretched out on the bed. The coverlet was spread over her as far as her lips. Above her head candles burned in sconces, casting a pitiless light on the grey, ashen face. If he had not known who it was, he would not have recognised her. The resemblance dawned on him only gradually. . . . Gradually the figure lying there became Anna, his Anna, and for the first time during these days of wretchedness and horror he felt tears spring to his eyes. A burning anguish tore his breast; he wanted to cry aloud, sink on his knees and kiss her hands. . . . And then he became aware that he was not alone. Someone else was kneeling beside the bed, his head buried in the coverlet, holding the dead woman's hand in both of his. At the same moment that Edward was in the act of drawing a step nearer, the head was raised. What could he say to *him*, the husband? But before he could think of anything, his right hand was seized by the kneeling man, who, pressing it hard, murmured in a tear-strangled voice, "Thank you, thank you." And again the head was bowed in grief and the mourner sobbed into the coverlet. Edward stood a few minutes and contemplated the face of the dead with a kind of cold, critical attention. His tears were again dried up. His sorrow grew suddenly hard and unemotional.

He felt that this encounter would one day seem to him something at once awful and ludicrous. It would have been too ridiculous if he and the sorrowing husband had sobbed together.

He turned to go. But at the door he paused and looked back. In the flickering of the candles he fancied he saw a smile playing about Anna's mouth. And all at once it became an estranged, contemptuous smile. He could understand it. The smile said, "I have loved you, and now you stand there like a stranger and disown me. Tell him that I belonged to you, that it is your right to kneel by the bed and kiss my hands. Tell him! Why don't you speak?"

But he dared not. He put his hand before his eyes so as not to see the smile. Then he stole out of the room on the tips of his toes, shutting the door behind him. Shuddering, he went through the bright little boudoir into the semi-darkness of the room where the relations and friends were gathered together, whispering. He might not linger in their midst. Quickly he hurried on, pushing his way through the anteroom till he gained the staircase. Then when he was out of the house he slunk stealthily along in the shadow of its walls and his steps became every minute more hurried. Something goaded him away from the neighbourhood of that house, and full of shame he hastened through the streets; for it seemed to him as if he were not privileged to mourn with the others—as if his dead love was driving him away because he had disowned her.

HOW OLD TIMOFEI DIED SINGING[1]

RAINER MARIA RILKE

(1875-1926)

WHAT a pleasure it is to tell stories to a lame man! Healthy people are so changeable; they look at things now from this, now from that angle, and, when you have been walking along with them on your right for an hour, they may suddenly answer you from your left, simply because it occurs to them that that is more polite and shows a more refined upbringing. With a lame man one has not this to fear. His immobility makes him resemble things, with which indeed he fosters many intimacies; makes him, so to speak, a thing far superior to other things, a thing that listens not only with its silence but also with its rare, quiet words and with its gentle, reverent feelings.

I like best telling stories to my friend Ewald. And I was very glad when from his accustomed window he called to me: "I must ask you something."

Quickly I went up and greeted him.

"Where did you get the story you told me last time?" he finally asked. "Out of a book?"

"Yes," I answered sadly, "the historians have kept it buried there, since it died; that is not so very long ago. Only a hundred years since, it lived—carelessly, for sure—on many lips. But the words that people use now, those heavy words one cannot sing, were its enemies and took from it one

---

[1] Translated by M. D. Herter Norton and Nora Purtscher-Wyden-bruck. Reprinted from *Stories of God* by Rainer Maria Rilke by permission of W. W. Norton & Company, Inc. Copyright, 1932, by W. W. Norton & Company, Inc. Published in England by Sidgwick and Jackson, Ltd.

mouth after another, so that in the end it lived, most secluded
and in poverty, on one pair of dry lips, as on a miserable
widow's portion. And there it died, leaving no heirs, and
was, as I have already said, buried with all honors in a book
where others of its family already lay."

"And it was very old when it died?" asked my friend, entering into the conceit.

"Four to five hundred years," I informed him truthfully;
"some of its relations attained an even greater age."

"How, without ever coming to rest in a book?" asked the
astonished Ewald.

I explained: "So far as I know, they were traveling from
mouth to mouth all the time."

"And did they never sleep?"

"Oh, yes, rising from the singer's lips, they might stay
now and then in some heart, where it was warm and dark."

"But were people so quiet that songs could sleep in their
hearts?" Ewald seemed thoroughly incredulous.

"They must have been. It is said that they spoke less,
danced dances of slowly growing intensity that had something soothing in their sway, and above all, they did not
laugh loudly, as one not infrequently hears them do to-day,
despite our generally advanced state of culture."

Ewald was on the point of asking another question, but
he suppressed it and smiled. "I ask and ask—but perhaps you
are about to tell me a story?" He looked at me expectantly.

"A story? I don't know. I only wanted to say that these
songs were the heritage of certain families. One had taken
it over and one passed it on, not quite untouched, with traces
of daily use yet still undamaged, like an old bible that is
handed down from father to son. A disinherited man differed
from his brothers who had come into their rights in that he
could not sing, or knew only a small part of the songs of his
father and grandfather, and lost with the other songs that
great piece of experience which all these *bylini* and *skaski*
represent to the people.

"Thus Yegor Timofeievitch, for instance, had married

against the will of his father, old Timofei, a beautiful young wife and had gone with her to Kiev, to the holy city, beside which the graves of the greatest martyrs of the Holy Orthodox Church are gathered. Father Timofei, who was known as the best singer within ten days' journey, cursed his son and told his neighbors he was often convinced that he had never had any such son at all. Nevertheless he grew dumb with sorrow and remorse. And he sent away all the young people who came crowding into his hut in order to become the heritors of the many songs that were locked up in the old man as in a dust-covered violin. 'Father, our little father, give us only one song or another. See, we will carry it into the villages and you shall hear it in every farmyard as soon as evening comes and the cattle in the stables are still.'

"The old man, who continually sat on the stove, shook his head all day long. He no longer heard well, and as he never knew whether one of the lads who always hung listening around his house now, had not just asked for a song again, he would sign with his white head tremulously: No, no, no, till he fell asleep, and even then a while—in sleep. He would gladly have done as the young men asked; he himself was sorry that his dumb, dead dust was to lie upon these songs, perhaps quite soon now. But had he tried to teach one of them something, he would surely have had to remember his own boy Yegorushka, and then—who knows what might have happened then? For only because he never spoke at all had no one seen him weep. They were there, the sobs, behind every word, and he always had to close his mouth very quickly and carefully, lest they should come out too.

"Old Timofei had begun very early to teach his only son Yegor a few songs, and as a boy of fifteen Yegor could already sing better and more than all the grown-up youths in the village and the neighborhood. At the same time the old man, mostly of a holiday when he was somewhat drunk, would say to the lad: 'Yegorushka, my little dove, I have already taught you to sing many songs, many bylini and also the legends of the Saints, one for every day almost. For as you know, I am the best singer of the whole government, and my father knew, so to speak, all the songs of the whole of Russia, and also Tartar stories as well. You are still very young, and so I have not yet told you the most beautiful bylini, in which the words are like ikons and not to be compared with ordinary words, and you have not yet learned to sing those melodies that no man ever, were he Cossack or peasant, has been able to listen to without weeping.'

"This Timofei repeated to his son every Sunday and on all the many holidays of the Russian year—that is, quite often. Until Yegor, after a violent scene with the old man, and simultaneously with the beautiful Ustionka, the daughter of a poor peasant, disappeared.

"In the third year after this event, Timofei fell ill, at the very time when one of those many pilgrimages that are always on their way from all parts of the vast empire to Kiev, was about to start. His neighbor Ossip came to see the sick man: 'I am going with the pilgrims, Timofei Ivanitch, permit me to embrace you before I go.' Ossip was not a friend of the old man, but now that he was starting on this long journey, he found it necessary to take leave of him as of a father. 'I have sometimes offended you,' he sobbed, 'forgive me, my little heart, it happened in drunkenness, and one cannot help that, as you know. Now I will pray for you and light a candle for you. Farewell, Timofei Ivanitch, my little father, perhaps you will get well again, if God wills it; then you will sing for us once more. Ah, yes, it is a long time since you have sung. What songs those were! The one about Diuk Stepanovitch, for instance, do you think I have forgotten it? How stupid you are! I still know it perfectly. Of course, not like you—you simply knew how to sing, one must admit. God gave you that, to another he gives something else. To me, for instance . . .'

"The old man, who was lying on the stove, turned round with a groan and made a movement as though he would say something. It sounded, very softly, like Yegor's name. Perhaps he wanted to send him a message. But when Ossip, from the door, asked: 'Did you say something, Timofei Ivanitch?' he lay quite still again and only shook his white head gently. All the same, God knows how it happened, hardly a year after Ossip had gone away, Yegor quite unexpectedly returned. The aged man did not recognize him at once, for it was dark in the hut, and the old eyes were reluctant to take in a new, unfamiliar figure. But when Timofei heard the stranger's voice, he started and jumped down from the stove on his rickety old legs. Yegor caught him, and they clasped each other in their arms. Timofei wept. The young man asked over and over again: 'Have you been ill a long time, Father?' When the old man had regained a little composure, he crept back on his stove and inquired in a changed, a severe tone: 'And your wife?'

"A pause. Yegor spat. 'I have sent her away, you know, with the child.' He was silent a while. 'One day Ossip comes to see me. "Ossip Nikoforovitch?" say I. "Yes," he answers, "it is I. Your father is sick, Yegor. He can no longer sing. It is all silent now in the village, as though it, our village, had no soul any more. Nothing knocks, nothing stirs, no one weeps any more, and there seems to be no real reason to laugh either." I think it over. What's to be done? So I call my wife. "Ustionka"—say I—"I must go home, no one else is singing there now, it is my turn. Father is sick." "Good," says Ustionka. "But I cannot take you with me," I explain, "Father, you know, won't have you. And probably I shall not come back to you either, once I am there again and singing." Ustionka understands me. "Well, God be with you. There are many pilgrims here now, they will give alms. God will help, Yegor." And so I went away. And now, Father, tell me all your songs.'

"The rumor spread that Yegor had come back and that old Timofei was singing again. But that autumn the wind went so violently through the village that none of those who passed by could tell for sure whether there really was singing in Timofei's house. And the door was not opened to any one who knocked. The two wanted to be alone. Yegor sat on the edge of the stove on which his father lay, now and then bringing his ear close to the old man's lips, for he was indeed singing. His aged voice, somewhat bent and trembling, bore all his most beautiful songs to Yegor, and Yegor would sometimes sway his head or swing his hanging legs, quite as though he were already singing himself. This went on for many days. Timofei kept finding song after song in his memory, each one more beautiful than the last; often, at night, he would wake his son and while he gestured uncertainly with his withered, twitching hands, he would sing a little song, and then another and yet another—till the lazy morning began to stir. Soon after singing the most beautiful, he died. He had often bitterly complained in his last days that he still carried a vast quantity of songs within him and had no time left to impart them to his son. He lay there with furrowed brow, in intense and fearful recollection, and his lips trembled with expectancy. From time to time he would sit upright, sway his head to and fro for a while, move his lips—and at length some faint little song would come forth; but now for the most part, he kept singing the same verses about Diuk Stepanovitch, which he particularly loved, and his son had to appear astonished and pretend he was hearing them for the first time, in order not to anger the old man.

"After old Timofei Ivanitch had died, the house, in which his son now lived alone, remained shut up for a time. Then, in the following spring, Yegor Timofeievitch, who now wore quite a long beard, stepped out of his door, and began to walk about the village and sing. Later he visited the neighboring villages too, and the peasants began to tell each other that Yegor had become at least as accomplished a singer as his father Timofei; for he knew a great number of grave and heroic songs and all those melodies to which no man, were he Cossack or peasant, could listen without weeping. Besides, his voice is supposed to have had such a soft and sorrowful tone as had never been heard from any other singer. And this quality always appeared, quite unexpectedly, in the refrain, wherefore it was particularly moving. So at least I have heard tell."

"Then he did not learn that tone from his father?" asked my friend Ewald after a while.

"No," I answered, "it is not known how he came by it."

I had already stepped away from the window, but the lame man moved again and called after me:

"Perhaps he was thinking of his wife and his child. Tell me, did he never send for them, his father being dead?"

"No, I don't think so. At least he was alone when he died."

THE BURNING OF EGLISWYL[1]

FRANK WEDEKIND

(1864-1918)

In the canton of Aargau, in the northern part of Switzer
land, there are more mountain castles than there are farm
yards in all the north of Germany. Every mountain top,
every crest is crowned with an old castle, or at least a ruin
of one. Within the circumference of a few miles there are
the castles Wildegg, Habsburg, Bruneck, Casteln, Wilden-
stein, Lenzburg, Liebegg, and Hallwyl. My father bought
the castle of Lenzburg when I was eight years old. The
little town of Lenzburg had, besides this old castle, a less
happy place of interest. This was the cantonal prison
modeled after an American type. And thus when the land
owners of the surrounding country have any heavy labor to
be performed, they hire the convicts, who have become so
accustomed to their lot that they almost never try to escape.
And among them there are some very dangerous criminals.

In the year 1876 there was a small landslide which blocked
one half of the street. In order to drain the place, pipes had to
be laid deep under the ground. My father secured a number
of convicts to perform the undertaking. A guard accompanied
them. Besides, my father was always on hand. As the men
were not permitted to smoke, he gave them chewing tobacco.
One day, a long, lead pipe was needed from the village. My
father took one of the prisoners with him to fetch it. I met
them on their return as I was coming from school. The three
of us walked slowly up the hillside, my father in the middle.

[1] Translated by F. Eisemann. From the *Princess Russalka* by Frank
Wedekind. Reprinted by permission of John W. Luce & Company.

"How long have you been in prison?" my father asked the convict.

"Seven years."

"And how much longer is your sentence?"

"Eight years."

"How did you get here?"

"Arson."

"You probably had debts, and wanted to get the insurance on your house?"

"I never owned a house, and never had any debts. I was a servant. But—but—." Then he told his story. He was born and committed his crime in Egliswyl. I was not more than twelve years old at the time, but his story made such an impression upon me that today, twenty years afterwards, I can remember it word for word.

"Amrai's Susan," began the prisoner, "there was a girl for you! There was nothing lacking in her. Every man in this world should have had his little fun with her. She was the bailiff's daughter, and the whole week through she was washed and combed, and she wore a white shirt. I was only farmer Suter's hired man and had always been boarded at the expense of the community. I never knew who my parents were. In fact, I knew nothing about men and women; all that I knew was about cattle: why they were on earth and how old they were. And until Amrai's Susan told me that her father had said that I was nineteen years old and would have to go to the army in two years, I knew nothing about myself. She was drawing water from the pump and I was holding Bethi by the halter because the milk boy had gone into the village. She looked at me so queerly that I turned around because I thought that she was perhaps talking about Bethi. 'You are nineteen years old,' I said to Bethi when I tied her up for the night. And from that moment I had a strange feeling.

"Amrai's Susan was the first. As far back as I can remember I had never dared to look at her squarely. I don't think I could have done it even in a dream. I used to look at her

only when her back was turned. And now she made such big
eyes. The next evening she told me that I should come to
the 'Egli' on the following Sunday. I told her that I had no
money but she said that made no difference. So on Sunday I
went to the 'Egli' and watched them dancing from the doorway. Then Amrai's Susan came with her little friend Marianne and they drew me into the hall. First Marianne had to
dance with me. At the beginning it was hard; I did not hold
her tight, but she was so clever that by the time we had
made three turns we were doing as well as any of the others.
And then I felt that something strange was going on within
me. After a while Amrai's Susan let her partner go and took
me, hot as I was, out of Marianne's arms and danced with
me until it grew dark. When there was an intermission she
gave me a glass of wine to keep me cool. After that I held
her so close that her shoulders were bent back and she did
not know what to do with her feet. After the dance she took
me with her by the hand. Marianne started a fuss because
no one was going with her. I took my shoes off in the street
and left them at the pump. The bailiff was taking his grog
at the 'Egli.' There were two roses painted on her bed. When
I came back to the stable and saw our five cows sleeping in
a row, I said to myself, 'It is all the same; man or beast!'

"Every night I climbed in and out of Susan's window. But
then there was Veronica, farmer Leser's daughter, a proud
creature, and the first girl in the whole village. On Sundays
she and her comrades would go up in the main street in the
village all in a row, so that no carriage could pass them. And
when a young fellow would come along, all seven of them
would stare at him until he had passed by; and once he was
gone they would laugh so that they could be heard way up in
the church. Veronica had had a lover now for a year. But
Ruodi Weber had been consumptive since the fall. Now he
could only dance three dances no matter how much wine he
had drunk at the 'Egli.' Then he would rest his elbows on
the table and not say a word. Thus when Veronica saw me
dance all night with Susan, without resting at all, she begged

Susan to let her have a dance with me. Susan didn't want to but I did, and so I danced with her. Susan ran outside and wept. And Veronica laughed; and I felt how warm she was. She was as solid as if she had been fed for the butcher. If she had been a three-year-old heifer I'd have given twenty napoleons for her. We went home arm in arm.

"When the clock struck one there was a knock outside her window. 'That's Ruodi Weber,' she said, and got up and went to the window to bid him good night so that he would not get the stable men. Then she told me that I ought not go with Susan any longer, and because I liked her so well I told her that I wouldn't. But the next day I felt as if I ought to go and see Susan anyway. And I went to see her that night and told her everything. Then she said that she was not like Veronica; as far as she was concerned I could go with any one I cared about, excepting one, her little friend Marianne. And because Susan was so good I said that I would do as she said. But the next day I thought it was mean of Susan to have told me not to go with Marianne.

"But then when our Muni was being shod on account of the ice, Marianne came to the smithy to say that her father was coming to get a potion for the bailiff's sick horse. Then I asked her whether I might come and see her. Marianne stood there as if rooted to the spot and gazed at the glowing coals; then she went softly up the stairs.

"At the 'Egli' on Sunday, there was a fight between big Veronica and Susan. I danced the whole afternoon with Marianne. And when the dance was over, they made up, and the four of us walked home together. They kept me in the middle for they were afraid that I would run away. And thus we went through the village on the following Sunday, and the boys cursed and swore, and the girls who were with them laughed, but stared at me because I was walking with the three prettiest girls in the village. Neither Veronica, Susan, nor Marianne looked to the left or right. They talked among themselves, however, and laughed so loud that they could be heard all over the village. The pastor who was coming along at this time pretended to see nothing. He looked at me, however, and I thought he was jealous.

"Marianne loved me so much that she gave me a pipe. I showed it to Susan and she gave me a large fur cap. Then I showed the cap to Veronica and she gave me a silver watch.

"And thus it happened that when the summer came around there was not a girl who danced at the 'Egli,' or one who went to the spinning room with whom I had not spent the night. During the day I worked well and it pleased farmer Suter. Every one wondered at how I had filled out in the last year. My shoulders were so broad that one could have hitched me to a plow. My arms were well developed too, and I had grown very smart with it all! 'Now he's ready for the recruits,' said farmer Suter, 'and they'll not send him back.'

"It was midsummer. One night when I opened the stable door I found farmer Suter's wife standing there. 'Where are you going, Hans?' 'Is that any of your business?' 'I'll tell farmer Suter!' Then I went back into the stable. Farmer Suter's wife was fifty-three, and her face was all wrinkled. I suddenly turned back and said to her: 'If you tell farmer Suter that I go out at night, I'll tell him that you did it once too.' She never came to the stable again and I went where I pleased.

"Then came haying time, then the harvest, and then the vintage; and it was during vintage time that the good Lord punished me, and made me an incendiary. It was over there, at Castle Wildegg. Because the vine dresser himself came from Egliswyl, he took all of his help from that village. It was a rich year, the last year that I carried the grapes. The vintage lasted three days. There were seven of us men, and twenty women folks. On the third day, in the evening, the owner of the castle brought a gypsy along with him. He had a fiddle, and we danced on the grass in the castle courtyard. The grooms strung lanterns, and then the maids also came out to dance. There was one—she was the chambermaid— who came from Suabia. She was slim and short; but her

eyes sank into my flesh so that were I to see them today I
would recognize them. I had only one dance with her, but
when we were leaving I met her coming along singing, arm
in arm with the fat cook. I heard that singing all night, as I
lay in the stable gazing into the lantern light. The next
evening I went to Wildegg again to get a basket that had
been forgotten; and then the little maid came down into the
lower courtyard with me and gave me her mouth to kiss.
When I left her I felt it here, in my breast; that is where it
hurt, and I did not know what the matter was as I had never
been ill before.

"The next evening I again went to see her, and I asked her
whether I might stay with her until morning, but she said
no. Then I wept. For three days I could do no work. Farmer
Suter said: 'What's the matter with Hans? He doesn't eat,
drink, or work any more.' Then I went down again that
night to Wildegg. At every step I felt better. The castle gate
was closed and everything was dark. There I sat until morning and did not return to Egliswyl; I hired myself out down
in the village. Every evening when it grew dark I went up
there, and if I but saw a corner of her apron I felt better.
During the week I drove with a load of wood to Lenzburg.
There I brought a ring so that I would have something to give
her the next time we met. She laughed when I gave it to her,
and she offered me her mouth to kiss. Then she told me that
I might come the day after next, when it was dark. And
when I was going down the mountain I said to myself: 'Up
there lies Egliswyl, and now you are a good man; now you
will succeed in life.' Until I again saw Marie—that was her
name—I worked as no farm hand ever worked before. And
while working I thought: 'When you come back from the
army you'll carry every penny to the savings bank until you
have enough to buy some land and build a little cottage.
Then you'll go up to the castle and ask Marie to marry you.
And if she says no, then you'll go to America and never wed.
But Marie will not say no; that would not be right, for if she
did not want you she ought to tell you so immediately, and

not ask you to come and see her again.' Morning and evening I said the same to myself; and I said to the cows: 'You don't understand such things. That is just the difference between man and beast.'

"And now I have pondered over it for seven years, and still I do not know what brought me down there to the prison, making me miss the best years of a man's life. Marie was a flighty little thing, and when we had made love for three weeks down in the lower courtyard, under the cliffs, and in the cold snow, she wanted to go where it was warmer, and I was not sorry. Then she showed me where I could clamber up the rocks to the little room where she slept alone. One night, when it was striking midnight down in the village, I climbed up to her, trembling for fear lest a stone should roll down among the bushes and awaken the castle folks. Marie softly opened and closed her window. Then for an hour not a word was spoken. And when I left her she was the same as when I had come.

"I dashed down over the cliffs. I had no more feeling in my hands or feet; and my throat felt as though the hangman's noose were around it. And I felt it in my chest, in my back, and in between: as if my insides were being torn out. And I felt poison surging through my veins. At first I wanted to drown myself, but then I thought: 'No! What does she think of me! What does she think of me! She did not cry and she did not laugh. She was as if frozen.' And then I thought of Amrai's Susan, of Veronica, of Marianne. 'It is their fault,' I said to myself, 'it is their fault.' It was not, though, and I knew it, but I said so to myself as I ran hither and thither through the streets of Egliswyl. I've been pretty bad at times during my seven years here, so bad that I have screamed and rolled on the ground until they locked me up in a place where there was neither light nor air. But at such times I used to think back to that night, and then I'd say to myself: 'They can do what they want with you here, for there is no suffering in God's world as great as what you went through on that night, and that, at least, is behind you.' Had

some one tied me to a bench and beaten me at that time I
would have thanked him for it. But there was no one. I came
down the mountain side. I howled and shrieked like an
animal in a slaughter house. And all I could see was flames,
which always grew hotter. It was as if I were in a burning
house. Wherever I looked hot flames beat into my face. And
the ground was so hot, in spite of the snow that had fallen,
that I could not stand still on one spot. And thus it drove me
on. At first I did not know what to do, but then suddenly I
knew. And then I felt better; but I kept on running for I
thought that the new day would break before I had done it.
I still saw nothing but flames. All the trees were crackling.
It was the biswind. 'It has come just at the right time,' I
thought. 'You must start in that corner where the wind comes
from so that it will spread well. The fire hydrant is frozen
too,' I thought. 'That is fine, that is fine!' When I came to the
village of Egliswyl I crept around the left side of it, for it
was from there that the wind was blowing; and I crept into
five houses, right up under the straw roofs. The third house
belonged to farmer Leser, and I thought of Veronica and
hoped that she would burn up too. Then I set fire to it. Now
I ran back. When I came to the woods there was a good
blaze, and my heart grew warm in it. I was still in the middle
of the woods when the fire bells began ringing in the little
town of Lenzburg; and on the Stanfberg, and over in Amris-
wyl. And then it went 'boom, boom.' That was the fireman on
the castle of Lenzburg who had shot off the cannon. When I
came out of the woods the heavens in back of me were red,
and I could hear the swishing of the fire hose down on the
highway. 'They can sprinkle a long while,' I thought, 'without any water'; and I kept on running down towards Wildegg. I clambered up the rocks, I don't know how, and
knocked softly at the window. Marie came.

"'Let me in,' I cried. 'Open, Marie!'

"Then she opened the window.

"'Do you know that it's burning?'

"'What is burning? Where is it burning?'

" 'Do you see, over there? The heavens are burning.'

" 'Oh, my God!'

" 'It is burning! The village is burning! The village of Egliswyl is burning! And I did it! See how it lights up. I set fire to five corners of it, Marie! Look look!'

"But she was still like ice. It did not seem to move her. Her face was white. She dressed hurriedly and awoke the whole castle, and she told them that she knew who had set fire to Egliswyl. Then she pointed to me. It was I, she said. I had wanted to hide in her room, but she despised me too much. Then they brought a strait jacket; I was still standing at the window, enjoying the crimson heavens. They took me down to the courtyard. Marie was there. She did not laugh —I am sure of that—yet I do not know why she didn't."

We had arrived at the top of the hill by this time, at the place where the landslide had occurred. Over there, but an hour away, lay the castle of Wildegg bathed in the afternoon sunlight. Perhaps my father would have liked to have sent me away during the story, but there had been no excuse for doing so. The convict stretched his bony body and placed the lead pipe on the grass.

Perhaps my father may have thought that I did not understand what the prisoner was talking about. And, in fact, my understanding of it did not come until much, much later. And by that time the prisoner must have been released.

THREE MINUTE NOVEL[1]

Heinrich Mann

(1871-1950)

When I was twenty-one I had my share in my father's estate paid to me, went to Paris, and, without any particular effort, spent it within a short time on women. My idea was to see life from the perspective of my own car, of a box at the opera, or of an enormous and expensive bed. I expected this to be of advantage to me in my writing, but I soon found that I was mistaken. It did not help me at all that I had everything; I continued to wish it. I led a sensuous life as though in a dream in which you know that you dream and yet crave for reality. At the side of a chic and much desired woman who favored me I moved as if beside the dissolving veils of my longing . . .

I had only a few thousand left when one night at a public dance, I foolishly opened my pocket book under the eyes of a young girl. She invited me and I followed her a distance to a musty house with slippery stairs and dripping walls. I had just hung my coat over a chair when the bed mat on which I stood, together with part of the floor, tilted, and I slipped into a shaft. It was fairly deep. A ledge enabled me to stop three or four feet below the room that I had just left, and to overhear the delight of a female and a male voice over my bequest. This, too, provided me with a perspective. It was not that upper-crust one for the sake of which I had come to Paris. It rather extended from the strange and evil depth of a dream. Still, there was something soothing about it.

There was scarcely any desire left in me to climb back into

[1] Translated by Victor Lange.

the light. Moreover, the drop lid snapped shut. I closed my eyes and let myself fall again and, contrary to all expectations, I did not break my neck but managed to get away through a canal. I escaped to Florence, where I had only one wish—to love that powdered Pierrot, who every night in a pantomime in the Teatro Pagliano sank to his knees before a milliner's block because he was too bashful to do it before the woman he loved; who won her, deceived her, and made her poor; who gambled and stole, and whose crimes, committed with the naïveté of a child, drew ever more melting circles about his innocently sinful eyes. At the end of a rather frosty April day, he finally died, delicate and corrupt, to the accompaniment of the light tears of a slender lithe music . . . I wished to love him; only, off stage, he was a renowned courtesan on whom Count Such-and-Such alone spent a thousand lire per month, which in Florence is a great deal of money. I went to her hairdresser, and for my last money he taught me his craft and sent me to her dressing room with rouge and powder. My services did not always please or satisfy her, and I felt the first touch of her lovely, full, and pointed hands in my face. One night when I was to fit her with a new wig, I dared to confess everything, and she dismissed me; I continued to dream of loving her . . .

Our further relations developed rapidly. Count Such-and-Such, from whom she received the thousand lire, suddenly and under protest abandoned her. He had already made most of his family unhappy: because of her, as he pretended. Others, too, declared that thanks to her they had been seriously damaged, and now just as she had dismissed me, she was dismissed by all of them, including her director. She was soon penniless and had to leave the hospital and, despised and harassed, be satisfied with what she could find in the street . . .

This was the time when she permitted me to provide a bed for her in my attic room at the end of the narrow and crowded Via dell'Agnolo. There she lay in the moonlit nights, her head against the dark wall and her hands for-

ever groping and moving in ghostly and shrill gestures like
sickly, moody flowers snapping for insects. I sat at the table
and wrote by the light of a candle. The air was filled with an
echoing, glittering, steel-blue silence; and the young Pierrot
powdered by the moon and sick unto death had stumbled
from his sinful journey directly into my room. How I wished
to love him. She opened her eyes, melting with gentle astonishment at her fate. Reluctantly she allowed me to take
care of her and all the time her searching eyes burned into
me. She despised me because I continued to stand by her.
She wanted me because she didn't understand me. Sometimes she was filled with horror, sometimes with passionate
desire, and sometimes with hatred. She tortured me, happy
because she could still be a little mean, still have a shadow
of revenge for what had happened to her. She cried on my
shoulder, and again her eyes seemed to ask me why I still
loved her. She did not receive an answer. I had never loved
her; I had only wished to love her.

One of those nights she died; I went down into the street
and in the darkness of the empty Via dell'Agnolo, and the
little guttery alley, I shed tears of which I was unspeakably
proud, and whose end I did not wish to experience . . . They
lasted not much less than an hour: an hour which in my
memory represents the best, the truest, the most beautiful
part of my life . . . But I was beginning to grow weary—and
I found leisure enough to fear for my life: in front of my
house I noticed two suspicious looking fellows. I walked
towards them, afraid to turn my back to them. One of them
had a squashed nose, oriental eyes, square shoulders, and
short, crooked legs. The other, who wore a thin jacket and
something black around his neck, was slender, dark, and
extraordinarily beautiful. He started to move, and, with
the other one beside him, approached me, his hand in his
inner breast pocket. His walk was that of the dead. As if
paralyzed, yet with fluttering senses, I made two steps. In
his pale, thick-lipped face—her face—I could see black and
stinging eyelashes. In his fist near the lapel of his jacket,

I noticed the handle of a knife. That my death was certain, I could see in his face, in the face of the dead: because the two of them had only one face; he was her brother. He had come from the suburb with one of his companions to liberate her from me because he thought that her love affair with me had made her neglect her business and that she had failed to provide money for her parents and himself.

Suddenly—I almost touched her brother—the two made a loop around me, left the road free, seemed not to know me and disappeared. I was completely bewildered, and no longer realized what was happening. At that moment I heard the trot of a third, who had come out of the dark. He was a slight man, who carried a coat over his arm and seemed to be in a hurry. Either because I was grateful, or had lost my head, or felt a sense of affinity to him, I took two long steps after him. In fear he lifted his left shoulder and began to run. He ran away from me. He seemed to take me for somebody I was not. Her brother, too, had mistaken me for somebody else. And I have the feeling that communication among people is always such a helpless and cruel confusion of errors as that night scene at the corner of the Via dell'Agnolo . . .

In Milan, my native town, they gave me some money for the piece I had written in those shady nights by the side of the sick woman whom I did not love. A gifted lady of rank attached herself to me. She said that she had always been searching; that her life was tragic, and that she simply had to love him who had written this piece. I thought to myself that this did not much concern me, but I was polite. She insisted that I owed her thanks; for no one in the world would ever understand me as she did. This I could not admit, I rebelled, and would not acknowledge my indebtedness. She repeated that her life was tragic, and that a plunge from the rock of Leukos would end it. I was indignant, flattered, and baffled. Why did I get involved in such things? I didn't want to have anything to do with her. I would not permit anybody to disturb my solitude. Those chic, much desired, and amorously inclined ladies of my youth had only touched me with dissolving veils. Pierrot had died like a reflection with the dust of the moon on her face. And now a body insisted upon entering my life, upon healing me, upon giving me reality, upon loving away my sufferings; yet, all interest in myself depended upon this suffering. A sick face is more noble than a healthy one. I was not inclined to give in. She could not understand it; she wanted to be happy, therefore she wanted to make me happy. In the end I found her only stupid, and maltreated her accordingly, resolutely, consciously, although I knew that I would be ashamed of this when the time came and that I would turn this shame into art . . .

When her crisis had passed and she began to turn away from me, I brought her back and compelled her to be my lover. It satisfied me to have her before me as proof of my unbroken solitude . . .

This solitude resembles a sudden quiet of the wind before sailing. As yet the sailors are climbing about the masts and the sides of the ship, lifting the anchor, untying the sails, when suddenly the sails fall limp, the ship does not stir, the men slide down, stand about, and look at each other . . . I suppose that in these pages unusual things have happened. But my mood is barren as if nothing had ever occurred. I seem to be watching a monotonous play in which people die forever in the most tedious manner. What is reality?

Reality was perhaps in the tears which I shed one night for almost an hour along the empty Via dell'Agnolo and, along the little guttery alleys. That hour was real—of a whole life, almost an hour. At least the first half hour was real. Perhaps . . . but I wonder.

DEATH IN VENICE[1]

Thomas Mann

(b. 1875)

1

On a spring afternoon of the year 19—, when our continent lay under such threatening weather for whole months, Gustav Aschenbach, or von Aschenbach as his name read officially after his fiftieth birthday, had left his apartment on the Prinzregentenstrasse in Munich and had gone for a long walk. Overwrought by the trying and precarious work of the forenoon—which had demanded a maximum wariness, prudence, penetration, and rigor of the will—the writer had not been able even after the noon meal to break the impetus of the productive mechanism within him, that *motus animi continuus* which constitutes, according to Cicero, the foundation of eloquence; and he had not attained the healing sleep which—what with the increasing exhaustion of his strength—he needed in the middle of each day. So he had gone outdoors soon after tea, in the hopes that air and movement would restore him and prepare him for a profitable evening.

It was the beginning of May, and after cold, damp weeks a false midsummer had set in. The English Gardens, although the foliage was still fresh and sparse, were as pungent as in August, and in the parts nearer the city had been full of conveyances and promenaders. At the Aumeister, which he had reached by quieter and quieter paths, Aschenbach had surveyed for a short time the Wirtsgarten with its

[1] Translated by Kenneth Burke. Copyright, 1925, by Alfred A Knopf, Inc.

lively crowds and its border of cabs and carriages. From here, as the sun was sinking, he had started home, outside the park, across the open fields; and since he felt tired and a storm was threatening from the direction of Föhring, he waited at the North Cemetery for the tram which would take him directly back to the city.

It happened that he found no one in the station or its vicinity. There was not a vehicle to be seen, either on the paved Ungererstrasse, with its solitary glistening rails stretching out towards Schwabing, or on the Föhringer Chaussee. Behind the fences of the stone-masons' establishments, where the crosses, memorial tablets, and monuments standing for sale formed a second, uninhabited burial ground, there was no sign of life; and opposite him the Byzantine structure of the Funeral Hall lay silent in the reflection of the departing day, its façade ornamented in luminous colors with Greek crosses and hieratic paintings, above which were displayed inscriptions symmetrically arranged in gold letters, and texts chosen to bear on the life beyond, such as, "They enter into the dwelling of the Lord," or, "The light of eternity shall shine upon them." And for some time, as he stood waiting, he found a grave diversion in spelling out the formulas and letting his mind's eye lose itself in their transparent mysticism, when, returning from his reveries, he noticed in the portico, above the two apocalyptic animals guarding the steps, a man whose somewhat unusual appearance gave his thoughts an entirely new direction.

Whether he had just now come out from the inside through the bronze door, or had approached and mounted from the outside unobserved, remained uncertain. Aschenbach, without applying himself especially to the matter, was inclined to believe the former. Of medium height, thin, smooth-shaven, and noticeably pug-nosed, the man belonged to the red-haired type and possessed the appropriate fresh milky complexion. Obviously, he was not of Bavarian extraction, since at least the white and straight-brimmed straw hat that covered his head gave his appearance the stamp of a foreigner, of some one who had come from a long distance. To be sure, he was wearing the customary knapsack strapped across his shoulders, and a belted suit of rough yellow wool; his left arm was resting on his thigh, and his gray storm cape was thrown across it. In his right hand he held a cane with an iron ferrule, which he had stuck diagonally into the ground, while, with his feet crossed, he was leaning his hip against the crook. His head was raised so that the Adam's-apple protruded hard and bare on a scrawny neck emerging from a loose sport-shirt. And he was staring sharply off into the distance, with colorless, red-lidded eyes between which stood two strong, vertical wrinkles peculiarly suited to his short turned-up nose. Thus—and perhaps his elevated position helped to give the impression—his bearing had something majestic and commanding about it, something bold, or even savage. For whether he was grimacing because he was blinded by the setting sun, or whether it was a case of a permanent distortion of the physiognomy, his lips seemed too short, they were so completely pulled back from his teeth that these were exposed even to the gums, and stood out white and long.

It is quite possible that Aschenbach, in his half-distracted, half-inquisitive examination of the stranger, had been somewhat inconsiderate, for he suddenly became aware that his look was being answered, and indeed so militantly, so straight in the eye, so plainly with the intention of driving the thing through to the very end and compelling him to capitulate, that he turned away uncomfortably and began walking along by the fences, deciding casually that he would pay no further attention to the man. The next minute he had forgotten him. But perhaps the exotic element in the stranger's appearance had worked on his imagination; or a new physical or spiritual influence of some sort had come into play. He was quite astonished to note a peculiar inner expansion, a kind of roving unrest, a youthful longing after far-off places: a feeling so vivid, so new, or so long dormant and neglected, that, with his hands behind his back and his eyes on the ground, he came to a sudden stop, and examined into the nature and purport of this emotion.

It was the desire for travel, nothing more; although, to be sure, it had attacked him violently, and was heightened to a passion, even to the point of an hallucination. His yearnings crystallized; his imagination, still in ferment from his hours of work, actually pictured all the marvels and terrors of a manifold world which it was suddenly struggling to conceive. He saw a landscape, a tropical swamp-land under a heavy, murky sky, damp, luxuriant and enormous, a kind of prehistoric wilderness of islands, bogs, and arms of water, sluggish with mud; he saw, near him and in the distance, the hairy shafts of palms rising out of a rank lecherous thicket, out of places where the plant-life was fat, swollen, and blossoming exorbitantly; he saw strangely misshapen trees lowering their roots into the ground, into stagnant pools with greenish reflections; and here, between floating flowers which were milk-white and large as dishes, birds of a strange nature, high-shouldered, with crooked bills, were standing in the muck, and looking motionlessly to one side; between dense, knotted stalks of bamboo he saw the glint from the eyes of a crouching tiger—and he felt his heart knocking with fear and with puzzling desires. Then the image disappeared: and with a shake of his head Aschenbach resumed his walk along past the fences of the stone-masons' establishments.

Since the time, at least, when he could command the means to enjoy the advantages of moving about the world as he pleased, he had considered traveling simply as a hygienic precaution which must be complied with now and then despite one's feelings and one's preferences. Too busy with the tasks arranged for him by his interest in his own ego and in the problems of Europe, too burdened with the onus of production, too little prone to diversion, and in no sense an amateur of the varied amusements of the great world, he had been thoroughly satisfied with such knowledge of the earth's surface as any one can get without mov-

ing far out of his own circle; and he had never even been
tempted to leave Europe. Especially now that his life was
slowly on the decline, and that the artist's fear of not having
finished—this uneasiness lest the clock run down before he
had done his part and given himself completely—could no
longer be waved aside as a mere whim, he had confined his
outer existence almost exclusively to the beautiful city
which had become his home and to the rough country-
house which he had built in the mountains and where he
spent the rainy summers.

Further, this thing which had laid hold of him so be-
latedly, but with such suddenness, was very readily moderated and adjusted by the force of his reason and of a
discipline which he had practiced since youth. He had intended carrying his life-work forward to a certain point before removing to the country. And the thought of knocking
about the world for months and neglecting his work during
this time, seemed much too lax and contrary to his plans;
it really could not be considered seriously. Yet he knew
only too well what the reasons were for this unexpected
temptation. It was the urge to escape—he admitted to himself—this yearning for the new and the remote, this appetite for freedom, for unburdening, for forgetfulness; it
was a pressure away from his work, from the steady drudg-
ery of a coldly passionate service. To be sure, he loved his
work and almost loved the enervating battle that was fought
daily between a proud tenacious will—so often tested—
and this growing weariness which no one was to suspect and
which must not betray itself in his productions by any sign
of weakness or negligence. But it seemed wise not to draw
the bow overtightly, and not to strangle by sheer obstinacy
so strongly persistent an appetite. He thought of his work,
thought of the place at which yesterday and now again to-
day he had been forced to leave off, and which, it seemed,
would yield neither to patience and coaxing nor to a definite
attack. He examined it again, trying to break through or to
circumvent the deadlock, but he gave up with a shudder of

repugnance. There was no unusual difficulty here; what balked him were the scruples of aversion, which took the form of a fastidious insatiability. Even as a young man this insatiability had meant to him the very nature, the fullest essence, of talent; and for that reason he had restrained and chilled his emotions, since he was aware that they incline to content themselves with a happy approximate, a state of semi-completion. Were these enslaved emotions now taking their vengeance on him, by leaving him in the lurch, by refusing to forward and lubricate his art; and were they bearing off with them every enjoyment, every live interest in form and expression?

Not that he was producing anything bad; his years gave him at least this advantage, that he felt himself at all times in full and easy possession of his craftsmanship. But while the nation honored him for this, he himself was not content; and it seemed to him that his work lacked the marks of that fiery and fluctuating emotionalism which is an enormous thing in one's favor, and which, while it argues an enjoyment on the part of the author, also constitutes, more than any depth of content, the enjoyment of the amateur. He feared the summer in the country, alone in the little house with the maid who prepared his meals, and the servant who brought them to him. He feared the familiar view of the mountain peaks and the slopes which would stand about him in his boredom and his discontent. Consequently there was need of a break in some new direction. If the summer was to be endurable and productive, he must attempt something out of his usual orbit; he must relax, get a change of air, bring an element of freshness into the blood. To travel, then—that much was settled. Not far, not all the way to the tigers. But one night on the sleeper, and a rest of three or four weeks at some pleasant popular resort in the South. . . .

He thought this out while the noise of the electric tram came nearer along the Ungererstrasse; and as he boarded it, he decided to devote the evening to the study of maps and time-tables. On the platform it occurred to him to look around for the man in the straw hat, his companion during that most significant time spent waiting at the station. But his whereabouts remained uncertain, as he was not to be seen either at the place where he was formerly standing, or anywhere else in the vicinity of the station, or on the car itself.

II

The author of that lucid and powerful prose epic built around the life of Frederick of Prussia; the tenacious artist who, after long application, wove rich, varied strands of human destiny together under one single predominating theme in the fictional tapestry known as "Maya"; the creator of that stark tale which is called "The Wretch" and which pointed out for an entire oncoming generation the possibility of some moral certainty beyond pure knowledge; finally, the writer (and this sums up briefly the works of his mature period) of the impassioned treatise on "Art and the Spirit," whose capacity for mustering facts, and, further, whose fluency in their presentation, led cautious judges to place this treatise alongside Schiller's conclusions on naïve and sentimental poetry—Gustav Aschenbach, then, was the son of a higher law official, and was born in L——, a leading city in the Province of Silesia. His forebears had been officers, magistrates, government functionaries, men who had led severe, steady lives serving their king, their state. A deeper strain of spirituality had been manifest in them once, in the person of a preacher; the preceding generation had brought a brisker, more sensuous blood into the family through the author's mother, daughter of a Bohemian bandmaster. The traces of foreignness in his features came from her. A marriage of sober painstaking conscientiousness with impulses of a darker, more fiery nature had had an artist as its result, and this particular artist.

Since his whole nature was centered around acquiring a reputation, he showed himself, if not exactly precocious, at least (thanks to the firmness and pithiness of his personality, his accent) ripened and adjusted to the public at an early age. Almost as a schoolboy he had made a name for himself. Within ten years he had learned to face the world through the medium of his writing-table, to discharge the obligations of his fame in a correspondence which (since many claims are pressed on the successful, the trustworthy) had to be brief as well as pleasant and to the point. At forty, wearied by the vicissitudes and the exertion of his own work, he had to manage a daily mail which bore the postmarks of countries in all parts of the world.

Equally removed from the banal and the eccentric, his talents were so constituted as to gain both the confidence of the general public and the stable admiration and sympathy of the critical. Thus even as a young man continually devoted to the pursuit of craftsmanship—and that of no ordinary kind—he had never known the careless freedom of youth. When, around thirty-five years of age, he had been taken ill in Vienna, one sharp observer said of him in company: "You see, Aschenbach has always lived like this," and the speaker contracted the fingers of his left hand into a fist: "never like this," and he let his open hand droop comfortably from the arm of his chair. That hit the mark; and the heroic, the ethical about it all was that he was not of a strong constitution, and though he was pledged by his nature to these steady efforts, he was not really born to them.

Considerations of ill health had kept him from attending school as a boy, and had compelled him to receive instruction at home. He had grown up alone, without comrades—and he was forced to realize soon enough that he belonged to a race which often lacked, not talent, but that physical substructure which talent relies on for its fullest fruition: a race accustomed to giving its best early, and seldom extending its faculties over the years. But his favorite phrase was "carrying through"; in his novel on Frederick he saw the pure apotheosis of this command, which struck him as the essential concept of the virtuous in action and passion. Also, he wished earnestly to grow old, since he had always maintained that the only artistry which can be called truly great, comprehensive—yes, even truly admirable—is that which is permitted to bear fruits characteristic of each stage in human development.

Since he must carry the responsibilities of his talent on frail shoulders, and wanted to go a long way, the primary requirement was discipline—and fortunately discipline was his direct inheritance from his father's side. By forty, fifty, or at an earlier age when others are still slashing about with enthusiasm, and are contentedly putting off to some later date the execution of plans on a large scale, he would start the day early, dashing cold water over his chest and back, and then, with a couple of tall wax candles in silver candlesticks at the head of his manuscript, he would pay out to his art, in two or three eager, scrupulous morning hours, the strength which he had accumulated in sleep. It was pardonable, indeed it was a direct tribute to the effectiveness of his moral scheme, that the uninitiated took his "Maya" world, and the massive epic machinery upon which the life of the hero Frederick was unrolled, as evidence of long breath and sustaining power. While actually they had been built up layer by layer, in small daily allotments, through hundreds and hundreds of single inspirations. And if they were so excellent in both composition and texture, it was solely because their creator had held out for years under the strain of one single work, with a steadiness of will and a tenacity comparable to that which conquered his native province; and because, finally, he had turned over his most vital and valuable hours to the problem of minute revision.

In order that a significant work of the mind may exert immediately some broad and deep effect, a secret relationship, or even conformity, must exist between the personal destiny of the author and the common destiny of his contemporaries. People do not know why they raise a work of art to fame. Far from being connoisseurs, they believe that they see in it hundreds of virtues which justify so much in-

terest; but the true reason for their applause is an unconscious sympathy. Aschenbach had once stated quite plainly
in some remote place that nearly everything great which
comes into being does so in spite of something—in spite of
sorrow or suffering, poverty, destitution, physical weakness, depravity, passion, or a thousand other handicaps. But
that was not merely an observation; it was a discovery, the
formula of his life and reputation, the key to his work. And
what wonder, then, that it was also the distinguishing moral
trait, the dominating gesture, of his most characteristic figures?

Years before, one shrewd analyst had written of the new
hero-type to which this author gave preference, and which
kept turning up in variations of one sort or another: he
called it the conception of "an intellectual and youthful mas-
culinity" which "stands motionless, haughty, ashamed, with
jaw set, while swords and spear-points beset the body." That
was beautiful and ingenious; and it was exact, although it
may have seemed to suggest too much passivity. For to be
poised against fatality, to meet adverse conditions gracefully, is more than simple endurance; it is an act of aggres-
sion, a positive triumph—and the figure of Sebastian is the
most beautiful figure, if not of art as a whole, at least of the
art of literature. Looking into this fictional world, one saw: a
delicate self-mastery by which any inner deterioration, any
biological decay was kept concealed from the eyes of the
world; a crude, vicious sensuality capable of fanning its
rising passions into pure flame, yes, even of mounting to
dominance in the realm of beauty; a pallid weakness which
draws from the glowing depths of the soul the strength to
bow whole arrogant peoples before the foot of the cross, or
before the feet of weakness itself; a charming manner maintained in his cold, strict service to form; a false, precarious
mode of living, and the keenly enervating melancholy and
artifice of the born deceiver—to observe such trials as this
was enough to make one question whether there really was
any heroism other than weakness. And, in any case, what

heroism could be more in keeping with the times? Gustav Aschenbach was the one poet among the many workers on the verge of exhaustion: the over-burdened, the used-up, the clingers-on, in short all those moralists of production who, delicately built and destitute of means, can rely for a time at least on will-power and the shrewd husbandry of their resources to secure the effects of greatness. There are many such: they are the heroes of the period. And they all found themselves in his works; here they were indeed, upheld, intensified, applauded; they were grateful to him, they acclaimed him.

In his time he had been young and raw; and, misled by his age, he had blundered in public. He had stumbled, had exposed himself; both in writing and in talk he had offended against caution and tact. But he had acquired the dignity which, as he insisted, is the innate goad and craving of every great talent; in fact, it could be said that his entire development had been a conscious undeviating progression away from the embarrassments of skepticism and irony, and towards dignity.

The general masses are satisfied by vigor and tangibility of treatment rather than by any close intellectual processes; but youth, with its passion for the absolute, can be arrested only by the problematical. And Aschenbach had been absolute, problematical, as only a youth could be. He had been a slave to the intellect, had played havoc with knowledge, had ground up his seed crops, had divulged secrets, had discredited talent, had betrayed art—yes, while his modelings were entertaining the faithful votaries, filling them with enthusiasm, making their lives more keen, this youthful artist was taking the breath away from the generation then in its twenties by his cynicisms on the questionable nature of art, and of artistry itself.

But it seems that nothing blunts the edge of a noble, robust mind more quickly and more thoroughly than the sharp and bitter corrosion of knowledge; and certainly the moody radicalism of the youth, no matter how conscientious, was

shallow in comparison with his firm determination as an
older man and a master to deny knowledge, to reject it, to
pass it with raised head, in so far as it is capable of crip-
pling, discouraging, or degrading to the slightest degree,
our will, acts, feelings, or even passions. How else could the
famous story of "The Wretch" be understood than as an
outburst of repugnance against the disreputable psycholo-
gism of the times: embodied in the figure of that soft and
stupid half-clown who pilfers a destiny for himself by guiding his wife (from powerlessness, from lasciviousness, from
ethical frailty) into the arms of an adolescent, and believes
that he may through profundity commit vileness? The ver-
bal pressure with which he here cast out the outcast announced the return from every moral skepticism, from all
fellow-feeling with the engulfed: it was the counter-move
to the laxity of the sympathetic principle that to understand
all is to forgive all—and the thing that was here well begun,
even nearly completed, was that "miracle of reborn ingenuousness" which was taken up a little later in one of the
author's dialogues expressly and not without a certain discreet emphasis. Strange coincidences! Was it as a result of
this rebirth, this new dignity and sternness, that his feeling
for beauty—a discriminating purity, simplicity, and evenness
of attack which henceforth gave his productions such an obvious, even such a deliberate stamp of mastery and classi-
cism—showed an almost excessive strengthening about this
time? But ethical resoluteness in the exclusion of science, of
emancipatory and restrictive knowledge—does this not in
turn signify a simplification, a reduction morally of the
world to too limited terms, and thus also a strengthened capacity for the forbidden, the evil, the morally impossible?
And does not form have two aspects? Is it not moral and
unmoral at once—moral in that it is the result and expression
of discipline, but unmoral, and even immoral, in that by
nature it contains an indifference to morality, is calculated,
in fact, to make morality bend beneath its proud and unen-
cumbered scepter?

Be that as it may. An evolution is a destiny; and why should his evolution, which had been upheld by the general confidence of a vast public, not run through a different course from one accomplished outside the luster and the entanglements of fame? Only chronic vagabondage will find it tedious and be inclined to scoff when a great talent outgrows the libertine chrysalis-stage, learns to seize upon and express the dignity of the mind, and superimposes a formal etiquette upon a solitude which had been filled with unchastened and rigidly isolated sufferings and struggles and had brought all this to a point of power and honor among men. Further, how much sport, defiance, indulgence there is in the self-formation of a talent! Gradually something official, didactic, crept into Gustav Aschenbach's productions, his style in later life fought shy of any abruptness and boldness, any subtle and unexpected contrasts; he inclined towards the fixed and standardized, the conventionally elegant, the conservative, the formal, the formulated, nearly. And, as is traditionally said of Louis XIV, with the advancing years he came to omit every common word from his vocabulary. At about this time it happened that the educational authorities included selected pages by him in their prescribed school readers. This was deeply sympathetic to his nature, and he did not decline when a German prince who had just mounted the throne raised the author of the "Frederick" to knighthood on the occasion of his fiftieth birthday. After a few years of unrest, a few tentative stopping-places here and there, he soon chose Munich as his permanent home, and lived there in a state of middle-class respectability such as fits in with the life of the mind in certain individual instances. The marriage which, when still young, he had contracted with a girl of an educated family came to an end with her death after a short period of happiness. He was left with a daughter, now married. He had never had a son.

Gustav von Aschenbach was somewhat below average height, dark, and smooth-shaven. His head seemed a bit too large in comparison with his almost dapper figure. His hair was brushed straight back, thinning out towards the crown, but very full about the temples, and strongly marked with gray; it framed a high, ridged forehead. Gold spectacles with rimless lenses cut into the bridge of his bold, heavy nose. The mouth was big, sometimes drooping, sometimes suddenly pinched and firm. His cheeks were thin and wrinkled, his well-formed chin had a slight cleft. This head, usually bent patiently to one side, seemed to have gone through momentous experiences, and yet it was his art which had produced those effects in his face, effects which are elsewhere the result of hard and agitated living. Behind this brow the brilliant repartee of the dialogue on war between Voltaire and the king had been born; these eyes, peering steadily and wearily from behind their glasses, had seen the bloody inferno of the lazaret in the Seven Years' War. Even as it applies to the individual, art is a heightened mode of existence. It gives deeper pleasures, it consumes more quickly. It carves into its servants' faces the marks of imaginary and spiritual adventures, and though their external activities may be as quiet as a cloister, it produces a lasting voluptuousness, overrefinement, fatigue, and curiosity of the nerves such as can barely result from a life filled with illicit passions and enjoyments.

III

Various matters of a literary and social nature delayed his departure until about two weeks after that walk in Munich. Finally he gave orders to have his country-house ready for occupancy within a month; and one day between the middle and the end of May he took the night train for Trieste, where he made a stop-over of only twenty-four hours, and embarked the following morning for Pola.

What he was hunting was something foreign and unrelated to himself which would at the same time be quickly within reach; and so he stopped at an island in the Adriatic

which had become well known in recent years. It lay not
far off the Istrian coast, with beautifully rugged cliffs front-
ing the open sea, and natives who dressed in variegated tatters and made strange sounds when they spoke. But rain
and a heavy atmosphere, a provincial and exclusively Austrian patronage at the hotel, and the lack of that restfully
intimate association with the sea which can be gotten only
by a soft, sandy beach, irritated him, and prevented him
from feeling that he had found the place he was looking for.
Something within was disturbing him, and drawing him he
was not sure where. He studied sailing dates, he looked
about him questioningly, and of a sudden, as a thing both
astounding and self-evident, his goal was before him. If
you wanted to reach over night the unique, the fabulously
different, where did you go? But that was plain. What was
he doing here? He had lost the trail. He had wanted to go
there. He did not delay in giving notice of his mistake in
stopping here. In the early morning mist, a week and a half
after his arrival on the island, a fast motor-boat was carrying him and his luggage back over the water to the naval
port, and he landed there just long enough to cross the gang-
plank to the damp deck of a ship which was lying under
steam ready for the voyage to Venice.

It was an old hulk flying the Italian flag, decrepit, sooty,
and mournful. In a cave-like, artificially lighted inside cabin
where Aschenbach, immediately upon boarding the ship,
was conducted by a dirty hunchbacked sailor, who smirked
politely, there was sitting behind a table, his hat cocked over
his forehead and a cigarette stump in the corner of his
mouth, a man with a goatee, and with the face of an old-
style circus director, who was taking down the particulars
of the passengers with professional grimaces and distribut-
ing the tickets. "To Venice!" he repeated Aschenbach's request, as he extended his arm and plunged his pen into the
pasty dregs of a precariously tilted inkwell. "To Venice,
first class! At your service, sir." And he wrote a generous
scrawl, sprinkled it with blue sand out of a box, let the sand

run off into a clay bowl, folded the paper with sallow, bony fingers, and began writing again. "A happily chosen destination!" he chatted on. "Ah, Venice! A splendid city! A city of irresistible attractiveness for the educated on account of its history as well as its present-day charms." The smooth rapidity of his movements and the empty words accompanying them had something anæsthetic and reassuring about them, much as though he feared lest the traveler might still be vacillating in his decision to go to Venice. He handled the cash briskly, and let the change fall on the spotted table-cover with the skill of a croupier. "A pleasant journey, sir!" he said with a theatrical bow. "Gentlemen, I have the honor of serving you!" he called out immediately after, with his arm upraised, and he acted as if business were in full swing, although no one else was there to require his attention. Aschenbach returned to the deck.

With one arm on the railing, he watched the passengers on board and the idlers who loitered around the dock waiting for the ship to sail. The second-class passengers, men and women, were huddled together on the foredeck, using boxes and bundles as seats. A group of young people made up the travelers on the first deck, clerks from Pola, it seemed, who had gathered in the greatest excitement for an excursion to Italy. They made a considerable fuss about themselves and their enterprise, chattered, laughed, enjoyed their own antics self-contentedly, and, leaning over the handrails, shouted flippantly and mockingly at their comrades who, with portfolios under their arms, were going up and down the waterfront on business and kept threatening the picnickers with their canes. One, in a bright yellow summer suit of ultrafashionable cut, with a red necktie, and a rakishly tilted Panama, surpassed all the others in his crowning good humor. But as soon as Aschenbach looked at him a bit more carefully, he discovered with a kind of horror that the youth was a cheat. He was old, that was unquestionable. There were wrinkles around his eyes and mouth. The faint crimson of the cheeks was paint, the hair under his brilliantly decorated straw hat was a wig; his neck was hollow and stringy, his turned-up mustache and the imperial on his chin were dyed; the full set of yellow teeth which he displayed when he laughed, a cheap artificial plate; and his hands, with signet rings on both index fingers, were those of an old man. Fascinated with loathing, Aschenbach watched him in his intercourse with his friends. Did they not know, did they not observe that he was old, that he was not entitled to wear their bright, foppish clothing, that he was not entitled to play at being one of them? Unquestioningly, and as quite the usual thing, it seemed, they allowed him among them, treating him as one of their own kind and returning his jovial nudges in the ribs without repugnance. How could that be? Aschenbach laid his hand on his forehead and closed his eyes; they were hot, since he had had too little sleep. He felt as though everything were not quite the same as usual, as though some dream-like estrangement, some peculiar distortion of the world, were beginning to take possession of him, and perhaps this could be stopped if he hid his face for a time and then looked around him again. Yet at this moment he felt as though he were swimming; and looking up with an unreasoned fear, he discovered that the heavy, lugubrious body of the ship was separating slowly from the walled bank. Inch by inch, with the driving and reversing of the engine, the strip of dirty glistening water widened between the dock and the side of the ship; and, after cumbersome maneuvering, the steamer finally turned its nose towards the open sea. Aschenbach crossed to the starboard side, where the hunchback had set up a deck-chair for him, and a steward in a spotted dress-coat asked after his wants.

The sky was gray, the wind damp. Harbor and islands had been left behind, and soon all land was lost in the haze. Flakes of coal dust, bloated with moisture, fell over the washed deck, which would not dry. After the first hour an awning was spread, since it had begun to rain.

Bundled up in his coat, a book in his lap, the traveler rested, and the hours passed unnoticed. It stopped raining; the canvas awning was removed. The horizon was unbroken.

The sea, empty, like an enormous disk, lay stretched under the curve of the sky. But in empty inarticulate space our senses lose also the dimensions of time, and we slip into the incommensurate. As he rested, strange shadowy figures, the old dandy, the goatee from the inside cabin, passed through his mind, with vague gestures, muddled dream-words—and he was asleep.

About noon he was called to a meal down in the corridor-like dining-hall into which the doors opened from the sleeping-cabins; he ate near the head of a long table, at the other end of which the clerks, including the old man, had been drinking with the boisterous captain since ten o'clock. The food was poor, and he finished rápidly. He felt driven outside to look at the sky, to see if it showed signs of being brighter above Venice.

He had kept thinking that this had to occur, since the city had always received him in full blaze. But sky and sea remained dreary and leaden, at times a misty rain fell, and here he was reaching by water a different Venice than he had ever found when approaching on land. He stood by the forestays, looking in the distance, waiting for land. He thought of the heavy-hearted, enthusiastic poet for whom the domes and bell towers of his dreams had once risen out of these waters; he relived in silence some of that reverence, happiness and sorrow which had been turned then into cautious song; and easily susceptible to sensations already molded, he asked himself wearily and earnestly whether some new enchantment and distraction, some belated adventure of the emotions, might still be held in store for this idle traveler.

Then the flat coast emerged on the right; the sea was alive with fishing-smacks; the bathers' island appeared; it dropped behind to the left, the steamer slowly entered the narrow port which is named after it; and on the lagoon, facing gay ramshackle houses, it stopped completely, since it had to wait for the barque of the health department.

An hour passed before it appeared. He had arrived, and yet he had not; no one was in any hurry, no one was driven by impatience. The young men from Pola, patriotically attracted by the military bugle calls which rang over the water from the vicinity of the public gardens, had come on deck and, warmed by their Asti, they burst out with cheers for the drilling *bersagliere*. But it was repulsive to see what a state the primped-up old man had been brought to by his comradeship with youth. His old head was not able to resist its wine like the young and robust: he was painfully drunk. With glazed eyes, a cigarette between his trembling fingers, he stood in one place, swaying backwards and forwards from giddiness, and balancing himself laboriously. Since he would have fallen at the first step, he did not trust himself from the spot—yet he showed a deplorable insolence, buttonholed every one who came near him, stammered, winked and tittered, lifted his wrinkled, ornamented index finger in a stupid attempt at bantering, while he licked the corners of his mouth with his tongue in the most abominably suggestive manner. Aschenbach observed him darkly, and a feeling of numbness came over him again, as though the world were displaying a faint but irresistible tendency to distort itself into the peculiar and the grotesque: a feeling which circumstances prevented him from surrendering himself to completely, for just then the pounding activity of the engines commenced again, and the ship, resuming a voyage which had been interrupted so near its completion, passed through the San Marco canal.

So he saw it again, the most remarkable of landing-places, that blinding composition of fantastic buildings which the Republic lays out before the eyes of approaching seafarers: the soft splendor of the palace, the Bridge of Sighs, on the bank the columns with lion and saint, the advancing, showy flank of the enchanted temple, the glimpse through to the archway, and the giant clock. And as he looked on he thought that to reach Venice by land, on the railroad, was like entering a palace from the rear, and that this most unreal of cities should not be approached except as he was now doing, by ship, over the high seas.

The engine stopped, gondolas pressed in, the gangway

was let down, customs officials climbed on board and dis-charged their duties perfunctorily; the disembarking could begin. Aschenbach made it understood that he wanted a gondola to take him and his luggage to the dock of those lit-tle steamers which ply between the city and the Lido, since he intended to locate near the sea. His plans were com-plied with, his wants were shouted down to the water, where the gondoliers were wrangling with one another in dialect. He was still hindered from descending; he was hin-dered by his trunk, which was being pulled and dragged with difficulty down the ladder-like steps. So that for some minutes he was not able to avoid the importunities of the atrocious old man, whose drunkenness gave him a sinister desire to do the foreigner parting honors. "We wish you a very agreeable visit," he bleated as he made an awkward bow. "We leave with pleasant recollections! *Au revoir, ex-cusez,* and *bon jour,* your excellency!" His mouth watered, he pressed his eyes shut, he licked the corners of his mouth, and the dyed imperial turned up about his senile lips. "Our compliments," he mumbled, with two fingertips on his mouth, "our compliments to our sweetheart, the dearest, prettiest sweetheart . . ." And suddenly his false upper teeth fell down on his lower lip. Aschenbach was able to escape. "To our sweetheart, our handsome sweetheart," he heard the cooing, hollow, stuttering voice behind him while, support-ing himself against the hand-rail, he went down the gang-way.

Who would not have to suppress a fleeting shudder, a vague timidity and uneasiness, if it were a matter of board-ing a Venetian gondola for the first time or after several years? The strange craft, an entirely unaltered survival from the times of balladry, with that peculiar blackness which is found elsewhere only in coffins—it suggests silent, criminal adventures in the rippling night, it suggests even more strongly death itself, the bier and the mournful fu-neral, and the last silent journey. And has it been observed that the seat of such a barque, this arm-chair of coffin-black

veneer and dull black upholstery, is the softest, most luxuriant, most lulling seat in the world? Aschenbach noted this
when he had relaxed at the feet of the gondolier, opposite
his luggage, which lay neatly assembled on the prow. The
rowers were still wrangling, harshly, incomprehensibly,
with threatening gestures. But the strange silence of this
canal city seemed to soften their voices, to disembody them,
and dissipate them over the water. It was warm here in
the harbor. Touched faintly by the warm breeze of the sirocco, leaning back against the limber portions of the cushions, the traveler closed his eyes in the enjoyment of a lassitude which was as unusual with him, as it was sweet. The
trip would be short, he thought; if only it went on for ever!
He felt himself glide with a gentle motion away from the
crowd and the confusion of voices.

It became quieter and quieter around him! There was
nothing to be heard but the splashing of the oar, the hollow
slapping of the waves against the prow of the boat as it stood
above the water black and bold and armed with its halberd-
like tip, and a third sound, of speaking, of whispering—the
whispering of the gondolier, who was talking to himself
between his teeth, fitfully, in words that were pressed out
by the exertion of his arms. Aschenbach looked up, and was
slightly astonished to discover that the lagoon was widening, and he was headed for the open sea. This seemed to indicate that he ought not to rest too much, but should see to
it that his wishes were carried out.

"To the steamer dock!" he repeated, turning around completely and looking into the face of the gondolier who stood
behind on a raised platform and towered up between him
and the dun-colored sky. He was a man of unpleasant, even
brutal appearance, dressed in sailor-blue, with a yellow
sash; a formless straw hat, its weave partially unraveled,
was tilted insolently on his head. The set of his face, the
blond curly mustache beneath a curtly turned-up nose, undoubtedly meant that he was not Italian. Although of somewhat frail build, so that one would not have thought him

especially well suited to his trade, he handled the oar with great energy, throwing his entire body into each stroke. Occasionally he drew back his lips from the exertion, and disclosed his white teeth. Wrinkling his reddish brows, he gazed on past his passenger, as he answered deliberately, almost gruffly: "You are going to the Lido." Aschenbach replied: "Of course. But I have just taken the gondola to get me across to San Marco. I want to use the *vaporetto*."

"You cannot use the *vaporetto*, sir."

"And why not?"

"Because the *vaporetto* will not haul luggage."

That was so; Aschenbach remembered. He was silent. But the fellow's harsh, presumptuous manner, so unusual towards a foreigner here, seemed unbearable. He said: "That is my affair. Perhaps I want to put my things in storage. You will turn back."

There was silence. The oar splashed, the water thudded against the bow. And the talking and whispering began again. The gondolier was talking to himself between his teeth.

What was to be done? This man was strangely insolent, and had an uncanny decisiveness; the traveler, alone with him on the water, saw no way of getting what he wanted. And besides, how softly he could rest, if only he did not become excited! Hadn't he wanted the trip to go on and on for ever? It was wisest to let things take their course, and the main thing was that he was comfortable. The poison of inertia seemed to be issuing from the seat, from this low, black-upholstered arm-chair, so gently cradled by the oarstrokes of the imperious gondolier behind him. The notion that he had fallen into the hands of a criminal passed dreamily across Aschenbach's mind—without the ability to summon his thoughts to an active defense. The possibility that it was all simply a plan for cheating him seemed more abhorrent. A feeling of duty or pride, a kind of recollection that one should prevent such things, gave him the strength to arouse himself once more. He asked: "What are you asking for the trip?"

Looking down upon him, the gondolier answered: "You will pay."

It was plain how this should be answered. Aschenbach said mechanically: "I shall pay you nothing, absolutely nothing, if you don't take me where I want to go."

"You want to go to the Lido."

"But not with you."

"I am rowing you well."

That is so, Aschenbach thought, and relaxed. That is so, you are rowing me well. Even if you do have designs on my cash, and send me down to Pluto with a blow of your oar from behind, you will have rowed me well.

But nothing like that happened. They were even joined by others: a boatload of musical brigands, men and women, who sang to guitar and mandolin, riding persistently side by side with the gondola and filling the silence over the water with their covetous foreign poetry. A hat was held out, and Aschenbach threw in money. Then they stopped singing, and rowed away. And again the muttering of the gondolier could be heard as he talked fitfully and jerkily to himself.

So they arrived, tossed in the wake of a steamer plying towards the city. Two municipal officers, their hands behind their backs, their faces turned in the direction of the lagoon, were walking back and forth on the bank. Aschenbach left the gondola at the dock, supported by that old man who is stationed with his grappling-hook at each one of Venice's landing-places. And since he had no small money, he crossed over to the hotel by the steamer wharf to get change and pay the rower what was due him. He got what he wanted in the lobby, he returned and found his traveling-bags in a cart on the dock, and gondola and gondolier had vanished.

"He got out in a hurry," said the old man with the grappling-hook. "A bad man, a man without a license, sir. He is the only gondolier who doesn't have a license. The others telephoned here."

Aschenbach shrugged his shoulders.

"The gentleman rode for nothing," the old man said, and held out his hat. Aschenbach tossed in a coin. He gave in-

structions to have his luggage taken to the beach hotel, and
followed the cart through the avenue, the white-blossomed
avenue which, lined on both sides with taverns, shops, and
boarding-houses, runs across the island to the shore.

He entered the spacious hotel from the rear, by the ter-
raced garden, and passed through the vestibule and the
lobby until he reached the desk. Since he had been announced, he was received with obliging promptness. A
manager, a small, frail, flatteringly polite man with a black
mustache and a French style frock-coat, accompanied him to
the third floor in the lift, and showed him his room, an
agreeable place furnished in cherry wood. It was decorated
with strong-smelling flowers, and its high windows afforded
a view out across the open sea. He stepped up to one of them
after the employee had left; and while his luggage was
being brought up and placed in the room behind him, he
looked down on the beach (it was comparatively deserted
in the afternoon) and on the sunless ocean which was at
flood-tide and was sending long low waves against the bank
in a calm regular rhythm.

The experiences of a man who lives alone and in silence
are both vaguer and more penetrating than those of people
in society; his thoughts are heavier, more odd, and touched
always with melancholy. Images and observations which
could easily be disposed of by a glance, a smile, an exchange
of opinion, will occupy him unbearably, sink deep into the
silence, become full of meaning, become life, adventure,
emotion. Loneliness ripens the eccentric, the daringly and
estrangingly beautiful, the poetic. But loneliness also ripens
the perverse, the disproportionate, the absurd, and the illicit.
—So, the things he had met with on the trip, the ugly old
fop with his twaddle about sweethearts, the lawbreaking gondolier who was cheated of his pay, still left the traveler uneasy. Without really providing any resistance to the mind,
without offering any solid stuff to think over, they were
nevertheless profoundly strange, as it seemed to him, and
disturbing precisely because of this contradiction. In the

meanwhile, he greeted the sea with his eyes, and felt pleasure at the knowledge that Venice was so conveniently near. Finally he turned away, bathed his face, left orders to the chambermaid for a few things he still needed done to make his comfort complete, and let himself be taken to the ground floor by the green-uniformed Swiss who operated the lift.

He took his tea on the terrace facing the ocean, then descended and followed the boardwalk for quite a way in the direction of the Hotel Excelsior. When he returned it seemed time to dress for dinner. He did this with his usual care and slowness, since he was accustomed to working over his toilet. And yet he came down a little early to the lobby, where he found a great many of the hotel guests assembled, mixing distantly and with a show of mutual indifference to one another, but all waiting for meal-time. He took a paper from the table, dropped into a leather chair, and observed the company; they differed agreeably from the guests where he had first stopped.

A wide and tolerantly inclusive horizon was spread out before him. Sounds of all the principal languages formed a subdued murmur. The accepted evening dress, a uniform of good manners, brought all human varieties into a fitting unity. There were Americans with their long wry features, large Russian families, English ladies, German children with French nurses. The Slavic element seemed to predominate. Polish was being spoken near by.

It was a group of children gathered around a little wicker table, under the protection of a teacher or governess: three young girls, apparently fifteen to seventeen, and a long-haired boy about fourteen years old. With astonishment Aschenbach noted that the boy was absolutely beautiful. His face, pale and reserved, framed with honey-colored hair, the straight sloping nose, the lovely mouth, the expression of sweet and godlike seriousness, recalled Greek sculpture of the noblest periods; and the complete purity of the form was accompanied by such a rare personal charm that, as he watched, he felt that he had never met with anything equally felicitous in nature or the plastic arts. He was further struck by the obviously intentional contrast with the principles of upbringing which showed in the sisters' attire and bearing. The three girls, the eldest of whom could be considered grown up, were dressed with a chasteness and severity bordering on disfigurement. Uniformly cloister-like costumes, of medium length, slate-colored, sober, and deliberately unbecoming in cut, with white turned-down collars as the only relief, suppressed every possible appeal of shapeliness. Their hair, brushed down flat and tight against the head, gave their faces a nun-like emptiness and lack of character. Surely this was a mother's influence, and it had not even occurred to her to apply the pedagogical strictness to the boy which she seemed to find necessary for her girls. It was clear that in his existence the first factors were gentleness and tenderness. The shears had been resolutely kept from his beautiful hair; like a Prince Charming's, it fell in curls over his forehead, his ears, and still deeper, across his neck. The English sailor suit, with its braids, stitchings, and embroideries, its puffy sleeves narrowing at the ends and fitting snugly about the fine wrists of his still childish but slender hands, gave the delicate figure something rich and luxurious. He was sitting, half profile to the observer, one foot in its black patent-leather shoe placed before the other, an elbow resting on the arm of his wicker chair, a cheek pressed against his fist, in a position of negligent good manners, entirely free of the almost subservient stiffness to which his sisters seemed accustomed. Did he have some illness? For his skin stood out as white as ivory against the golden darkness of the surrounding curls. Or was he simply a pampered favorite child, made this way by a doting and moody love? Aschenbach inclined to believe the latter. Almost every artist is born with a rich and treacherous tendency to recognize injustices which have created beauty, and to meet aristocratic distinction with sympathy and reverence.

A waiter passed through and announced in English that the meal was ready. Gradually the guests disappeared through the glass door into the dining-hall. Stragglers crossed, coming from the entrance, or the lifts. Inside, they had already begun serving, but the young Poles were still waiting around the little wicker table; and Aschenbach, comfortably propped in his deep chair, and with this beauty before his eyes, stayed with them.

The governess, a small corpulent middle-class woman with a red face, finally gave the sign to rise. With lifted brows, she pushed back her chair and bowed, as a large woman dressed in gray and richly jeweled with pearls entered the lobby. This woman was advancing with coolness and precision; her lightly powdered hair and the lines of her dress were arranged with the simplicity which always signifies taste in those quarters where devoutness is taken as one element of dignity. She might have been the wife of some high German official. Except that her jewelry added something fantastically lavish to her appearance; indeed, it was almost priceless, and consisted of ear pendants and a very long triple chain of softly glowing pearls, as large as cherries.

The children had risen promptly. They bent over to kiss the hand of their mother who, with a distant smile on her well-preserved though somewhat tired and peaked features, looked over their heads and directed a few words to the governess in French. Then she walked to the glass door. The children followed her: the girls in the order of their age, after them the governess, the boy last. For some reason or other he turned around before crossing the sill, and since no one else was in the lobby his strange dusky eyes met those of Aschenbach, who, his newspaper on his knees, lost in thought, was gazing after the group.

What he saw had not been unusual in the slightest detail. They had not preceded the mother to the table; they had waited, greeted her with respect, and observed the customary forms on entering the room. But it had taken place so pointedly, with such an accent of training, duty, and self-respect, that Aschenbach felt peculiarly touched by it all.

He delayed for a few moments, then he too crossed into the dining-room, and was assigned to his table, which, as he noted with a brief touch of regret, was very far removed from that of the Polish family.

Weary, and yet intellectually active, he entertained himself during the lengthy meal with abstract, or even transcendental things; he thought over the secret union which the lawful must enter upon with the individual for human beauty to result, from this he passed into general problems of form and art, and at the end he found that his thoughts and discoveries were like the seemingly felicitous promptings of a dream which, when the mind is sobered, are seen to be completely empty and unfit. After the meal, smoking, sitting, taking an occasional turn in the park with its smell of nightfall, he went to bed early and spent the night in a sleep deep and unbroken, but often enlivened with the apparitions of dreams.

The weather did not improve any the following day. A land breeze was blowing. Under a cloudy ashen sky, the sea lay in dull peacefulness; it seemed shriveled up, with a close, dreary horizon, and it had retreated from the beach, baring the long ribs of several sandbanks. As Aschenbach opened his window, he thought that he could detect the foul smell of the lagoon.

He felt depressed. He thought already of leaving. Once, years ago, after several weeks of spring here, this same weather had afflicted him, and impaired his health so seriously that he had to abandon Venice like a fugitive. Was not this old feverish unrest again setting in, the pressure in the temples, the heaviness of the eyelids? It would be annoying to change his residence still another time; but if the wind did not turn, he could not stay here. To be safe, he did not unpack completely. He breakfasted at nine in the buffet-room provided for this purpose between the lobby and the dining-room.

That formal silence reigned here which is the ambition of large hotels. The waiters who were serving walked about on soft soles. Nothing was audible but the tinkling of the tea-things, a word half whispered. In one corner, obliquely across from the door, and two tables removed from his own, Aschenbach observed the Polish girls with their governess. Erect and red-eyed, their ash-blond hair freshly smoothed down, dressed in stiff blue linen with little white cuffs and turned-down collars—they were sitting there, handing around a glass of marmalade. They had almost finished their breakfast. The boy was missing.

Aschenbach smiled. "Well, little Phæacian!" he thought. "You seem to be enjoying the pleasant privilege of having your sleep out." And, suddenly exhilarated, he recited to himself the line: "A frequent change of dress; warm baths, and rest."

He breakfasted without haste. From the porter, who entered the hall holding his braided cap in his hand, he received some forwarded mail; and while he smoked a cigarette he opened a few letters. In this way it happeend that he was present at the entrance of the late sleeper who was being waited for over yonder.

He came through the glass door and crossed the room in silence to his sisters' table. His approach—the way he held the upper part of his body, and bent his knees, the movement of his white-shod feet—had an extraordinary charm; he walked very lightly, at once timid and proud, and this became still more lovely through the childish embarrassment with which, twice as he proceeded, he turned his face towards the center of the room, raising and lowering his eyes. Smiling, with something half muttered in his soft vague tongue, he took his place; and now, as he turned his full profile to the observer, Aschenbach was again astonished, terrified even, by the really godlike beauty of this human child. To-day the boy was wearing a light blouse of blue and white striped cotton goods, with a red silk tie in front, and closed at the neck by a plain white high collar. This collar lacked the distinctiveness of the blouse, but above it the flowering head was poised with an incomparable seductive-

ness—the head of an Eros, in blended yellows of Parian
marble, with fine serious brows, the temples and ears covered softly by the abrupt encroachment of his curls.

"Good, good!" Aschenbach thought, with that deliberate
expert appraisal which artists sometimes employ as a subter-
fuge when they have been carried away with delight before
a masterwork. And he thought further: "Really, if the sea
and the beach weren't waiting for me, I should stay here as
long as you stayed!" But he went then, passed through the
lobby under the inspection of the servants, down the wide
terrace, and straight across the boardwalk to the section of
the beach reserved for the hotel guests. The barefoot old
man in dungarees and straw hat who was functioning here
as bathing-master assigned him to the bath-house he had
rented; a table and a seat were placed on the sandy board
platform, and he made himself comfortable in the lounge
chair which he had drawn closer to the sea, out into the
waxen yellow sand.

More than ever before, he was entertained and amused
by the sights on the beach, this spectacle of carefree, civilized
people getting sensuous enjoyment at the very edge of the
elements. The gray flat sea was already alive with wading
children, swimmers, a motley of figures lying on the sandbanks with arms bent behind their heads. Others were rowing about in little red and blue striped boats without keels;
they were continually upsetting, amid laughter. Before the
long stretches of bathing-houses, where people were sitting
on the platforms as though on small verandas, there was a
play of movement against the line of rest and inertness behind—visits and chatter, fastidious morning elegance alongside the nakedness which, boldly at ease, was enjoying the
freedom which the place afforded. Farther in front, on the
damp firm sand, people were parading about in white bath-
ing-cloaks, in ample, brilliantly colored wrappers. An elaborate sand pile to the right, erected by children, had flags in
the colors of all nations planted around it. Venders of shells,
cakes, and fruit spread out their wares, kneeling. To the left,

before one of the bathing-houses which stood at right angles to the others and to the sea, a Russian family was encamped: men with beards and large teeth, slow delicate women, a Baltic girl sitting by an easel and painting the sea amidst exclamations of despair, two ugly good-natured children, an old maidservant who wore a kerchief on her head and had the alert scraping manners of a slave. Delighted and appreciative, they were living there, patiently calling the names of the two rowdy disobedient children, using their scanty Italian to joke with the humorous old man from whom they were buying candy, kissing one another on the cheek, and not in the least concerned with any one who might be observing their community.

"Yes, I shall stay," Aschenbach thought. "Where would things be better?" And, his hands folded in his lap, he let his eyes lose themselves in the expanses of the sea, his gaze gliding, swimming, and failing in the monotone mist of the wilderness of space. He loved the ocean for deep-seated reasons: because of that yearning for rest, when the hard-pressed artist hungers to shut out the exacting multiplicities of experience and hide himself on the breast of the simple, the vast; and because of a forbidden hankering—seductive, by virtue of its being directly opposed to his obligations— after the incommunicable, the incommensurate, the eternal, the non-existent. To be at rest in the face of perfection is the hunger of every one who is aiming at excellence; and what is the non-existent but a form of perfection? But now, just as his dreams were so far out in vacancy, suddenly the horizontal fringe of the sea was broken by a human figure; and as he brought his eyes back from the unbounded, and focused them, it was the lovely boy who was there, coming from the left and passing him on the sand. He was bare-footed, ready for wading, his slender legs exposed above the knees; he walked slowly, but as lightly and proudly as though it were the customary thing for him to move about without shoes; and he was looking around him towards the line of bathing-houses opposite. But as soon as he had noticed the

Russian family, occupied with their own harmony and contentment, a cloud of scorn and detestation passed over his face. His brow darkened, his mouth was compressed, he gave his lips an embittered twist to one side so that the cheek was distorted and the forehead became so heavily furrowed that the eyes seemed sunken beneath its pressure: malicious and glowering, they spoke the language of hate. He looked down, looked back once more threateningly, then with his shoulder made an abrupt gesture of disdain and dismissal, and left the enemy behind him.

A kind of pudency or confusion, something like respect and shyness, caused Aschenbach to turn away as though he had seen nothing. For the earnest-minded who have been casual observers of some passion, struggle against making use, even to themselves, of what they have seen. But he was both cheered and unstrung—which is to say, he was happy. This childish fanaticism, directed against the most good-natured possible aspect of life—it brought the divinely arbitrary into human relationships; it made a delightful natural picture which had appealed only to the eye now seem worthy of a deeper sympathy; and it gave the figure of this half-grown boy, who had already been important enough by his sheer beauty, something to offset him still further, and to make one take him more seriously than his years justified. Still looking away, Aschenbach could hear the boy's voice, the shrill, somewhat weak voice with which, in the distance now, he was trying to call hello to his playfellows busied around the sand pile. They answered him, shouting back his name, or some affectionate nickname; and Aschenbach listened with a certain curiosity, without being able to catch anything more definite than two melodic syllables like "Adgio," or still more frequently "Adgiu," with a ringing *u*-sound prolonged at the end. He was pleased with the resonance of this; he found it adequate to the subject. He repeated it silently and, satisfied, turned to his letters and manuscripts.

His small portable writing-desk on his knees, he began

writing with his fountain pen an answer to this or that bit
of correspondence. But after the first fifteen minutes he
found it a pity to abandon the situation—the most enjoyable
he could think of—in this manner and waste it in activities
which did not interest him. He tossed the writing materials
to one side, and he faced the ocean again; soon afterwards,
diverted by the childish voices around the sand heap, he
revolved his head comfortably along the back of the chair
towards the right, to discover where that excellent little
Adgio might be and what he was doing.

He was found at a glance; the red tie on his breast was
not to be overlooked. Busied with the others in laying an
old plank across the damp moat of the sand castle, he was
nodding, and shouting instructions for this work. There
were about ten companions with him, boys and girls of his
age, and a few younger ones who were chattering with one
another in Polish, French, and in several Balkan tongues.
But it was his name which rang out most often. He was
openly in demand, sought after, admired. One boy especially, like him a Pole, a stocky fellow who was called something like "Jaschu," with sleek black hair and a belted linen
coat, seemed to be his closest vassal and friend. When the
work on the sand structure was finished for the time being,
they walked arm-in-arm along the beach and the boy who
was called "Jaschu" kissed the beauty.

Aschenbach was half minded to raise a warning finger. "I
advise you, Cristobulus," he thought, smiling, "to travel
for a year! For you need that much time at least to get over
it." And then he breakfasted on large ripe strawberries which
he got from a peddler. It had become very warm, although
the sun could no longer penetrate the blanket of mist in the
sky. Laziness clogged his brain, even while his senses delighted in the numbing, drugging distractions of the ocean's
stillness. To guess, to puzzle out just what name it was that
sounded something like "Adgio," seemed to the sober man
an appropriate ambition, a thoroughly comprehensive pur-
suit. And with the aid of a few scrappy recollections of Polish

he decided that they must mean "Tadzio," the shortened form of "Tadeusz," and sounding like "Tadziu" when it is called.

Tadzio was bathing. Aschenbach, who had lost sight of him, spied his head and the arm with which he was propelling himself, far out in the water; for the sea must have been smooth for a long distance out. But already people seemed worried about him; women's voices were calling after him from the bathing-houses, uttering this name again and again. It almost dominated the beach like a battle-cry, and with its soft consonants, its long-drawn u-note at the end, it had something at once sweet and wild about it: "Tadziu! Tadziu!" He turned back; beating the resistant water into a foam with his legs, he hurried, his head bent down over the waves. And to see how this living figure, graceful and clean-cut in its advance, with dripping curls, and lovely as some frail god, came up out of the depths of sky and sea, rose and separated from the elements—this spectacle aroused a sense of myth, it was like some poet's recovery of time at its beginning, of the origin of forms and the birth of gods. Aschenbach listened with closed eyes to this song ringing within him, and he thought again that it was pleasant here, and that he would like to remain.

Later Tadzio was resting from his bath; he lay in the sand, wrapped in his white robe, which was drawn under the right shoulder, his head supported on his bare arm. And even when Aschenbach was not observing him, but was reading a few pages in his book, he hardly ever forgot that this boy was lying there and that it would cost him only a slight turn of his head to the right to behold the mystery. It seemed that he was sitting here just to keep watch over his repose— busied with his own concerns, and yet constantly aware of this noble picture at his right, not far in the distance. And he was stirred by a paternal affection, the profound leaning which those who have devoted their thoughts to the creation of beauty feel towards those who possess beauty itself.

A little past noon he left the beach, returned to the hotel, and was taken up to his room. He stayed there for some time in front of the mirror, looking at his gray hair, his tired, sharp features. At this moment he thought of his reputation, and of the fact that he was often recognized on the streets and observed with respect, thanks to the sure aim and the appealing finish of his words. He called up all the exterior successes of his talent which he could think of, remembering also his elevation to the knighthood. Then he went down to the dining-hall for lunch, and ate at his little table. As he was riding up in the lift, after the meal was ended, a group of young people just coming from breakfast pressed into the swaying cage after him, and Tadzio entered too. He stood quite near to Aschenbach, for the first time so near that Aschenbach could see him, not with the aloofness of a picture, but in minute detail, in all his human particularities. The boy was addressed by some one or other, and as he was answering with an indescribably agreeable smile he stepped out again, on the second floor, walking backwards, and with his eyes lowered. "Beauty makes modest," Aschenbach thought, and he tried insistently to explain why this was so. But he had noticed that Tadzio's teeth were not all they should be; they were somewhat jagged and pale. The enamel did not look healthy; it had a peculiar brittleness and transparency, as is often the case with anæmics. "He is very frail, he is sickly," Aschenbach thought. "In all probability he will not grow old." And he refused to reckon with the feeling of gratification or reassurance which accompanied this notion.

He spent two hours in his room, and in the afternoon he rode in the *vaporetto* across the foul-smelling lagoon to Venice. He got off at San Marco, took tea on the Piazza, and then, in accord with his schedule for the day, he went for a walk through the streets. Yet it was this walk which produced a complete reversal in his attitudes and his plans.

An offensive sultriness lay over the streets. The air was so heavy that the smells pouring out of homes, stores, and eating-houses became mixed with oil, vapors, clouds of perfumes, and still other odors—and these would not blow away, but hung in layers. Cigarette smoke remained suspended, disappearing very slowly. The crush of people along the narrow streets irritated rather than entertained the walker. The farther he went, the more he was depressed by the repulsive condition resulting from the combination of sea air and sirocco, which was at the same time both stimulating and enervating. He broke into an uncomfortable sweat. His eyes failed him, his chest became tight, he had a fever, the blood was pounding in his head. He fled from the crowded business streets across a bridge into the walks of the poor. On a quiet square, one of those forgotten and enchanting places which lie in the interior of Venice, he rested at the brink of a well, dried his forehead, and realized that he would have to leave here.

For the second and last time it had been demonstrated that this city in this kind of weather was decidedly unhealthy for him. It seemed foolish to attempt a stubborn resistance, while the prospects for a change of wind were completely uncertain. A quick decision was called for. It was not possible to go home this soon. Neither summer nor winter quarters were prepared to receive him. But this was not the only place where there were sea and beach; and elsewhere these could be found without the lagoon and its malarial mists. He remembered a little watering-place not far from Trieste which had been praised to him. Why not there? And without delay, so that this new change of location would still have time to do him some good. He pronounced this as good as settled, and stood up. At the next gondola station he took a boat back to San Marco, and was led through the dreary labyrinth of canals, under fancy marble balconies flanked with lions, around the corners of smooth walls, past the sorrowing façades of palaces which mirrored large dilapidated business-signs in the pulsing water. He had trouble arriving there, for the gondolier, who was in league with lace-makers and glass-blowers, was always trying to land him for inspections and purchases; and just as the bizarre

trip through Venice would begin to cast its spell, the greedy
business sense of the sunken Queen did all it could to destroy
the illusion.

When he had returned to the hotel, he announced at the
office before dinner that unforeseen developments necessi-
tated his departure the following morning. He was assured
of their regrets. He settled his accounts. He dined and spent
the warm evening reading the newspapers in a rocking-chair
on the rear terrace. Before going to bed he got his luggage
all ready for departure.

He did not sleep so well as he might, since the impending
break-up made him restless. When he opened the window in
the morning, the sky was as overcast as ever, but the air
seemed fresher, and he was already beginning to repent.
Hadn't his decision been somewhat hasty and uncalled for,
the result of a passing diffidence and indisposition? If he had
delayed a little, if, instead of surrendering so easily, he had
made some attempt to adjust himself to the air of Venice
or to wait for an improvement in the weather, he would not
be so rushed and inconvenienced, but could anticipate
another forenoon on the beach like yesterday's. Too late.
Now he would have to go on wanting what he had wanted
yesterday. He dressed, and at about eight o'clock rode down
to the ground-floor for breakfast.

As he entered, the buffet-room was still empty of guests.
A few came in while he sat waiting for his order. With his
tea-cup to his lips, he saw the Polish girls and their governess appear: rigid, with morning freshness, their eyes still
red, they walked across to their table in the corner by the
window. Immediately afterwards, the porter approached
him, cap in hand, and warned him that it was time to go. The
automobile is ready to take him and the other passengers
to the Hotel Excelsior, and from here the motorboat will
bring the ladies and gentlemen to the station through the
company's private canal. Time is pressing.—Aschenbach
found that it was doing nothing of the sort. It was still over
an hour before his train left. He was irritated by this hotel

custom of hustling departing guests out of the house, and indicated to the porter that he wished to finish his breakfast in peace. The man retired hesitatingly, to appear again five minutes later. It is impossible for the car to wait any longer. Then he would take a cab, and carry his trunk with him, Aschenbach replied in anger. He would use the public steamboat at the proper time, and he requested that it be left to him personally to worry about his departure. The employee bowed himself away. Pleased with the way he had warded off these importunate warnings, Aschenbach finished his meal at leisure; in fact, he even had the waiter bring him a newspaper. The time had become quite short when he finally arose. It was fitting that at the same moment Tadzio should come through the glass door.

On the way to his table he walked in the opposite direction to Aschenbach, lowering his eyes modestly before the man with the gray hair and high forehead, only to raise them again, in his delicious manner, soft and full upon him —and he had passed. "Good-by, Tadzio!" Aschenbach thought. "I did not see much of you." He did what was unusual with him, really formed the words on his lips and spoke them to himself; then he added: "God bless you!"— After this he left, distributed tips, was ushered out by the small gentle manager in the French frock-coat, and made off from the hotel on foot, as he had come, going along the white blossoming avenue which crossed the island to the steamer bridge, accompanied by the house servant carrying his hand luggage. He arrived, took his place—and then followed a painful journey through all the depths of regret.

It was the familiar trip across the lagoon, past San Marco, up the Grand Canal. Aschenbach sat on the circular bench at the bow, his arm supported against the railing, shading his eyes with his hand. The public gardens were left behind, the Piazzetta opened up once more in princely splendor and was gone, then came the great flock of palaces, and as the channel made a turn the magnificently slung marble arch of the Rialto came into view. The traveler was watching; his emotions were in conflict. The atmosphere of the city, this slightly foul smell of sea and swamp which he had been so anxious to avoid—he breathed it now in deep, exquisitely painful draughts. Was it possible that he had not known, had not considered, just how much he was attached to all this? What had been a partial misgiving this morning, a faint doubt as to the advisability of his move, now became a distress, a positive misery, a spiritual hunger, and so bitter that it frequently brought tears to his eyes, while he told himself that he could not possibly have foreseen it. Hardest of all to bear, at times completely insufferable, was the thought that he would never see Venice again, that this was a leave-taking for ever. Since it had been shown for the second time that the city affected his health, since he was compelled for the second time to get away in all haste, from now on he would have to consider it a place impossible and forbidden to him, a place which he was not equal to, and which it would be foolish for him to visit again. Yes, he felt that if he left now, he would be shamefaced and defiant enough never to see again the beloved city which had twice caused him a physical breakdown. And of a sudden this struggle between his desires and his physical strength seemed to the aging man so grave and important, his physical defeat seemed so dishonorable, so much a challenge to hold out at any cost, that he could not understand the ready submissiveness of the day before, when he had decided to give in without attempting any serious resistance.

Meanwhile the steamboat was nearing the station; pain and perplexity increased, he became distracted. In his affliction, he felt that it was impossible to leave, and just as impossible to turn back. The conflict was intense as he entered the station. It was very late; there was not a moment to lose if he was to catch the train. He wanted to, and he did not want to. But time was pressing; it drove him on. He hurried to get his ticket, and looked about in the tumult of the hall for the officer on duty here from the hotel. The man appeared and announced that the large trunk had been transferred. Transferred already? Yes, thank you—to Como. To Como? And in the midst of hasty running back and forth, angry questions and confused answers, it came to light that the trunk had already been sent with other foreign baggage from the express office of the Hotel Excelsior in a completely wrong direction.

Aschenbach had difficulty in preserving the expression which was required under these circumstances. He was almost convulsed with an adventurous delight, an unbelievable hilarity. The employee rushed off to see if it were still possible to stop the trunk, and, as was to be expected, he returned with nothing accomplished. Aschenbach declared that he did not want to travel without his trunk, but had decided to go back and wait at the beach hotel for its return. Was the company's motorboat still at the station? The man assured him that it was lying at the door. With Italian volubility he persuaded the clerk at the ticket window to redeem the canceled ticket, he swore that they would act speedily, that no time or money would be spared in recovering the trunk promptly, and—so the strange thing happened that, twenty minutes after his arrival at the station, the traveler found himself again on the Grand Canal, returning to the Lido.

Here was an adventure, wonderful, abashing, and comically dreamlike, beyond belief: places which he had just bid farewell to for ever in the most abject misery—yet he had been turned and driven back by fate, and was seeing them again in the same hour! The spray from the prow washing between gondolas and steamers with an absurd agility, the speedy little craft shot ahead to its goal, while the lone passenger was hiding the nervousness and ebullience of a truant boy under a mask of resigned anger. From time to time he shook with laughter at this mishap which, as he told himself, could not have turned out better for a child of destiny. There were explanations to be given, expressions of astonishment to be faced—and then, he told himself, everything would be all right; then a misfortune would be avoided, a grave error rectified. And all that he had thought he was leaving behind him would be open to him again, there at his disposal. . . . And, to cap it all, was the rapidity of the ride deceiving him, or was the wind really coming from the sea?

The waves beat against the walls of the narrow canal which runs through the island to the Hotel Excelsior. An autmobile omnibus was awaiting his return there, and took him above the rippling sea straight to the beach hotel. The little manager with mustache and long-tailed frock-coat came down the stairs to meet him.

He ingratiatingly regretted the episode, spoke of it as highly painful to him and the establishment, but firmly approved of Aschenbach's decision to wait here for the baggage. Of course his room had been given up, but there was another one, just as good, which he could occupy immediately. *"Pas de chance, Monsieur,"* the Swiss elevator boy smiled as they were ascending. And so the fugitive was established again, in a room almost identical with the other in its location and furnishings.

Tired out by the confusion of this strange forenoon, he distributed the contents of his hand-bag about the room and dropped into an arm-chair by the open window. The sea had become a pale green, the air seemed thinner and purer; the beach with its cabins and boats, seemed to have color, although the sky was still gray. Aschenbach looked out, his hands folded in his lap; he was content to be back, but shook his head disapprovingly at his irresolution, his failure to know his own mind. He sat here for the better part of an hour, resting and dreaming vaguely. About noon he saw Tadzio in a striped linen suit with a red tie, coming back from the sea across the private beach and along the boardwalk to the hotel. Aschenbach recognized him from this altitude before he had actually set eyes on him; he was about to think some such words as "Well, Tadzio, there you are again!" but at the same moment he felt this careless greeting go dumb before the truth in his heart. He felt the exhilaration of his blood, a conflict of pain and pleasure, and he realized that it was Tadzio who had made it so difficult for him to leave.

He sat very still, entirely unobserved from this height, and looked within himself. His features were alert, his eyebrows raised, and an attentive, keenly inquisitive smile distended his mouth. Then he raised his head, lifted both hands, which had hung relaxed over the arms of the chair, and in a slow twisting movement turned the palms upward—as though to suggest an opening and spreading outward of his arms. It was a spontaneous act of welcome, of calm acceptance.

IV

Day after day now the naked god with the hot cheeks drove his fire-breathing quadriga across the expanses of the sky, and his yellow locks fluttered in the assault of the east wind. A white silk sheen stretched over the slowly simmering Ponto. The sand glowed. Beneath the quaking silver blue of the ether, rust-colored canvases were spread in front of the bathing-houses, and the afternoons were spent in the sharply demarcated spots of shade which they cast. But it was also delightful in the evening, when the vegetation in the park had the smell of balsam, and the stars were working through their courses above, and the soft persistent murmur of the sea came up enchantingly through the night. Such evenings contained the cheering promise that more sunny days of casual idleness would follow, dotted with countless closely interspersed possibilities of well-timed accidents.

The guest who was detained here by such an accommodating mishap did not consider the return of his property as sufficient grounds for another departure. He suffered some inconvenience for two days, and had to appear for meals in the large dining-room in his traveling-clothes. When the strayed luggage was finally deposited in his room again, he unpacked completely and filled the closet and drawers with his belongings; he had decided to remain here indefinitely, content now that he could pass the hours on the beach in a silk suit and appear for dinner at his little table again in appropriate evening dress.

The comfortable rhythm of this life had already cast its spell over him; he was soon enticed by the ease, the mild splendor, of his program. Indeed, what a place to be in, when the usual allurement of living in watering-places on southern shores was coupled with the immediate nearness of the most wonderful of all cities! Aschenbach was not a lover of pleasure. Whenever there was some call for him to take a holiday, to indulge himself, to have a good time—and this was especially true at an earlier age—restlessness and repugnance soon drove him back to his rigorous toil, the faithful sober efforts of his daily routine. Except that this place was bewitching him, relaxing his will, making him happy. In the mornings, under the shelter of his bathing-house, letting his eyes roam dreamily in the blue of the southern sea; or on a warm night as he leaned back against the cushions of the gondola carrying him under the broad starry sky home to the Lido from the Piazza di San Marco after long hours of idleness—and the brilliant lights, the melting notes of the serenade were being left behind—he often recalled his place in the mountains, the scene of his battles in the summer, where the clouds blew low across his garden, and terrifying storms put out the lamps at night, and the crows which he fed were swinging in the tops of the pine-trees. Then everything seemed just right to him, as though he were lifted into the Elysian fields, on the borders of the earth, where man enjoys the easiest life, where there is no snow or winter, nor storms and pouring rains, but where Oceanus continually sends forth gentle cooling breezes, and the days pass in a blessed inactivity, without work, without effort, devoted wholly to the sun and to the feast-days of the sun.

Aschenbach saw the boy Tadzio frequently, almost constantly. Owing to the limited range of territory and the regularity of their lives, the beauty was near him at short intervals throughout the day. He saw him, met him, everywhere: in the lower rooms of the hotel, on the cooling water trips to the city and back, in the arcades of the square, and at times when he was especially lucky ran across him on the streets. But principally, and with the most gratifying regularity, the forenoon on the beach allowed him to admire and study this rare spectacle at his leisure. Yes, it was this guaranty of happiness, this daily recurrence of good fortune, which made his stay here so precious, and gave him such pleasure in the constant procession of sunny days.

He was up as early as he used to be when under the driving pressure of work, and was on the beach before most people, when the sun was still mild and the sea lay blinding white in the dreaminess of morning. He spoke amiably to the guard of the private beach, and also spoke familiarly to the barefoot, white-bearded old man who had prepared his place for him, stretching the brown canopy and bringing the furniture of the cabin out on the platform. Then he took his seat. There would now be three or four hours in which the sun mounted and gained terrific strength, the sea a deeper and deeper blue, and he might look at Tadzio.

He saw him approaching from the left, along the edge of the sea; he saw him as he stepped out backwards from among the cabins; or he would suddenly find, with a shock of pleasure, that he had missed his coming, that he was already here in the blue and white bathing-suit which was his only garment now while on the beach, that he had already commenced his usual activities in the sun and the sand—a pleasantly trifling, idle, and unstable manner of living, a mixture of rest and play. Tadzio would saunter about, wade, dig, catch things, lie down, go for a swim, all the while being kept under surveillance by the women on the platform who made his name ring out in their falsetto voices: "Tadziu! Tadziu!" Then he would come running to them with a look of eagerness, to tell them what he had seen, what he had experienced, or to show them what he had found or caught:

mussels, sea-horses, jelly-fish, and crabs that ran sideways. Aschenbach did not understand a word he said, and though it might have been the most ordinary thing in the world, it was a vague harmony in his ear. So the foreignness of the boy's speech turned it into music, a wanton sun poured its prodigal splendor down over him, and his figure was always set off against the background of an intense sea-blue.

This piquant body was so freely exhibited that his eyes soon knew every line and posture. He was continually re-discovering with new pleasure all this familiar beauty, and his astonishment at its delicate appeal to his senses was un-ending. The boy was called to greet a guest who was paying his respects to the ladies at the bathing-house. He came run-ning, running wet perhaps out of the water, tossed back his curls, and as he held out his hand, resting on one leg and raising his other foot on the toes, the set of his body was delightful; it had a charming expectancy about it, a well-meaning shyness, a winsomeness which showed his aristo-cratic training. . . . He lay stretched full length, his bath towel slung across his shoulders, his delicately chiseled arm supported in the sand, his chin in his palm; the boy called Jaschu was squatting near him and making up to him—and nothing could be more enchanting than the smile of his eyes and lips when the leader glanced up at his inferior, his serv-ant. . . . He stood on the edge of the sea, alone, apart from his people, quite near to Aschenbach—erect, his hands locked across the back of his neck, he swayed slowly on the balls of his feet, looked dreamily into the blueness of sea and sky, while tiny waves rolled up and bathed his feet. His honey-colored hair clung in rings about his neck and temples. The sun made the down on his back glitter; the fine etching of the ribs, the symmetry of the chest, were emphasized by the tightness of the suit across the buttocks. His armpits were still as smooth as those of a statue; the hollows of his knees glistened, and their bluish veins made his body seem built of some clearer stuff. What rigor, what precision of thought were expressed in this erect, youthfully perfect body! Yet the pure and strenuous will which, darkly at work, could bring such godlike sculpture to the light—was not he, the artist, familiar with this? Did it not operate in him too when he, under the press of frugal passions, would free from the marble mass of speech some slender form which he had seen in the mind and which he put before his fellows as a statue and a mirror of intellectual beauty?

Statue and mirror! His eyes took in the noble form there bordered with blue; and with a rush of enthusiasm he felt that in this spectacle he was catching the beautiful itself, form as the thought of God, the one pure perfection which lives in the mind, and which, in this symbol and likeness, had been placed here quietly and simply as an object of devotion. That was drunkenness; and eagerly, without thinking, the aging artist welcomed it. His mind was in travail; all that he had learned dropped back into flux; his understanding threw up age-old thoughts which he had inherited with youth though they had never before lived with their own fire. Is it not written that the sun diverts our attention from intellectual to sensual things? Reason and understanding, it is said, become so numbed and enchanted that the soul forgets everything out of delight with its immediate circumstances, and in astonishment becomes attached to the most beautiful object shined on by the sun; indeed, only with the aid of a body is it capable then of raising itself to higher considerations. To be sure, Amor did as the instructors of mathematics who show backward children tangible representations of the pure forms—similarly the god, in order to make the spiritual visible for us, readily utilized the form and color of man's youth, and as a reminder he adorned these with the reflected splendor of beauty which, when we behold it, makes us flare up in pain and hope.

His enthusiasm suggested these things, put him in the mood for them. And from the noise of the sea and the luster of the sun he wove himself a charming picture. Here was the old plane-tree, not far from the walls of Athens—a holy, shadowy place filled with the smell of *agnus castus* blossoms and decorated with ornament and images sacred to Achelous and the Nymphs. Clear and pure, the brook at the foot of the spreading tree fell across the smooth pebbles; the cicadas were fiddling. But on the grass, which was like a pillow gently sloping to the head, two people were stretched out, in hiding from the heat of the day: an older man and a youth, one ugly and one beautiful, wisdom next to loveliness. And amid gallantries and skillfully engaging banter, Socrates was instructing Phædrus in matters of desire and virtue. He spoke to him of the hot terror which the initiate suffer when their eyes light on an image of the eternal beauty; spoke of the greed of the impious and the wicked who cannot think beauty when they see its likeness, and who are incapable of reverence; spoke of the holy distress which befalls the noble-minded when a god-like countenance, a perfect body, appears before them; they tremble and grow distracted, and hardly dare to raise their eyes, and they honor the man who possesses this beauty, yes, if they were not afraid of being thought downright madmen they would sacrifice to the beloved as to the image of a god. For beauty, my Phædrus, beauty alone is both lovely and visible at once; it is, mark me, the only form of the spiritual which we can receive through the senses. Else what would become of us if the divine, if reason and virtue and truth, should appear to us through the senses? Should we not perish and be consumed with love, as Semele once was with Zeus? Thus, beauty is the sensitive man's access to the spirit—but only a road, a means simply, little Phædrus. . . . And then this crafty suitor made the neatest remark of all; it was this, that the lover is more divine than the beloved, since the god is in the one, but not in the other—perhaps the most delicate, the most derisive thought which has ever been framed, and the one from which spring all the cunning and the profound-est pleasures of desire.

Writers are happiest with an idea which can become all emotion, and an emotion all idea. Just such a pulsating idea, such a precise emotion, belonged to the lonely man at this

moment, was at his call. Nature, it ran, shivers with ecstasy
when the spirit bows in homage before beauty. Suddenly
he wanted to write. Eros loves idleness, they say, and he is
suited only to idleness. But at this point in the crisis the
affliction became a stimulus towards productivity. The incentive hardly mattered. A request, an agitation for an open
statement on a certain large burning issue of culture and
taste, was going about the intellectual world, and had finally
caught up with the traveler here. He was familiar with the
subject, it had touched his own experience; and suddenly
he felt an irresistible desire to display it in the light of his
own version. And he even went so far as to prefer working
in Tadzio's presence, taking the scope of the boy as a stand-
ard for his writing, making his style follow the lines of this
body which seemed godlike to him, and carrying his beauty
over into the spiritual just as the eagle once carried the
Trojan stag up into the ether. Never had his joy in words
been more sweet. He had never been so aware that Eros is
in the word as during those perilously precious hours when,
at his crude table under the canopy, facing the idol and
listening to the music of his voice, he followed Tadzio's
beauty in the forming of his little tract, a page and a half of
choice prose which was soon to excite the admiration of
many through its clarity, its poise, and the vigorous curve
of its emotion. Certainly it is better for people to know only
the beautiful product as finished, and not in its conception,
its conditions of origin. For knowledge of the sources from
which the artist derives his inspiration would often confuse
and alienate, and in this way detract from the effects of his
mastery. Strange hours! Strangely enervating efforts! Rare
creative intercourse between the spirit and body! When
Aschenbach put away his work and started back from the
beach, he felt exhausted, or in dispersion even; and it was
as though his conscience were complaining after some trans-
gression.

The following morning, as he was about to leave the
hotel, he looked off from the steps and noticed that Tadzio,

who was alone and was already on his way towards the sea, was just approaching the private beach. He was half tempted by the simple notion of seizing this opportunity to strike up a casual friendly acquaintanceship with the boy who had been the unconscious source of so much agitation and up-heaval; he wanted to address him, and enjoy the answering look in his eyes. The boy was sauntering along, he could be overtaken; and Aschenbach quickened his pace. He reached him on the boardwalk behind the bathing-houses; was about to lay a hand on his head and shoulders; and some word or other, an amiable phrase in French, was on the tip of his tongue. But he felt that his heart, due also perhaps to his rapid stride, was beating like a hammer; and he was so short of breath that his voice would have been tight and trembling. He hesitated, he tried to get himself under control. Sud-denly he became afraid that he had been walking too long so close behind the boy. He was afraid of arousing curiosity and causing him to look back questioningly. He made one more spurt, failed, surrendered, and passed with bowed head.

"Too late!" he thought immediately. Too late! Yet was it too late? This step which he had just been on the verge of taking would very possibly have put things on a sound, free and easy basis, and would have restored him to wholesome soberness. But the fact was that Aschenbach did not want soberness: his intoxication was too precious. Who can ex-plain the stamp and the nature of the artist? Who can under-stand this deep instinctive welding of discipline and license? For to be unable to want wholesome soberness, is license. Aschenbach was no longer given to self-criticism. His tastes, the mental caliber of his years, his self-respect, ripeness, and a belated simplicity made him unwilling to dismember his motives and to debate whether his impulses were the result of conscientiousness or of dissolution and weakness. He was embarrassed, as he feared that some one or other, if only the guard on the beach, must have observed his pur-suit and defeat. He was very much afraid of the ridiculous.

Further, he joked with himself about his comically pious distress. "Downed," he thought, "downed like a rooster, with his wings hanging miserably in the battle. It really is a god who can, at one sight of his loveliness, break our courage this way and force down our pride so thoroughly. . . ." He toyed and skirmished with his emotions, and was far too haughty to be afraid of them.

He had already ceased thinking about the time when the vacation period which he had fixed for himself would expire; the thought of going home never even suggested itself. He had sent for an ample supply of money. His only concern was with the possible departure of the Polish family; by a casual questioning of the hotel barber he had contrived to learn that these people had come here only a short time before his own arrival. The sun browned his face and hands, the invigorating salt breezes made him feel fresher. Once he had been in the habit of expending on his work every bit of nourishment which food, sleep, or nature could provide him; and similarly now he was generous and uneconomical, letting pass off as elation and emotion all the daily strengthening derived from the sun, idleness, and sea air.

His sleep was fitful; the preciously uniform days were separated by short nights of happy unrest. He did retire early, for at nine o'clock, when Tadzio had disappeared from the scene, the day seemed over. But at the first gray of dawn he was awakened by a gently insistent shock; he suddenly remembered his adventure, he could no longer remain in bed; he arose and, clad lightly against the chill of morning, he sat down by the open window to await the rising of the sun. Toned by his sleep, he watched this miraculous event with reverence. Sky, earth, and sea still lay in glassy, ghostlike twilight; a dying star still floated in the emptiness of space. But a breeze started up, a winged message from habitations beyond reach, telling that Eos was rising from beside her husband. And that first sweet reddening in the farthest stretches of sky and sea took place by which the sentiency of creation is announced. The goddess was approaching, the seductress of youth who stole Cleitus and Cephalus, and despite the envy of all the Olympians enjoyed the love of handsome Orion. A strewing of roses began there on the edge of the world, an unutterably pure glowing and blooming. Childish clouds, lighted and shined through, floated like busy little Cupids in the rosy, bluish mist. Purple fell upon the sea, which seemed to be simmering, and washing the color towards him. Golden spears shot up into the sky from behind. The splendor caught fire, silently; with godlike power an intense flame of licking tongues broke out—and with rattling hoofs the brother's sacred chargers mounted the horizon. Lighted by the god's brilliance, he sat there, keeping watch alone. He closed his eyes, letting this glory play against the lids. Past emotions, precious early afflictions and yearnings which had been stifled by his rigorous program of living, were now returning in such strange new forms. With an embarrassed, astonished smile, he recognized them. He was thinking, dreaming; slowly his lips formed a name. And still smiling, with his face turned upwards, hands folded in his lap, he fell asleep again in his chair.

But the day which began with such fiery solemnity underwent a strange mythical transformation. Where did the breeze originate which suddenly began playing so gently and insinuatingly, like some whispered suggestion, about his ears and temples? Little white choppy clouds stood in the sky in scattered clumps, like the pasturing herds of the gods. A stronger wind arose, and the steeds of Poseidon came prancing up, and along with them the steers which belonged to the blue-locked god, bellowing and lowering their horns as they ran. Yet among the detritus of the more distant beach, waves were hopping forward like agile goats. He was caught in the enchantment of a sacredly distorted world full of Panic life—and he dreamed delicate legends. Often, when the sun was sinking behind Venice, he would sit on a bench in the park observing Tadzio, who was dressed in a white suit with a colored sash and was playing ball on the smooth gravel—and it was Hyacinth that he seemed to be watching. Hyacinth who was to die because two gods loved him. Yes, he felt Zephyr's aching jealousy of the rival who forgot the oracle, the bow, and the lyre, in order to play for ever with this beauty. He saw the discus, guided by a pitiless envy, strike the lovely head; he too, growing pale, caught the drooping body—and the flower, sprung from this sweet blood, bore the inscription of his unending grief.

Nothing is more unusual and strained than the relationship between people who know each other only with their eyes, who meet daily, even hourly, and yet are compelled, by force of custom or their own caprices, to say no word or make no move of acknowledgment, but to maintain the appearance of an aloof unconcern. There is a restlessness and a surcharged curiosity existing between them, the hysteria of an unsatisfied, unnaturally repressed desire for acquaintanceship and intercourse; and especially there is a kind of tense respect. For one person loves and honors another so long as he cannot judge him, and desire is an evidence of incomplete knowledge

Some kind of familiarity had necessarily to form itself between Aschenbach and young Tadzio; and it gave the elderly man keen pleasure to see that his sympathies and interests were not left completely unanswered. For example, when the boy appeared on the beach in the morning and was going towards his family's bathing-house, what had induced him never to use the boardwalk on the far side of it any more, but to stroll along the front path, through the sand, past Aschenbach's habitual place, and often unnecessarily close to him, almost touching his table, or his chair even? Did the attraction, the fascination of an overpowering emotion have such an effect upon the frail unthinking object of it? Aschenbach watched daily for Tadzio to approach; and sometimes he acted as though he were occupied when this event was taking place, and he let the boy pass unobserved. But at other times he would look up, and their glances met. They were both in deep earnest when this occurred. Nothing in

the elderly man's cultivated and dignified expression betrayed any inner movement; but there was a searching look
in Tadzio's eyes, a thoughtful questioning—he began to
falter, looked down, then looked up again charmingly, and,
when he had passed, something in his bearing seemed to
indicate that it was only his breeding which kept him from
turning around.

Once, however, one evening, things turned out differently.
The Polish children and their governess had been missing
at dinner in the large hall; Aschenbach had noted this uneasily. After the meal, disturbed by their absence, Aschenbach was walking in evening dress and straw hat in front
of the hotel at the foot of the terrace, when suddenly he saw
the nunlike sisters appear in the light of the arc-lamp, accompanied by their governess and with Tadzio a few steps
behind. Evidently they were coming from the steamer pier
after having dined for some reason in the city. It must have
been cool on the water; Tadzio was wearing a dark blue
sailor overcoat with gold buttons, and on his head he had a
cap to match. The sun and sea air had not browned him;
his skin still had the same yellow marble color as at first. It
even seemed paler to-day than usual, whether from the coolness or from the blanching moonlight of the lamps. His
regular eyebrows showed up more sharply, the darkness of
his eyes was deeper. It is hard to say how beautiful he was;
and Aschenbach was distressed, as he had often been before,
by the thought that words can only evaluate sensuous beauty,
but not re-give it.

He had not been prepared for this rich spectacle; it came
unhoped for. He had no time to entrench himself behind an
expression of repose and dignity. Pleasure, surprise, admiration must have shown on his face as his eyes met those of the
boy—and at this moment it happened that Tadzio smiled,
smiled to him, eloquently, familiarly, charmingly, without
concealment; and during the smile his lips slowly opened.
It was the smile of Narcissus bent over the reflecting water,
that deep, fascinated, magnetic smile with which he

stretches out his arms to the image of his own beauty—a smile distorted ever so little, distorted at the hopelessness of his efforts to kiss the pure lips of the shadow. It was coquettish, inquisitive, and slightly tortured. It was infatuated, and infatuating.

He had received this smile, and he hurried away as though he carried a fatal gift. He was so broken up that he was compelled to escape the light of the terrace and the front garden; he hastily hunted out the darkness of the park in the rear. Strangely indignant and tender admonitions wrung themselves out of him: "You dare not smile like that! Listen, no one dare smile like that to another!" He threw himself down on a bench; in a frenzy he breathed the night smell of the vegetation. And leaning back, his arms loose, overwhelmed, with frequent chills running through him, he whispered the fixed formula of desire—impossible in this case, absurd, abject, ridiculous, and yet holy, even in this case venerable: "I love you!"

V

During his fourth week at the Lido, Gustav von Aschenbach made several sinister observations touching on the world about him. First, it seemed to him that as the season progressed the number of guests at the hotel was diminishing rather than increasing; and German especially seemed to be dropping away, so that finally he heard nothing but foreign sounds at table and on the beach. Then one day in conversation with the barber, whom he visited often, he caught a word which startled him. The man had mentioned a German family that left soon after their arrival; he added glibly and flatteringly: "But you are staying, sir. You have no fear of the plague." Aschenbach looked at him. "The plague?" he repeated. The gossiper was silent, made out as though busy with other things, ignored the question. When it was put more insistently, he declared that he knew nothing, and with embarrassing volubility he tried to change the subject.

That was about noon. In the afternoon there was a calm, and Aschenbach rode to Venice under an intense sun. For he was driven by a mania to follow the Polish children whom he had seen with their governess taking the road to the steamer pier. He did not find the idol at San Marco. But while sitting over his tea at his little round iron table on the shady side of the square, he suddenly detected a peculiar odor in the air which, it seemed to him now, he had noticed for days without being consciously aware of it. The smell was sweetish and drug-like, suggesting sickness, and wounds, and a suspicious cleanliness. He tested and examined it thoughtfully, finished his luncheon, and left the square on the side opposite the church. The smell was stronger where the street narrowed. On the corners printed posters were hung, giving municipal warnings against certain diseases of the gastric system liable to occur at this season, against the eating of oysters and clams, and also against the water of the canals. The euphemistic nature of the announcement was palpable. Groups of people had collected in silence on the bridge and squares; and the foreigner stood among them, scenting and invesitgating.

At a little shop he inquired about the fatal smell, asking the proprietor, who was leaning against his door surrounded by coral chains and imitation amethyst jewelry. The man measured him with heavy eyes, and brightened up hastily. "A matter of precaution, sir!" he answered with a gesture. "A regulation of the police which must be taken for what it is worth. This weather is oppressive, the sirocco is not good for the health. In short, you understand—an exaggerated prudence perhaps." Aschenbach thanked him and went on. Also on the steamer back to the Lido he caught the smell of the disinfectant.

Returning to the hotel, he went immediately to the periodical stand in the lobby and ran through the papers. He found nothing in the foreign language press. The domestic press spoke of rumors, produced hazy statistics, repeated official denials and questioned their truthfulness. This explained the departure of the German and Austrian guests. Obviously, the subjects of the other nations knew nothing, suspected nothing, were not yet uneasy. "To keep it quiet!" Aschenbach thought angrily, as he threw the papers back on the table. "To keep that quiet!" But at the same moment he was filled with satisfaction over the adventure that was to befall the world about him. For passion, like crime, is not suited to the secure daily rounds of order and well-being; and every slackening in the *bourgeois* structure, every disorder and affliction of the world, must be held welcome, since they bring with them a vague promise of advantage. So Aschenbach felt a dark contentment with what was taking place, under cover of the authorities, in the dirty alleys of Venice. This wicked secret of the city was welded with his own secret, and he too was involved in keeping it hidden. For in his infatuation he cared about nothing but the possibility of Tadzio's leaving, and he realized with something like terror that he would not know how to go on living if this occurred.

Lately he had not been relying simply on good luck and the daily routine for his chances to be near the boy and look at him. He pursued him, stalked him. On Sundays, for instance, the Poles never appeared on the beach. He guessed that they must be attending mass at San Marco. He hurried there; and, stepping from the heat of the square into the golden twilight of the church, he found the boy he was hunting, bowed over a *prie-dieu,* praying. Then he stood in the background, on the cracked mosaic floor, with people on all sides kneeling, murmuring, and making the sign of the cross. And the compact grandeur of this oriental temple weighed heavily on his senses. In front, the richly orna-mented priest was conducting the office, moving about and singing; incense poured forth, clouding the weak little flame of the candle on the altar—and with the sweet, stuffy sacrifi-cial odor another seemed to commingle faintly: the smell of the infested city. But through the smoke and the sparkle Aschenbach saw how the boy there in front turned his head, hunted him out, and looked at him.

When the crowd was streaming out through the opened portals into the brilliant square with its swarms of pigeons, the lover hid in the vestibule; he kept under cover, he lay in wait. He saw the Poles quit the church, saw how the children took ceremonious leave of their mother, and how she turned towards the Piazzetta on her way home. He made sure that the boy, the nunlike sisters, and the governess took the road to the right through the gateway of the clock tower and into the Merceria. And after giving them a slight start, he followed, followed them furtively on their walk through Venice. He had to stand still when they stopped, had to take flight in shops and courts to let them pass when they turned back. He lost them; hot and exhausted, he hunted them over bridges and down dirty blind-alleys—and he underwent minutes of deadly agony when suddenly he saw them coming towards him in a narrow passage where escape was impossible. Yet it could not be said that he suffered. He was drunk, and his steps followed the promptings of the demon who delights in treading human reason and dignity underfoot.

In one place Tadzio and his companions took a gondola; and shortly after they had pushed off from the shore, Aschenbach, who had hidden behind some structure, a well, while they were climbing in, now did the same. He spoke in a hurried undertone as he directed the rower, with the promise of a generous tip, to follow unnoticed and at a distance that gondola which was just rounding the corner. And he thrilled when the man, with the roguish willingness of an accomplice, assured him in the same tone that his wishes would be carried out, carried out faithfully.

Leaning back against the soft black cushions, he rocked and glided towards the other black-beaked craft where his passion was drawing him. At times it escaped; then he felt worried and uneasy. But his pilot, as though skilled in such commissions, was always able through sly maneuvers, speedy diagonals and shortcuts, to bring the quest into view again. The air was quiet and smelly, the sun burned down strong through the slate-colored mist. Water slapped against the wood and stone. The call of the gondolier, half warning, half greeting, was answered with a strange obedience far away in the silence of the labyrinth. White and purple umbels with the scent of almonds hung down from little elevated gardens over crumbling walls. Arabian window-casings were outlined through the murkiness. The marble steps of a church descended into the water; a beggar squatted there, protesting his misery, holding out his hat, and showing the whites of his eyes as though he were blind. An antiquarian in front of his den fawned on the passer-by and invited him to stop in the hopes of swindling him. That was Venice, the flatteringly and suspiciously beautiful—this city, half legend, half snare for strangers; in its foul air art once flourished gluttonously, and had suggested to its musicians seductive notes which cradle and lull. The adventurer felt as though his eyes were taking in this same luxury, as though his ears were being won by just such melodies. He recalled too that the city was diseased and was concealing this through greed —and he peered more eagerly after the retreating gondola.

Thus, in his infatuation, he wanted simply to pursue uninterrupted the object that aroused him, to dream of it when it was not there, and, after the fashion of lovers, to speak softly to its mere outline. Loneliness, strangeness, and the joy of a deep belated intoxication encouraged him and prompted him to accept even the remotest things without reserve or shame—with the result that as he returned late in the evening from Venice, he stopped on the second floor of the hotel before the door of the boy's room, laid his head in utter drunkenness against the hinge of the door, and for a long time could not drag himself away despite the danger of being caught and embarrassed in such a mad situation.

Yet there were still moments of relief when he came partly to his senses. "Where to!" he would think, alarmed. "Where to!" Like every man whose natural abilities stimulate an aristocratic interest in his ancestry, he was accustomed to think of his forebears in connection with the accomplishments

and successes of his life, to assure himself of their approval,
their satisfaction, their undeniable respect. He thought of
them now, entangled as he was in such an illicit experience,
caught in such exotic transgressions. He thought of their
characteristic rigidity of principle, their scrupulous mas-
culinity—and he smiled dejectedly. What would they say?
But then, what would they have said to his whole life, which
was almost degenerate in its departure from theirs, this life
under the bane of art—a life against which he himself had
once issued such youthful mockeries out of loyalty to his
fathers, but which at bottom had been so much like theirs!
He too had served, he too had been a soldier and a warrior
like many of them—for art was a war, a destructive battle,
and one was not equal to it for long, these days. A life of
self-conquest and of in-spite-ofs, a rigid, sober, and unyield-
ing life which he had formed into the symbol of a delicate
and timely heroism. He might well call it masculine, or brave;
and it almost seemed as though the Eros mastering him were
somehow peculiarly adapted and inclined to such a life. Had
not this Eros stood in high repute among the bravest of
people; was it not true that precisely through bravery he had
flourished in their cities? Numerous war heroes of antiquity
had willingly borne his yoke, for nothing was deemed a disgrace which the god imposed; and acts which would have
been rebuked as the sign of cowardice if they had been done
for other purposes—prostrations, oaths, entreaties, abject-
ness—such things did not bring shame upon the lover, but
rather he reaped praise for them.

In this way his infatuation determined the course of his
thoughts, in this way he tried to uphold himself, to preserve
his respect. But at the same time, selfish and calculating, he
turned his attention to the unclean transactions here in Venice, this adventure of the outer world which conspired darkly
with his own and which fed his passion with vague lawless
hopes.

Bent on getting reliable news of the condition and progress
of the pestilence, he ransacked the local papers in the city

cafés, as they had been missing from the reading-table of the
hotel lobby for several days now. Statements alternated with
disavowals. The number of the sick and dead was supposed
to reach twenty, forty, or even a hundred and more—and
immediately afterwards every instance of the plague would
be either flatly denied or attributed to completely isolated
cases which had crept in from the outside. There were scattered admonitions, protests against the dangerous conduct
of foreign authorities. Certainty was impossible. Nevertheless
the lone man felt especially entitled to participate in the
secret; and although he was excluded, he derived a grotesque satisfaction from putting embarrassing questions to
those who did know, and, as they were pledged to silence,
forcing them into deliberate lies. One day at breakfast in
the large dining-hall he entered into a conversation with the
manager, that softly-treading little man in the French frock-
coat who was moving amiably and solicitously about among
the diners and had stopped at Aschenbach's table for a few
passing words. Just why, the guest asked negligently and
casually, had disinfectants become so prevalent in Venice recently? "It has to do," was the evasive answer, "with a police
regulation, and is intended to prevent any inconveniences
or disturbances to the public health which might result from
the exceptionally warm and threatening weather." . . . "The
police are to be congratulated," Aschenbach answered; and
after the exchange of a few remarks on the weather, the
manager left.

Yet that same day, in the evening, after dinner, it happened
that a little band of strolling singers from the city gave a
performance in the front garden of the hotel. Two men and
two women, they stood by the iron post of an arc-lamp and
turned their whitened faces up towards the large terrace
where the guests were enjoying this folk-recital over their
coffee and cooling drinks. The hotel personnel, bellboys,
waiters, and clerks from the office, could be seen listening by
the doors of the vestibule. The Russian family, eager and
precise in their amusements, had had wicker chairs placed

in the garden in order to be nearer the performers; and they were sitting here in an appreciative semicircle. Behind the ladies and gentlemen, in her turban-like kerchief, stood the old slave.

Mandolin, guitar, harmonica, and a squeaky violin were responding to the touch of the virtuoso beggars. Instrumental numbers alternated with songs, as when the younger of the women, with a sharp trembling voice, joined with the sweetly falsetto tenor in a languishing love duet. But the real talent and leader of the group was undoubtedly the other of the two men, the one with the guitar. He was a kind of *buffo* baritone, with not much of a voice, although he did have a gift for pantomime, and a remarkable comic energy. Often, with his large instrument under his arm, he would leave the rest of the group and, still acting, would intrude on the platform, where his antics were rewarded with encouraging laughter. Especially the Russians in their seats down front seemed to be enchanted with so much southern mobility, and their applause incited him to let himself out more and more boldly and assertively.

Aschenbach sat on the balustrade, cooling his lips now and then with a mixture of pomegranate juice and soda which glowed ruby-red in his glass in front of him. His nerves took in the miserable notes, the vulgar crooning melodies; for passion lames the sense of discrimination, and surrenders in all seriousness to appeals which, in sober moments, are either humorously allowed for or rejected with annoyance. At the clown's antics his features had twisted into a set painful smile. He sat there relaxed, although inwardly he was intensely awake; for six paces from him Tadzio was leaning against the stone hand-rail.

In the white belted coat which he often wore at meal times, he was standing in a position of spontaneous and inborn gracefulness, his left forearm on the railing, feet crossed, the right hand on a supporting hip; and he looked down at the street-singers with an expression which was hardly a smile, but only an aloof curiosity, a polite amiability. Often he would stand erect and, expanding his chest, would draw the white smock down under his leather belt with a beautiful gesture. And then too, the aging man observed with a tumult of fright and triumph how he would often turn his head over the left shoulder in the direction of his admirer, carefully and hesitatingly, or even with abruptness as though to attack by surprise. He did not met Aschenbach's eyes, for a mean precaution compelled the transgressor to keep from staring at him: in the background of the terrace the women who guarded Tadzio were sitting, and things had reached a point where the lover had to fear he might be noticed and suspected. Yes, he had often observed with a kind of numbness how, when Tadzio was near him, on the beach, in the hotel lobby, in the Piazza San Marco, they called him back, they were set on keeping him at a distance—and this wounded him frightfully, causing his pride unknown tortures which his conscience would not permit him to evade.

Meanwhile the guitar-player had begun a solo to his own accompaniment, a street-ballad popular throughout Italy. It had several strophes, and the entire company joined each time in the refrain, all singing and playing, while he managed to give a plastic and dramatic twist to the performance. Of slight build, with thin and impoverished features, he stood on the gravel, apart from his companions, in an attitude of insolent bravado, his shabby felt hat on the back of his head so that a bunch of his red hair jutted out from under the brim. And to the thrumming of the strings he flung his jokes up at the terrace in a penetrating recitative; while the veins were swelling on his forehead from the exertion of his performance. He did not seem of Venetian stock, but rather of the race of Neapolitan comedians, half pimp, half entertainer, brutal and audacious, dangerous and amusing. His song was stupid enough so far as the words went; but in his mouth, by his gestures, the movements of his body, his way of blinking significantly and letting the tongue play across his lips, it acquired something ambiguous, something vaguely repulsive. In addition to the customary civilian dress, he was wearing a sport shirt; and his skinny neck protruded above the soft collar, baring a noticeably large and active Adam's-apple. He was pale and snub-nosed. It was hard to fix an age to his beardless features, which seemed furrowed with grimaces and depravity; and the two wrinkles standing arrogantly, harshly, almost savagely between his reddish eyebrows were strangely suited to the smirk on his mobile lips. Yet what really prompted the lonely man to pay him keen attention was the observation that the questionable figure seemed also to provide its own questionable atmosphere. For each time they came to the refrain the singer, amid buffoonery and familiar handshakes, began a grotesque circular march which brought him immediately beneath Aschenbach's place; and each time this happened there blew up to the terrace from his clothes and body a strong carbolic smell.

After the song was ended, he began collecting money. He started with the Russians, who were evidently willing to spend, and then came up the stairs. Up here he showed himself just as humble as he had been bold during the performance. Cringing and bowing, he stole about among the tables, and a smile of obsequious cunning exposed his strong teeth, while the two wrinkles still stood ominously between his red eyebrows. This singular character collecting money to live on—they eyed him with a curiosity and a kind of repugnance, they tossed coins into his felt hat with the tips of their fingers, and were careful not to touch him. The elimination of the physical distance between the comedian and the audience, no matter how great the enjoyment may have been, always causes a certain uneasiness. He felt it, and tried to excuse it by groveling. He came up to Aschenbach, and along with him the smell, which no one else seemed concerned about.

"Listen!" the recluse said in an undertone, almost mechanically. "They are disinfecting Venice. Why?" The jester answered hoarsely: "On account of the police. That is a precaution, sir, with such heat, and the sirocco. The sirocco is oppressive. It is not good for the health." He spoke as though astonished that any one could ask such things and demonstrated with his open hand how oppressive the sirocco was. "Then there is no plague in Venice?" Aschenbach asked quietly, between his teeth. The clown's muscular features fell into a grimace of comical embarrassment. "A plague? What kind of plague? Perhaps our police are a plague? You like to joke! A plague! Of all things! A precautionary measure, you understand! A police regulation against the effects of the oppressive weather." He gesticulated. "Very well," Aschenbach said several times curtly and quietly; and he quickly dropped an unduly large coin into the hat. Then with his eyes he signaled the man to leave. He obeyed, smirking and bowing. But he had not reached the stairs before two hotel employees threw themselves upon him, and with their faces close to his began a whispered cross-examination. He shrugged his shoulders; he gave assurances, he swore that he had kept quiet—that was evident. He was released, and he returned to the garden; then, after a short conference with his companions, he stepped out once more for a final song of thanks and leavetaking.

It was a rousing song which the recluse never recalled having heard before, a "big number" in incomprehensible dialect, with a laugh refrain in which the troupe joined regularly at the tops of their voices. At this point both the words and the accompaniment of the instruments stopped, with nothing left but a laugh which was somehow arranged rhythmically although very naturally done—and the soloist especially showed great talent in giving it a most deceptive vitality. At the renewal of his professional distance from the audience, he recovered all his boldness again, and the artificial laugh that he directed up towards the terrace was derisive. Even before the end of the articulate portion of the strophe, he seemed to struggle against an irresistible tickling. He gulped, his voice trembled, he pressed his hand over his mouth, he contorted his shoulders; and at the proper moment the ungovernable laugh broke out of him, burst into such

real cackles that it was infectious and communicated itself
to the audience, so that on the terrace also an unfounded
hilarity, living off itself alone, started up. But this seemed
to double the singer's exuberance. He bent his knees, he
slapped his thighs, he nearly split himself; he no longer
laughed, he shrieked. He pointed up with his finger, as
though nothing were more comic than the laughing guests
there, and finally every one in the garden and on the veranda
was laughing, even to the waiters, bellboys, and house-
servants in the doorways.

Aschenbach was no longer resting in his chair; he sat upright, as if attempting to defend himself, or to escape. But
the laughter, the whiffs of the hospital smell, and the boy's
nearness combined to put him into a trance that held his
mind and his senses hopelessly captive. In the general movement and distraction he ventured to glance across at Tadzio,
and as he did so he dared observe that the boy, in reply to
his glance, was equally serious, much as though he had modeled his conduct and expression after those of one man, and
the prevalent mood had no effect on him since this one man
was not part of it. This portentous childish obedience had
something so disarming and overpowering about it that the
gray-haired man could hardly restrain himself from burying
his face in his hands. It had also seemed to him that Tadzio's
occasional stretching and quick breathing indicated a complaint, a congestion, of the lungs. "He is sickly, he will probably not grow old," he thought repeatedly with that positive-
ness which is often a peculiar relief to desire and passion.
And along with pure solicitude he had a feeling of rakish
gratification.

Meanwhile the Venetians had ended and were leaving. Applause accompanied them, and their leader did not miss the
opportunity to cover his retreat with further jests. His bows,
the kisses he blew, were laughed at—and so he doubled
them. When his companions were already gone, he acted as
though he had hurt himself by backing into a lamppost, and
he crept though the gate seemingly crippled with pain. Then

he suddenly threw off the mask of comic hard luck, stood upright, hurried away jauntily, stuck out his tongue insolently at the guests on the terrace, and slipped into the darkness. The company was breaking up; Tadzio had been missing from the balustrade for some time. But, to the displeasure of the waiters, the lonely man sat for a long while over the remains of his pomegranate drink. Night advanced. Time was crumbling. In the house of his parents many years back there had been an hourglass—of a sudden he saw the fragile and expressive instrument again, as though it were standing in front of him. Fine and noiseless the rust-red sand was running through the glass neck; and since it was getting low in the upper half, a speedy little vortex had been formed there.

As early as the following day, in the afternoon, he had made new progress in his obstinate baiting of the people he met—and this time he had all possible success. He walked from the Piazza of St. Mark's into the English traveling-bureau located there; and after changing some money at the cash desk, he put on the expression of a distrustful foreigner and launched his fatal question at the attendant clerk. He was a Britisher; he wore a woolen suit, and was still young, with close-set eyes, and had that characteristic stolid reliability which is so peculiarly and strikingly appealing in the tricky, nimble-witted South. He began: "No reason for alarm, sir. A regulation without any serious significance. Such measures are often taken to anticipate the unhealthy effects of the heat and the sirocco . . ." But as he raised his blue eyes, he met the stare of the foreigner, a tired and somwhat unhappy stare focused on his lips with a touch of scorn. Then the Englishman blushed. "At least," he continued in an emotional undertone, "that is the official explanation which people here are content to accept. I will admit that there is something more behind it." And then in his frank and leisurely manner he told the truth.

For several years now Indian cholera had shown a heightened tendency to spread and migrate. Hatched in the warm swamps of the Ganges delta, rising with the noxious breath of that luxuriant, unfit primitive world and island wilderness which is shunned by humans and where the tiger crouches in the bamboo thickets, the plague had raged continuously and with unusual strength in Hindustan, had reached eastwards to China, westward to Afghanistan and Persia, and, following the chief caravan routes, had carried its terrors to Astrachan, and even to Moscow. But while Europe was trembling lest the specter continue its advance from there across the country, it had been transported over the sea by Syrian merchantmen, and had turned up almost simultaneously in several Mediterranean ports, had raised its head in Toulon and Malaga, had showed its mask several times in Palermo and Naples, and seemed permanently entrenched through Calabria and Apulia. The north of the peninsula had been spared. Yet in the middle of this May in Venice the frightful vibrions were found on one and the same day in the blackish wasted bodies of a cabin boy and a woman who sold greengroceries. The cases were kept secret. But within a week there were ten, twenty, thirty more, and in various sections. A man from the Austrian provinces who had made a pleasure trip to Venice for a few days, returned to his home town and died with unmistakable symptoms—and that is how the first reports of the pestilence in the lagoon city got into the German newspapers. The Venetian authorities answered that the city's health conditions had never been better, and took the most necessary preventive measures. But probably the food supply had been infected. Denied and glossed over, death was eating its way along the narrow streets, and its dissemination was especially favored by the premature summer heat which made the water of the canals lukewarm. Yes, it seemed as though the plague had got renewed strength, as though the tenacity and fruitfulness of its stimuli had doubled. Cases of recovery were rare. Out of a hundred attacks, eighty were fatal, and in the most horrible manner. For the plague moved with utter savagery, and often showed that most dangerous form which is called "the drying."

Water from the blood vessels collected in pockets, and the blood was unable to carry this off. Within a few hours the victim was parched, his blood became as thick as glue, and he stifled amid cramps and hoarse groans. Lucky for him if, as sometimes happened, the attack took the form of a light discomfiture followed by a profound coma from which he seldom or never awakened. At the beginning of June the pest-house of the Ospedale Civico had quietly filled; there was not much room left in the two orphan asylums, and a frightfully active commerce was kept up between the wharf of the Fondamenta Nuove and San Michele, the burial island. But there was the fear of a general drop in prosperity. The recently opened art exhibit in the public gardens was to be considered, along with the heavy losses which, in case of panic or unfavorable rumors, would threaten business, the hotels, the entire elaborate system for exploiting foreigners —and as these considerations evidently carried more weight than love of truth or respect for international agreements, the city authorities upheld obstinately their policy of silence and denial. The chief health officer had resigned from his post in indignation, and been promptly replaced by a more tractable personality. The people knew this; and the corruption of their superiors, together with the predominating insecurity, the exceptional condition into which the prevalence of death had plunged the city, induced a certain demoralization of the lower classes, encouraging shady and antisocial impulses which manifested themselves in license, profligacy, and a rising crime wave. Contrary to custom, many drunkards were seen in the evenings; it was said that at night nasty mobs made the streets unsafe. Burglaries and even murders became frequent, for it had already been proved on two occasions that persons who had presumably fallen victim to the plague had in reality been dispatched with poison by their own relatives. And professional debauchery assumed abnormal obtrusive proportions such as had never been known here before, and to an extent which is usually found only in the southern parts of the country and in the Orient.

The Englishman pronounced the final verdict on these facts. "You would do well," he concluded, "to leave to-day rather than to-morrow. It cannot be much more than a couple of days before a quarantine zone is declared." "Thank you," Aschenbach said, and left the office.

The square lay sunless and stifling. Unsuspecting foreigners sat in front of the cafés or stood among the pigeons in front of the church and watched the swarms of birds flapping their wings, crowding one another, and pecking at grains of corn offered them in open palms. The recluse was feverishly excited, triumphant in his possession of the truth. But it had left him with a bad taste in his mouth, and a weird horror in his heart. As he walked up and down the flagstones of the gorgeous court, he was weighing an action which would meet the situation and would absolve him. This evening after dinner he could approach the woman with the pearls and make her a speech; he had figured it out word for word: "Permit a foreigner, madam, to give you some useful advice, a warning, which is being withheld from you through self-interest. Leave immediately with Tadzio and your daughters! Venice is full of the plague." Then he could lay a farewell hand on the head of this tool of a mocking divinity, turn away, and flee this morass. But he felt at the same time that he was very far from seriously desiring such a move. He would retract it, would disengage himself from it. . . . But when we are distracted we loathe most the thought of retracing our steps. He recalled a white building, ornamented with inscriptions which glistened in the evening and in whose transparent mysticism his mind's eye had lost itself— and then that strange wanderer's form which had awakened in the aging man the roving hankerings of youth after the foreign and the remote. And the thought of return, the thought of prudence and soberness, effort, mastery, disgusted him to such an extent that his face was distorted with an expression of physical nausea. "It must be kept silent!" he whispered heavily. And: "I will keep silent!" The consciousness of his share in the facts and the guilt intoxicated him, much as a little wine intoxicates a tired brain. The picture of the diseased and neglected city hovering desolately before him aroused vague hopes beyond the bounds of reason, but with an egregious sweetness. What was the scant happiness he had dreamed of a moment ago, compared with these expectations? What were art and virtue worth to him, over against the advantages of chaos? He kept silent, and remained in Venice.

This same night he had a frightful dream, if one can designate as a dream a bodily and mental experience which occurred to him in the deepest sleep, completely independent of him, and with a physical realness, although he never saw himself present or moving about among the incidents; but their stage rather was his soul itself, and they broke in from without, trampling down his resistance—a profound and spiritual resistance—by sheer force; and when they had passed through, they left his substance, the culture of his lifetime, crushed and annihilated behind them.

It began with anguish, anguish and desire, and a frightened curiosity as to what was coming. It was night, and his senses were on the watch. From far off a grumble, an uproar, was approaching, a jumble of noises. Clanking, blaring, and dull thunder, with shrill shouts and a definite whine in a long-drawn-out *u*-sound—all this was sweetly, ominously interspersed and dominated by the deep cooing of wickedly persistent flutes which charmed the bowels in a shamelessly penetrative manner. But he knew one word; it was veiled, and yet would name what was approaching: "The foreign god!" Vaporous fire began to glow; then he recognized mountains like those about his summer-house. And in the scattered light, from high up in the woods, among tree-trunks and crumbling moss-grown rocks—people, beasts, a throng, a raging mob plunged twisting and whirling downwards, and made the hill swarm with bodies, flames, tumult, and a riotous round dance. Women, tripped by overlong fur draperies which hung from their waists, were holding up tambourines and beating on them, their groaning heads flung back. Others swung sparking firebrands and

bare daggers, or wore hissing snakes about the middle of
their bodies, or shrieking held their breasts in their two
hands. Men with horns on their foreheads, shaggy-haired,
girded with hides, bent back their necks and raised their
arms and thighs, clashed brass cymbals and beat furiously
at kettledrums, while smooth boys prodded he-goats with
wreathed sticks, climbing on their horns and falling off with
shouts when they bounded. And the bacchantes wailed the
word with the soft consonants and the drawn-out *u*-sound,
at once sweet and savage, like nothing ever heard before. In
one place it rang out as though piped into the air by stags,
and it was echoed in another by many voices, in wild triumph
—with it they incited one another to dance and to fling out
their arms and legs, and it was never silent. But everything
was pierced and dominated by the deep coaxing flute. He
who was fighting against this experience—did it not coax
him too with its shameless penetration, into the feast and
the excesses of the extreme sacrifice? His repugnance, his
fear, were keen—he was honorably set on defending himself
to the very last against the barbarian, the foe to intellectual
poise and dignity. But the noise, the howling, multiplied by
the resonant walls of the hills, grew, took the upper hand,
swelled to a fury of rapture. Odors oppressed the senses,
the pungent smell of the bucks, the scent of moist bodies,
and a waft of stagnant water, with another smell, something
familiar, the smell of wounds and prevalent disease. At the
beating of the drum his heart fluttered, his head was spinning, he was caught in a frenzy, in a blinding deafening
lewdness—and he yearned to join the ranks of the god. The
obscene symbol, huge, wooden, was uncovered and raised
up; then they howled the magic word with more abandon.
Foaming at the mouth, they raged, teased one another with
ruttish gestures and caressing hands; laughing and groaning,
they stuck the goads into one another's flesh and licked the
blood from their limbs. But the dreamer now was with them,
in them, and he belonged to the foreign god. Yes, they were
he himself, as they hurled themselves biting and tearing

upon the animals, got entangled in steaming rags, and fell in promiscuous unions on the torn moss, in sacrifice to their god. And his soul tasted the unchastity and fury of decay.

When he awakened from the affliction of this dream he was unnerved, shattered, and hopelessly under the power of the demon. He no longer avoided the inquisitive glances of other people; he did not care if he was exciting their suspicions. And as a matter of fact they were fleeing, traveling elsewhere. Numerous bathing-houses stood empty, the occupants of the dining-hall became more and more scattered, and in the city now one rarely saw a foreigner. The truth seemed to have leaked out; the panic, despite the reticence of those whose interests were involved, seemed no longer avoidable. But the woman with the pearls remained with her family, either because the rumors had not yet reached her, or because she was too proud and fearless to heed them. Tadzio remained. And to Aschenbach, in his infatuation, it seemed at times as though flight and death might remove all the disturbing elements of life around them, and he stay here alone with the boy. Yes, by the sea in the forenoon when his eyes rested heavily, irresponsibly, unwaveringly on the thing he coveted, or when, as the day was ending, he followed shamelessly after him through streets where the hideous death lurked in secret—at such times the atrocious seemed to him rich in possibilities, and laws of morality had dropped away.

Like any lover, he wanted to please; and he felt a bitter anguish lest it might not be possible. He added bright youthful details to his dress, he put on jewels, and used perfumes. During the day he often spent much time over his toilet, and came to the table strikingly dressed, excited, and in suspense. In the light of the sweet youthfulness which had done this to him, he detested his aging body. The sight of his gray hair, his sharp features, plunged him into shame and hopelessness. It induced him to attempt rejuvenating his body and appearance. He often visited the hotel barber.

Beneath the barber's apron, leaning back in the chair

under the gossiper's expert hands, he winced to observe his reflection in the mirror.

"Gray," he said, making a wry face.

"A little," the man answered. "Due entirely to a slight neglect, an indifference to outward things, which is conceivable in people of importance, but it is not exactly praiseworthy. And all the less so since such persons are above prejudice in matters of nature or art. If the moral objections of certain people to the art of cosmetics were to be logically extended to the care of the teeth, they would give no slight offense. And after all, we are just as old as we feel, and under some circumstances gray hair would actually stand for more of an untruth than the despised correction. In your case, sir, you are entitled to the natural color of your hair. Will you permit me simply to return what belongs to you?"

"How is that?" Aschanbach asked.

Then the orator washed his client's hair with two kinds of water, one clear and one dark, and it was as black as in youth. Following this, he curled it with irons into soft waves, stepped back, and eyed his work.

"All that is left now," he said, "would be to freshen up the skin a little."

And like some one who cannot finish, cannot satisfy himself, he passed with quickening energy from one manipulation to another. Aschenbach rested comfortably, incapable of resistance, or rather his hopes aroused by what was taking place. In the glass he saw his brows arch more evenly and decisively. His eyes became longer; their brilliance was heightened by a light touching-up of the lids. A little lower, where the skin had been a leatherish brown, he saw a delicate crimson tint grow beneath a deft application of color. His lips, bloodless a little while past, became full, and as red as raspberries. The furrows in the cheeks and about the mouth, the wrinkles of the eyes, disappeared beneath lotions and cream. With a knocking heart he beheld a blossoming youth. Finally the beauty specialist declared himself content, after the manner of such people, by obsequiously thanking the man he had been serving. "A trifling assistance," he said, as he applied one parting touch. "Now the gentleman can fall in love unhesitatingly." He walked away, fascinated; he was happy as in a dream, timid and bewildered. His necktie was red, his broad-brimmed straw hat was trimmed with a variegated band.

A tepid storm wind had risen. It was raining sparsely and at intervals, but the air was damp, thick, and filled with the smell of things rotting. All around him he heard a fluttering, pattering, and swishing; and under the fever of his cosmetics it seemed to him as though evil wind-spirits were haunting the place, impure sea-birds which rooted and gnawed at the food of the condemned and befouled it with their droppings. For the sultriness destroyed his appetite, and the fancy suggested itself that the foods were poisoned with contaminating substances. Tracking the boy one afternoon, Aschenbach had plunged deep into the tangled center of the diseased city. He was becoming uncertain of where he was, since the alleys, waterways, bridges, and little squares of the labyrinth were all so much alike, and he was no longer even sure of directions. He was absorbed with the problem of keeping the pursued figure in sight. And, driven to disgraceful subterfuges, flattening himself against walls, hiding behind the backs of other people, for a long time he did not notice the weariness, the exhaustion, with which emotion and the continual suspense had taxed his mind and his body. Tadzio walked behind his companions. He always allowed the governess and the nunlike sisters to precede him in the narrow places; and, loitering behind alone, he would turn his head occasionally to look over his shoulder and make sure by a glance of his peculiarly dark-gray eyes that his admirer was following. He saw him, and did not betray him. Drunk with the knowledge of this, lured forward by those eyes, led meekly by his passion, the lover stole after his unseemly hope—but finally he was cheated and lost sight of him. The Poles had crossed a short arching bridge; the height of the curve hid them from the pursuer, and when he himself had arrived there he no longer saw them. He hunted for them vainly in three directions, straight ahead and to either side along the narrow dirty wharf. In the end he was so tired and unnerved that he had to give up the search.

His head was on fire, his body was covered with a sticky sweat, his knees trembled. He could no longer endure the thirst that was torturing him, and he looked around for some immediate relief. From a little vegetable store he bought some fruit—strawberries, soft and overly ripe—and he ate them as he walked. A very charming, forsaken little square opened up before him. He recognized it; here he had made his frustrated plans for flight weeks ago. He let himself sink down on the steps of the cistern in the middle of the square, and laid his head against the stone cylinder. It was quiet; grass was growing up through the pavement; refuse was scattered about. Among the weatherbeaten, unusually tall houses surrounding him there was one like a palace, with little lion-covered balconies, and Gothic windows with blank emptiness behind them. On the ground floor of another house was a drug store. Warm gusts of wind occasionally carried the smell of carbolic acid.

He sat there, he, the master, the artist of dignity, the author of "The Wretch," a work which had, in such accurate symbols, denounced vagabondage and the depths of misery, had denied all sympathy with the engulfed, and had cast out the outcast; the man who had arrived and, victor over his own knowledge, had outgrown all irony and acclimatized himself to the obligations of public confidence; whose reputation was official, whose name had been knighted, and on whose style boys were urged to pattern themselves—he sat there. His eyelids were shut; only now and then a mocking uneasy side-glance slipped out from beneath them. And his loose lips, set off by the cosmetics, formed isolated words of the strange dream-logic created by his half-slumbering brain.

"For beauty, Phædrus, mark me, beauty alone is both divine and visible at once; and thus it is the road of the sensuous; it is, little Phædrus, the road of the artist to the spiritual. But do you now believe, my dear, that they can ever attain wisdom and true human dignity for whom the road to the spiritual leads through the senses? Or do you believe rather (I leave the choice to you) that this is a pleasant but perilous road, a really wrong and sinful road, which necessarily leads astray? For you must know that we poets cannot take the road of beauty without having Eros join us and set himself up as our leader. Indeed, we may even be heroes after our fashion, and hardened warriors, though we be like women, for passion is our exaltation, and our desire must remain love—that is our pleasure and our disgrace. You now see, do you not, that we poets cannot be wise and dignified? That we necessarily go astray, necessarily remain lascivious, and adventurers in emotion? The mastery of our style is all lies and foolishness, our renown and honor are a farce, the confidence of the masses in us is highly ridiculous, and the training of the public and of youth through art is a precarious undertaking which should be forbidden. For how, indeed, could he be a fit instructor who is born with a natural leaning towards the precipice? We might well disavow it and reach after dignity, but wherever we turn it attracts us. Let us, say, renounce the dissolvent of knowledge, since knowledge, Phædrus, has no dignity or strength. It is aware, it understands and pardons, but without reserve and form. It feels sympathy with the precipice, it *is* the precipice. This, then, we abandon with firmness, and from now on our efforts matter only by their yield of beauty, or, in other words, simplicity, greatness, and new rigor, form, and a second type of openness. But form and openness, Phædrus, lead to intoxication and to desire, lead the noble perhaps into sinister revels of emotion which his own beautiful rigor rejects as infamous, lead to the precipice—yes, they too lead to the precipice. They lead us poets there, I say, since we cannot force ourselves, since we can merely let ourselves out. And now I am going, Phædrus. You stay here; and when you no longer see me, then you go too."

A few days later, as Gustav von Aschenbach was not feeling well, he left the beach hotel at a later hour in the morning than usual. He had to fight against certain attacks of vertigo which were only partially physical and were accompanied by a pronounced malaise, a feeling of bafflement and hopelessness—while he was not certain whether this had to do with conditions outside him or with his own nature. In the lobby he noticed a large pile of luggage ready for shipment; he asked the doorkeeper who it was that was leaving, and heard in answer the Polish title which he had learned secretly. He accepted this without any alteration of his sunken features, with that curt elevation of the head by which one acknowledges something he does not need to know. Then he asked: "When?" The answer was: "After lunch." He nodded, and went to the beach.

It was not very inviting. Rippling patches of rain retreated across the wide flat water separating the beach from the first long sandbank. An air of autumn, of things past their prime, seemed to lie over the pleasure spot which had once been so alive with color and was now almost abandoned. The sand was no longer kept clean. A camera, seemingly without an owner, stood on its tripod by the edge of the sea; and a black cloth thrown over it was flapping noisily in the wind.

Tadzio, with the three or four companions still left, was moving about to the right in front of his family's cabin. And midway between the sea and the row of bathing-houses, lying back in his chair with a robe over his knees, Aschenbach looked at him once more. The game, which was not being supervised since the women were probably occupied with preparations for the journey, seemed to have no rules, and it was degenerating. The stocky boy with the sleek black hair who was called Jaschu had been angered and blinded by sand flung in his face. He forced Tadzio into a wrestling match which quickly ended in the fall of the beauty, who was weaker. But as though, in the hour of parting, the servile feelings of the inferior had turned to merciless brutality and were trying to get vengeance for a long period of slavery, the victor did not let go of the boy underneath, but knelt on

his back and pressed his face so persistently into the sand
that Tadzio, already breathless from the struggle, was in
danger of strangling. His attempts to shake off the weight
were fitful; for moments they stopped entirely and were
resumed again as mere twitchings. Enraged, Aschenbach
was about to spring to the rescue, when the torturer finally
released his victim. Tadzio, very pale, raised himself half-
way and sat motionless for several minutes, resting on one
arm with rumpled hair and glowering eyes. Then he stood
up completely, and moved slowly away. They called him,
cheerfully at first, then anxiously and imploringly; he did
not listen. The swarthy boy, who seemed to regret his excesses
immediately afterwards, caught up with him and tried to
placate him. A movement of the shoulder put him at his
distance. Tadzio went down obliquely to the water. He was
barefoot, and wore his striped linen suit with the red bow.
He lingered on the edge of the water with his head down,
drawing figures in the wet sand with one toe; then he went
into the shallows, which did not cover his knees in the deepest place, crossed them leisurely, and arrived at the sandbank. He stood there a moment, his face turned to the open
sea; soon after, he began stepping slowly to the left along the
narrow stretch of exposed ground. Separated from the main-
land by the expanse of water, separated from his companions
by a proud moodiness, he moved along, a strongly isolated
and unrelated figure with fluttering hair—placed out there
in the sea, the wind, against the vague mists. He stopped
once more to look around. And suddenly, as though at some
recollection, some impulse, with one hand on his hip he
turned the upper part of his body in a beautiful twist which
began from the base—and he looked over his shoulder towards the shore. The watcher sat there, as he had sat once
before when for the first time those twilight-gray eyes had
turned at the doorway and met his own. His head, against
the back of the chair, had slowly followed the movements of
the boy walking yonder. Now, simultaneously with this
glance it rose and sank on his breast, so that his eyes looked

out from underneath, while his face took on the loose, inwardly relaxed expression of deep sleep. But it seemed to him as though the pale and lovely lure out there were smiling to him, nodding to him; as though, removing his hand from his hip, he were signaling to come out, were vaguely guiding towards egregious promises. And, as often before, he stood up to follow him.

Some minutes passed before any one hurried to the aid of the man who had collapsed into one corner of his chair. He was brought to his room. And on the same day a respectfully shocked world received the news of his death.

A COUNTRY DOCTOR[1]

Franz Kafka

(1883-1924)

I was in great perplexity; I had to start on an urgent journey; a seriously ill patient was waiting for me in a village ten miles off; a thick blizzard of snow filled all the wide spaces between him and me; I had a gig, a light gig with big wheels, exactly right for our country roads; muffled in furs, my bag of instruments in my hand, I was in the courtyard all ready for the journey; but there was no horse to be had, no horse. My own horse had died in the night, worn out by the fatigues of this icy winter; my servant girl was now running round the village trying to borrow a horse; but it was hopeless, I knew it, and I stood there forlornly, with the snow gathering more and more thickly upon me, more and more unable to move. In the gateway the girl appeared, alone, and waved the lantern; of course, who would lend a horse at this time for such a journey? I strode through the courtyard once more; I could see no way out; in my confused distress I kicked at the dilapidated door of the yearlong uninhabited pigsty. It flew open and flapped to and fro on its hinges. A steam and smell as of horses came out from it. A dim stable lantern was swinging inside from a rope. A man, crouching on his hams in that low space, showed an open blue-eyed face. "Shall I yoke up?" he asked, crawling out on all fours. I did not know what to say and merely stooped down to see what else was in the sty. The servant girl was standing be-

[1] Translated by Willa and Edwin Muir. Reprinted by permission of the publisher from *The Penal Colony*, copyright 1948 by Schocken Books, Inc.

side me. "You never know what you're going to find in your own house," she said, and we both laughed. "Hey there, Brother, hey there, Sister!" called the groom, and two horses, enormous creatures with powerful flanks, one after the other, their legs tucked close to their bodies, each well-shaped head lowered like a camel's, by sheer strength of buttocking squeezed out through the door hole which they filled entirely. But at once they were standing up, their legs long and their bodies steaming thickly. "Give him a hand," I said, and the willing girl hurried to help the groom with the harnessing. Yet hardly was she beside him when the groom clipped hold of her and pushed his face against hers. She screamed and fled back to me; on her cheek stood out in red the marks of two rows of teeth. "You brute," I yelled in fury, "do you want a whipping?" but in the same moment reflected that the man was a stranger; that I did not know where he came from, and that of his own free will he was helping me out when everyone else had failed me. As if he knew my thoughts he took no offense at my threat but, still busied with the horses, only turned round once towards me. "Get in," he said then, and indeed: everything was ready. A magnificent pair of horses, I observed, such as I had never sat behind, and I climbed in happily. "But I'll drive, you don't know the way," I said. "Of course," said he, "I'm not coming with you anyway I'm staying with Rose." "No," shrieked Rose, fleeing into the house with a justified presentiment that her fate was inescapable; I heard the door chain rattle as she put it up; I heard the key turn in the lock; I could see, moreover, how she put out the lights in the entrance hall and in further flight all through the rooms to keep herself from being discovered. "You're coming with me," I said to the groom, "or I won't go, urgent as my journey is. I'm not thinking of paying for it by handing the girl over to you." "Gee up!" he said; clapped his hands; the gig whirled off like a log in a freshet; I could just hear the door of my house splitting and bursting as the groom charged at it and then I was deafened and blinded by a storming rush that

steadily buffeted all my senses. But this only for a moment,
since, as if my patient's farmyard had opened out just before
my courtyard gate, I was already there; the horses had come
quietly to a standstill; the blizzard had stopped; moonlight
all around; my patient's parents hurried out of the house,
his sister behind them; I was almost lifted out of the gig;
from their confused ejaculations I gathered not a word; in
the sickroom the air was almost unbreathable; the neglected
stove was smoking; I wanted to push open a window; but
first I had to look at my patient. Gaunt, without any fever,
not cold, not warm, with vacant eyes, without a shirt, the
youngster heaved himself up from under the feather bedding, threw his arms round my neck, and whispered in my
ear: "Doctor, let me die." I glanced round the room; no one
had heard it; the parents were leaning forward in silence
waiting for my verdict; the sister had set a chair for my
handbag; I opened the bag and hunted among my instruments; the boy kept clutching at me from his bed to remind
me of his entreaty; I picked up a pair of tweezers, examined
them in the candlelight and laid them down again. "Yes," I
thought blasphemously, "in cases like this the gods are helpful, send the missing horse, add to it a second because of the
urgency, and to crown everything bestow even a groom—"
And only now did I remember Rose again; what was I to
do, how could I rescue her, how could I pull her away from
under that groom at ten miles' distance, with a team of
horses I couldn't control. These horses, now, they had somehow slipped the reins loose, pushed the windows open from
outside, I did not know how; each of them had stuck a
head in at a window and, quite unmoved by the startled
cries of the family, stood eyeing the patient. "Better go back
at once," I thought, as if the horses were summoning me to
the return journey, yet I permitted the patient's sister, who
fancied that I was dazed by the heat, to take my fur coat
from me. A glass of rum was poured out for me, the old
man clapped me on the shoulder, a familiarity justified by
this offer of his treasure. I shook my head; in the narrow
confines of the old man's thoughts I felt ill; that was my only

reason for refusing the drink. The mother stood by the bedside and cajoled me towards it; I yielded, and, while one of
the horses whinnied loudly to the ceiling, laid my head to the
boy's breast, which shivered under my wet beard. I confirmed what I already knew; the boy was quite sound, something a little wrong with his circulation, saturated with coffee
by his solicitous mother, but sound and best turned out of
bed with one shove. I am no world reformer and so I let him
lie. I was the district doctor and did my duty to the utter-
most, to the point where it became almost too much. I was
badly paid and yet generous and helpful to the poor. I had
still to see that Rose was all right, and then the boy might
have his way and I wanted to die too. What was I doing
there in that endless winter! My horse was dead, and not a
single person in the village would lend me another. I had
to get my team out of the pigsty; if they hadn't chanced to
be horses I should have had to travel with swine. That was
how it was. And I nodded to the family. They knew nothing
about it, and, had they known, would not have believed
it. To write prescriptions is easy, but to come to an understanding with people is hard. Well, this should be the end
of my visit, I had once more been called out needlessly, I
was used to that, the whole district made my life a torment
with my night bell, but that I should have to sacrifice Rose
this time as well, the pretty girl who had lived in my house
for years almost without my noticing her—that sacrifice was
too much to ask, and I had somehow to get it reasoned out
in my head with the help of what craft I could muster, in
order not to let fly at this family, which with the best will in
the world could not restore Rose to me. But as I shut my bag
and put an arm out for my fur coat, the family meanwhile
standing together, the father sniffing at the glass of rum in
his hand, the mother, apparently disappointed in me—why,
what do people expect?—biting her lips with tears in her
eyes, the sister fluttering a blood-soaked towel, I was somehow ready to admit conditionally that the boy might be ill
after all. I went towards him, he welcomed me smiling as if
I were bringing him the most nourishing invalid broth—ah,

now both horses were whinnying together; the noise, I suppose, was ordained by heaven to assist my examination of the patient—and this time I discovered that the boy was indeed ill. In his right side, near the hip, was an open wound as big as the palm of my hand. Rose-red, in many variations of shade, dark in the hollows, lighter at the edges, softly granulated, with irregular clots of blood, open as a surface mine to the daylight. That was how it looked from a distance. But on a closer inspection there was another complication. I could not help a low whistle of surprise. Worms, as thick and as long as my little finger, themselves rose-red and blood-spotted as well, were wriggling from their fastness in the interior of the wound towards the light, with small white heads and many little legs. Poor boy, you were past helping. I had discovered your great wound; this blossom in your side was destroying you. The family was pleased; they saw me busying myself; the sister told the mother, the mother the father, the father told several guests who were coming in, through the moonlight at the open door, walking on tiptoe, keeping their balance with outstretched arms. "Will you save me?" whispered the boy with a sob, quite blinded by the life within his wound. That is what people are like in my district. Always expecting the impossible from the doctor. They have lost their ancient beliefs; the parson sits at home and unravels his vestments, one after another; but the doctor is supposed to be omnipotent with his merciful surgeon's hand. Well, as it pleases them; I have not thrust my services on them; if they misuse me for sacred ends, I let that happen to me too; what better do I want, old country doctor that I am, bereft of my servant girl! And so they came, the family and the village elders, and stripped my clothes off me; a school choir with the teacher at the head of it stood before the house and sang these words to an utterly simple tune:

> Strip his clothes off, then he'll heal us,
> If he doesn't, kill him dead!
> Only a doctor, only a doctor.

Then my clothes were off and I looked at the people quietly, my fingers in my beard and my head cocked to one side. I was altogether composed and equal to the situation and remained so, although it was no help to me, since they now took me by the head and feet and carried me to the bed. They laid me down in it next to the wall, on the side of the wound. Then they all left the room; the door was shut; the singing stopped; clouds covered the moon; the bedding was warm around me; the horses' heads in the open windows wavered like shadows. "Do you know," said a voice in my ear, "I have very little confidence in you. Why, you were only blown in here, you didn't come on your own feet. Instead of helping me, you're cramping me on my deathbed. What I'd like best is to scratch your eyes out." "Right," I said, "it is a shame. And yet I am a doctor. What am I to do? Believe me, it is not too easy for me either." "Am I supposed to be content with this apology? Oh, I must be, I can't help it. I always have to put up with things. A fine wound is all I brought into the world; that was my sole endowment." "My young friend," said I, "your mistake is: you have not a wide enough view. I have been in all the sickrooms, far and wide, and I tell you: your wound is not so bad. Done in a tight corner with two strokes of the ax. Many a one proffers his side and can hardly hear the ax in the forest, far less that it is coming nearer to him." "Is that really so, or are you deluding me in my fever?" "It is really so, take the word of honor of an official doctor." And he took it and lay still. But now it was time for me to think of escaping. The horses were still standing faithfully in their places. My clothes, my fur coat, my bag were quickly collected; I didn't want to waste time dressing; if the horses raced home as they had come, I should only be springing, as it were, out of this bed into my own. Obediently a horse backed away from the window; I threw my bundle into the gig; the fur coat missed its mark and was caught on a hook only by the sleeve. Good enough. I swung myself on to the horse. With the reins loosely trailing, one horse barely fastened to the other, the gig swaying behind, my fur coat last of all in the snow. "Gee up!" I said, but there was no galloping; slowly, like old men, we crawled through the snowy wastes; a long time echoed behind us the new but faulty song of the children:

> O be joyful, all you patients,
> The doctor's laid in bed beside you!

Never shall I reach home at this rate; my flourishing practice is done for; my successor is robbing me, but in vain, for he cannot take my place; in my house the disgusting groom is raging; Rose is his victim; I do not want to think about it any more. Naked, exposed to the frost of this most unhappy of ages, with an earthly vehicle, unearthly horses, old man that I am, I wander astray. My fur coat is hanging from the back of the gig, but I cannot reach it, and none of my limber pack of patients lifts a finger. Betrayed! Betrayed! A false alarm on the night bell once answered—it cannot be made good, not ever.

MODERN LIBRARY GIANTS

A series of full-sized library editions of books that formerly were available only in cumbersome and expensive sets.
THE MODERN LIBRARY GIANTS REPRESENT A SELECTION OF THE WORLD'S GREATEST BOOKS

These volumes contain from 600 to 1,400 pages each

Interior by Melanie Kahane, A. I. D.

No modern library is complete
without THE AMERICAN
COLLEGE DICTIONARY